K'ATSINA

Forge Books by Lana M. Harrigan

Ácoma
K'atsina

K'ATSINA

A Novel of Rebellion

LANA M. HARRIGAN

A TOM DOHERTY ASSOCIATES BOOK
New York

K'ATSINA

A Forge Book
Published by Tom Doherty Associates, LLC
175 Fifth Avenue
New York, NY 10010

www.tor.com

Forge® is a registered trademark of Tom Doherty Associates, LLC.

Interior drawings by Gary Moeller
Maps by Ellisa H. Mitchell

Library of Congress Cataloging-in-Publication Data

Harrigan, Lana M.
    K'atsina / Lana M. Harrigan.
      p.   cm.
    "A Tom Doherty Associates book"
    ISBN 0-312-86260-1 (hc)
    ISBN 0-312-87277-1 (pbk)
    1. Mexico—History—Spanish colony, 1540–1810—Fiction.
2. Inquisition—Mexico—History—17th century—Fiction.   3. New
Mexico—History—To 1848—Fiction.   4. Pueblo Revolt, 1680—Fiction.
5. Ácoma Indians—Fiction.   I. Title.
PS3558.A6258K38   1998
813'.54—dc21   98-7609
                                                                          CIP

First Hardcover Edition: September 1998
First Trade Paperback Edition: September 2000

Printed in the United States of America

0 9 8 7 6 5 4 3 2 1

For my parents
Georgia and Frederick Moeller
with love

Contents

It comes alive
It comes alive, live, live.
In the south mountain
The jaguar comes alive, comes alive.

With this animal of prey
Comes the power,
  comes the deer
    comes the antelope
Comes the power of good fortune
      in the hunt.

    —Acoma prayer to give power
      and spirit to a hunting fetish

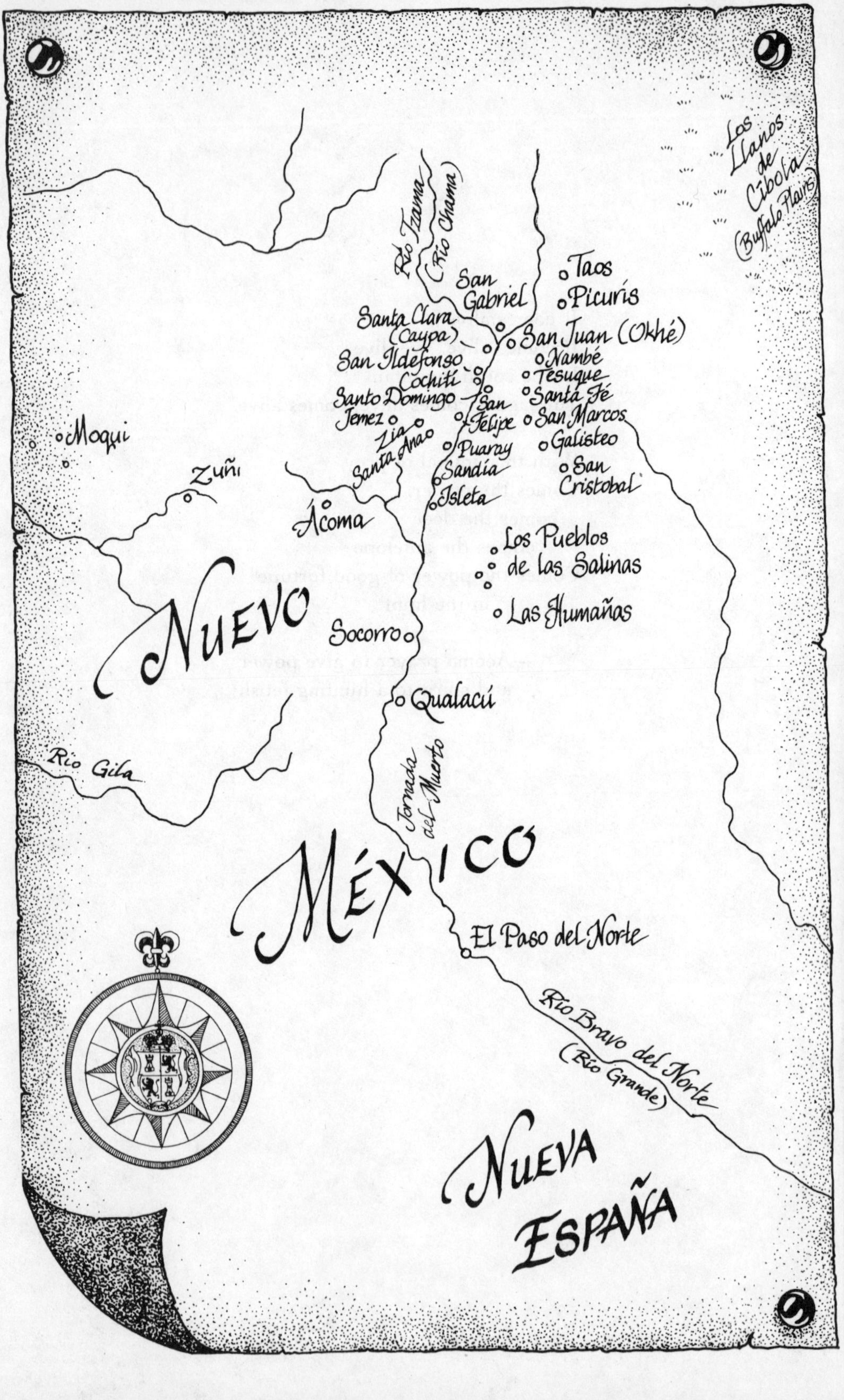
Los Llanos de Cíbola (Buffalo Plains)
Río Izama (Río Chama)
San Gabriel
Taos
Picurís
Santa Clara (Caypa)
San Juan (Okhé)
San Ildefonso
Nambé
Cochití
Tesuque
Santo Domingo
Santa Fé
San Felipe
San Marcos
Jemez
Zia
Santa Ana
Moqui
Puaray
Galisteo
Sandía
San Cristobal
Zuñi
Isleta
Ácoma
Los Pueblos de las Salinas
Las Humañas
Socorro
Qualacú
Río Gila
Jornada del Muerto
Nuevo México
El Paso del Norte
Río Bravo del Norte (Río Grande)
Nueva España

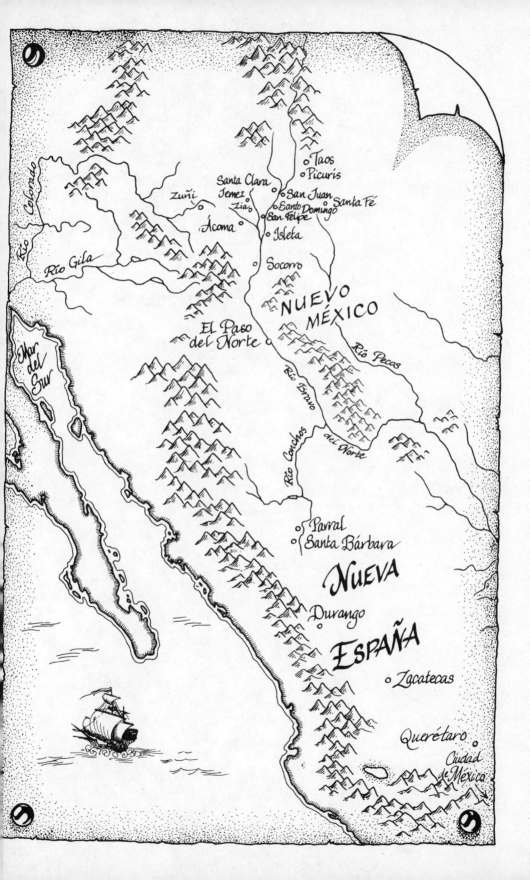

Historical Preface

As the Black Death ravaged Europe and a fierce tribe of Aztec warriors founded a city in a lake on a part of the globe Europeans did not yet know existed, the Ácoma had already lived for a century on a high mesa far to the north of the Aztec city in the lake. Dwellings rose three and four stories high on the Ácoma's sandstone citadel, women skillfully crafted thin-walled pots with intricate black and white geometric designs, and men wove soft cloth from the cotton they cultivated in irrigated fields.

Two centuries later, far to the south of the Ácoma, well-armed men in armor set foot on the previously unknown continent, and their leader burned his ships so that none of his soldiers might have second thoughts about marching inland to conquer a fabled city in the lake, said to abound in gold. When Hernán Cortés entered Tenochtitlán and laid eyes upon the riches of the Aztec city and its ruler Moctezuma, his imagination and the imagination of all of Europe flamed like the crucible of an alchemist, burning with the possibility of other cities, just as rich, in the newly discovered other half of the world.

In Tenochtitlán, the Spanish conquistadors marveled at the sumptuous palaces, the enormous pyramids, bathed in sacrificial human blood, and the thousands of inhabitants whose rulers adorned themselves with gold, jewels, and extraordinary cloaks of multicolored iridescent feathers. If this city existed in the land they christened New Spain, could they not expect to find others of equal magnificence?

A few years later, four starving men dressed in rags reignited that fire of the imagination when they brought news of large cities leagues to the north of the Valley of Mexico. Álvar Núñez Cabeza de Vaca and his companions, shipwrecked on a distant coast, had made their tortuous way to the settlements of northern Mexico and told the stories that they had been told by the natives they met. The viceroy in Mexico City sent a Franciscan, Fray Marcos de Niza, to investigate the validity of these new tales, and although Fray Marcos may have disappointed truth, he did not disappoint the imagination of the conquerors of the New World. He returned with the story of having seen, at a distance, seven cities of burnished gold and was told that farther on lay the kingdom of Acus.

In 1540, Francisco Vásquez de Coronado set out to find these seven mythic Cities of Cíbola, but what he found instead were villages of mud and stone, and Fray Marcos was branded a liar. Although not of gold, the village called "Acus" by the friar captured the attention of one of Coronado's lieutenants. After he saw it, he wrote that it was the greatest stronghold ever witnessed in the world, so formidable, that it was nearly impossible to climb to the village that sat upon the top of the rose-pink sandstone *peñol*.

Fifty years passed during which a number of small groups of intrepid soldiers and friars ventured into the land of Cíbola, but their tracks little disturbed the soil of what was being called "the New Mexico"—until 1598. That year, a rich silver miner from Zacatecas by the name of Juan de Oñate gathered soldiers, colonists, and Franciscan priests to lay claim to the land, settle and Christianize it for the King of Spain.

Trailed by many solid-wheeled carts and hundreds of horses, cattle, and other stock, Oñate marched into the land of the pueblos, conquering them peacefully, excepting the lofty pueblo of Áco. Juan de Zaldívar, nephew of Oñate and second in command of the *conquista*, along with a dozen of his men, met their death in the high-perched mesa village when they attempted to take food from the unwilling Ácoma.

To avenge the murder of his nephew, the first governor of *Nuevo México* ordered his other nephew Vicente, younger brother of Juan, west to the treasonous village to exact payment for their deed.

And pay the Ácoma did—dearly. By dragging a small cannon up the south, more sloping side, of the mesa, Zaldívar was able to fire into the village and subjugate it. Hundreds of Ácoma were massacred; the remainder were herded to the pueblo of Santo Domingo where they stood trial for treason against the King of Spain. Their punishment was brutal: All men over the age of twenty-five had their right foot cut off and were made slaves for twenty years; women, girls, and boys above the age of twelve likewise were condemned to two decades of servitude.

The mesa village lay in smoldering ruins, but from the rubble and ashes it rose to life again like the mythical bird of Greek legend, however, only to sustain legends of its own . . .

Part One

LA MÁSCARA
The Masquerade, 1640

Chapter 1

The air hung warm and humid from the downpour of rain the previous day, but that afternoon the sky was blue crystal. The languid, heavily sweet and sensuous scent of *yolloxochitl* flowers wafted through the packed streets, and the fragrance of a hundred other flowers mingled with the varied odors of the crowds of onlookers and with the wet refuse of the gutters.

Augustín adjusted the mask of lacquered flames so that he could see better from behind it, then seated the headdress of iridescent green-gold feathers of the *quetzal* bird more firmly on his head. He reached down and grasped his sword, slashed it left, right. He was sweating. The August sun marched relentlessly, fed by the blood of fearless warriors, according to mythology. Perspiration beaded on his oiled skin and slithered like a water serpent down his muscles.

He nodded to the platform carriers. "I'm ready." One of his costumed colleagues laced his fingers together to give him a step up, but Augustín leaped onto the platform unassisted.

The black robed guidon carrier shouted, "Shoulder bars! Ready! Lift!"

Standing on top, Augustín lurched momentarily as the seminarians hoisted the scarlet-streamered platform onto their shoulders. He crossed himself. "Let me do this well," he whispered behind his mask. A knot twisted in his stomach. He felt no fear of his performance today. This particular sensation he recognized well—it was the same knot that had coiled in his stomach when he was just a boy and looked at himself in the polished metal mirror, wondering if anyone could tell from his face what he wanted no one to know. He sucked in a deep breath of air, straightened his shoulders, and as his cape billowed out behind him, willed the knot away. He looked out on the procession as it moved down the street ahead of him.

Native reed flutes and handmade drums filled the cloying air with a throbbing exotic music enticing the crowds to move to the exhorting rhythm. There came a wild throng of natives clad only in *maxtlatl*, a strip of cloth worn around the hips, the loose end of which hung like a miniature apron covering the wearer's crotch. Their bronze bodies were daubed with clay paints of bright earth colors, and they danced and chanted as they led the parade through the streets. People pushed and shoved to get a better view of the spectacle, while children were lifted onto shoulders. Those who were fortunate to have a balcony from which to view the parade of the *máscara* could see more readily the magnificence that followed.

Triumphal arches bedecked with bright fuchsia flowers were carried by Indian pages of San Gregorio, the gold medallions that hung around their necks flashing brilliantly in the afternoon sun. Behind the arches came fearsome masked warriors who symbolized the southern stars. The dancers were clearly natives of this valley of Mexico, but the masked warriors gave evidence of their Castilian blood from skin tones that were far from copper. The warriors carried gilded weapons and flourished them with grace and studied bellicosity.

Banners of crimson satin with gold tassels fluttered, making the embroidered gold Aztec hieroglyphics sparkle like small bursts of flame, adding to the ferocity of the serpents and wild beasts depicted there. Symbolism pervaded every aspect of the moving pageant, from the blood-red crimson that represented the sacrificial rites of the feared former rulers of the valley of Anahuac to the abundance of gilt that flashed and shone like the burning orb it signified.

Nothing had been spared to make the *máscara* the most lavish, the most intricate, the most splendidly moving of all the many parades that had taken place in years past. All the people in the city, as well as those from leagues around, thronged to the wide, paved thoroughfares to witness the immensely popular form of entertainment that made the City of Mexico far more exciting than many of its European counterparts.

The Jesuit schools of San Ildefonso and the Colegio Máximo, with students known for their superior intelligence and erudition, could be counted on to prepare a magnificent parade steeped in allegorical allusion and symbolism. This time they had outdone themselves, for the entrance of a new viceroy into the city called for a lavish celebration. The seventeenth viceroy of Mexico was younger than the nobles the king had usually sent to govern his New World realm. The populace was expecting an exciting court life in the viceregal capital during his tenure as the king's emissary to the land in which the great Moctezuma had once reigned supreme.

For over one hundred and twenty years, Spain had ruled the land that had once lived in fear of the warring, bloodthirsty Aztecs who fought their *guerras floridas* to obtain the thousands of captives necessary for their religious rites of human sacrifice. In 1519, when Cortés entered the capital of Tenochtitlán, the City in the Lake, he had been nauseated by the stench of the black, rotting blood that covered the stones of the sacrificial pyramids. On a convex altar located on the flat top of a massive pyramid, the chief priest or *topiltzin*, a razor-sharp obsidian knife in his hand, would slice open the chest of his living victim and yank out the warm, palpitating heart while five other priests secured the arms, legs, and head of the unfortunate captive whose blood would spout over the altar and flow down the steps.

The Aztec gods daily demanded the red liquid of life so that they in turn might sustain the dwellers on earth. The sun was a young, handsome god called "Huitzilopochtli" who each day traveled across the sky in fierce battle with the stars and moon. In order that he might triumph in his daily battle and thus continue to shine, the sun god had to have *chalchiuatl*, warm human blood, which was supplied to him daily by the priests. The handsome god was helped in his heavenly struggle by the souls of fearless warriors who had died in battle or in sacrifice. It was imperative that the sun shine and therefore, that man provide the sustenance for him.

The Jesuit students and seminarians availed themselves of the rich, bloody lore of the pre-Columbian Aztec dynasty for the pageant they were presenting to the new viceroy, Don Diego López Cabrera y Bobadilla, Duque de Escalona y Marqués de Villena who had made his grand entry into Mexico City on August 18 of that year of 1640.

A relative of the Duke of Bragança of the Portuguese nobility, the new viceroy would be fêted by all groups wishing for viceregal favor. The festivities for Don Diego would last weeks. That particular August day he would witness the allegorical *máscara* of the Jesuits, and the sumptuousness and complex symbolism of it would be carefully explained to him by a Jesuit Father who had been assigned to the viceregal entourage strictly for that purpose. The powerful Jesuits would want the new viceroy to fully appreciate the *máscara* so carefully and expensively conceived for him.

"Look!" people shouted with enthusiasm as an enormous platform on wheels, pulled by handsome white steeds caparisoned with scarlet silk and golden fringe, rolled down the street carrying a large rectangular stone upon which a mock sacrifice was being carried out before the eyes of the crowd. A red viscous liquid took the place of real blood, and to the delight and horror of the onlookers, the seminarians, looking little like themselves in their Aztec costumes, played out their bloody drama on the rolling stage.

Those on balconies were the first to see the tall, amazing platform approaching behind the *carro* with its sacrificial stone. Musicians and feathered dancers separated them. Thirty black satin-clad seminarians, their faces concealed behind frightful black and red masks, carried a large platform on their shoulders. Streamers of scarlet taffeta fluttered down on them from the edges of the lustrous deck. They walked slowly and in step. Brilliant red flowers covered the entire perimeter of the stage and at its back rose a huge, beaten and gilded tin disk whose reflected light leaped and sparkled and blinded like the sun it portrayed. On either side of the sun rose terrible fiery serpents, symbolizing the daily strife the sungod Huitzilopochtli must undergo.

In the middle of the platform stood the god. His body gleamed in the sunlight from the oil that had been rubbed on him. He was tall and naked, save a golden *maxtlatl* that covered his manhood and a golden cape that streamed out behind him from his broad shoulders. He was lean, but the muscles of his thighs stood out taut in his warlike, regal stance. A fierce mask of flames covered his face, and in his dark glinting hair lay a crown of iridescent feathers. He carried a huge, golden sword that he wielded with grace and dexterity as he moved and leaped on the high, man-carried platform in simulated battle against a host of silver stars that ringed the stage.

Whispers flew through the crowd as the spectators caught a glimpse of the sun god. "Who is he?" they asked. "Who is the man that portrays Huit-zilopochtli? Surely he is not a Jesuit."

"Madre de Dios," whispered a woman whose provocative clothes implied questionable virtue. *"¡Qué hombre más lindo!* What a man like that could do for a woman, eh?"

Another near her laughed and echoed her sentiments. "That one would never have to pay to warm my bed!" She snorted and tossed her head. "The men with their velvet cloaks and ruffles of lace! Bah! They hide ugly, white, pudgy bodies beneath all their finery. But that one," she said, her eyes fixed brightly on the oiled body of the sun god, *"that* one is truly a man."

Another spectator standing nearby who had overheard the comments of the two women remarked with some irony, "That body is undoubtedly chastely covered by a Jesuit cassock every day except today, and he may not be the man you think he is!"

One of the women laughed knowingly and turned to him, "Ah, *Señor,* I can vouch for the fact that many of the good Fathers are men indeed!"

As the pageant passed directly in front of that group of onlookers, Huit-zilopochtli now stood in full view. His presence exerted a powerful influence on the people. Some stood silent in apparent awe while others voiced their surprise at the physical beauty of the mortal, who seemed as if he might have truly been a god, riding high above them on the shoulder-held platform.

Women of scant virtue were not the only members of the gentler sex who commented on the appearance of the sun god. Many whispers were shielded behind a gloved hand or a lace-edged fan. But the comments were the same, *"¡Qué hombre más lindo!* Who is he? Surely he is not a Jesuit dressed like *that*!"

"Mamá!" a little girl shouted, "that's him! That's our tutor!"

"No, *mi hijita,"* her mother laughed, "it could not be."

"But it *is, Mamá,"* the little girl insisted as she pulled at her mother's hand. "I saw him practicing with a golden sword last weekend when we were in the country."

"I didn't see him," her older brother said.

The mother leaned against the balcony railing, looking toward the approaching platform. "There are similarities in stature, yes, and the hair color might be the same, but it is not possible, *mi hija*. It is certainly someone else."

"Well, I think it's him," the girl insisted, "and I'm going to ask him." She clutched the wrought-iron railing of the balcony. "Isn't he grand-looking?"

On another balcony the Duque de Escalona stroked his small goatee. "I must commend you, Padre," he said with a slight bow of his head. "The *máscara* is truly magnificent. It is most kind of Your Reverence to explain the symbolism to me. Scarcely had I imagined such a rich lore of the heathen. I dare say the only thing one hears in España is of the bloodthirsty sacrifices formerly committed by the natives."

The black-robed Jesuit smiled in satisfaction. "I am flattered Your Excellency approves of the pageant."

It was at that moment the scarlet taffeta-covered platform bearing Huitzilopochtli came into the viceroy's view from his favored position on the balcony of the palace. The hammered gilt-covered disk of sun that rose behind the Aztec deity flashed brilliantly as the masked god lunged and spun, wielding his golden sword in mortal combat against the southern stars.

"*Nombre de Dios*. What is this?" the viceroy asked as he saw the approaching man-carried platform and its fierce, half-naked warrior.

"That," the Jesuit Father answered with authority, pronouncing the name with careful precision, "is Huitzilopochtli, the sun god of the Aztecs." His voice rose so that he might be heard above the clamor of the crowd as he related in exacting detail the theogony of the former rulers of the city the Duque de Escalona now ruled in the name of the King of Spain.

"What we have attempted to do," the Jesuit continued with emphasis, "is to allegorize the beliefs of the heathen in light of Christian theology. Thus, Huitzilopochtli's daily battle is that of the 'good' or the 'light' against 'evil' or the forces of darkness. As the pageant proceeds you will see the symbols of the Aztecs become the symbols of the true faith. Thus the blood is the blood of Christ that He shed for us. So what we have here is not merely an exposition of the ancient Aztec culture, but rather a statement of the greatness of God."

The viceroy leaned forward to get a better view. The stage with its masked warrior seemed to hold his attention more than the erudite explications of the Jesuit Father beside him. The platform came to a halt in front of the balcony of the palace where they stood. The glistening, masked god sliced the air with his golden sword in a flurry of well-studied, graceful moves. He went to his knees as he finished, facing the balcony with its important guests. His sword went tip down onto the platform, the vertical hilt making the age-old symbol of the soldier's cross. The god bowed in homage to the new viceroy, the iridescent feathers of his headdress shimmering in the sunlight.

"*¡Magnífico, magnífico!*" the viceroy shouted, clapping and voicing his approval of the brilliant pageant the Jesuits were presenting in honor of his arrival in the city.

He turned to the priest beside him. "Who is the sun god? A swordsman of some repute, a young nobleman, perhaps?" He did not pause to allow the Jesuit Father to respond as he continued emphatically. "Bring him tomorrow. I am having audiences with men of the realm who might be of use to my viceroyalty. I don't want to surround myself with sycophants from Spain who know nothing about this country I am to govern. There might be a place at court for a man such as this one."

The priest smiled and paused for effect. "But he is one of *ours*, Excellency." There was a trace of smugness at the corners of his lips. "I will have him summoned."

The Duque turned to the priest, his surprise unhidden. "A *Jesuit*?"

The impeccable, black-robed Father nodded, smiling with satisfaction. "Yes, he has just finished seminary and has begun his regency. A brilliant young man, that one."

The viceroy looked down at the warrior, naked save only the golden piece of cloth that encircled his hips, and the priest spoke as if he had read the viceroy's thoughts. "There are few of the religious who are more morally correct than that young man, Excellency. He is an asset to the Order in every respect."

"So you are Augustín," the Duque de Escalona said a day later as the seminarian straightened from his bow.

"Yes, Your Excellency," he replied quietly, still shocked that the viceroy had requested to meet him.

"You are taller than I imagined from watching you on the platform."

Augustín gave a brief nod and clasped his hands together more tightly in an attempt to hide his severe discomfort, not knowing how to respond to a viceroy. He glanced at the Jesuit father who had explained the *máscara* to the Duque and who had escorted him to the viceregal residence that day, but the priest gave him no indication that he should speak.

The Duque stroked his goatee. "You cut an imposing figure even in your cassock with its thirty-three buttons down the front. My Jesuit tutor told me when I was young that they symbolize the number of years of Christ's life on earth." Augustín nodded again, and the viceroy motioned with his hand. "But, the robe of a religious directs the thoughts to the spiritual and not to the worldly or physical." The Duque fixed him with his eyes. "I judge you to be a man of intelligence, but I see nothing of conceit. You give an impression of a steeled self-control."

Augustín held his face impassive the way his grandfather had taught him long ago to do in unsettling circumstances. There was a moment of silence, but before Augustín felt compelled to speak, the Jesuit father spoke, instead. "Not only is this young man an outstanding athlete at our *casa de campo* in the country at which our seminarians spend weekends so that the body may serve as a proper vessel for the soul, but he likewise performs the spiritual exercises of our father Loyola with rigor and humility." For a moment Augustín was surprised at the flattering words from his superior but realized just as quickly that the priest was not attempting to praise him as much as he was to extol the virtues of the Order. They would want the new viceroy to look favorably on the Society of Jesus. "As our founder admonished all Jesuits," the black-robed father continued, "this young man is a dedicated soldier of the Lord in the hospitals and dark prisons of this city where we carry out our efforts to help humanity. And, as we require of all our seminarians, he is working toward the spiritual perfection that our father Ignatius envisioned when he began the Order."

"High praise, indeed," the Duque said to Augustín who fought to conceal his growing discomfort. "I called you here because I wished to compliment you on your superb portrayal of the Aztec sun god. It was a most impressive representation of the *máscara* you and your fellow seminarians presented on my behalf."

Augustín shifted his weight from one foot to the other, felt the eyes of the priest on him, and replied quietly, "I am pleased Your Excellency found the *máscara* worthy of esteem, but I am afraid my representation does not deserve such high praise."

The viceroy laughed good-naturedly. "Indeed it does, Don Augustín, the representation was so powerful, it is easy to understand how one might worship such a warrior as the true God."

Augustín knew that his discomfort now showed clearly in his face, and he looked down. "It was not my intention the god be worthy of glorification. Only God in Heaven is due such veneration."

As if regretting his words, the Duque put a hand on his shoulder. "Your portrayal was a glorification of our Lord." The viceroy turned to the Jesuit Father. "Isn't that right, Padre?"

"Of course," the priest answered smoothly, "there is no need for self-recrimination, Augustín. Anything less than total effort on your part would have been a disservice to the God who granted you all your abilities."

Relieved that the audience with the viceroy had finally ended, Augustín walked quickly from the viceregal residence through the crowded marketplace of the square whose eastern side it formed. But in spite of what the priest had said, Augustín knew that he was not entirely without guilt.

Smells of the *zócalo*—freshly baked corn tortillas, roasting chiles, fermenting *pulque*, none-too-fresh slaughtered meat—wafted up to him, but he was oblivious to the people who pushed through the square making their sundry purchases.

He had enjoyed portraying Huitzilopochtli too much. He had devoted too much time to practicing with the gilded sword. It was not necessary in such a *máscara* to be totally proficient in one's representation. He had felt an exuberance, a heady puissance as he stood on the platform above the crowds and exhibited his swordsmanship, and he had been fully aware of his effect on the crowds. He had heard the shouts of praise and felt a deep satisfaction with the enthusiastic adulation of the spectators. Yes, he had sinned, even if it was a minor sin.

He sidestepped a ragged little urchin who leaped to grab a *zapote* that had fallen from a basket. He realized he was as susceptible as anyone to the vanities of the world and tapped his chest over his heart. He could not do a spiritual exercise of an entire month because of his teaching duties, but he would request a week free so that he might meditate on pride and attempt to conquer his own. He should not feel those feelings.

He had gone to confession last night after the *máscara* knowing his culpability and had told his old confessor of his sin.

"True," Padre de la Cruz acknowledged, but his voice had not been harsh, "*fue pecado*, but do not regret having performed in the parade, Augustín, rather, you should welcome it as God's grace. Through this *máscara*, you have been given a better understanding of man's frailties and of the continual necessity of *Dios* in each of our lives."

From the first, when Augustín, as a scared, ten-year-old boy from a village in the farthest reaches of northern New Spain, had arrived in Mexico City to be given into his care, Padre Guillermo de la Cruz had shaped his life. Partly because of the old priest he had worked incessantly to perfect himself—and partly for the other reason that lay hidden within him. He studied with absolute intensity, trying never to shirk the smallest detail of his responsibilities, educational or communal. The *padre* was like a father to him, praising his efforts and accomplishments, but always adding that perfection was God's alone. "Man will always need *Dios* no matter how sinless he may appear," his old mentor had said to him many, many times.

Augustín looked up at the ominous, rain-threatening sky and remembered vividly his arrival in the viceregal capital ten years ago that spring. The rains had started the summer before he arrived and had not stopped. One might have thought that God had broken his promise to Noah not to destroy the earth by flood again. The many canals that crisscrossed the city rose and overflowed their banks, making rivers of the streets. The only way to traverse the city was by canoe; Mass was said from balconies. Hundreds of Spaniards died; thousands of natives lost their lives in the inundation. A stench of death and destruction pervaded the city, and the statue of the Virgin of Guadalupe was brought by canoe to the cathedral in hopes that she could stop the horror. It had all been a sight of awe and terror to a boy from a high desert so far away.

That summer the sickness began. Many people fled the city to the higher, more salutary air of Puebla, and the King of Spain sent his approval to move the capital if it was deemed best. Augustín was sick for days. He knew Padre de la Cruz had despaired of his life, but in the end he lived, and the priest had always attributed it to a miracle of God.

He had felt so alone and afraid in that huge, bustling city that he and the *padre* became close, much like father and son. Above all, he strove to make his mentor proud of him.

After he recovered from the sickness, he began at once in a Jesuit school. Many of his classmates complained, but he loved school, devoured books voraciously, and was happy. For the first time he belonged. He was part of a group; he was not standing on the outside looking in. He remembered the village high on a solitary mesa and remembered the hurt as he stood and wished he could be a part of the games the other children — those with eyes darker than his — played.

As the years had passed in the viceregal capital, he found it increasingly more difficult to remember the remote village of Áco perched in the western reaches of the province of *Nuevo México* far to the north. Every three years he wrote a letter to his grandfather and to Padre Ramírez, which he sent with the mission supply caravan. But even those treasured men were more like a dream than reality, and when he was fourteen he had entered the novitiate. That had been his consuming desire from the start. He wanted to be a Jesuit and devote his life to study, but Padre de la Cruz had not seemed as pleased as he had expected when he told the old priest of his wish. The *padre* grilled him and tried to make the life of a Jesuit seem unattractive.

"But why then are *you* one?" Augustín asked, and when the *padre* gave his reasons, Augustín said those, too, were his own.

"Hijo, ¡no!"

Augustín looked back toward the urgent shout. A well-dressed woman cried with distress as a small boy of two or three darted toward the busy coach-filled street that paralleled one side of the *zócalo*. A dark-skinned nurse-maid ran after the child while the mother wailed, unable to run, hampered by her elegant long clothing.

With two quick strides, Augustín intercepted the swift-legged little boy, sweeping him up in his arms.

"Not so fast, *chicuelo*," he laughed. The small boy wriggled to get loose, but Augustín held him securely and delivered him into the arms of the nurse-maid who came rushing up.

The mother reached them, leaned over and hugged her baby as the nurse-maid held the squirming little boy.

"Hijito, you gave me such a fright," the mother said, her voice trembling with emotion. She smoothed the child's hair with her hand and kissed him on both chubby cheeks.

She turned toward the Jesuit seminarian. *"Gracias, Padre*, from the bottom of my heart."

"No hay de que, Señora," Augustín said, surprised when he saw how young she was. She could not have been older than eighteen or nineteen and yet she already had a child of two or three years of age and from her waistline appeared to be expecting another.

He gave a small bow. *"Con permiso,"* he said and continued on his way.

The young mother was pretty with bright cheeks, her child a mirror image of her, and Augustín remembered other words of his old mentor.

"There will come a day, Augustín, when your body will hunger for a woman." He had turned red as the priest explained in sharp detail what the vow of celibacy required.

"You will experience a desire so strong that you will feel it consuming you, and you will want to join your body to that of a woman. It is not evil, Augustín, it is natural, for God created man and woman to love each other and to give life to children. But when you make the decision to become a priest you must renounce the love of a woman in order to dedicate your entire being to Christ as one of his disciples. It is not a decision to be made lightly. It requires a difficult sacrifice. Never will you have a son of your own blood to raise; you will have no descendants." Augustín did not tell his mentor that he wanted no descendants.

Kneeling in confession that day long ago, he had told Padre de la Cruz of his shame—he wanted the priest to know the worst about him. But he did not tell him of his belief that there was something wrong within him that absolution could not wash away.

Chapter 2

Augustín glanced up again at the heavy sky, grateful that the day before had been filled with sun for the *máscara* parade. He hoped he could reach the Salvatierra house before the rain began in earnest, as it most certainly would before long. He knew from the note he received that the family was impatiently awaiting him.

At first he had deplored the thought of tutoring a wealthy Creole's pampered son. It had seemed demeaning. Studying for the Jesuit priesthood was rigorous and challenging. Teaching Latin and Greek verbs to a lazy child was not. He had just completed his years as a scholastic and philosopher, and now he was in his regency, during which he would teach for three years to gain experience—and a part of his teaching duties included tutoring the son of Don Rodrigo de Salvatierra. Following this period of regency, three more years of intense theological study were required before ordination. And then the final year of tertianship, a year spent in isolation and meditation.

He had looked forward to all the rigors—save tutoring a spoiled child.

"We must be realists," Padre de la Cruz told him. "Salvatierra is a wealthy man. He has it in his power to aid the work of the Church to an enormous degree. He wishes a Jesuit tutor for his son. We will give him a Jesuit tutor, and in return the Profesa will benefit richly."

"But why me?" Augustín asked bluntly, not at all with the obedience the Jesuits instilled in their members.

"Why not you?" the *padre* said. "There is no Jesuit so lofty that he may scorn any task as beneath him—no matter how mean or humble or degrading or uninteresting. Remember that, Augustín."

"Yes, forgive me for my presumption."

"Besides," Padre de la Cruz said as he placed his hand on Augustín's shoulder, his tone less authoritative, "you are one of the best students and a

promising teacher. Why should we not give Señor Salvatierra one of our
very best?"

The onerous task Augustín had expected became, however, a source of satisfaction for him. The comradeship and friendship of the Jesuit schools had
given him a much desired sense of belonging. The friendship that had grown
with the Salvatierra family gave him even more.

Both mother and father welcomed him as if he were an esteemed member
of the family. Weekends he was invited to join the family at their estate
outside Mexico City, and it was there he had been able to engage in the one
thing he loved next to books: riding horses. Don Rodrigo made him a present
of a beautiful silver-gray Arabian. It was a dream of his youth come true,
but he had sadly informed his benefactor that he could not own such a
treasure because of his vow of poverty.

"Nonsense," Don Rodrigo replied. "While the horse remains here, it is
yours. There is no need for a formality of papers. The Arabian is yours for
your enjoyment—it has nothing to do with your vows. If you wish to think
of it as mine, you may do so, but as far as I'm concerned, the horse is yours."
Augustín accepted the handsome animal on those terms and whenever other
duties permitted, and he received approval, he would spend the weekends at
the *hacienda* riding until exhaustion. He liked the exhilaration, the feel of the
sweat, the feel of his muscles, hardened with the exertion. He could forget
everything while he was riding. Nothing intruded.

He felt a drop of rain on his cheek and increased his pace.

The boy he was to tutor was pampered and spoiled, as he had fully expected him to be, but he was bright and Augustín determined, before he even
saw him, that he was going to teach and Luís was going to learn, and learn
well. He had approached the task as a challenge and would not accept defeat.

He discovered at the first lesson that he was not the first tutor the boy
had had, and it was obvious Luís did not expect him to be the last. It appeared the ten-year-old had been able to intimidate his other tutors, and
hoping he had made his eyes cold and steely, Augustín let the pampered son
know immediately who was in charge.

Augustín smiled to himself remembering. Perhaps the other tutors had
been fearful the wealthy father would not be forthcoming with funds if they
made things unpleasant for the son, but he had not cared. He did not want
the job anyway. A show of physical force had been required on a few occasions to make clear that he expected to be obeyed. Once, he pulled Luís
up out of his chair by his shirtfront, lifting him until he looked directly into
the boy's terrified eyes. It was obvious no one had ever dared lay hands on
him before, and it had been difficult not to smile at the sight of the young,
astonished face.

Slightly recovered, Luís had spoken petulantly, "I'm going to tell my father
how I have been mistreated."

"Fine, let us go tell him now." It was clear the boy's threat had been only that, but Augustín pulled him up by the arm and dragged him to his father's study nonetheless.

"Explain the situation," he said firmly to Luís.

Amid a great deal of pauses and stammering, the boy told the story and looked none too good in the recounting.

Don Rodrigo was not at all sympathetic. He stood up from his large desk and looked directly at his son. "Whatever methods Don Augustín employs in his teaching have my full approval, Luís. Remember that!" Following that episode there were few major clashes with the boy, but he still did not apply himself as Augustín might have wished. Help in that respect had come in an unexpected form.

Luís resisted education, but his young sister was avid to learn. The parents, however, saw no need to waste the seminarian's time on a daughter — the son was the one who would need an education; the son was the one the family pinned its hopes on to achieve stunning success.

The son would need a fine education, though it alone would not be sufficient to reach the social levels to which his parents aspired. Neither was money sufficient. Of that, Don Rodrigo had an abundance, for his mines at Ixmiquilpan had seen to that. What he desired above all was a title — not so much for himself, but for his son. Then all the doors would open. First, though, the son must receive the proper educational background.

In the years he had lived in Mexico City, Augustín had learned well the enmity that existed between the *criollos* — Spaniards of pure European blood born in the New World — and *gachupines*, the peninsulars, born in España, the mother country.

The native-born Creoles could never hope to achieve the highest positions in the New World, for those were always filled by Spaniards from the peninsula who had succeeded in obtaining their appointment by flattery, friends, or familial connections at the court in Madrid. The prejudice against Creoles was perpetuated and justified by the statement that the New World had an enervating effect on its inhabitants, sapping their physical and mental prowess.

Augustín was perfectly aware of the fallacy in that belief. In the viceregal capital there was an overabundance of examples of peninsulars devoid of any abilities whatsoever, but that did not change the situation. Ill feelings grew continually, for the *criollos* did not quietly abide their commonly accepted inferiority. Their envy of the privileges of those born in the motherland fired their desires to seek ways to overcome their Creole status.

One of the most common methods was to marry a *gachupín*, whether male or female, but there were few women in New Spain who had been born in España, so most frequently, a family would seek a husband from the mother country for a daughter. At the moment, however, Don Rodrigo was not concerned about marriage, for his son was only ten and his daughter eight. He was determined to see that his son had the best of everything and that included an education.

One day in the room in which the son had his lessons, the little girl had given her presence away by a sneeze. Augustín found her hiding next to a bookcase behind an oversized chair.

Her large eyes brimmed with tears and her mouth quivered as she tried to be brave, expecting a severe reprimand from her brother's strict tutor. Augustín smiled at her, but the tears welled up over her bottom lashes and spilled down her cheeks. In a plaintive little voice she sobbed, "I want to study like Luís!"

Her head dropped to her chest and she stood there weeping, her small shoulders shaking. She was a pitiful sight. Augustín's chest constricted with tenderness for her. He reached down and picked her up, smoothing her tousled, honey-colored hair and pressed her head against his shoulder.

"Don't cry, Antonia," he said gently, "don't cry."

Over his shoulder, he spoke to Luís. "You may have fifteen minutes. Don't be late in returning!" The boy was out of the door in an instant, mumbling a quick "gracias."

Augustín sat down in the chair behind which the girl had been hiding. He held her on his lap. "Now, tell me," he said quietly, lifting her chin so that she would look at him, "what is this about your wanting to study?" The little girl gulped for air, trying to stop her crying.

"I want to study like Luís," she said poignantly. "He doesn't even want to learn things, but he gets to anyway. I would work hard, but they won't let me!" She buried her face again in the seminarian's shoulder. "I wish I were a boy!" she wailed. "They get everything."

He patted her, an immense feeling of tenderness welling within him for the despondent little child. "Antonia, don't cry," he said softly. "Do not wish to be a boy. Dios made both boys and girls; he loves and wants you both. He made little girls more beautiful than little boys so that they would grow up into beautiful women and men would take care of them."

She sat up straight and full of anger and looked directly at him, her eyes indignant. "I want to take care of myself! But most of all I want to learn. Why can't I learn? You're like everyone else!"

With that scathing remark, she pushed herself off his lap and began to cry again as she stood there in front of him.

"First of all," he said sternly, "if you want people to take you seriously, you must learn not to cry."

The abruptness of his words stilled her sobs. He leaned forward, lifted her face, wiped the tears away with his thumbs, and smoothed back her hair from her face. "Now," he said, "tell me why you think you should be allowed to study."

She swallowed, and her light hazel eyes were wide and large as she looked at him solemnly. "I am as smart as my brother. I know I am. I want to work, he doesn't. I will be a good student. I will learn the things my father wants my brother to learn, and when I grow up I can help him if my brother won't."

She raised her chin a little higher. "But I don't care what you say, it's better to be a boy than a girl." He laughed at her young defiance, and she was not pleased. "I am not crying, but still you laugh at me," she said.

"I'm sorry, you are absolutely right. Forgive me. I should not have laughed. Tell me, now, what have you learned from behind this chair?"

Without hesitation she reeled off the declension of the Latin pronoun he had just been teaching her brother before she was discovered.

He was dumbfounded and wanted to laugh with surprise but did not. He looked at her seriously and asked her to decline a word he had worked on the previous day with her brother. Without a single mistake, she recited it.

"Excellent. Would you like for me to ask your father to permit you to study alongside your brother?"

She threw her arms around his neck and hugged him with all her strength. "Yes, yes, yes!"

A sly smile touched her lips. "Who knows," she whispered, "maybe my brother will start to work harder if there is a *girl* to show him up."

In the end that had been one of the arguments he used to convince Antonia's father to let her study, and as it turned out, the little girl was correct. At first Luís scoffed and made fun of her, but when she began to do better than he, his pride would not allow a mere girl — and younger, at that — to surpass him.

It had all worked out for the best, and in the process Augustín became more like a member of the family. Each time he arrived, he was welcomed with a warmth that surpassed mere politeness or friendship. Antonia adored him — that he knew — and he reciprocated. She was eager to learn and please her tutor in the bargain. She always ran to him when she saw him and grabbed his hand, something bubbling from her lips that she had been saving to tell him.

He was quick to realize that he was the only person who listened to her. Her parents loved her but they had no expectations for her as they had for her brother; therefore the things she had to say to them they treated like a bird's song — something one heard but did not stop to consider, much less answer. He, on the other hand, listened to her song, heard the words, and responded.

He was less than a block from the Salvatierras' house when the rain began. Nevertheless by the time he reached the door, he was soaked through. The servant let him in and Doña María Luisa came running with towels.

"Oh, you poor thing," she said, as she handed him a towel and began to help dry his garments as they dripped onto the marble floor, but his clothes were much too soaked for a few towels to have any effect.

"Come," she said, in the voice of an overly protective mother, "you must get out of that wet clothing or you will catch a chill." He started to protest, but she was insistent. "I won't have you getting sick. What would I do with the children if you were not here to give them their lessons?"

Obediently he followed her up the long stairs to Don Rodrigo's room. She took a dressing gown from an armoire and laid it on the ornate bed. "Now you get out of that wet cassock and put on this robe, for we are all anxious to hear about this meeting of yours with the viceroy," she said with excitement.

After a delay, María Luisa sent a servant for him.

The *criada* returned and spoke hesitantly to her mistress, "The seminarian says that he has been soaked through, *Señora*, and the cassock is not the only piece of his clothing that is wet. He regrets that he does not have the proper attire in which to appear in public."

"Bah!" Don Rodrigo responded with a laugh as he walked into the *sala*. "He is family. There is no need to stand on ceremony!"

And with that the elder Salvatierra went to the marble stairway and headed to the second-floor bedrooms. When he entered, he found the seminarian dressed in his robe standing by the dark green brocade drapes staring out the window at the downpour.

"Augustín," he said, good-naturedly, "don't hide in the bedroom just because your clothes are wet. You must tell us about your audience with the viceroy and who you were in the *máscara*. You kept it secret before the parade, but you gave your word you would tell us afterward if we hadn't spotted you."

Augustín smiled weakly. "I know I promised to tell you everything as soon as possible, but I cannot very well appear like this in polite company."

Don Rodrigo laughed. "Modest, my dear Augustín, after that *máscara*? Little Antonia thinks she knows who you were."

He grinned and winked, and Augustín colored perceptibly. "Come now. You are a member of the family. That robe covers any indecency. Besides, they will tear me limb from limb if I go back downstairs without you. Everyone is waiting for you in the *sala*. We have not seen you since before the *máscara*. Then, when you sent the note saying that you would not be coming for the children's lesson until late today because the viceroy had requested your presence, well, there has been nothing *else* talked about in this house. Even Luís could not hide his eagerness for your arrival."

"Perhaps I should contrive to see the viceroy more often if it makes Luís anxious for his lesson."

"Fine idea, except that María Luisa would take up all your time quizzing you about the new Duque de Escalona and the doings of the court, and you would have no time to put Luís through his materials! But come now," Don Rodrigo said, "let's go downstairs."

Augustín hesitated, looking down at his attire again. He did not even have shoes.

Don Rodrigo went to the armoire and rummaged among the shoes and boots, finding a pair of backless slippers. "At least you won't have to go unshod. Here."

He reluctantly followed Don Rodrigo down the stairs. When he reached the bottom, Antonia came flying to him, her face beaming. He forgot his discomfort and picked her up as he always did when he came to the house. She kissed his cheek in her usual greeting.

Normally consumed by the intellectual and mental, he paid scarce attention to his own feelings. The charitable works he did were not done so much from the heart as from the mind knowing that compassion is necessary in this difficult life and that human suffering should be abolished if possible. He had not wished ill of anyone and had in fact prayed for the well-being of many, whether they were prisoners in the jails of Mexico City, syphilitic patients in the hospital, wealthy widows on their deathbed fearful of what God had in store for them, or his own colleagues who were troubled by a difficult problem. Though he was concerned for all those with affliction and did whatever was in his power to do for them, they had never touched the most interior part of him.

This was so until the little daughter of the Salvatierra family opened a small window into his heart—a window that he had sought previously to keep closed in order to protect himself from pain. The child's adoration was something new, and he gave of himself to her in a way he had not done before for others.

He set Antonia down in the *sala* as he accepted a frothy, perfumed cup of hot *chocolatl* from the servant.

"See, *Mamá*, see!" Antonia laughed happily, "I was right!" She pointed to Augustín's legs that could be seen below the robe. "See, those are the same legs as Huitzi . . . , Huitzi . . ."

"Huitzilopochtli," Luís supplied in the condescending tone of an older brother.

"I think you are right, *mija*," Don Rodrigo laughed. "Come now, tell us, Augustín. Were you the masked god with the golden sword?"

Augustín took the chair offered him. He brought the cup of chocolate to his lips hoping to hide his discomfort.

"Tell us," they all chorused.

"Yes."

Antonia clapped her hands. "I was right. I was right. I told you so."

Luís had a look of awe on his face. "*Híjole*," he whistled, "you really know how to use a sword!"

Don Rodrigo laughed and turned to his son. "Maybe we should get Augustín to teach you swordsmanship instead of your fencing master."

María Luisa changed the subject. "Tell us," she broke in, clasping her hands together on the pale yellow silk of her skirt, "what did the viceroy want of you?"

Color spread across Augustín's face again. The viceroy wanted to meet him to commend him on his performance as Huitzilopochtli. How could he tell them that?

Luís unknowingly came to his rescue. "I'll bet the viceroy wanted to meet the person who was so good with the sword of gold!"

He nodded and responded quietly, "Yes, something like that."

Don Rodrigo clapped him on the shoulder. "You're too modest, Augustín. Are you going to make us drag all the details out of you?"

"What's the Duque like?" María Luisa asked eagerly. "We only caught a glimpse of him on his entry into the city. As yet we haven't been invited to the palace. If we were *gachupines* we would have been there already." This last she added with asperity, her mouth forming a hard line.

"We would be wiping the viceroy's *culo* if we were *gachupines*," her husband said bitterly, and María Luisa gasped.

"Rodrigo, not before the children!" she said sharply.

Augustín spoke up to keep the conversation away from the enmity *criollos* felt for peninsulars. "The Duque seems like a reasonable man. One of the reasons he wanted to see me, according to the Jesuit Father, was that he thought perhaps I was a native swordsman, and they might be able to use such a person at court."

"Oh, did he really?" Don Rodrigo said, his interest perking up.

"Yes, he seemed quite taken by everything about the valley of Mexico."

The air remained heavy with moisture but the rain had stopped by the time he started back to San Ildefonso. Clouds lowered over the city, obscuring the twilight. He would be up late. He must finish the letters. The mission supply caravan for *Nuevo México* would be departing shortly for its triennial journey that required half a year to reach its far destination.

Fray Tomás Manso, who oversaw the purchasing of the great quantities of supplies that the caravan loaded into its heavy, mule- and oxen-drawn carts, had left word for Augustín that he should have his letter ready in the event the caravan might depart ahead of schedule.

Every three years the caravan carried a letter from the seminarian to the Franciscan Juan Ramírez at the pueblo of Ácoma.

As a boy, Augustín had traveled in the caravan that rumbled south from Santa Fé to Mexico City in the fall of 1629, and Fray Manso, who had journeyed in that same cart train, had known only the brief story that Padre Ramírez had told about the boy. Neither did Manso know that the sealed packet from the seminarian to Juan Ramírez in reality contained two letters: one to the priest and one to an aging Ácoma native.

Augustín wrote telling of his progress in his studies and a few anecdotes of his life. This letter would describe the family for which he was now tutor, but when he wrote the letters, he wrote them to a memory, yellowed and faded like some of the letters he had in a small silver box that contained his past.

Over half his life had been lived in the opulent viceregal capital, and he could scarcely remember the high, barren rock that had once been his home. Sometimes he felt a constriction in his chest when he thought about the grandfather who had allowed him to journey to Mexico City to study. Many times he had in the silence of a prayer thanked his grandfather for this sacrifice. He always included the old man, his aunt, and the priest at Ácoma in his petitions. He had done it for so long that they were more like words in a prayer than the names of living people.

When Augustín received letters from the priest and his grandfather, he was enveloped in a kind of irreality. It was as if he were reading a letter out of someone else's distant past, as if he were holding fog or mist between his hands.

After he had read the letters, he put them in the silver box that contained his past. Then he would take the stone fetish from its small deerskin pouch in the bottom of the box and finger it carefully as he also did a piece of mulberry silk ribbon, and a small, carved bead of coral. He would finish by taking the rosary that had belonged to a grandmother he had never known, and would pray with it before carefully replacing it in the box that for another three years would remain unopened.

Augustín let the candle wax drip onto the folded paper, pressed a seal into it, and closed his eyes.

Part Two

EL PEÑOL

The Rock, 1629

Chapter 3

"They come!"

The word spread swiftly throughout the village as if blown like particles on the wind, and the words caught in their throats like the fine, pale sand ground by the wind from the high rock mesa on which they lived.

"They come! They bring the large rolling baskets with them."

Another voice questioned. "Why? What do they want this time?"

No one spoke the words, but all remembered. The weather-hewn copper faces were emotionless. Thirty growing seasons had not yet obliterated the memory of that other time. Nor would a hundred growing seasons, nor a hundred more. The memory was as much a part of them as was the story of Iyatiku, the mother of them all. It was tribal memory, and tribal memory was difficult to erase, withstanding as it did even the erosive wind of time. The sharp edges might be worn smooth, but the memory remained cast in stone much like the sheer rock that was their home.

The man limped as he walked toward the precipitous drop of the mesa's edge. He held the hand of a young boy, nine or ten growing seasons old. The man looked older than the fifty some growing seasons of his life—not that his back was bowed, for he held himself arrow-straight, nor was his hair dusted with the gray ashes of time.

The suns of cloudless skies, brilliantly blue, and the harsh winter winds that had nothing in their path to ease their biting edges as they blew across the exposed village on the bare mesa top had etched permanent lines on the man's high-cheekboned face, but neither the sun nor the wind could claim authorship of the man's appearance of great age.

As his aged eyes looked out across the valley floor, it was as if he had stood that same way looking into the distance that reached back years into the past. The years were ten and twenty and thirty, but they were more than many lifetimes to him. The man could have told the boy that through the eyes may pass uncounted years, more swift than the sharp-shinned hawk's high-velocity stoop that sends it earthward toward an unsuspecting prairie rodent, but he said nothing.

The boy clutched the man's hand tightly, sensing instinctively the future that would be acted upon by the past. A tiny shiver ran through him. It had its source in apprehension but also in anticipation. He had seen one or two of them from a distance, as he peeked from a housetop, but in spite of his grandfather's attempts to dissemble, the boy knew the old man did not want the pale ones to see him. His aunt, too, kept him busy when one of the strangers happened to the valley and climbed to the top of the mesa where their village perched. But this time it was different. This time there were more of them, and they brought with them odd, rolling *carretas*, as his grandfather called them, that lumbered across the dry, rough terrain, their loud creaks and groans rising stridently and clearly to the mesa top.

Why had his grandfather taught him their language if he did not want the strangers to see him, he who looked more like the strangers than like the people of the mesa? His grandfather told him he must learn the strangers' language so that, when the day came for the boy to die, he could talk with his grandmother, who would have loved him very much.

They had a place, the pale ones, where they went when they died. There his grandmother was. It disturbed the boy that his grandfather did not know for sure if the ones with copper skin went there, too. Where would he go when he died? Would he go to live among the pale ones whom he resembled but did not know, or would he go among those with whom he had lived all his life? His grandfather was very wise; he knew everything—why did he not know this, too?

Surely there must be an answer somewhere in those many bound leaves that were his grandfather's treasure and now also his own. For as long as he could remember he would go to the carefully stacked leaves and take a volume, turning each leaf carefully as he had seen his grandfather do. His grandfather had taught him that the marks on the leaves talked, and when he looked at them a whole new world opened up for him behind his eyes.

People, things, and places that were like dreams filled his head, but his grandfather said they were real. Somewhere, farther than his mind could even grasp, were all the things that the marks on the leaves told him. The leaves talked to him as the other children in the village would not.

He wanted someone to talk to; he wanted to play with the other children but they laughed at him and called him names. When he was younger they had pushed him, too, and pinched him, but no longer. No one dared to touch him now. He was a head taller than any boy his age and taller than some boys three years his senior. They stayed away from him now, knowing that he had no fear and that he could rub any of their faces into the dusty street. They knew, too, that the steel-bladed knife of the pale ones that his grandfather had given him and which he carried at his waist could be used faster than the eye could follow, for they had seen it used.

Mastya was just as quick and just as cunning as the gray fox for whom he was named. Arrows were pulled from the gray fox quiver he wore on his back with a quiet swiftness none could match. And he was always the first on the valley floor, reaching it before the cold winter sun did, running tirelessly in the brittle, frozen dawn air dressed only in rabbit fur moccasins and a breechclout.

His chest was not even heaving when at last he scaled the sheer mesa wall and reentered the village. Nor did he shiver when he broke the ice on the frozen pool of water on the mesa top, dipped in the pottery jug and poured its icy contents over himself to bathe, but none of the rigors through which he put himself would be enough to gain admission into the K'atsina society. He had no birthright. There would be no uncle to come to his dwelling to carry him on his back to the *kiva,* where the initiation would take place. He knew the prayers. He knew how to sprinkle cornmeal to the cardinal directions and how to make a prayer stick to send to Wenimats. He knew the prayer to sing during a hunt. He knew that it was necessary to feed the smooth black fetish he carried in his small pouch. When he made a kill, the fetish was to eat first, renewing its power to help him track and secure game, and he knew he must also feed earth mother with some of the blood of his kill. He knew all these things, and the village was the only home he knew. But he could not be Ácoma; he could never be Ácoma. His mother was not a person of the mesa top.

He knew the story of his birth and it caused him much shame, although his grandfather had said it was not shameful. His grandfather told him everything—everything. They had made a mistake, his grandmother and himself, his grandfather had said. They should have told the boy who was his father everything from the beginning, then it might not have happened.

And there was the pale ones' god, *Dios.* He was difficult to understand. He was not like the K'atsina who sent the clouds that brought the rain for their crops. They were not difficult to understand. They were K'atsina. Without them the rain would not come, the crops of the Ácoma would die, and with no food to eat, the Ácoma would die, but the pale god—one could not be sure what he did. The boy's grandfather told him that his grandmother, who lay on the top of a high rock pinnacle to the west, believed in the pale god. She said he had a purpose but that man sometimes did not understand what it was, but if one prayed to him, he would provide.

Mastya knew he had a name his grandfather had given him, a name only he, his grandfather, and his aunt knew. Sometimes he whispered it to himself.

"Augustín, Augustín."

He liked the sound. It had a clear ring like a pebble tinging against the blade of the knife his grandfather had given him—a knife of the strangers that had been his father's.

His grandfather had even taught him some of the prayers the pale god understood and told him that he should repeat the strange words that started "Ave Maria" and "Pater Noster." And he showed him how to touch himself on the forehead, chest, and shoulders to make the sign of the crossed sticks that were so important to the god. He told him also about the men who had nailed the god onto crossed sticks, but his grandfather said he did not understand it.

"Why do you tell it to me?" Mastya asked him once.

"Your grandmother would have wanted me to," was his grandfather's reply.

Once, a pale stranger who wore a long robe came to the village to talk about the man on the crossed sticks, but he did not stay. The silent hostility of the villagers was patently obvious, and though the man made pious protestations about returning, everyone saw the fear he tried to hide, and they knew he would not be back.

Mastya would have liked to ask him about the man on the crossed sticks, for he was very curious, and he would like to have spoken the language he had learned—the language he could speak to no one but himself, his grandfather, and his aunt. He knew, however, that his grandfather did not want the pale ones to see him, so he stayed on the rooftop terrace and watched the man as he gestured with his hands, the breeze lifting and whipping his long robe about his ankles.

He would also have liked to see the pale one's village. How he would have liked to see other places that he knew existed.

La villa de la Santa Fé—the name rolled off his lips. His grandfather had even lived there, but that was long ago. The *villa* had been the home of his father, also, and his mother and his grandmother, but now they were dead, resting under piles of stones on the top of a high rock pinnacle to the west of Áco.

He had been to the pinnacle once or twice with his grandfather, and it was difficult climbing when he was smaller. He remembered distinctly the feel of the rocks cutting into his knees as he mimicked his grandfather and knelt on the sharp stones of the top. Crossed sticks marked each grave and his grandfather pointed out under which pile lay his father, his mother, and his grandmother.

"You have your grandmother's eyes." His grandfather's voice had a faraway sound to it. "They were gray, the color of the dove, and her hair was the color of wet pine bark."

Mastya's eyes moved from his grandfather's face. There was an emotion there he had never seen before and he had an uneasy feeling that he had been privy to something that was not for him to see.

"Your father was tall and beautiful," his grandfather said, "like you will be, and he rode the horse better than any of the pale ones. Perhaps one day you, too, may ride the swift animal."

The story his grandfather told him of the strange *caballos* the pale ones had brought into their land fascinated Mastya. He was about six growing seasons when he saw the first one. He felt bewitched by the huge animal that stamped and snorted. He slipped off his housetop unseen and made his way down a little-used rock crevice, hiding behind boulders and stones until he was not too distant from where the horses stood at the bottom of the mesa, guarded by a man dressed in metal plate. From his secret spot, Mastya watched for a long time, aching to know how it felt to ride like the wind across the valley floor on the back of the powerful animal.

"Your mother, too," his grandfather continued, "loved the horses and rode as well as a man."

Mastya's chest filled with pride at the thought. "But why do the Ácoma not have any of the wonderful beasts?"

"The pale ones keep them for themselves. They do not want the people to have them."

"Why not?"

"Perhaps they are afraid the people will become strong and make them leave the land."

"Do you want them to leave?"

"At one time I wanted them to go. I hated the pale ones. I would gladly have killed them all."

"But what about grandmother? She was a pale one. Did you hate her?"

A smile touched the corners of his grandfather's lips, and he reached out and stroked the boy's hair. "No, I loved your grandmother. Had it not been for her, I would not have had you to keep me company in my old age."

Mastya saw the emotion in his grandfather's eyes, and he threw his arms around him and hugged him fiercely. "I wish Grandmother, and Father, and Mother could be here with us, too," the little boy said. He felt his grandfather nod, but he did not see the look in the man's eyes that showed clearly that it could never have been.

"But we have Auntie Siya," Mastya said, trying to sound cheerful, knowing instinctively his grandfather's loneliness, for it was his also.

"Yes," his grandfather replied, smiling, "we have Auntie Siya. She has taken care of you since you were born."

The boy said, "I like the rabbit stew Auntie Siya makes."

His grandfather laughed.

As Mastya stood clutching his grandfather's hand and staring intently into the distance where the carts labored noisily across the terrain, he too, like the rest of the wary Ácoma, wondered why the strangers had come.

"Are they going to fill the rolling baskets with our cornmeal?" Mastya asked in a whisper.

"I do not know," his grandfather said.

"But what if we don't have enough? Will they do like they did last time?"

Unconsciously his eyes moved to his grandfather's lame foot, encased in a moccasin only half the size of the one on his left foot.

His grandfather saw the path the boy's eyes took. His face was solemn but gentle, wearing no hate. "They may have cut off my foot, but I have my life. There are still Ácoma on this mesa. We still have our K'atsina. That is what matters. Always remember that, my grandson."

The boy nodded solemnly, swallowing. He knew by heart the story of the massacre. His grandfather had told it many times upon his request. There was a fascination in the horror of it.

It was hard for him to visualize his grandfather as a young man of twenty-five growing seasons. To him, his grandfather had always been old, very old and wise, but his grandfather had been a young man when it happened. He had a young wife — a young wife with child. That was in the first year the pale ones came to stay. They came to Áco, a small group of them, wanting cornmeal. One of the metal-clothed men killed a woman over a turkey she did not want to give him. Filled with anger, the people of the village killed the small group of strangers who demanded the food the Ácoma needed for their own sustenance.

Mastya slipped a small, pale pink coral bead from his leather pouch and rolled it between his fingers. His grandfather had given it to him. It was one of the boy's prized possessions along with the obsidian fetish with its tiny eye of turquoise. The pink bead was delicately carved, like a flower. Mastya rubbed it between his fingers and looked at it. The tiny bead had belonged to the leader of the small group of pale ones. The man had been fingering a string of the same beads when he was killed by the Ácoma, a heavy rock hurled against his head. Later, Mastya's grandfather had found the pink bead lying in the dust, and when he made Mastya's medicine pouch he took the bead from his own pouch and put it in Mastya's.

A large group of the pale ones returned to Áco to avenge the death of the others. They brought a thundering weapon made of metal and as big around as a tree trunk. It sent fire and destruction into the village. More Ácoma than the fingers of one hundred hands were killed, and the survivors were herded back to the village of the pale ones at Santo Domingo. That was where his grandfather's foot had been cut off along with those of the other Ácoma men, and they were made slaves for twenty years, as were his auntie Siya and the other women.

Mastya slipped the bead back into the pouch. It was at the village of Ohké where his grandfather had come to be the slave of the pale woman. His grandfather had gotten sickness in the wound of his foot and the woman had cared for him, and he had lived, but he hated her and hated the pale ones who had made him lame, but she would not hate him back.

It was here the look on his grandfather's face always changed as he told the story. His grandfather began to love the woman and the hate went away, and Mastya's father was born, but they had not told their child who his real parents were. The boy did not know that the Ácoma and the pale woman were his father and mother. He thought his own mother had died when he was born and the pale woman had taken pity on him and raised him in her house.

Not telling him was what caused the shame, Mastya's grandfather told him. For that reason, his grandfather had told Mastya everything. Mastya knew that his father and mother were . . . he could not bring his mind to say it. He was glad the people in the village did not know. It was bad enough that he carried the blood of the pale ones. How much worse would it be if they knew the other? His grandfather tried to tell him it did not matter, but was that why his grandfather did not want any of the pale ones to see his grandson?

At times Mastya looked at his reflection in the cool, clear water trapped in the stone pools on the mesa top or looked at his reflection in the shiny, polished piece of metal Auntie Siya had brought with her when she returned from living among the pale ones. He did not look like the Ácoma, but he did not look bad to himself. He did not see anything in his face that showed the shame.

His skin was lighter than the Ácoma, but his face had their same high cheekbones. His eyes were not Ácoma, that was true. They were the color of the gray fox's fur or the dove, like his grandmother's, so his grandfather told him. His hair was dark, but if he took the shiny piece of metal out into the sun and looked at himself, it appeared as if his hair caught fire, flickering and smoldering like the coals in the bottom of a dying campfire. His grandfather did not talk much about Mastya's mother, but he had said that her hair was the color of flames—bright, leaping flames.

Mastya wondered what it would have been like had his mother and father lived. He sometimes wondered what it would be like to live far away; to live where he was the same as everyone else, somewhere where he belonged, somewhere where he could have friends. He wanted friends; he wanted to belong; he wanted someone to talk to. Was there any such place? He loved his grandfather and his aunt, and he knew that they loved him absolutely, but he would have liked to have had a friend. But he did not and so sought friendship in the leaves with marks on them.

Little by little, the bound leaves had arrived. They had been his grandmother's, and when she died, she willed them to one of the pale women, a friend named Dorotea, in the *villa* of the pale ones. Auntie Siya had lived in this woman's house, and when she returned to Áco, the pale woman began to send the bound leaves, called *libros*, to give to Mastya's grandfather, for the woman knew he had learned to read the marks.

If ever an Ácoma went to the *villa*, they returned with bound leaves for Mastya's grandfather, and occasionally a villager from some other pueblo would come to Áco, a basket filled with *libros* on his back, which the pale woman had paid him to carry on the long journey.

At last they all arrived. The woman wrote to ask after the boy and prayed that one day she might see the grandchild of her dearest friend. She closed, saying that if they ever needed for anything, they were to contact her immediately. It was signed, DOROTEA.

Mastya's grandfather had taught him how to read the marks, lamenting that he could not teach him more when the boy had learned everything the grandfather knew, but Mastya continued to spend hours with the leaves until he knew more than the grandfather, learning the meanings by seeing the words in different places. There were some, however, that Mastya could never succeed in deciphering and he longed to know them. They were like the little prickly stickers that one might get in the fingers if he were not careful gathering the purplish fruit of the *ibitsha:* The thorns were not painful but were a constant source of irritation until they finally worked their way out. Mastya wondered if any of the pale ones might be able to unlock the meaning of those words.

When the group of pale ones reached the base of the awe-inspiring citadel, the rays of the sun were lengthening, bringing to prominence the steep, vertical crags of the massive stone mesa. It seemed impossible that it had once been conquered.

A delegation of Ácoma descended to the valley floor. It might have been a sign of peace but more probably was an attempt to forestall the pale ones from climbing up to the village.

There was still some time. It was not yet necessary for Mastya to return to his dwelling and remain out of sight in the event any pale ones chose to come into the village. Scores of Ácoma lined the edges of the high rock, looking down at the unwelcome visitors, wondering why so many had come this time.

The armor of the thirty-some strangers mirrored the golden rays of the sun, and the embossed plates of their weapons snatched shards of the lengthening light and flashed random glints of it upward to the mesa top.

A lean, vigorous man broke away from the group of pale ones. His long, blue habit was gray with dust. It was obvious he had walked the entire distance from the *villa* of the pale ones. Behind him, three more long-robes dismounted from their mules but did not follow him. With long, bold strides the dust-clad priest approached the delegation of Ácoma who stood silent and unwelcoming.

He stopped in front of them and looked levelly at each one. Then he made the sign of the cross over them. Their faces were stolid and unfriendly, revealing nothing of their thoughts. He lifted his eyes to the mesa top and made the sign of the cross over the people assembled there, first to the left, then to the center, then to the right. He looked back at the men in front of him. Slowly he lifted the heavy silver crucifix that hung around his neck and kissed it.

The silence was as ominous as the rocky crags. Then to the astonishment of the Ácoma, evidenced only by a flickering in their dark eyes, the priest fell to his knees, inclined his head to the ground and kissed the soil of Áco.

"I have come to stay." He spoke loudly so that those on the mesa top might hear. Someone had taught him the Queres words.

The delegation of Ácoma men did not stop him as he walked past them and made his way among the boulders to the crevice pathway by which to reach the mesa top. The priest was lost from sight for a moment behind the rugged rocks. As a group, the metal-plated Spaniards moved forward, their weapons poised, their bodies erect and tense. The priest emerged from behind the rocks, never looking back. As he began to climb, the Ácoma above leaned over the edge, watching his progress.

Suddenly there was a scream, and the priest's head flew up, his eyes filled with horror, attaching instantly to that which held all eyes, native and foreign. A small form, arms and legs flailing grotesquely, plummeted from above.

As the body hit, a loud, shrieking wail rent the air from above, the women keening shrilly with their lament. The small form lay inert. The priest scrambled madly down, clawing over the rocks to reach the body that had fallen only a few yards from him.

It was a girl child he saw, a beautiful, square-faced little girl of about five or six. There was no evidence of life but she looked as if she might only have been sleeping, for the cruel rocks had not smashed the small body. She lay on a pocket of sand the wind had ground from the towering rock of pink sandstone that had been her home. The priest knelt beside her, making the sign of the cross on her forehead as his lips began the prayers, but they stopped in midsentence, frozen in astonishment. The girl's eyelids fluttered and then blinked open.

"My God in Heaven," the priest whispered, breaking into a broad smile as he gathered up the little girl and clutched her to his chest. Juan Ramírez's eyes closed and his lips moved in fervent prayer as he held her.

Thank You, Lord, for Your blessed mercy in saving this innocent child. Thank You for allowing her to fall to the sand instead of to the rocks that would surely have killed her. Thank You for this sign of Your power. I will give my life that these people may know of Your salvation.

He looked down at the little girl and smiled at her. She looked with fear at him, but he stroked her cheek and murmured reassuringly in broken Queres. He rose to his feet, lifting her with him, and carried her across the rocks. A cheer rose from the Spaniards below and there were shouts from the Ácoma when they saw her. He began to climb upward along the path again. Her arms went round his neck and held tightly as he climbed. He reached the series of ladders and began the final ascent, the girl held in one arm as he climbed with the other.

"Father, look out!" came the horrified shout of the Spaniards below.

Ramírez heard the crashing noise of the large rock before his eyes saw it hurtling down from above. The little girl screamed and clutched hard at him. He pressed her against the ladder, protecting her with his own body as best he could.

"*Santa María,* have mercy on us," he gasped.

He felt sharp splinters bite into his face as the careening stone crashed against a rock that jutted out only a foot or so from them. His ears rang from the impact, and he heard in the distance the rock as it continued on its unimpeded course downward. The little girl whimpered with fear.

He whispered soothingly to her in Castilian, wishing he knew more than a handful of words in her language. It was then he heard the shouting and the jangling of armor from down below. He jerked his head around and saw with shock the soldiers as they shoved the delegation of Ácoma with their arquebuses and surrounded them. He heard the angry shouts of the Ácoma from above when they saw their leaders herded together.

"Release those men immediately!" Ramírez bellowed to the soldiers below. "How dare you insult their hospitality!"

"But Father," the captain of the guard shouted up to him, "I don't think that rock fell of its own accord."

"I say it did!" Juan Ramírez shouted with anger, his voice like iron. "Release those men!"

The soldiers backed away from the delegation of Ácoma, and the shouts from above ceased. Only then did the priest resume his ascent, the little girl on his arm. There was absolute silence when he finally stepped onto the mesa top with the child.

The Ácoma backed away, leaving an open semicircle around him. From the crowd a woman ran toward him, crying, her arms outstretched toward the child. Juan Ramírez gave the little girl into her mother's arms. The woman cried and babbled as she hugged the child.

At last the little girl pushed herself out of her mother's arms and walked back to where the friar stood. Timidly, she took his hand, bent her face toward it and breathed on it in the sign of welcome.

He made the sign of the cross on her forehead with his thumb and blessed her. As timidly as her daughter, the mother approached the priest and made the same sign of welcome, and he blessed her.

He looked out at the surrounding crowd. The copper faces were unfriendly, perhaps even hostile. He repeated the words in their language he had spoken down below. There was absolute assurance in his voice.

"I have come to stay."

Chapter 4

Juan Ramírez did not see the young boy, well to the back of the crowd, who watched him intently. Mastya had not returned to his house, for the tumult and confusion of the events had given him the opportunity to stay.

He had stood by his grandfather and watched in horror and fascination as the daughter of Sweet Corn Deer Woman fell and as the long-robe miraculously made her live again. Then some moments later, from where Mastya stood with the rest of the Ácoma on the summit, it appeared as if the falling rock had smashed against the man in the dark blue robe who held the girl, but when the man did not fall but rather resumed his ascent as if he had been untouched, murmurs surged through the crowd on the mesa top, their awe and trepidation palpable in the clear air.

Had the god of the pale strangers done these things? Mastya wondered in amazement. Was he real? Not until that moment had the pale ones' god ever been anything to Mastya other than something that his grandfather had talked about upon a few occasions.

Mastya would have liked to ask the long-robe if his god had done the things he had just witnessed, but he did not dare.

The long-robe stood and gazed at the village, taking in everything before he turned and looked out across the valley. He raised his arms toward the sky, transfixed by the magnificence of the view. There was a look of serene satisfaction on his face as he began to walk toward the village. The Ácoma did not impede his way nor that of the group of the Spaniards from down below who began to ascend the rock of Áco, sounds of their clanking armor drifting clearly up the steep sides of the mesa.

"I will go to the house now," Mastya whispered to his grandfather. The old man nodded, and Mastya trotted down one of the house rows and quickly disappeared. His grandfather remained a part of the crowd that followed slowly and watched the long-robed priest as he walked through the village, surveying it. At one point he turned to the crowd.

"Does anyone here speak Castilian?" he asked in a loud voice.

There was not a murmur. All eyes looked at him without expression; even the eyes of Mastya's grandfather belied not a flicker of understanding. The priest turned away and continued his walking.

He traversed the house rows and when he had reached the south side of the village he turned back to gaze for long moments at the multistoried earth-colored dwellings. He looked around him and then walked toward the east. Again he surveyed the village, then walked to the edge of the precipitous cliff and looked out over the valley and toward the mesa that lined the eastern horizon. By that time the other Spaniards had reached the mesa top, and the priest went to meet them. They stood as a group in one of the village plazas.

A man who appeared to be the leader of the Spaniards stood arrogantly and authoritatively in the center, and next to him the royal notary began to speak in a commanding voice. He paused for a moment and a *mestizo* who stood nearby began to translate in the Queres language.

"Know ye, people of Ácoma," he said in a loud, carrying voice, "you have before you the new governor of the province of *Nuevo México*, Don Francisco Manuel de Silva Nieto. Your chiefs will now present themselves to render homage unto the said governor. And know ye likewise," the voice had taken on a harsh tone that indicated the Spanish authorities would brook no resistance, "you will render homage unto the Reverend Father, Fray Juan Ramírez, who has come to live among you to bring salvation to your souls. You will accept him into your village and you will provide him with the necessities of his person and likewise those pertaining to the Church."

There was a moment of heavy silence. The governor looked out at the hostile faces of the Ácoma and was again unsure of the wisdom of allowing the priest to stay to convert the natives. He did not want to have to make a retaliatory attack on the citadel village, should the heathen kill the zealous priest.

Vicente de Zaldívar might have succeeded once, but Governor Silva did not see how it had been possible, for the village appeared impregnable to him. No, he would not relish having to attack such a rock fortress.

The Ácoma began to murmur among themselves. Again the *mestizo* spoke, commanding the chiefs to come forward. At length, several natives separated themselves from the crowd and approached the Spanish delegation. They knelt first in front of the governor. He motioned toward the blue-robed priest who stood next to him, and the natives likewise knelt before Juan Ramírez, breathing on his hand as was the Ácoma custom.

The governor then spoke to the *mestizo* translator. "Tell them that we will accept any gifts they wish to give as we are on our way to the pueblo of Zuñi, and traveling requires many provisions." The *mestizo* duly translated, and again there was murmuring among the Ácoma.

Distant mesas deepened to shadowed indigo and the sun sat on the western ledge, soon to drop below it. The governor was aware that only a few hours of light were left even though it was late spring and the days were lengthening.

One of the Ácoma chiefs spoke to the *mestizo* translator. "Would your leader wish to spend the night in the village? In that way, the people might bring him the provisions."

The governor listened as he eyed the enigmatic, copper faces watching him. The last thing he wanted to do was to be surrounded by several hundred unfriendly heathen when the dark curtain of night fell over the isolated, eagle's nest of a village.

But he would not let them think he was afraid. "Thank them for their hospitality," he said, "but I have already given orders to make camp below. They may deliver their gifts there in the morning."

Juan Ramírez spoke. "Governor, I am remaining here on the mesa top tonight. This is now my home; this is where I have come to live."

"I admire your zeal, *Padre*," the governor said, "but I think it would be wise for you to spend this first night down below in camp. I am posting plenty of guards in case of treachery. I don't like the looks on these heathens' faces. If nothing happens and the natives show their friendliness by offering adequate provisions tomorrow morning, then you may stay and try to convert these savages. However, if they show the slightest indication of ill will, you should choose to labor elsewhere in the province. The Lord doesn't need another martyr."

"I have promised God I will convert this pueblo," the priest said. "If martyrdom is my lot, I accept it joyfully. As for this night, I am spending it here where I will spend the rest of the days God grants me."

The governor laughed harshly. "There's nothing you friars like better than martyrdom, is there?"

"We do not fear it," Juan Ramírez replied. "Our Lord took care of that for us, didn't He, Governor?"

Silva snorted. "If martyrdom is what you want, it looks to me like you've come to the right place." He made a contemptuous gesture toward the natives and turned his back on Juan Ramírez.

A sliver of moon illuminated the mesa top with a faint light, outlining the kneeling form of the long-robed stranger. Various young men of the village had been detailed to watch him throughout the night. To their astonishment, he never moved from his kneeling position. Once or twice he appeared to sway, but then he would hold himself straight and his lips continued in their unceasing movement.

The sentries kept to the shadows not making their presence known. It would have been so easy to have sent an arrow through his back.

Later, all the men made their way quietly to Mauharots. There in the head *kiva* many spoke. The voices of the young were raised in anger.

"Kill the priest," they said with vehemence, "before he has a chance to interfere with and destroy our ceremonials as the long-robes in the other villages have done!"

"He is just one man. The others leave tomorrow. We must not allow this stranger to remain in our midst!"

"And if we kill him?" one of the old ones had asked. "Does that mean that another will not come to take his place?"

It was the words of one who had most reason to hate the Spaniards that finally influenced the group in their decision. The *kiva* was a hollow of silence when he rose to speak. His voice was as sharp as a sliver of obsidian.

"For as long as I walk the dust of this earth, I will carry the symbol of Áco's revolt against the pale intruder into our land." Rohona motioned to his maimed foot. "I have hated the strangers; I have wished to see them all dead, rotting upon the earth for *macawi* to feed upon." He paused. "But more than to see their death, I wish to see the life of Áco. I wish for the K'atsina to continue to dance upon our rock for the growing seasons ten times the number of fingers on a man, ten times the number of fingers on ten men.

"The strangers took only my foot and those of the other men left alive after the battle of thirty growing seasons ago. Would they still take only the foot, or this time would they take the whole life as well and leave no Ácoma to witness the sunrise upon our lofty village? Would never more an Ácoma child be held before the sun on its fourth day of life?

"The strangers have their *kawa*, their swift animals to ride, they have knives of the shiny wonder rock and sticks that send fire and death great distances. They are few, but they count for many because of the things of war they possess. If we kill one of them, many Ácoma will suffer, but if we allow the long-robe to stay, how many Ácoma will suffer? Let him remain for now. He is just one man alone. What can he do? But men of Áco, I tell you, and *this* is the most difficult part—many times more difficult than killing the long-robe or being killed by his protectors—let us preserve all that is best of Áco while the long-robe is in our midst. That is the challenge. That is the true challenge."

Some did not like his words. Others did not grasp the full meaning of the point he was attempting to make, but whatever the differences were, the consensus was that the long-robe would not die, at least not that night. There were even those who had been profoundly affected by the events of the afternoon, which pointed to special powers that the long-robe might possess.

Shadowy figures moved silently in the faint light of the predawn. Just as silently, the words had spread: throughout the night the long-robe had not moved from his kneeling position facing the east mountain. His lips had moved the entire time.

All knew that the man was undoubtedly asking his god for something and all knew the power of prayer. Did they not ask the K'atsina for rain and plentiful harvests, and did not the K'atsina hear their prayers and respond? Would not the stranger's god respond to the long-robe's prayer?

The people stood in the shadows watching the kneeling man, keenly aware of the man's conviction and uneasy because of it. One young man kept touching his knife in a nervous gesture.

Rohona approached him and spoke quietly. "There is no honor in it, my son." The young man dropped his hand and looked away.

The Ácoma were not guided by thoughts of a heaven or a hell awaiting in the future. Their concern was the present, and the present was this stranger in their midst praying to a god they knew nothing about. They would not understand the concept of salvation the stranger brought them. Prayer, though, they understood well.

Suddenly Juan Ramírez realized the night had fled. He had not been aware of the faint gray spreading out across the east. He had not noticed the stars beginning to fade. One does not persevere through a nightlong vigil by awaiting the dawn; one concentrates only on the prayer on one's lips. This, any Ácoma warrior undergoing a vigil would have understood.

He lifted his head and straightened his back. The heavy weariness that had begun to gnaw at him faded and the cold that had made his muscles ache, he no longer noticed. Colors of vibrant pink burst like blooms of the beautiful, sensuous flowers that bedecked the floating barges of Mexico City's many canals, and the beauty of the dawn gave fragrance to the soul just as the flowers perfumed the air of the ancient city of the Aztecs.

It was but a pinpoint at first, but rapidly the light spread like a semicircular halo crowning the long mesa, and the priest knew exactly where the sun would make its blinding appearance.

He raised his arms and in a clear, steady voice poured out his joy and praise in the words of the "Canticle of the Sun," the prayer that St. Francis himself, the father of all Franciscan priests, had given them.

The friar's words rang out: "Praised be my Lord with all His creatures, and especially our brother the Sun, who brings the day. He signifies to us Thee! and, for our sister the Moon, for our brother the Wind; and for Air and Land. And for our sister Water, who is very serviceable unto us, and precious and clear. And for our brother Fire. And for our mother the Earth, which doth sustain us and keep us and bringeth forth divers fruits and flowers of many colors . . ."

Had the Ácoma comprehended the words he spoke, they might have joined their voices with his, for they would have understood that prayer. They themselves offered very similar ones, for they knew the importance of the sun and wind and water and fire and duly thanked the creators of them. One Ácoma did understand the words of the prayer in their full beauty, but they troubled him more than the other Castilian prayers he knew. With a prayer like that, the long-robe was more dangerous than Rohona had thought.

Danger lay in understanding. If the Ácoma did not understand the religion the priest brought, it would never take the place of their own traditions and ceremonies, but if they could understand the message the long-robe taught, it might supplant the beliefs that had given life to Áco since the beginning. For a moment Rohona wondered whether he had been right to speak against killing the priest.

The prayer finished, the brilliant light blinding in its brightness, the priest rose. His legs, stiff with cold and cramped from kneeling all night, buckled, and he fell headlong to the ground. Slowly and painfully he pushed himself to his knees and then to his feet. He wobbled for a few seconds as he tried to stand and then crumpled again. With effort, he made it to his feet once more, his balance still impaired, as the pain of the blood surging newly through his legs was excruciating, but he kept to his feet.

"I will endure anything, Lord," he shouted, as if in defiance. "I welcome any trial!" He spread his arms out from his sides and looked exultantly into the blinding sun. "This is where I shall build my church!"

That night Juan Ramírez wrapped himself in a coarse woolen blanket and lay down on the hard ground where he would build his house of worship. He was glad the governor and his entourage had departed.

The Ácoma had taken down baskets of corn, a few *mantas*, and some turkeys to the Spaniards. The gifts were not lavish, but they had been sufficient to satisfy the governor.

Silva was relieved that the priest had survived the night and voiced his opinion to Ramírez. "*Padre*, I'm still not entirely confident these heathen won't try to kill you once the soldiers and I have gone."

"It makes not the slightest difference," the friar said, his voice steely.

Silva shrugged. "I shall call the translator to order the Ácoma to help carry all the accouterments for your church and dwelling up to the top of this damnable rock."

"I do not want any orders given. If I need help in transporting the things, I will arrange it."

And so the governor and soldiers departed, unloading the carts of all the priest's supplies and stacking the contents in a huge pile at the base of the mesa, supplies sufficient for three years: forty-five gallons of sacramental wine, eighty-five and a half pounds of prepared candle wax, twenty-six gallons of oil for illuminating the Holy Sacrament, eight more for the friar, four gallons of vinegar, one hundred yards of sackcloth, one ream of paper, awls, needles, knives, scissors, one dozen horseshoes, three pairs of sandals, two pairs of woolen stockings, thirty-five pesos' worth of medicines, five boxes of conserves, twenty-five pounds of sugar, three ounces of saffron, one pound of pepper, six ounces of cinnamon, ten and a half pounds of raisins, six pounds of almonds, two jugs of Campeche honey, altarcloths, one small bell to sound the Sanctus, one bell two hundred pounds in weight, iron framework from which to hang the bell, one pair of gilded wooden processional candleholders, cassocks, one rug for the altar steps, one copper vessel for the Holy Water, one wafer box, two and a half pounds of incense, three pesos' worth of soap, an iron utensil for making the host wafers, a set of clarions and bassoons, a trumpet, a book of chants, ten axes, adzes, spits, hoes, saw, chisel, one large latch for the church door, ten pounds of steel, six hundred tinned nails for the church door, seven other kinds of nails in great quantity for building the church, frying pans, *metate*, pewter plates and bowls, a cauldron, bacon, cheese, dried shrimp, haddock, dogfish, beans, lentils, salt, six hundred pounds of flour, corn, chile, smoked oysters, garlic, onions, and lard.

In addition, left at the base of the mesa were the heifers, a bull calf, ten sheep, two goats, and the *padre*'s mule, which he did not ride on the journey to Ácoma.

All that, save the animals, would have to be transported over three hundred and fifty feet from the base of the mesa to its top. It was an enormous task, but Ramírez did not intend to ask for help. If anyone offered of their own free will, he would gladly accept. No one did.

The first day the priest spent building makeshift pens for the animals at the base of the cliff. He chose small cul-de-sacs that would require only a fence across the mouth, and riding the mule, he set out for a small arroyo nearby that had scrub juniper and piñon growing near it. He cut as much as he thought the mule could drag and then led the animal with its heavy load back to the mesa.

After holes were dug, he placed the larger posts in them, wiring together a few cross poles through which he wove the smaller branches. He prayed that all would hold. If nothing scared the animals, the barrier would probably be sufficient, but there was nothing he could do if the Ácoma decided to sabotage his work. He would have to hope they didn't.

There was no time left in the first day to transport any of his belongings to the mesa top, and so he had slept on the hard ground wrapped only in a rough woolen blanket. He had never expected to be accepted with open arms into the unfriendly village, but he was surprised at his feelings of depression at the end of that first day. No one had approached him; he was avoided as if he might have been a leper. Never before had he felt such intense isolation.

How weak we are, Lord, he prayed, *and how filled with pride in spite of our best intentions. I knew the natives would not accept me freely, and yet I am disappointed that they did not. Help me, Lord, not to desire anything from them, but to think only of bringing them Your love.*

For a week he toiled from sunup to sundown, carrying load after load to the top and stacking it on the spot he had chosen for his church. There were still many things left to be transported. Some of them, such as the two-hundred-pound bell, he had no idea how he would get to the top. Daily he said Mass at the makeshift altar he had erected. He knew now that he was being watched, not out of interest, he was certain, but probably to see if what he did might affect the village adversely in some way.

He was not going to be like the majority of the other priests who crammed their religion down the natives' throats. He was going to let them come to him of their own free will; it was going to be *their* desire to embrace the faith that brought them to him.

With his habit tucked up in his belt to make climbing easier, he continued his sunup-to-sundown labor. A swift but violent downpour made him aware of the fact that he needed shelter not so much for his person, although that would be necessary when winter arrived, but for the many things he had brought with him for the furnishing of his church, much of which would be ruined if left exposed to the elements. So he began to transport rocks and dirt and sand from wherever he could find them. He made some forms, and mixing water with clay, sand, and weeds, he made mud bricks that he set out to dry.

When he saw how few he could make and how slowly the task progressed, he was dismayed at the thought of how long building the church would take. Could he endure that long? What could he do to show the people the love that God offered them? How could he make them of their own free will embrace the faith and, desiring a worthy tabernacle in which to practice it, help with the construction of it? For one thing, he must learn their language so he could communicate the message of the Gospel to them. But how was he going to learn Queres if the villagers continued to avoid him?

Days passed and each night he wrapped himself in his coarse woolen blanket and fell into an exhausted sleep. Not yet did he have all his belongings to the top of the mesa. All the heaviest things still remained. The days did not have enough hours for him. The animals he had brought needed tending, and they had to eat. The valley surrounding the mesa was semi-arid and pasture was not abundant, making it necessary for the animals to range some distance to find food. He was thankful, at least, that the natives had not bothered his stock.

He must build up a herd of cattle and sheep. With animals to sell, he could buy more things for his church than the meager number of articles his Franciscan superiors and the Crown supplied. And he would teach the natives husbandry so that they, too, might reap the benefits. Not only did he wish to bring them the message of God, he wished also to bring them a better life.

What he did not realize was that they already felt they had a good life there upon their high-perched rock. None of the Ácoma saw an advantage in the strange new animals, and none offered their help in tending them.

Once or twice the priest had caught a fleeting glimpse of movement behind some of the rocks above the animal pens. He hoped it indicated interest in the animals and that perhaps eventually the person or persons would become brave enough to come out of hiding so he could talk to them about the animals. He desperately needed help.

The adobe bricks he was making for a small shelter were taking too long to produce. All the dirt had to be transported from the valley floor to the mesa top on his back, and with an iron knife to trade, he had bartered for one of the baskets the Ácoma used to transport things from down below. He lined the basket with a piece of *jerga* to keep every precious piece of sand and dirt in it.

At times he thought he could not carry one more heavy basketful of dirt up the steep cliff wall. Constantly he prayed for patience and fortitude. The only reward he received was that he felt perhaps the Ácoma's hostility toward him was diminishing. The faces no longer seemed quite so unfriendly. Were they perhaps becoming used to his presence? It was a meager reward for the long, hard days of toil and strain and loneliness.

After one particularly difficult day, he wrapped himself in his woolen blanket and lay down on the rough ground with a feeling of despair. He had not even been able to say his prayers properly. They had issued from his mouth mechanically and with no thought to their meaning.

It had been a terrible day. The proportions of mud, sand, and weeds must have been wrong in the last set of adobes he had made, for they all had cracked. One of the sheep had gone astray, and he had not been able to find it. The wolves undoubtedly would, and once they got a taste of mutton, might they not come looking for more? But the crowning blow came at sundown.

He had been attempting to make one more journey up the steep cliff with a load of heavy nails, hinges, and iron horseshoes. In the gathering darkness, he had made a misstep and had fallen several feet. Not only had he painfully sprained his ankle, but he had also wrenched his back so that only with difficulty and pain could he stand upright. After that he left the nails and other things below as he torturously made his way to the top. His supper had been a handful of finely ground, parched sweet corn, stirred into a cup of water. As he lay on the cold, hard ground, his faith plummeted momentarily.

"No!" he spoke vehemently, struggling painfully to his feet. "No! I will not give up! I know you are testing me, Lord, but I will not break so easily!" His voice was defiant. "Give me more tribulations, Lord, heap them on my back! I will not fail you!"

He rummaged through his things and brought out a slender switch. He threw the blanket to the side and painfully pulled off his habit and the rough shirt he wore under it. Dressed only in his loose priest's trousers, he limped slowly across the mesa top toward the south. He chose a spot on the edge of a deep crevasse. He could not see the bottom, but he knew the jagged rocks that must lie below. He knelt on the very edge of the sheer drop. If he lost his balance or fell asleep, he would topple down into the deadly precipice.

He crossed himself. "I am unworthy, Father," he said as he struck the first blow across his bare shoulders. He winced at the pain, but his lips continued to move as his hand sent the slender whip down across his flesh. The pain was blinding but he did not cease.

Eventually he lost all sensation save a trickling of blood down his back.

He had little memory after that, except that he became aware of the lightening sky. Suddenly a thought came to him. "A road! A road! There must be a road!" he shouted.

He felt joyful and light-headed as he pushed himself to his feet. His trousers were stiff with his blood. Staggering, he returned to the blanket he had thrown off the night before.

"Thank You, Lord," he whispered, before he pitched forward onto it and lay unmoving as the sun crowned East Mountain.

Chapter 5

Slowly and silently they gathered. Their faces bore no hostility, only curiosity. They had seen the day-after-day solitary laboring of the pale, long-robed stranger. Industry was counted as a virtue among the Pueblo Indians, rising at dawn the sign of a good man. They had seen him tend his strange animals, make his mud bricks, carry his heavy loads, and pray to his god. Not once had he asked for food from them nor tried to take away any of their ceremonies. They could understand many of the things he did. They understood hard work; they understood the vigil and the self-inflicted physical pain. All were actions worthy of a warrior. A silent admiration for the lone, stoic man developed, and although he did not know it, the beginning of a kind of acceptance.

A woman came out of the crowd and approached the sleeping or unconscious priest. With her was a young girl of five or six. The woman knelt beside the man with the blood-encrusted back and very gently applied something to the welts that covered his shoulders. He winced occasionally but did not wake while she completed her ministrations.

The sun's rays slanted almost horizontally, bathing the long house rows in a burnished light when Juan Ramírez finally awoke. Something smelled wonderful. He opened his eyes slowly and started to get up, aware instantly of the excruciating pain in his body. Once more he attempted to rise and succeeded in reaching a sitting position. His fingers went gingerly to his throbbing shoulders. Something sticky covered his fingertips. He assumed it was blood, but when he looked at his fingers, he saw bits of what might have been ground up leaves in some kind of a sticky, pungent-smelling base. What was on his back? What had been the delicious odor that woke him? Was it merely part of a cruel dream?

He glanced around him. Then he saw it: a small pottery bowl filled with what looked like stew. He reached for it and began greedily to eat the chunks of meat and squash with his fingers. He lifted the bowl to his lips and drank the rest of the contents. Nothing that he could remember had ever tasted so good. As he set the bowl down, the full impact of what had happened hit him.

He went to his knees and poured out his thanks to *Dios* more deeply than he ever had. Someone among the Ácoma had taken pity on him. Someone had doctored his lacerated back; someone had left him food. And he remembered the road. Yes, the road! Through his pain and suffering had come blessings, and somehow his back no longer seemed so painful.

He struggled to his feet and rummaged among his belongings until he found a small, flat wooden box. Gritting his teeth against the pain, he put on his coarse shirt and then his dusty habit. Taking the bowl and the small box, he walked toward the houses. He did not know the language, but at the base of each dwelling he called out. When someone would appear on the rooftop above him, he would hold out the bowl asking, "*¿Es tuyo?* Is it yours?"

He was afraid he would never know who his benefactor had been, but finally a woman indicated the bowl was hers. The priest smiled at her and held up the small, flat box, making signs for her to take it. The woman descended the ladder to the ground, and it was then that he saw the young girl on the roof. It was the little girl who had fallen from the cliff the day he arrived, the girl who had been miraculously saved by landing on the sand that had drifted next to the sharp rocks. Her mother had been the one who had taken pity on him.

Hesitantly the woman approached him. He handed her the pottery bowl and pried off the top of the tiny wooden crate. He took a dried peach from the small box.

"Eat," he said. "Good," and he pointed to his mouth. The woman took the wrinkled object and looked at it suspiciously. He took a peach from the box and chewed it, smacking his lips.

"Good," he said and smiled. The look on her face was distrustful, but to the priest's surprise, she bit into the peach.

Slowly she chewed the piece of dried fruit. She smiled, and he smiled in return. The woman said something to the girl on the roof, and like a little squirrel, the child scrambled down the ladder. The priest held out a dried peach to her. She did not hesitate but bit into it immediately. He handed the small box to the mother.

"Thank you," he said, motioning to the bowl she held. "Thank you for the food." She said something in her language and then mounted the ladder with her daughter.

It was by now too late for him to accomplish anything that day, for the sun was sinking. He would, however, go down and check the animals. He grieved over the lost sheep. Each one was precious, for who knew how many would survive the winter? His ankle was tender, but he made it down the side of the mesa and limped to the animal pens.

Someone had brought water! The two logs he had hollowed as troughs were filled, and it had not rained. He crossed himself and said again a silent prayer of thanksgiving. He had been so struck by the water that he failed to count the sheep. Had he been Indian he would have noticed immediately the small moccasin tracks that led to the pen.

"*¡Santa María!*" he whispered as he counted the animals. "It is not possible," he said with a shake of his head. "But it is. I cannot believe it. Praise the Lord!"

He counted for a second time. All of the sheep were miraculously in the pen. Had God found the missing one for him or had one of the Ácoma found and returned it? Once more he thought he saw a fleeting movement in the rocks above the pens. Perhaps he had someone who helped him look after the sheep.

He climbed to the mesa top, but it felt rather as if he might have been soaring. His prayers were long that night and every word he spoke came from deep within, with as much intensity as he had ever spoken them. On the following day, he would address the problem of the road. He lay down on the hard ground as if it were the softest bed in the entire Spanish dominion.

It was toward late afternoon the next day that Juan Ramírez managed to gather together a fair number of people in one of the open spaces in the village. The men had just returned from the newly planted fields that lined the arroyos in the valley. He began to talk slowly and loudly, making many motions in pantomime. He felt certain that there must be at least one person who understood a few Castilian words. Some of them undoubtedly had lived among the Spaniards, for he had been told in the *villa de Santa Fé* of Ácoma slaves who had served Spanish masters.

"I have seen you carry your heavy loads," he said, as he acted out putting a basket on his back and trudging along under the heavy weight. "You have seen me," he added, pointing to himself.

"It is difficult to climb the mesa." He made the motion of climbing. "You must bring all your wood from the valley to the top on your back. You must carry down your seed corn. You must carry back up your fresh ears of corn, as well as squash and beans. The deer you hunt, you must transport to the top. The clay to make your pots must come up on your backs. It is difficult and dangerous for the old and the very young."

He talked and pantomimed. "I am going to build a huge house here on the mesa top for God and for you. It will be a beautiful house, but it will take much work. All things will have to be carried to the top." He paused. "Ácoma needs a road. I need a road."

From their faces he knew they did not understand. He repeated his motions but there was still no comprehension. He looked around quickly, searching for something that might explain his meaning. Seeing a stick and a rock, he picked them up and inclined the stick on the rock. Using two fingers of his hand as legs, he "walked" up the stick. "See?" he said expectantly.

But the Ácoma had heard enough from the foolish priest and began to wander away.

Finally the priest was alone in the square, his arms hanging limply at his sides. How was he going to make them see the value of a road? That night he prayed once again for patience.

The next morning he determined to walk the entire perimeter of the mesa's base to find the best place where a road might be built. He would not give up. A road to the top was absolutely vital. He saddled his mule and began the circuit. In the late afternoon he approached the animal pens from which he had started. Something made him dismount and tie the mule to a rock. Quietly, keeping to the boulders, he approached the enclosures and when he reached the sheep's pen he peered through the fence structure. There sat a young boy, hunkered down on his heels, running his hands over the wooly back of one of the sheep.

He was not shocked to see a boy in the sheep pen because he assumed the fleeting movement he had seen among the rocks was not an adult, but he was stunned by the color of the boy's skin. At that moment the boy became aware of a presence, leaped agilely to his feet and scrambled up the rocks.

"Wait!" the priest shouted. "Wait!"

Juan Ramírez pulled up his habit and tucked it up at his waist as he ran up one side of the rocks. He scrambled as fast as he could but by the time he reached the back part of the pen, the agile boy had disappeared among the crevices. The priest stood still for a moment. What was a boy of obvious Spanish parentage doing living in this pueblo, so hostile to its conquerors? Why had he never seen the light-skinned boy before? He must find out who he was.

That night his thoughts were not on the road and the obstacle it presented. His mind was fully absorbed by the vision of the boy fleeing through the rocks.

Ramírez rose before dawn and made his way down off the mesa. His ankle had recovered, but the pain in his back shot through his body when his clothing caught on the healing wounds there.

Darkness still mantled the valley and the mesa when he reached the sheep pen. He stationed himself behind a large rock above the enclosure. He did not hold out much hope that the boy would come back. The priest was certain someone did not want the child's presence in the village known.

His muscles cramped in the confined space and he was not sure whether or not he could remain much longer. The sun had just risen, but his side of the mesa was still in shadow. When he was just about to give up and stretch his cramped legs, he heard a noise in the pen below. He peered around the boulder. There was the boy in the pen. How had he gotten in there without the priest hearing him?

Juan Ramírez moved his legs to get the blood flowing again, then carefully moved around the boulder. About six feet below was the pen and the boy. The priest jumped and the boy looked up, startled at the sound of the flapping habit. The friar hit the ground with a thud, rolling and grasping at the boy who had started to flee. In a tumble of dust and amid the bleating of scared animals, Ramírez managed to grab the boy's moccasined foot.

The boy put up a valiant struggle, but the priest was in his prime. Days of toil and the long walk from Mexico City to *Nuevo México* had hardened him. Although the boy was tall for his years, he was no match for the toughened priest and Ramírez held him to the ground and sat on him to still his thrashings.

"Who are you?" the priest asked the boy when he had quieted.

Large gray eyes looked at Ramírez. Defiance tried to hide the fear.

"I'm not going to hurt you. If I let you up, will you promise not to run away?"

The boy did not answer, but the priest rose anyway and dusted off his habit. The boy pushed himself to a sitting position, and Ramírez squatted down in front of him.

"Do you speak Spanish?" he asked the solemn boy. "Who are your parents? Why do you live here with the Ácoma?"

Still the boy did not answer. Ramírez pointed at the sheep.

"*Oveja,*" he said and repeated it, "*oveja. Do you like the *oveja*?"

The friar rose and walked over to the animals. He pulled one from the group and brought it over to the boy. He saw the boy's eyes light up.

"This one is yours."

The boy put his arms around the sheep's neck and buried his fingers in its deep wool.

"It is yours," the priest reiterated.

"*Mi oveja,*" the boy whispered in the language he spoke only to himself.

Ramírez was dumbfounded. "You speak Castilian," he said, squatting down beside the boy again and taking him by the shoulder. The boy looked at the priest hesitantly and the friar was vividly aware of his fear. He took the boy's face in his hands.

"Do not be afraid, my son. I will not hurt you. I only want to know you. Do you speak my language?"

The boy's eyes were enormous. "*Sí, Padre,*" he whispered.

Ramírez smiled and laughed joyfully, and turning his face toward the sky and lifting his arms to heaven said, "Will Your wonders never cease?!"

He turned back to the boy. "Who are you? Where are your parents?"

"I am Mastya. My father and mother are dead."

"Then with whom do you live?"

"With my grandfather."

"Who taught you to speak Castilian?"

"My grandfather, but I read it better than I speak." The boy looked down at his feet.

"You read?" Ramírez asked and crossed himself as he whispered, "My God in Heaven."

He wrote the word *libro* with his finger in the dirt. "What does this mean?"

"Book."

"And this?" the priest queried, writing *oveja*.

"Sheep."

"And this?" He wrote *Dios el Padre*.

"God the Father." The boy looked at him and began to recite, "Our Father who art in Heaven, Hallowed be Thy name . . ."

Tears formed in the priest's eyes.

The boy continued, "Hail Mary, full of grace, the Lord is with thee. Blessed art thou among women and blessed is the fruit of thy womb Jesus."

Ramírez went to his knees, crossing himself. Timidly the boy imitated him. As the priest finished pouring out his gratefulness to his lord, he turned toward the boy who knelt beside him. With his thumb, he made the sign of the cross on the boy's forehead.

"The blessing of God Almighty, Father, Son, and Holy Spirit be upon you, now and always."

The boy took the priest's hand and breathed gently on it.

"Will you take me to your grandfather?" Ramírez asked him.

"You promise you will not tell other pale ones that I am here?" the boy asked with worry. "My grandfather fears that I may be seen by a pale one."

Ramírez put his hand over the crucifix that hung from his neck. "I promise."

Together, they climbed to the mesa top, and the boy led the priest down the streets to a dwelling. He called up in Queres. Instantly a man and woman were at the roof's edge, looking with shock at the boy and the priest together.

Rohona's worst fears had been realized.

Chapter 6

The two faces looking down on Juan Ramírez were unfriendly, but the priest smiled and asked, "May I come up?"

The boy's grandfather gave a grunt, and taking that as a grudging invitation, the priest started up the ladder.

Once on the roof, a motion of the grandfather's hand invited him to sit. The boy moved close to his grandfather. There was a long awkward silence. Ramírez did not know the etiquette of the situation but did not want to sit in silence when he hungered for information.

"I caught the boy at the sheep pen, and I learned that he speaks Castilian and that you were the one who taught him."

Rohona made no response. The priest had not asked a question.

"The boy recited the 'Our Father' and 'Hail Mary,' which I assume you also taught him."

Again Rohona did not respond; nothing had been asked of him.

The priest continued, undaunted. "Are you a Christian?" he asked the grandfather directly.

"I am Ácoma," Rohona said, which he knew was not an answer to the question. He had had the water poured over his head, but he did not feel Christian; he did not know whether the pale ones would still consider him a *cristiano* or not. The water seemed very important to them—as presenting a child on the fourth day of its life to the sun was important to the Ácoma.

"Why did you teach the boy the prayers, then?" Ramírez asked bluntly.

"His grandmother would have wanted."

"Then his grandmother was Spanish?"

Rohona grunted affirmatively.

"The boy says his mother and father are dead," the priest continued. The grandfather made no response.

Here was a frustrating man to talk to, Ramírez thought, but at least he understood Castilian and would answer questions if asked directly. It was a start. "When did they die?" he asked.

"When the boy was born."

Rohona thought the priest rude with his unceasing questions, but it would be impolite to ask him to leave once he was invited into the house. So he sat, his face a mask of stone.

"How did they die?"

"The mother died from the birth; the father fell off the cliff."

"Then they were here at Ácoma?"

"Ácoma is not the name of the village. The village is Áco, the White Rock. The Ácoma are the people of the White Rock."

Ramírez was embarrassed at his mistake.

"Thank you for explaining that to me. I have a great desire to learn the language of Áco. I would appreciate your help so that I might not make mistakes."

Rohona made no response. Ramírez knew that he should probably leave, but he could not give up this opportunity. He had no idea if or when he might be able to talk to the boy's grandfather again.

"The boy told me that you taught him how to read. Never did I expect to find anyone in Áco who knew how to read, and now I find that there are two who can."

Mastya said excitedly, "Auntie Siya knows how to read, too."

The priest looked at the woman who sat with downcast eyes. "Will wonders never cease!" he said, smiling. He turned to the boy. "Do you have any books?"

The boy looked up hesitantly at his grandfather. The old man nodded his approval.

"Yes," the boy said proudly, "we have many."

"Many? May I see them?"

Again the grandfather nodded.

The boy rose. "Come, *Padre*, I will show you."

Ramírez followed the boy inside the room off the roof terrace. Light entered the shadowy room through the doorway. Gradually the priest's eyes became accustomed to the dim interior. Dried rings of squash and strips of dried meat hung from the roof. From the walls hung moccasins, a fur quiver of arrows, baskets, and objects whose purpose he did not know. On the floor near the walls were rolled up hides, pottery jugs of varying sizes, and a grinding stone. Against the back wall in the corner were the books.

The priest could not believe his eyes. There were at least as many as he had been able to bring with him. Some of the other friars had complained that he had brought too many on the long journey, but books were important to Juan Ramírez. Mastya's were stacked in the corner on crude shelves made of flat rocks spanned by small pine logs, but they were obviously well cared for.

"What a treasure you do have," Ramírez said with a smile, putting his hand on the boy's shoulder. "You have every right to be proud of them." The boy beamed.

"Can you read all of these?" Ramírez asked as he took a book off the shelves.

"I have read all of them," the boy said proudly. "Some several times." Then he added with embarrassment, "Some I have read the words but I do not understand the meaning. There are words I want to know very badly."

"Would you like for me to teach you?"

"Oh, yes. If my grandfather would consent."

"We will ask him." The priest squatted down in front of the books and looked at the various titles. "These books were your Spanish grandmother's?"

"Yes."

Nothing was said for long moments.

"Your grandmother must have been a well-educated woman. Plays by Rueda, here is Gil Vicente, *La Celestina,* the *Coplas* of Jorge Manrique, the Portuguese Jorge de Montemayor, Garcilaso. The *Cantigas de Santa María.* Nebrija's grammar. Even the Greeks and Romans are here in translation — Homer, Ovid, Aristotle, the *Meditations* of the philosopher-emperor Marcus Aurelius, and even the *Gallic Wars* of Caesar."

Ramírez was talking to himself more than to the boy. "How incredible that such a woman was here in this isolated place."

There was much the priest wanted to know about the background of the gray-eyed boy who could read.

"I have other books," he said to the boy, "and you are welcome to borrow them. If I teach you Castilian words you don't know, will you teach me to speak the language of Áco?"

"Yes! I will teach you. I will try very hard to be a good teacher."

Ramírez laughed and clapped the boy gently on the shoulder. Together they went back outside onto the roof where the grandfather and aunt still sat.

The priest dropped to a sitting position again. "The woman who owned those books must have been a special person," he said and saw a flicker in the grandfather's eyes. "Did you love her?"

The grandfather looked directly at the priest. "Yes."

Color rose to Ramírez's face. He was embarrassed by his rudeness. "Forgive me, I did not mean to pry. It's just that I never expected to find anyone here who could speak Castilian much less read it. In my own joy at finding people who speak my language, I have overstepped my bounds. I regret my prying. Please forgive me. I must go. I have already taken up too much of your time. Thank you for your hospitality."

He rose but the grandfather motioned for him to sit again.

"Won't you partake of some food with us?" the grandfather asked.

Ramírez nodded as the aunt rose and went to the small fireplace at one corner of the rooftop.

"Why do you come to Áco?" the old man asked as bluntly as Juan Ramírez had asked his questions.

The priest stammered momentarily. "I came to bring you salvation."

"What do the Ácoma need with that?"

"We all need salvation so that when we die we will not go to Hell."

"The Ácoma do not go to your Hell when they die."

"How do you know that?"

"Iyatiku is our mother; she gave us the earth and the things on it. She did not make a Hell."

Ramírez did not debate the statement. "I have come to bring you a message of salvation that God has given us. When you understand it, you will then know why you need it."

"The man on the crossed sticks?"

"Yes. Our Lord, *Jesús Cristo,* who died for us."

"A dead man?" the grandfather snorted.

"The message is that He lives," Ramírez said and then changed the subject.

"The boy would like to know more of the words in the books. I have offered to teach him, if you will permit it, and he might help me to learn the language of Áco."

The grandfather did not need to look at the boy to know what was in his eyes. He had seen it already. Joy and excitement sparkled there.

The grandfather was fully aware of the void the books filled in his beautiful grandson's life. In the absence of friends and playmates, the leaves with marks were the boy's companions. A great uneasiness welled in Rohona. He feared for the boy he had raised, feared for the grandson he loved so intensely. He turned to look at Mastya, then turned back to face the priest. The silence hung like a stone around their necks.

When the grandfather spoke at last, his voice was as soft as the soughing of the wind in pine needles.

"You may teach the boy. He has a Spanish name, too—Augustín. I gave him a name his grandmother would have liked. I chose it from a great saint of her god, the son of a Christian mother and a pagan father."

"Saint Augustine of Hippo."

"Yes," Rohona said. "Now we eat."

In silence they ate the rabbit stew and the thin, gray sheets of paperlike bread Siya had prepared. When they finished, Ramírez spoke. "Thank you for the food, thank you for the opportunity to speak my language, thank you for allowing me to teach the boy." He rose. It was almost noon. The late spring sun was hot on his back, and the sweat had made his clothes stick painfully to his healing shoulders, but he did not mind.

❈   ❈   ❈

The days began to pass much more quickly now. The presence of the boy added a dimension to the priest's life he had never known. He was constantly astounded by his intelligence. Never before had he seen a child with such a voracious appetite for knowledge, such a desire to learn, and with a mind of such wonderful retentive powers and budding logic. Ramírez knew that within a few years Mastya would have learned all that he could teach him.

Besides the lessons, the priest enjoyed the boy's companionship in tending the animals. Mastya talked constantly as if a dam had broken. The priest smiled as question after question poured from the boy's lips. He loved the animals and became the shepherd the friar so desperately needed. The grandfather had given his consent, so with book in hand, Mastya would take the sheep to look for pasture.

Ramírez grew troubled by one thing, however. He quickly saw that Mastya lived as an outcast among the Ácoma. He had no friends or companions his own age, and the priest saw his deep loneliness and grieved over it.

What would become of him, Ramírez worried. He could give Mastya friendship, but that was not the same as friends one's own age. Perhaps if the boy looked more Indian, he would have been accepted. He had traces of his Indian ancestry, which added to his fine looks, but in different circumstances, the priest knew that there would be few who could discern the boy's heritage. Take him out of his native clothing and dress him in that of Europe—he might be mistaken for a prince but never for the member of a remote tribe of Indians who lived in a mud village perched high on a barren mesa in the vastness of *Nuevo México*.

Black-lashed, clear gray eyes looked out of a high-cheekboned face, but his skin was light with only a faint touch of bronze, and his hair was of a deep, burning auburn color. Mastya's loneliness probably appeared as aloofness to all but the grandfather, the aunt, and the priest. No one, however, could mistake the intelligence that shone from the boy's eyes.

The priest became a frequent visitor to Mastya's household. Sometimes he and the grandfather scarcely talked, but more and more, a few sentences would grow into a long discussion that lasted well into the night. Ramírez came to realize that Mastya's intelligence did not come solely from his Spanish grandmother. The priest's respect for the grandfather grew every time he had a conversation with the old man. The grandfather, too, was acquiring a grudging respect for the priest, although the friar did not know it.

The days were more pleasant, but the euphoria of finding someone who spoke Castilian began to dim when the priest realized that he was no nearer his goal than when he arrived. Indeed, he had made a tentative friendship with the grandfather, aunt, and boy, and the mother of the girl who had fallen brought him food occasionally, but not a soul had been saved. Many priests reported hundreds of baptisms within their first few weeks at a pueblo, but did the parents—or the priests, for that matter—really understand their responsibility toward their baptized children? Was baptism merely enough to convert a pueblo?

Ramírez talked to the grandfather about the road that had earlier met with such indifference among the Ácoma, but he was unable to convince the old man of its practicality or necessity.

"We have lived at Áco without needing a road since the beginning," the grandfather said. "Why do we need one now?"

"When you are older, it will become more and more difficult to climb the steep wall of this mesa. If there were a road, you could continue to go down to the valley without difficulty," the priest countered.

"But if I continue to climb, my legs will stay strong."

"Every day I watch the Ácoma go down to the valley to gather their firewood or carry their tools for working in the fields. The corn, when it is ripe, they have to carry on their backs up the side of the mesa. Deer, game, piñon nuts likewise must be transported with difficulty. How much easier the life of the Ácoma would be with a road."

"We have carried these things up the cliff from the time of our ancestors. We can continue to carry them."

"But don't you want to make the life of the Ácoma less burdensome?"

"It is not a burden to the Ácoma. It is a part of our life. We do not think about it. We chose to live on Áco; we choose to climb up and down. And we are safe from our enemies here. They, too, must climb the steep walls of Áco. With a road, they could come more readily to attack us."

"A road could easily be defended by only a few men. Its advantages far outweigh its disadvantages."

"The walls of Áco have served us well. They will continue to serve us well."

"But I am going to build a great church here. Many things will have to be brought to the top that cannot be carried on a back."

"Ah, there is the necessity for the road. You need the road, not the Ácoma."

"Yes. I need the road. But it would benefit the Ácoma, too."

"That is not so easy to see as the other reason."

With that the conversation ended, and Juan Ramírez was no nearer his goal than previously. How was he going to get the road? How was he going to get the Ácoma to come to him of their own free will to accept the faith?

Gradually he learned a few Queres words and phrases. Mastya was a good teacher in spite of his youth. Each evening Ramírez would make a list of things he wanted to learn to say. The following morning he would ask the boy and then write them phonetically as best he could. Throughout the day he would practice and commit them to memory. Soon he would know enough to preach a short, simple sermon. But there was so much to do—how would he ever find the time to carry on the ministries of the Church?

There were the animals to care for. Indeed Mastya was of immeasurable help tending them, but still they required time on his part, and he had planted a small patch of wheat and barley near an arroyo beside the cornfields of the Ácoma. Gradually the adobe bricks were accumulating, but there were still so few.

Frustration haunted him, and he had constantly to battle against it. Every morning he said a lonely Mass at dawn, accompanied only by Mastya. He could count one soul saved, but he cherished that one soul. He knew that if he never saved another soul at Áco, his coming had been worth it for the boy alone — a boy taught Christian prayers by a grandfather who did not even believe in *Dios*. Ramírez hoped that the special woman who was the boy's grandmother, wherever she might be, could see her beautiful grandson and know that he was a Christian.

As Mastya and the priest began to develop a friendship through books and animals, the boy timidly began asking questions concerning the friar's god. Mastya had always been curious about that god of his grandmother's for whom he knew a few prayers. But the only gods who were real for him were the K'atsina of his grandfather and the Ácoma.

The boy quickly became attached to the priest, his only source of friendship outside his grandfather and aunt. The priest knew all the words Mastya longed to know, and the Spaniard made the books more fascinating by bringing understanding to them. Padre Ramírez had new books for Mastya to read and taught him how to write on a thin sheet of slick gray-black rock.

Mastya asked the endless questions that were always on his tongue. One had been: "Why are the crossed sticks so important?"

"Once long ago," the priest explained, "people took the son of God and mocked him. They put a cruel crown of thorns upon his head, and nailed him onto crossed sticks to die, but *Dios* still loved men in spite of what they had done to his son. *Dios* allowed the bad men to kill his son, but on the third day, the son came back to life."

Ramírez laid his hand on Mastya's shoulder. "If you love *Dios*, you no longer have to fear death because *Dios* has conquered it. So that when you die, you will die only to this earth, and then you will come to life again and live with *Jesús Cristo* forever."

"But how do you love this god?"

"By doing His will."

"And what is that?"

"You must love others even if they are bad to you. You must show others God's love so they will love Him. And you must come to *Dios*'s table."

"Where is this table?"

Ramírez pointed to the altar he had constructed. The boy was silent for long moments. "I would like to go to that table. May I, *Padre*?"

"Yes," Ramírez said, "but first you must prepare before you may go, and I must talk to your grandfather."

*   *   *

With a heaviness in his heart, Rohona had witnessed the growing friendship of his grandson and the priest. He feared for Áco if the priest were successful. Would all the traditions turn to dust and blow away? Would the K'atsina be replaced by the god of the strangers? Would prayers never more be sent to Wenimats to feed the K'atsina? Would the clouds that brought the rain never return if the Ácoma did not dance upon mother earth and sing their prayers? Would Iyatiku and all she had given them be forgotten?

When Rohona gave his consent that his grandson might accept the god of his grandmother, his fears grew and gnawed within him. Should they have killed the priest in the first place as some had wanted? Should all the Indians unite and push the hated foreigners out, keeping the ancient ceremonies and traditions protected?

The answer Rohona knew. The people of the land might push the Spaniards out if they united, but more would come, and more again, bringing their guns, big and small. He had read the book by the powerful warrior named Caesar, about the wars against barbarians. He had not understood much and it had been very difficult, but one thing he had learned from that book and others: there are many, many men who live outside the land of the Pueblos, and they fight to conquer. Some of them had come into the land of the Ácoma, but even if these eventually went away, others would follow.

The most important thing, Rohona knew, was that no matter what happened, Áco must survive. He must direct all his energies toward that purpose.

When he made the decision to allow the priest to teach his grandson about the god of the pale ones, however, it was not the welfare of Áco that determined his response. He did it for the woman with hair the color of wet pine bark. He did it for her and for the boy himself.

Mastya had asked him many questions about the god of his grandmother—questions Rohona had been unable to answer.

If the boy truly wished to know the god of the Castilians, Rohona would not forbid it.

The woman said the pale god had a purpose for all he did. At one time Rohona had attempted to understand the purpose, but he had been unable and had given up. Was it the purpose of the god that the grandson of the gray-eyed woman become what they called a *cristiano*? Rohona did not know. That was what bothered him about the Castilian god; he did not know him.

Perhaps if Mastya came to understand, he could explain it to him some day.

Juan Ramírez baptized the boy in the presence of the grandfather and the aunt. He wished all three could receive the water of salvation. Others of the village watched the ceremony from afar. Would it mean anything to them that the Ácoma grandfather had allowed his grandson to be baptized? Ramírez was afraid it would not. The boy was an outcast because of his Spanish blood; undoubtedly they would not consider that an Ácoma had accepted the Christian god. He must see if the mother of the girl who fell might be persuaded to allow her daughter to receive the holy water.

After the baptism, the priest began in earnest to catechize the boy. Never had there been a more joyful task, for Mastya learned with a rapidity that left Ramírez immeasurably pleased, and he thanked his lord each night for having given into his unworthy hands such a treasure. A boy with the intelligence of this one could rise in Mexico City to any height.

Ramírez had begun to think of himself and the boy in a partnership for the spiritual conversion of the Ácoma. Mastya spoke the Queres of Áco and already had a faith in and understanding of God that surpassed many adults who had lived all their lives as Christians. Yes, the two of them together would be a powerful Christianizing force. The boy would continue to teach him the language of the people, and he could write sermons that Mastya would translate, and his message would reach the people more quickly. The boy would also be able to judge the mood of the people; he could explain their traditions to the priest; he would know what examples the people would understand.

The priest would send for more books. He would teach the boy and together they would explore many topics. When he was older, the boy might serve as his secretary. Ramírez had many such dreams as he prepared the boy for his first confession prior to the first communion for which the boy appeared so anxious.

But the friar had not been prepared for Mastya's confession.

Ramírez kissed his stole and draped it around his neck. In the open air, the boy knelt on one side of a small latticed grate while the priest seated himself on a stool on the opposite side. In a soft, tentative voice Mastya spoke the formula he had been taught. He confessed the sins all children confess, and the priest explained whether they were important sins or not. The friar was preparing to say the absolution when the boy began to sob.

"Father, that is not all. I am so ashamed, so ashamed."

Ramírez sat in stunned silence as the boy poured forth the words of his shame.

Mastya told it just as his grandfather had told him. "My grandfather loved a Spanish woman in San Gabriel before the *villa* of Santa Fé was built, and she had a child, a son. Her god answered her prayers and provided a way for my grandfather and her to raise the child together, although she was married to a captain in Oñate's army. The son was raised in his mother's household, not knowing she was his real mother, for he had been told he was an orphan upon whom she had taken pity."

Mastya swallowed but continued. "The woman later had a daughter who looked like the Spanish captain, her husband. The two children grew up together, very fond of each other, but the fondness turned to love and a child was conceived. When they learned of their own parentage before the baby was born, the boy and girl fled to Áco. Their mother followed them but she was killed when her horse fell. The girl died the night her baby was born, and the next morning Grandfather found his son, the father of the child, at the base of the cliff, dead. They did not know whether it was by accident or purpose."

Mastya's voice was no more than a whisper. "I am the baby that was born that night, *Padre*. My mother and father were brother and sister!"

Chapter 7

Padre Ramírez prayed silently. The boy's father was an illegitimate half-breed and the boy, the product of an incestuous relationship between brother and half-sister.

"God must have killed my grandmother because she sinned and my mother and father because they sinned," Mastya sobbed. "He won't want me because I am an abomination!" With that, he pushed himself to his feet and ran from the makeshift confessional.

The priest leaped up, grabbing his garments, and tore after him. Mastya tried to wrench away but they both fell to the hard, dusty ground. Mastya went limp, his shoulders shaking in his grief, and Ramírez pushed himself to a sitting position and pulled the boy into his arms.

"Mastya, God does not hate you, He loves you. He wants you to be His more than anyone. Why do you think He sent me here? To tell you that He loves you, that you are not a sin. You are one of His proudest creations. The water of baptism has washed away sin, and you are free. God loves you, and you are free to love Him."

"I do love Him, *Padre*," Mastya whispered, his shoulders jerking.

The next week was the hardest week in Juan Ramírez's life. He spent many hours on his knees in prayer.

The boy's grandmother said You had a purpose, and I believe You do, he prayed. *Show me what it is, please, Lord, or at least show me what I must do.*

From the beginning he had seen the boy's quick intelligence and Mastya had been a tremendous help to him in caring for the animals and in teaching him the beginning of a Queres vocabulary. The boy would be an even greater help in the future, and the *padre* acknowledged freely another benefit: companionship.

Loneliness and isolation had been the priest's daily fare until he had discovered the boy. From that day on, he could count on the presence of a young, quick-witted lad to lift his spirits. He was someone to talk to, someone to teach the things that Fray Ramírez had to teach, someone to care about. That last was the difficult part. The priest had begun to care about the boy as if he were his own, and because of that the decision he had to make was all the more painful.

Mastya was reading from the *Meditations* of the philosopher Marcus Aurelius. Of all the books from his grandmother, it was the one his grandfather esteemed the most. As Mastya read, he began comparing what the Roman philosopher-emperor had written with many of the things the *padre* had taught him about being a Christian. The boy delighted in the many similarities but was quick to note the divergencies. He endeavored to translate the philosopher's precepts into Christian precepts.

He would read, "Begin the morning by saying to yourself, I shall meet with the busybody, the ungrateful, arrogant, deceitful, envious, unsocial. All these things happen to them by reason of their ignorance of what is good and evil. But I who have seen the nature of the good that it is beautiful and of the bad that it is ugly, and the nature of he who does wrong, that it is like me, not of the same blood or seed, but that it has the same intelligence and the same portion of the divinity, I cannot be harmed by any of them, for no one can fix on me what is ugly, nor can I be angry with my kinsman, nor hate him. For we have been born for a common task, like feet, like hands, like eyelids, like the rows of the upper and lower teeth. To act against one another then is contrary to nature; and it is acting against one another to become angry and to turn away."

Then Mastya would say, "Nature is God, isn't it, *Padre*? God has made all of us so we should not hate others for it is against God, isn't it?"

The priest smiled, but a worry began to nag at him. What would become of this boy? He was a brilliant child. What would happen to him when he grew up? How could he survive in Áco as an outcast? What would become of him when his grandfather died?

It was through Mastya's interpreting of Marcus Aurelius in light of Christian theology, however, that it occurred to the priest that the boy should have the opportunity to fulfill his potential completely, by studying in a center of learning where he would benefit from the very best teachers. Mastya should study in the capital of New Spain. He should study in Mexico City, and little as he liked it, Ramírez knew who the teacher should be.

It was a painful decision for the priest to make. It meant that he would lose the boy's companionship, his help with the animals and with the language. His vision for the future, the intelligent boy by his side, working with him to convert the Ácoma, would not come to pass. He would be left alone once more to face the obstacles of bringing the understanding of God to a heathen people.

He tried to think of all the reasons why the boy should not go to Mexico. Perhaps God wanted the boy to aid in the conversion of the pueblo. It would be cruel to send a young boy so far away from his home into an alien culture, and he did not want to lose the boy who was quickly becoming like a son to him. This last was a more powerful reason than he wanted to admit, but in the end he did admit it. He prayed for guidance from God, but he was filled with anxiety.

It was the boy finally, or *Dios* acting through the words of Marcus Aurelius, that allowed the *padre* to make his decision.

Mastya was reading a passage about prayer. The philosopher had said, "Either the gods have no power or they have power. If they have no power, why do you pray to them? But if they have power, why do you not pray for them to give you the faculty of not fearing any of the things that you fear?"

The Roman had gone on to explain how one might change his prayer and thereby find help. Mastya's voice was clear as he read, "A person prays thus: How shall I not lose my little son? You should pray like this: How shall I not be afraid to lose him? In other words, turn your prayers around, and see what happens."

And that is exactly what Fray Ramírez prayed: "How shall I not be afraid to lose him?"

He *was* afraid, but he found an answer to the question: Think only of the welfare of the boy and what would serve Mastya best.

The boy would be best served by having the opportunity to develop his potential to its greatest; he should have the benefit of the best teachers so that he might soar with his accomplishments and find the full expression of himself through that which he loved and through that at which he truly excelled.

Although the boy was young and it seemed a cruelty to send him from his home at such a tender age, would he not be benefited by the opportunity to belong, to have friends his own age, friends who would become his close companions? Was he not an outcast in his own village, shunned by those of all ages? Would his spirit flower at Áco? What would become of him there? How could he survive if his aunt and grandfather were gone?

With those thoughts Juan Ramírez made his decision, and once his decision had been made, it meant he must convince the grandfather of its necessity.

He repeated the question of the philosopher to the grandfather and added, "It served me well and perhaps may likewise serve again when you consider my proposition."

The grandfather's face belied none of the emotions that tore through his heart as he listened. When the priest finished what he had to say, Rohona spoke.

"I will think."

Ramírez left, knowing that the decision he had made had been infinitely easier than the one the grandfather must make.

The morning after the conversation with the priest, Rohona rose early, and taking the pouch of food Siya prepared for him, he left the village, telling her that he might be gone for some days. He must go to the rock. There he must think.

Rohona's limp seemed worse as he trudged across the valley floor. With great difficulty he climbed the rock to where they lay. His heart was just as heavy as it had been when he carried them up there. He knelt in front of the rocks that covered the woman with gray eyes. The crude cross of piñon wood showed clearly its age as it had weathered the wind, the dust, the rain, the sun, the snow of the ever-passing seasons.

"I have a heavy heart, Mia," he said. "I must make a decision that will rip that very heart from my breast. I hope you will help me.

"Oh, my son." He turned to the cairn that lay on one side of the woman he called Mia. "Oh, my beautiful son, whom I loved so much and whose son I love so much. The herb I drank to take away the memory of the dead has not worked. Some days I do not think of you nor of your mother nor of your sister, but they are few the days I do not remember. Oh, my son, you would be so proud of your son. He is tall and beautiful and has the gray eyes. He is swift, more swift than any of the boys in the village his age. The gray fox for which he is named has given him much hunting power although he is still very young. The gray fox has also given him his cleverness, for the boy is more clever than I have seen in boy or man.

"Oh, flame-haired one," Rohona said as he turned to the pile of stones on the opposite side of the woman, "your son is beautiful. He does not have the bright flame of your hair; his is more like the deep embers of the fire. I would that he had your joy when you were young, for he is a solemn, lonely boy. Siya and I have tried to give him happiness, but he has a need we cannot fill. Perhaps it is a need that a mother could have filled or that a woman may someday fill. I do not know, but I pray that it may be so."

He turned back to the middle grave of stones. "Oh, Mia, how I wish you could see him. You would love him as much as I do. I hope your god allows you to look upon him. I put the water on his head as you would have wanted, but there is a priest in the village now, and he did it again, so you can rest assured that it is done properly. The priest has taught the boy about your god, and the boy loves your god. You would be very happy. Oh, Mia, how I miss you!

"Ten growing seasons have passed since I held you in my arms and waited for your god to save you. But he did not and the great emptiness I knew at your death has not lessened through the years. In the fall when I see the trees on a riverbank or high on a mountainside turn golden, I think of our love. When I am in the piñon forest during an unexpected afternoon shower,

I remember your hair, the color of wet pine bark, and my sorrow becomes one with the falling raindrops."

Tears slid down Rohona's cheeks. "I wish I could love your god, Mia, for I know it would make you happy. But I do not like the way he acts — and now he has done *this* to me! I prayed to be able to keep my little grandson to love and raise. And now your god sends a priest to the village to take him away from me. I wish I had never heard of your god, for he makes my mind battle inside, for I do not understand what he does. The K'atsina I understand."

Rohona's head slumped onto his chest, and he was silent for long moments.

Suddenly he lifted his head and shouted defiantly at the sky, "You *will not* take my grandson!"

But then the silence returned, and he began to sing a slow, mournful chant. He sang of his grief to the earth, the sun, the wind, the rain, and he sang prayers to the K'atsina for all they gave the people and him. The breeze lifted his song and spiraled it into the air like thin ribbons of smoke.

The long rays of the setting sun outlined in bronze the solitary figure seated on the barren rock four times the height of a man. When the brilliant sun of morning rose after its nightlong journey, it illuminated again the solitary figure.

Another day passed.

On the third day Rohona, his voice quavering, asked the question posed by the philosopher-emperor.

"How shall I not be afraid to lose him?"

The question led him to the same answer to which the priest had been led.

Rohona thought of Mastya and nothing more. He did not think about the Castilian god, nor himself, nor the priest, nor Áco. That which gave the boy his only happiness were the leaves with marks. That which gave the boy his greatest pain was loneliness and the lack of friends and of belonging. The years were rushing by. What would become of his beautiful grandson when he was dead and the boy was left alone there on the bare rock where he was an outcast?

And so his decision was made. It did not ease the heaviness in his heart, for that was for himself, but it did ease the heaviness in his soul.

Rohona sent Siya and the boy to fetch water and sent for the priest.

Juan Ramírez could discern nothing on the grandfather's face that would indicate what his decision had been.

Slowly and carefully Rohona wrapped some dark, dried leaves into a piece of cornhusk. With an ember from the fire he lit it. After he had drawn on it, he passed it to the priest. Ramírez took the cornhusk without hesitating and likewise drew the aromatic smoke into his mouth. They sat smoking in complete silence.

"Now I pray," Rohona said. He began a soft, high chant asking the K'atsina that good things might be given unto his grandson.

"Now you pray," he said to the priest when he had finished his chant.

Fray Ramírez crossed himself. "In the name of the Father, Son, and Holy Spirit. May the decision made here today be the best for the boy Mastya and for Your greater glory, Amen."

The two men looked at each other across the gulf of their cultures, bound by a single thought.

"My grandson goes to the homeland of his grandmother," Rohona said.

The priest sat stunned, never really expecting that the grandfather would allow his young grandson to be taken from his village, his culture, his home. He closed his eyes and offered a silent prayer of gratitude, then said, "I pray this is the best decision for the boy."

"That, too, is my prayer," Rohona said. "Now, how do you propose that the boy will make the long journey?"

"The mission supply caravan will be returning this fall. The same caravan with which I arrived, now goes back. It will leave Santa Fé in several months and will arrive in Mexico City in the spring of next year. There is a priest, an older man, returning with the caravan to the provincial headquarters. He is a good man. I will give Mastya into his care, and he will see that the boy gets safely to Mexico. When the caravan reaches the city, Fray Benavides will give Mastya into the care of the best teacher in Mexico City and perhaps the most intelligent man in New Spain. He is a Jesuit, Padre Guillermo de la Cruz. With him Mastya will have the finest education available in the New World."

Fray Ramírez did not tell the grandfather how painful the decision had been to send Augustín to a Jesuit. He did not tell the grandfather of the enmity between the Franciscans and the Society of Jesus or that he could scarcely bear to give the young boy over into the power of a Jesuit.

Guillermo de la Cruz was a friend if Jesuit and Franciscan could be friends. Ramírez, whether he liked to admit it or not, knew that the Jesuits had by far the best educational system in Mexico City, and Guillermo de la Cruz was that system's best mind and teacher. The Jesuit would see to it that Mastya received the finest education possible, for the Jesuit was a *cazador*, a hunter of gifted young boys who under his tutelage became the outstanding minds of New Spain. The Jesuit, once he saw the boy's talent, would spare nothing in the way of his education. And besides all that, the education the Jesuits provided was free to those they accepted.

"We must now turn to the question of getting Augustín to the *villa* of Santa Fé," Juan Ramírez said.

"I have made the journey," Rohona said, "but I am now too old and crippled. I shall ask Siya if she will go. She will not want to give the boy

up, but she will want to go so that she may have more time with him before
he departs."

"I, too, will go," the priest said, "so that I may see to all the details
necessary for his journey."

Rohona nodded in approval. "In the *villa* there is a woman who was the
very good friend of the boy's grandmother. She knows all there is to know
about us. It was she who sent the grandmother's books to me. She is very
discreet. She will want to see the boy and Siya, for Siya lived in her house
for many years. Her name is Dorotea de Inojosa."

"I will take the boy to her," Ramírez said. "I think it is arranged, then.
Save telling the boy, that is."

"Are you not forgetting one thing, *Padre*?" Rohona asked.

The friar looked startled.

"How are you going to explain the boy to the Spaniards in the *villa*? Will
it be detrimental to him if they know that his father and mother were brother
and sister?"

The priest swallowed. He had been so concerned about other things that
the question had never occurred to him. Of course it would be a benefit to
the boy if the Spaniards knew nothing. But how would he explain a boy
with so much obvious European blood?

At length he said, "I think for the boy's sake, the Spaniards do not need
to know his story, but I must have some explanation to give them. Although
we are taught not to lie, I think in this case it will not hurt. Who knows
what harm might come from the truth? I will say that he is the child of a
half-Ácoma girl who had been sired by a Spaniard when her mother had
been a slave. Knowing human nature, I am sure that was not uncommon."

Rohona nodded, keeping his bitterness hidden. Ramírez continued. "This
girl, in turn, suffered the fate of her mother, thus bearing a child that was
one quarter Ácoma, three quarters Spanish. That accounts for the boy's obvious European parentage, but it leaves no means for determining the Spanish ancestors. I will say his mother died; he is an orphan."

Emotion did show in Rohona's eyes then, and the priest perceived a small
glint of fear. "*Padre*," Rohona said, "do you have the power to keep the boy
out of the hands of the civil authorities?"

"Yes," the priest answered. "Why?"

"It is well known what they do with orphans. They make them into
slaves."

Shock showed on Ramírez' face. The grandfather continued. "The governor's men come into the villages and take away all the orphans they can
discover, even though a family may be caring for the child like a son or
daughter. They take the child to the *villa* and make it a slave. They say they
are taking it to teach it about their god. But they make it work like a slave,
and if the child runs away they hunt it down like a slave. I do not want my
grandson to be made a slave."

The priest put his hand over the crucifix he wore.

"I swear by Almighty God that no one, *no one,* will make your grandson a slave. He has the immunity of the Church. Whoever might dare threaten to take him will incur excommunication and the fires of Hell!"

Mastya quickly accepted the decision and looked to it with anticipation. Now he would see with his own eyes what he had read in the bound leaves.

Only his aunt could not be consoled.

"I will write you letters, Auntie Siya," Mastya said. "I will tell you all about it and about all the wonderful books I am reading. And when I have learned everything, I will come back."

He did not know that the mission supply train went only every three years from the capital of New Spain to *Nuevo México.* His aunt knew, however, that once he left, he would never return.

On the saint's day of San Esteban, Mastya first set eyes on the *villa* of Santa Fé. He was sorely disappointed.

"I thought it would be a grand city like I have read about—with tall, beautiful buildings made out of a rock called marble. Áco is just as pretty as this village. Look, none of the houses are over one story except for the *torreones.* They're all just brown and mud-plastered. There's nothing grand at all about this place. It's no city!"

"Wait till you get to the *Ciudad de México,*" Juan Ramírez said. "There you will see magnificent buildings—the viceroy's palace, the Marqués del Valle's palace, the cathedral being built, and hundreds of beautiful churches. There are wide paved avenues that cross the lake by which you will enter the city, and you will see gilded coaches pass through the streets. Boats bedecked with the most beautiful flowers your eyes have ever seen float through the many canals that crisscross the city. Yes, wait until you get to Mexico City, then you *will* have something grand to witness."

They went first to the house of Señora Dorotea, to which Siya led them. It was Dorotea who opened the door. The priest had to step quickly to her side, for it appeared that she would faint, but she recovered from the initial shock of looking into the gray eyes of the boy.

Tears sprang to her eyes. "You are her grandson!" she exclaimed, throwing her arms around the neck of the bewildered young boy. She embraced him, sobbing while the boy stood unmoving, embarrassed.

At length Dorotea released him and wiped the tears off her cheeks with the backs of her hands. "I knew your grandmother, *hijito,*" she said, touching his cheek. "She was the best friend I have ever had."

Turning, she embraced the boy's aunt who stood at his side, and the tears flowed again. "Oh, Siya," she whispered, "how good it is to see you."

The Ácoma woman's eyes likewise filled with tears as she hugged her former mistress. "Señora Dorotea, it has been a long time. It is good to see you, too."

Dorotea turned back to the priest. "Excuse me, Father, I did not mean to create such a scene. It is just that I am overcome with emotion."

She looked back at the solemn-faced young boy and took his hand. "What a beautiful boy you are. How proud your grandmother would have been of you. Please," she said to the priest, motioning for them to come in, "I am forgetting my manners, letting you stand on the doorstep."

"I am Juan Ramírez," the priest said as he entered.

"Yes, of course," Dorotea responded, "you are the one who chose Ácoma."

Juan Ramírez laughed. "Yes," he said, "but when I arrived there, I was informed the village is Áco, the people are the Ácoma. I have much to learn."

Dorotea smiled. "Áco. I shall not forget. Father, I think you will be a good priest for them."

"I pray that God will grant it," he replied. "*Señora,*" he continued quietly, "if you have servants in the house, I think it might be wise that they not know immediately of our presence until we have a chance to talk in privacy."

"Yes, of course, Father," Dorotea replied, a sudden look of concern passing over her features, "please be seated. They are out back, I think. I will see to them. Excuse me for a moment."

As the Spanish woman left the room, the boy's eyes sped around it, looking at everything. His face filled with wonder at the many things the Spanish *sala* contained.

Juan Ramírez sat down on a leather-covered chair. "You may sit, too," he said to the boy who stood stiffly. Mastya sank to sit on the floor, eyeing the strange thing on which the priest perched. Juan Ramírez laughed.

"No, Augustín," the priest said, using Mastya's Spanish name, "you must learn to sit on chairs as they do in the viceregal capital. In books you have read about chairs, now you will learn to use them."

Hesitantly the boy rose and gingerly, as if he expected it to break, sat down upon the chair to which the priest pointed. "You will also have to learn to sleep in a bed, eat at a table, and use utensils to eat your food." Juan Ramírez smiled with encouragement, but the boy's face retained its solemnness.

Shortly Dorotea returned, walking quickly into the room, her happiness obvious. Siya sat down next to Mastya, and Dorotea pulled up a chair to sit opposite them. She smiled at the boy, and it appeared she would have liked to hug him again, but she refrained and pushed a wisp of hair from her face.

Her eyes were still clear brown, but strands of gray were seeking to dominate the chestnut color of her hair. Her hands were red and rough, clear evidence of the work life in *Nuevo México* required of even a Spanish lady, wife of one of the leading citizens of the provincial capital. The bones were prominent in her sun-weathered face; her body was lean, attesting to the fact that food was never overly abundant in that harsh, arid climate. She was just less than fifty, but it would have been difficult to pinpoint her age, for when she smiled, she seemed younger, although there was a quality to her that spoke of the many rigors and the pain she had suffered.

She turned to Juan Ramírez. "Where do we begin?"

Chapter 8

Throughout the afternoon, Dorotea learned the story of everything that had happened in the ten years since her best friend rode in haste from Santa Fé in search of her two runaway children.

Dorotea was enchanted with the priest's description of the boy's intelligence, and she approved wholeheartedly of the decision to send him to Mexico, but she clasped Siya's hands in sympathy.

"I certainly hope that Fray Benavides, who is in charge of the caravan, will not balk at the cost of another mouth to feed on the journey to Mexico City," Ramírez said. "Once in the capital, Guillermo de la Cruz will see to all the boy's necessities. The Jesuits do not lack for funds."

"There is no need to worry about money, Father." Dorotea rose and walked to a heavy buffet that stood along one wall and withdrew a small box. From beneath the other papers in it, she withdrew a yellowed piece, which she handed to the priest.

"It is the will of the boy's grandmother," she said. "She wrote it before she left for Áco. Everything she possessed, she gave to me in the event of her death because she knew that if any of the ones she loved ever needed anything, I would see they got it. After she died, I gradually liquidated all her possessions and kept careful tally so that my husband Isidro would never know that he had not benefited from her estate.

"With every mission supply caravan returning south, I have sent goods through one of the fathers without anyone else's knowledge. In Parral, the priest would deliver the goods to a trustworthy man who sold them for gold. When the next mission supply caravan came north—which is usually every three years—with it would come a small cryptic note indicating the amount of gold *pesos* accumulated. Fray Alberto de la Concepción in Parral has the money. I never wanted it here. I kept it there in case I might ever need it. Now it will be put to good use."

She handed another small piece of paper to Padre Ramírez. "This is the most recent tally. All of it, of course, is Augustín's. It will be enough to pay his expenses on the journey and leave a nice sum in excess."

The friar looked at Dorotea after reading the figures. "With this money the boy should have no problems as long as others do not know of the inheritance you have saved for him. The only problem facing us now is the lie I intend to tell the officials. I pray they take it at face value and are not overly curious about the boy."

"He will stay here, of course," Dorotea said, "and I shall exercise utmost care that nothing is done to draw attention to him. It is logical for him to be here, for you may say that Siya mentioned my name to you, as she had been my servant for many years."

"I will go alone, first, to see the Father Commissary and tell him of the situation, and I will also say the *señora* is going to pay the boy's expenses out of Christian piety," Ramírez said.

"Thank God my husband is away. This might be impossible if he were here. Please tell the Father Commissary not to mention that I am supplying the money, for if my husband heard about it, even though it is not his own, there would be terrible trouble. The Father Commissary will understand, for my husband is an enemy of the Church."

"Rest assured, *Señora*, God is on our side and nothing shall go wrong."

After the priest left, Dorotea talked to Mastya about his grandmother, his father when he was a boy, and his flame-haired mother. Gradually the boy's frightened demeanor relaxed. His shame did not seem so intense to him, although the woman knew of it.

Dorotea brought an embossed silver box to him. "This is yours," she said. "I have kept it all these years as a remembrance. Now it is yours."

His fingers trembling, Mastya opened the lid. From within he took a rosary with a silver crucifix.

"That was your grandmother's. She gave it to me before she left. The other things I later found in the silver box."

The boy took out a tiny folded piece of silk. Inside lay a lock of dark hair tied with a silk thread.

"That is a lock of your father's hair when he was a baby," Dorotea said. The boy opened another tiny folded piece of silk. He had never seen hair the color of the little curled lock that lay within. "That is your mother's. She had bright, flame-colored hair that was always a mass of wild, blowing curls."

From beneath the folded pieces of silk, Mastya took an ancient, golden cottonwood leaf that appeared as if it had been dipped in wax. With his other hand he removed from the box a piece of mulberry-colored silk ribbon.

"I do not know the significance of the leaf," Dorotea said, "but the ribbon is from a beautiful purple dress your mother wore on the day Don Juan de

Oñate took possession of *Nuevo México* in 1598. The box is yours, Augustín. It was obviously precious to your grandmother, and I am sure she would want you to have it."

Mastya delicately replaced all the items in the small silver box and closed it.

"*Gracias,* Señora Dorotea."

Tears sprang to her eyes. "What a silly old woman I am!" She wiped them away. "Well, now," she said, "we are going to have to make you some fine clothes for the capital of the viceroy!"

A week passed and Juan Ramírez delayed his return to Áco. To his great relief, everything had been arranged with little difficulty. There was nothing that held him in the *villa* save the desire for companionship and the feeling of being among his own.

When asked how the conversion at Áco was going, he invariably said, "Well," but in his heart, he knew that the conversion of the Ácoma was no closer than when he had arrived. In the *villa* he heard stories of the good success other friars were having in the various pueblos, and he rejoiced at the souls reaped by the Church and wished he had some to add to that number. But he wanted the Ácoma to come to him of their own free will; he did not want to herd them to Mass like sheep.

Mastya was now wearing European clothes; he slept in a bed, sat easily on chairs, and ate with much less awkwardness as he used the strange utensils of the Spaniards. He absorbed everything he saw. When Dorotea smiled at him, there was a sadness in her eyes she could not hide. She loved the boy and hated to see him leave so soon.

Although she was past the time of hope, she still grieved over having no child of her own, and although she despised and feared her husband, she had wanted a child from him. When Siya lived with them, Isidro had used her vilely, but Dorotea had hoped the girl would become pregnant so that she might have a baby in the house even if it was not her own. But it had not come to pass. When the boy's grandmother rode to Áco in search of her two children who had fled upon learning the truth about themselves, Siya, whose twenty years of servitude were over, rode with her to show her the way to the high mesa.

Dorotea grieved over the loss of Siya's companionship, for the two women had become close. Dorotea had not since had a close friend, Spanish or Indian, although many Indian girls had passed through the house.

The aridity of the land and its lack of mineral wealth had forced the colonists to look to any source of revenue, ill-got or other. It was soon learned what had market value in the mining towns of northern Mexico with which there was some trade. Tanned hides, woven cotton *mantas,* salt, and piñon nuts found ready sale there. Another commodity that brought good return for the seller was Indian slaves. Spanish law for the Indies forbade making slaves of natives, but the heathen Indians who did not live in pueblos—the nomads called "Apache de Návajo"—were fair game as far as the colonists were concerned. Slave raids, frequently veiled in the guise of retaliatory attacks for some Apache offense, had become commonplace.

Isidro Inojosa was one of the most frequent organizers of such forays, the object of which were women, as well as girls and boys under the age of twelve. Older boys and men were too much trouble, for they always attempted to escape and were often successful. Inojosa's quarry was always young girls of twelve or thirteen. He brought them to live in his house in Santa Fé, and nightly Dorotea had to cover her ears with her hands to shut out the screams as he raped them. In the morning she would go to the room that might have two or three of the poor hurt things, and she would shudder at the cruel bites and bruises that sometimes covered their bodies. Afterward she went to the church and prayed. It was always the same prayer.

First she asked God to take pity on the poor girls. Then she prayed for her own salvation; she could not make herself pray for her husband's. Inevitably the question followed, "Why? Why do you allow a man like Isidro to live?" And then she would say the Act of Contrition, thinking that God was punishing her for her own offenses by making her a witness to such cruelty. But what could she do? Many had been the times she had contemplated stabbing a knife into her husband's chest while he slept, but she had never been able to conquer the commandment that "thou shalt not kill." She knew it was a sin to hate, but she hated her husband, hated his evil face with its black piercing eyes and its disfiguring facial scar, hated his cruel nature. She had thought about escaping, but where in that godforsaken land could she escape to? There was the money in Parral but she could never have made it that far alone. She had even contemplated the unthinkable: She had wanted to take her own life, but the thought of eternal damnation was too onerous.

Instead she had prayed for strength, saying, "I know you must be testing me, Lord, but please, I beg you, give me strength to endure and give me understanding. If I have offended you, tell me how. Do not inflict punishment on the helpless girls if the sins are mine."

When her husband tired of the young girls, but more appropriately, when it became obvious that they were not becoming pregnant from his nightly attacks, he sent them to Mexico to be sold as slaves. He was accustomed to getting whatever he wanted by force, but what he wanted most was a male heir. He called Dorotea the barren old hag; he had not spoken her Christian name in years. She would have thought that listening to his abuse for so long would have made her insensitive to it, but each time he spoke the epithet, she shriveled inside.

Then one day the belly of one of the girls had begun to grow. Isidro had finally shown some kindness, if only to cease subjecting the girl to his nightly attacks. He instructed Dorotea to feed the girl well, and he waited for his heir to appear.

As he waited for the birthing, he paced and demanded angrily, "Why is it taking so long?"

The baby girl was born near dawn, and Dorotea took the child to him. "It is a girl," she said but recoiled at the rage that flared in his eyes and clasped the baby tightly to her.

His face suffused with crimson and the facial scar stood out like an ugly white welt, disfiguring even more the rage that contorted his face. He grabbed a silver candelabra from the table and hurled it against the wall. She ran back into the room from which she had come, closing the door behind her. Terrible sounds of wood splintering made her cringe with fear as she clutched the tiny baby, but her husband made no attempt to enter the room. The noises finally ceased and in the distance she heard a door slam and breathed a sigh of relief.

She knew a happiness like she had never known. There was a child in the house, no matter that the mother was an Apache slave, the father a man she loathed. She would love the child and care for it as if it were her own. She laid the baby next to its mother, and overcome with fatigue from the night's vigil, sought her own bed.

She thought the screaming was a nightmare, but suddenly she was awake, and it was very real. Sunlight poured in the window and she did not know how long she had slept, but she ran from her room, knowing from whence came the screams. She stopped abruptly at the open door of the girl's room and looked in horror as Isidro held the lifeless baby in his hands. He turned and looked at her, no emotion on his evil face.

"The child is dead. It must have suffocated." He dropped the lifeless baby onto the bed. The terrified young mother picked up the infant and cradled it against her chest and sobbed uncontrollably.

Isidro brushed past Dorotea as she stood frozen in horror. Then as if coming out of a dream, she ran to the child and dipped her hand in a pottery bowl of water that had been left at the bedside of the girl.

"I baptize thee in the name of the Father, Son, and Holy Spirit," Dorotea whispered as she let the drops of water fall on the baby's forehead. There were large red finger marks on the child's face.

"What happened?" she asked, although the Apache girl understood only a handful of Castilian words. There must have been comprehension for the girl put her hand over the dead baby's face and pointed in the direction in which the father had gone.

"No!" Dorotea gasped, but the girl's black eyes looked solemnly at her and she nodded yes.

Dorotea took the baby from the girl, wrapped it in a blanket and put it in the tiny cradle she had had a carpenter make before the child was born. She combed her hair, wiped away her tears and went to seek the priest at the Santa Fé convent. She asked to say confession, and he granted it. The priest was stunned at what she revealed.

"Please help me so that Isidro can be apprehended."

"There is nothing I can do, *Señora*. Did you see your husband commit the act?"

"No," she whispered.

"Who will take the word of a heathen girl who cannot speak Castilian against that of a Spanish *encomendero*?" She knew the answer.

"Vengeance is mine, sayeth the Lord. In His good time He will punish the guilty. Let us give the child a Christian burial and commend its soul to Heaven."

And so it had been done. Three days later her husband took the Apache girl south to sell her along with some other goods. She did not survive the trip.

Dorotea thanked God that Isidro was away from Santa Fé when Augustín arrived. She was terrified that he would have recognized the boy's parentage—the gray eyes were unmistakable. God knows what her husband might do to the boy or say to the authorities if he saw him. She was grateful also that Augustín would not have to be witness to her husband's depravity, but the longer the caravan delayed its departure, the more her trepidation grew. Isidro had gone to Taos and was usually gone for weeks, but who knew when he would return? She could not shake the apprehension that had taken hold of her.

Reluctantly Juan Ramírez left Santa Fé. He would have liked to stay to see the boy off on his journey, but there was no good reason to. Dorotea had not told him of her fears, and Fray Benavides assured him he would attend to the boy's welfare.

Ramírez knew that while Mastya awaited the preparation of the caravan for its return trip to Mexico City he could not possibly have a better place to stay than the home of the Señora Dorotea. The priest was grateful that the boy would be in the company of the mature priest Benavides as well as three other Franciscans who were making the return journey. They would see to it that he did not come under the influence of any of the soldiers escorting the caravan nor the *mestizos* who had charge of herding the stock that would be sold in northern Mexico. He was less than pleased that two prisoners of the Holy Office were being taken in chains to Mexico City to appear before the tribunal of the Inquisition. He hoped the boy would not be adversely affected by the sight of men in chains whose crimes were against the Church.

The Inquisition had reached *Nuevo México* three years previously, Fray Benavides carrying the papers of his appointment as Commissary of the Holy Office.

On January 25, 1626, the first Edict of Faith was read at the Santa Fé church, Benavides had told him proudly. Now the friar was on his way back to Mexico City, a chest of papers in his possession to present before the Tribunal. The chest contained all the depositions of denunciations and the evidence accumulated in his three years in the province. Only the judges of the Inquisition's Tribunal in the capital of New Spain could hear complaints and rule on them. The accusations Fray Benavides carried with him ranged from heresy to bigamy and from sorcery to pacts with the devil and evil-sounding language.

The Inquisition had its tainted hands full trying to purify the faith throughout the vast domain over which it wielded its ever-more powerful control, but Juan Ramírez had seen its cruelty and its greedy confiscation of the accuseds' worldly goods. Examples of Christian charity would go farther toward helping purify the faith in Ramírez's view, but he did not say that to Benavides. To do so would have been foolhardy not only for himself but for Mastya. He wanted no one casting a suspicion on the young boy with the unusual background.

Although Padre Ramírez departed for Áco, Siya stayed behind. Dorotea had urged her to remain until Augustín left, and it had not been difficult to persuade her. The time evaporated more quickly than either of the women had imagined. Dorotea felt a sense of relief but desolation also. She had grown to treasure the boy she would never see again.

The aspens high on the Sangre de Cristos that jutted up behind the *villa* had begun to make their visual announcement of the changing seasons, and patches of yellow and gold appeared upon the mountainsides. The caravan was prepared. After early Mass on the morrow, it would depart. Dorotea crossed herself.

Darkness fell and she lit the *candelabro*. She looked at Augustín and tried to smile. She took his face in her hands.

"Oh, my darling boy, how I will miss you," she said. "*Dios te bendiga, hijito*. I know He has wonderful things in store for you in the city of Mexico."

She heard the wind rise as she dropped her hands and looked at Siya. "Fall is coming," she said.

Then terror etched her face. She heard the sounds carried on the wind, and her face became as white as the winding cloth of the dead.

"It's him," she whispered. Horror washed across Siya's face in that instant also. Mastya saw the looks on the two women's faces and his eyes widened in fear.

"Quick," Dorotea said, "we must hide you both. Isidro will surely recognize Augustín once he sees his eyes, and God knows what will happen then."

She grabbed the boy's hand and ran to her bedroom. She threw open a large wooden trunk and yanked out some blankets. "*Hijito,* I don't have time to explain. Hide in here, and for the love of God, do not make a sound."

Mastya climbed swiftly into the trunk and curled up in a ball as Dorotea closed the lid. "He mustn't see you either," she said to Siya. "Come, we will hide you in the *armario*."

Dorotea pulled the garments in the clothes closet down to cover Siya and closed the door. She shoved the blankets she had taken from the trunk under the bed, then scurried from the room pulling the door shut behind her. She ran to the *sala*, grabbed a rosary from the long buffet, and ran to the kneeler in front of a small statue of the Virgin that sat in a *nicho* in the wall. She fell to her knees, dropped her head onto her hands, and tried to quiet her heavy breathing.

The door was shoved open and the chill night air swirled into the room. She jerked involuntarily and looked up.

Her husband, his face contorted in a grimace by the long scar that crossed his cheek to the corner of his mouth, slammed the door and turned to her.

"You look like you have just seen a ghost."

"You startled me," she said, keeping her voice even as she kissed the rosary and stood, pushing back the hair that had escaped from the knot at the nape of her neck.

"Get me something to eat," he demanded. "We would have been home by noon if the goddamned axle on the *carreta* hadn't broken."

"Of, course," Dorotea said, turning quickly away from him, knowing her face had paled. "It will only take a moment."

She scurried from the room and once in the kitchen leaned heavily against the table trying to quiet the pounding of her heart. She went to the hearth and with fumbling fingers pulled a heavy iron pot from the low fire and ladled beans into a bowl. From a cloth she unwrapped corn tortillas. She carried the food back to the *sala* and placed it on the long table. He sat down and noisily began to eat. She could not look at him and fought the desire to look at the closed door of her room where Siya and the boy were hidden.

"Where's my drink?"

His piercing black eyes narrowed. "What's the matter with you, *mujer*? You're as jumpy as an unbroken mule."

"It's nothing," she lied, thinking madly of something to say. "It's just that Fray Benavides warned us at Mass that there are people practicing sorcery here in the *villa*, and he told us to beware at night. You have been gone for days, and I, I . . ." Her words trailed off.

"Bah!" he spat. "You and your goddamned priests."

She quickly got his drink and sighed with relief when he finished his food, pushed himself away from the table, and rose with a yawn. "*Dios*, am I tired," he growled. He walked slowly to his room, and she heard the bed groan as he flopped down on it. She thanked God they did not share the same room.

She left the dishes on the table, blew out the candles in the *candelabro*, and went swiftly to her own room where she closed the door softly and climbed into bed fully dressed. The minutes dragged unmercifully. After what seemed like hours, she rose and tiptoed to Isidro's room where she heard the sounds of his snoring. When she had reached her room again and closed the door, she went to the *armario*.

"Come," she whispered as she opened the door and helped Siya out. "We must get Augustín to the *convento*. He will be safe there." Siya nodded in the darkness.

"*Hijo,*" Dorotea whispered when she opened the trunk, "we must go to the *convento* tonight. You must stay with Fray Benavides until tomorrow."

She hugged him tightly after he had stepped out of the trunk. She found three shawls and they tiptoed from the room and across the *sala* to the door. The squeak of the door opening sounded like a cannon shot in her ears, but after a few moments she heard no noise from the interior of the house and pulled the door slowly closed. They scurried across the plaza. Dorotea knocked softly on the door of the *convento*. Long moments passed. She knocked again and again. Finally the sacristan came.

"*¿Qué quiere?*" he asked suspiciously.

"It's Señora de Inojosa. Let me in. I must speak to Fray Benavides."

The sacristan opened the door and they rushed in.

"*Momentito,*" he said. "I will fetch him."

"Oh, *Padre,*" Dorotea sighed with relief as Fray Benavides came hurrying into the room. "My husband returned tonight. I hid Siya and the boy until it was safe to come. They must stay here tonight. I fear for them if . . ."

"Calm yourself, *hija,*" the friar said gently as he heard the agitation in her voice. "Of course they may stay here tonight. Have no fear. The caravan leaves as soon as early Mass is over in the morning, and the boy's things were all packed just this evening."

"Thank you, Father," Dorotea said, taking a deep breath. She hugged Siya and then Augustín. "*Hasta la mañanita.*"

The fall air was brisk and pungent with the smell of piñon smoke. Dorotea wrapped her shawl closely about her as she hurried to early Mass that autumn day of 1629. She slipped into church, knelt, and began to pray. Before long Siya and Augustín came and knelt beside her as people began to fill the church.

Dorotea prayed for the well-being of the boy and a quick, safe journey for the caravan. Many prayers were offered that morning, though none as fervent as hers.

When the Mass ended, the entire village saw the lumbering carts off. Dorotea could not keep from glancing over her shoulder every few minutes, terrified Isidro would appear.

Both women embraced the young, solemn-faced boy as they tried to restrain their tears, but they were not successful. Each knew it was the last time they would see the handsome, gray-eyed boy, and they grieved deeply.

Mastya mounted the mule that Padre Ramírez had bought for him with the money on credit Dorotea had given him.

In the weeks he had spent in Santa Fé, besides learning to sleep in a bed, and eat at a table with utensils, Mastya learned another aspect of Castilian culture: to ride a horse.

It was the sole thing in Santa Fé he loved. Señora Dorotea was kind and

good to him, and she had made delicious things for him to eat out of ingre-
dients he had never before tasted. There was wheat flour, sugar, apples,
grapes, honey, milk from cows, and strange spices. But what he truly loved
were the horses, and every minute he was permitted, he spent at the corrals.

An old man there cared for the horses. His eyes had a thin white film
partially covering them and he could scarcely see, but he knew everything
about the magnificent beasts, and his hands alone could discover any hurt
or defect. He was the only friend Mastya had made in the *villa* save Señora
Dorotea.

In just a few short weeks the old man, called Domingo, had taught Mastya
many things, and the boy learned quickly. One day after the boy had ridden,
the old man put his hand on his shoulder.

"You remind me of another boy I once taught to ride a horse," he said,
his eyes misting with the memory.

And so, when Padre Ramírez bought a mule for Mastya to ride on the
journey, it was a sad disappointment. He had not anticipated he would ride
one of the slow, balking, unattractive animals. He had hoped for a fast, sleek,
beautiful *caballo*.

One day I will have one, he promised himself.

As the lumbering caravan disappeared in a cloud of dust in the distance,
Dorotea fell to her knees and dissolved into tears.

"God be with thee, *hijito*. God be with thee."

Part Three

EL JESUITA

The Jesuit, 1641

Chapter 9

The runner crossed the village at a dog trot, the same pace at which he had begun the journey at Isleta. He mounted the several steps and genuflected briefly as he stepped inside the cool interior and crossed himself. It took a moment for his eyes to become accustomed to the shadows. His moccasined feet made no sound on the packed dirt floor as he walked toward the hand-carved altar. A gray-haired figure in a well-worn blue habit knelt there. The Indian went to his knees beside the priest and crossed himself again.

Juan Ramírez raised his head and turned toward the young runner. "Were there the leaves with marks?" he asked in Queres. The Indian nodded and the priest smiled. "Thank you, Dyatyu, thank you."

Ramírez fingered the letter and looked at the beautiful script as he walked from the church to his quarters that were connected on the north side of the massive church wall. He entered his room and climbed the ladder to the roof. He sat in a chair and looked out toward the east, toward the mountains, looking into the distance as if trying to see something human eyes could never reach. The spring sun was warm on his skin as he sat there for long moments. At last he broke the seal on the letter.

"*Querido Padre,*" it began. "Dear Father," father in the sense of priest, but it meant father to Juan Ramírez in its other sense, for he had felt a closeness for the boy as if he might have been his own son.

He should have taken the other letter immediately to the man who was the grandfather, for surely that letter had priority, but he could not keep from reading his own before anything else:

Dear Father,
    I hope this letter finds you in the best of health as my prayers always request. How proud I felt upon reading your last letter to hear that

your church is finally completed. What a monument to God and to you, *Padre,* as His servant, to have converted the pueblo of the Ácoma.

Fray Manso has told me that it is the finest church in the entire province, surpassing even that of Santa Fé and Santo Domingo. I know that what you wrote me is true, but to think of the Ácoma transporting those enormous *vigas* on their shoulders from a place so distant as North Mountain and never letting the beams touch the ground is astonishing. The church must be a marvelous edifice with its thick, massive walls, the carved *vigas,* and the clerestory that provides that light reach the interior.

I am still amazed to hear that they built the road you wanted. I know you call it only a path, but what a miracle you have wrought there upon the White Rock.

Now I must recount to you a *máscara* that we staged in honor of the new Viceroy. It was an allegorical *tour de force . . .*

Ramírez read on, devouring the details of the pageant, picturing it vividly as it wound its way through the streets of the Mexico City he knew so well. For a fleeting moment he would like to have set foot in the exciting, busy capital. He finished the letter sadly and would have liked to indulge himself in rereading it before taking the grandfather's letter to him, but he knew he had already delayed too long.

Rohona heard the priest call up the greeting and responded with pleasure for him to climb the ladder to the terrace roof. The two had become best of friends although neither would probably have acknowledged it to the other. Many were the hours they sat and talked, discussing every aspect of life, each usually taking a different side in the discussions that were frequently amicable, devil's advocate debates.

He saw what the priest carried in his hand and Rohona knew he was getting old. Every time a letter arrived, it became increasingly more difficult to keep the moisture from coming to his eyes. He had a desire so deep and sharp inside him that he had constantly to keep it in check so that he did not succumb to tears. He would have given anything to see his handsome grandson, but it was an impossible desire.

His hands trembled and his eyes blurred when he opened the letter and first began to read, but a smile of pride came to his face as he read on:

The Jesuits have a *casa de campo* outside Mexico City where on weekends and holidays we go to exercise our bodies and fill our lungs with fresh, clean air. You would be surprised at the many races and games much like the ones in which the ancient Greeks participated. The running of the Ácoma across the valley floor that I did so much as a child gives me the distinct advantage over the others that I still enjoy today. Knowing the value you place on the ability to run great distances without tiring, I try to keep in practice, although I am afraid I would not measure up to the standards of the White Rock.

Do you still read, Grandfather? Is the Roman philosopher Marcus Aurelius the one you spend most of your time with? I imagine your copy is very well-worn by now. If you ever need another, you have just to send me word, and I will send one with the next mission supply caravan.

The smile slipped from Rohona's face.

I am so disturbed, Grandfather, to hear about the increasing attacks of the ruthless Apaches. Cannot the Spanish authorities do anything to protect the pueblos against the marauders? I am thankful Padre Ramírez is at Áco to help protect the people from the exploitation of the Spaniards whose duty it is to protect the natives, not to use them for their own profit. How the villages near Santa Fé must suffer under the heavy yoke of labor required of them. Can nothing be done? Do both the clergy and the civilians exploit the pueblos as much as the friar writes? I know the good Father does not lie, but I find it difficult to believe that the natives do not protest or rise against the Spanish oppressors.

I wish you could see the valley of Mexico; it is very beautiful. The estate of the family of the children whom I tutor is outside the city and especially lovely. There I get to indulge in horseback riding. Sometimes on my rides with the children we take along a lunch that we eat by a spring, which are quite abundant there . . .

Rohona read on wishing the letter would not end. For long moments afterward, he sat silently, his eyes closed. Ramírez politely waited, saying nothing.

The grandfather wished the priest would not write about the troubles in the land, for they only served to cause the boy anxiety about their welfare. Rohona was glad the boy did not know the extent of the misery in which many of the villages lived, but he did agree with his grandson that the Ácoma were fortunate to have the friar. Rohona could not say that the priest had brought contentment to the Ácoma by bringing them his foreign god, but he had not caused them harm as had the priests in many of the other villages, and Padre Ramírez had never made an attempt to stop their ceremonials.

Rohona opened his eyes, and looked at the friar. "The boy is well, it seems," he said with satisfaction.

"Yes, he must be an outstanding young man. The Jesuits are very fortunate indeed. I knew that once they saw his intelligence, they would see to it he stayed within their fold, but I suppose it does not matter, for we all serve the same Lord."

The grandfather had no concept of how one group of long-robes differed from another. What mattered to him was that the boy was happy.

Juan Ramírez smoothed his well-worn habit—Augustín's would be crisp and black. The friar felt emotion well in him but fought it back.

"I wish I could have seen the boy Luís's face when Augustín pulled him up by the shirtfront!" Ramírez said with a laugh.

Rohona chuckled, for his letter had also contained the description of the confrontation.

"It seems that the tutoring has become a pleasant job now, though," the priest continued.

Rohona nodded. "He wrote he has made a bow and some arrows for the son, hoping to develop a better rapport with him. And my grandson appears to get a great deal of pleasure out of horseback riding at the family's estate outside the city." Rohona paused and looked off into the distance, remembering others who had loved to ride like the wind.

Juan Ramírez knew that both he and the grandfather were having difficulty keeping their emotions in check. He tried to make his voice light.

"It pleases me that our boy has the warmth and friendship of the family. He says he hopes to make a scholar of the son but must truthfully admit, however, that it is the little daughter of the family who makes him strive most concentratedly on providing the best education he can. He says she reminds him of himself and his own thirst for learning."

"He always had his nose in a book." Rohona raised his hands in mock despair. "I finally gave up telling him it would ruin his eyes!"

"It doesn't appear that it has yet."

"Now," the grandfather said, "we must write our letters so that the carts may carry them back to Mexico when they return in the fall." His eyes misted. "Now we wait for three more summers until the next letter shall arrive."

"You speak Nahuatl?" the viceroy asked Augustín.

"Yes, Excellency. All Jesuit seminarians in New Spain must master at least one indigenous language. We learn them at our novitiate in Tepotzotlán—which itself is a village of natives."

"And you know others?"

"Sí, Excelencia. Otomí and the language of the fierce Tarahumaras in the mountains of the north—beyond Durango and near Parral."

"Why their language if they are so fierce and far away?"

"I had once thought I would like to carry the Gospel to that area of New Spain." Augustín did not tell the viceroy that he would have then been closer to a place called Áco where he might at least have had the opportunity to visit clandestinely. He would have had to go on the sly because the province of *Nuevo México* was solely the domain of the Franciscans, and even a visiting Jesuit was barred from entering.

"But you have changed your mind?" the viceroy asked.

"After ordination I will happily go wherever my Provincial sends me, but I expect I won't be given missionary work."

"And why is that?"

Augustín looked down with discomfort at the question, and the viceroy laughed. "Of course your superiors would not send one of their brightest minds off among the heathen."

Why was the viceroy taking such an interest in him? Why did he so often summon him to the viceregal palace when all he did there was spend half an hour or so answering the Duque's questions about all manner of things in the capital and in New Spain itself.

Augustín looked up. His face must have revealed his curiosity because the viceroy said, "You wish to ask *me* a question for a change?"

Augustín started to say no but said instead, "I am honored and flattered that Your Excellency summons me to audiences in the viceregal palace, but I am not worthy of the honor you bestow on me. I am not even an ordained priest yet; I cannot possibly supply you with proper information or guidance, and yet I feel you wish something of me."

The viceroy looked at him levelly. "I am surrounded by supplicants. Everyone wants something from *me*—even the religious. Every order is at my door, trying to jockey for my favor. You, on the other hand, want nothing, stand to gain nothing. I do not mean it in a deprecatory way, but you have no power. There is little, if anything, I could ever do for you—you are under the strict discipline of your vows and your order—they are your rulers in a very real sense, not I. Therefore, when I ask you questions, I am seeking answers that are unbiased."

"But I am a Jesuit, Excellency. I will have their bias whether I realize it or not."

"True, but Jesuits are the best educated of all the religious and much more broad and open-minded than most. Besides, I essentially plucked you off the street—no one pushed you at me nor did you come seeking something from me. For a man in my position, I can't tell you how difficult it is to get an honest view of a new place. You seemed intelligent and unpretentious."

The viceroy sat back and fingered his stiff, curled mustache.

"Thank you, Excellency, but there are honest and much wiser men than I here in the capital."

"Who, for example? How am I to find these men when I am beset on all sides by people being pushed at me?"

"My confessor, for example," Augustín said. "He is one of the wisest, most brutally honest men I know." He smiled thinking about Padre de la Cruz. "Excellency, he would tell you what he thought whether you had asked or not, and even if you told him you did not want to know, he would tell you anyway."

The Duque roared with laughter. "I've been so accustomed to people telling me what they think I want to hear, that perhaps I couldn't take the blunt truth!" His demeanor changed and he became serious. "I would like for you to bring this *padre* to me if you would. I do not particularly care for the priest who was put forward as a 'suitable' viceregal confessor for me."

"As you wish."

"Now," the viceroy said, "who are some of these other wise men in the city to whom you referred?"

"Wise in what particular way, *Excelencia*?"

"Men knowledgeable in government, politics, business, trade—anything that concerns the affairs of New Spain. Men from whom I might learn important details about this land that I have been entrusted to govern for the king."

"As an example, perhaps, the status of mining?" Augustín asked.

"Absolutely," the Duque said with enthusiasm, sitting forward on his velvet-covered chair. "Mining, especially. The king is *máximamente* interested in the status of the mines. New World silver is vital for the royal coffers—without it the mother country would be at the mercy of the rest of those upstart European countries bent on stealing our hard-won New World possessions and their riches."

"Don Rodrigo de Salvatierra, the father of the children I tutor, is *sumamente rico* from his mines in Ixmiquilpan. He is a good businessman and will know the status of silver mining as well as anyone."

"Tell me about this Salvatierra and his mines."

Chapter 10

Augustín related information to the Duque of what he knew about Don Rodrigo's mining background and talked on at some length about the family itself and the talents of the young brother and sister he tutored. He realized with chagrin that in talking about the children he had veered from the subject in which the viceroy was most interested.

"Forgive me, Excellency," he said. "I did not mean to take up your valuable time with frivolous matters. It's just that I enjoy teaching the children and I forgot myself."

"That's quite all right," the Duque said good-naturedly, rising to indicate the audience was over. "I get bored talking about weighty matters all the time anyway. If you would be so kind," he continued, paying Augustín an honor by accompanying him to the door of the *salón*, "I would appreciate it if you could bring your 'brutal' confessor the next time you come."

Augustín smiled. "But of course, Excellency."

"The viceroy?" The wrinkles around Guillermo de la Cruz's bright blue eyes deepened with mirth. "Wants a lowly seminarian to bring me to him?" He chuckled. "Aren't *you* moving in exalted circles these days! Preparing yourself to join the ranks of the power brokers of the Church?"

Augustín knew his old mentor was only being light-hearted with his jesting, nonetheless he felt ill at ease. "I told him you were brutal," he said, trying to imitate the other's levity.

The *padre* burst into laughter, which became a paroxysm of coughing, and Augustín ran to fetch a glass of water.

When the priest could speak once more he said to Augustín, "I don't think the viceroy has much to worry about from an old man who can't even laugh without choking, do you?"

"So you will go with me to see him?"

"Could even *I* do otherwise? I am as much bound by the vow of obedience as you are. Can you imagine what the Provincial would say if I refused a meeting with the Duque de Escalona y Marqués de Villena? — particularly now that self-righteous, power-hungry bishop Juan de Palafox is here? He detests Jesuits because we owe our allegiance to the Pope himself, and no bishop, however lofty, has control over us. That was how our father Loyola wanted it — a spiritual army for the Pope. So you see, Augustín, even if I personally preferred not to have an audience with the viceroy, I would be duty-bound to be of whatever service I could because His Holiness is very much interested in bringing Our Lord to the New World." The old priest chuckled. "Besides, Bonifaz would skin me alive if I didn't go!"

The audience with the viceroy and Padre de la Cruz had gone exceedingly well. The Duque de Escalona now unburdened his conscience and sought guidance and absolution from a Jesuit Father. Padre Luís Bonifaz, the Provincial of the Order, was pleased one of the Society's own had the ear of the viceroy; the viceroy was content he had guidance he could trust; and Augustín was happy that the Duque would have the benefit of his mentor's wisdom.

The servant opened the door and when she saw the liveried page standing there, she smothered a gasp and dropped an awkward curtsy before she took the heavy sealed envelope handed her.

"*¿Qué fue?*" María Luisa asked when she saw the look on the *criada*'s face. "What is the matter, Concepción?"

The servant's voice came out as a croak as she extended the silver tray on which she had laid the letter. "It's for the *señor* and *señora*."

María Luisa took the expensive-looking letter on which her husband's and her names were written with elegant flourishes. "*Dulce Virgen,*" she whispered when she turned the envelope over and saw the coat-of-arms pressed in the wax seal.

"Rodrigo! Rodrigo!" she shouted. Her knees weakened and she sought the sofa in the *sala,* sinking down on it, clutching the letter to her chest.

"Go!" she said with urgency to the maid. "Get Don Rodrigo. I don't trust my legs."

The servant scurried from the room. María Luisa looked at the names on the envelope, turned it over and looked again at the seal.

Her husband rushed into the room, his face questioning, and she wordlessly handed him the envelope. His reaction was much the same as hers, only he chose the mantel to lean against for support. Slowly and carefully he pried up the wax seal, opened the envelope, and read silently.

María Luisa crossed herself. "What does it say?"

"El Marqués de Villena requests the pleasure of our company for tea next Thursday at the *palacio real* — and the children are invited."

"The Blessed Mother has answered my prayers," María Luisa whispered.

Her husband joined her on the sofa, rereading the invitation, and then handed it to her.

She glanced down at the invitation. "Oh, Rodrigo, our dreams are coming true."

He took her hand and kissed it. "Yes, dearest wife — and to think the *virrey* wants us to bring the children!" He leaned back against the sofa. "Without a doubt we have Augustín to thank for this good fortune. All the doors will open now."

Augustín came to the house to escort them to the viceroy's palace. Father and mother were filled with nervousness, but it appeared it had not infected Luís and Antonia, for they were engrossed in a game of colored *palillos*. Augustín was glad he had talked to the children about the viceroy and told them that although he was a duke and a marquis, the viceroy was simply a nice man who wanted to meet them and wanted them to enjoy some sweets at the *palacio real*.

"Just be polite the way your *mamá* has taught you," he had admonished them. "Treat the Duque as you would treat any of your parents' friends."

"But *Mamá* will want me to wear a fancy dress," Antonia had protested.

"That she will, Little One," Augustín said, "and you must wear it without complaint. Your *mamá* will have too many other things to worry about without having to plead with you for days. Do I have your solemn promise you won't complain?" She nodded but with apparent reluctance.

"It is a pleasure to meet the mother of such outstanding children whose accomplishments Don Augustín has recounted to me," the Duque said as he kissed María Luisa's hand.

She stammered a "thank you" and found nothing else to say, and it was then her husband's turn to lack elegant words upon his introduction to the seventeenth viceroy of New Spain, but the Duque de Escalona seemed not to notice as he turned to the children.

"And you must be the brilliant young girl of whom your tutor has spoken," he said as he took Antonia's hand, then bent and kissed it as he had her mother's. "But, tell me, why would such a beautiful little girl want to study Latin and Greek?"

She looked directly at him. "*Scientia ipse voluptas,* Señor Virrey."

Although her father did not understand the Latin words, he turned red with embarrassment at her forwardness; her mother blanched, Augustín smiled, and the viceroy laughed.

"I'm afraid my Latin is a little rusty," the Duque said, turning to Augustín. "Perhaps your tutor would oblige me with the translation."

"Knowledge itself is pleasure."

"Well said, Señorita Antonia!" The Duque turned to Luís. "Do you have an edifying Latin phrase for me, also, young man?"

Luís looked at the floor, shifted his weight from one foot to the other, hesitated. "*Mens bona regnum possidet.*"

The viceroy smiled and turned again to Augustín for a translation.

"A good mind possesses a kingdom."

"*¡Magnífico!*" The Duque clapped his hands. "Wonderful *dicho* for a ruler — or anyone! I shall remember that. Such talented children. Don Rodrigo, you have much to be proud of. My sincerest congratulations on raising such fine children. They will do you proud, no doubt."

After the family tea at the viceregal palace, Don Rodrigo found himself invited upon several occasions for audiences with the viceroy to discuss silver mining. The viceroy's secretary was also present, sitting at a small desk.

"And what would you say is most vital in the *industria minera* as far as the king is concerned?" the Duque asked at the first audience.

"That depends, Excellency," Don Rodrigo said. He clasped his hands together so that the viceroy might not catch a telltale tremor of his nervousness. "There are three major things that can impede or even bring to a halt the flow of the royal fifth into the king's treasury."

"Go on," the viceroy said when Salvatierra hesitated momentarily.

"First," Don Rodrigo continued, "there must be a constant and adequate supply of mercury for the mines. Your priority should be . . ." He swallowed. "I beg you pardon, Excellency, I did not mean to sound as if I were telling you what to do. Forgive my presumption."

"No, no. Please be frank. That's why I asked you here." The Duque gestured with his hand. "Please, go on."

"Mercury is essential for the extraction of the *plata* from the ore. Do you know how that is done here in New Spain?" The viceroy shook his head. "We grind the silver-containing ore very fine until we have a sort of mineral flour, then moisten the flour and spread it in a paved patio. This is where the amalgamation takes place. We begin by adding *sal blanca* — muriate of soda — and after that has sat for several days, the mercury is mixed in. We add other substances to enhance the chemical reaction and then stir the paste by having horses or mules run on it or we use men who tramp on it, much like they do for expressing the juice from grapes for making wine. But the silver process takes much longer. The men can tramp barefoot for days in the paste. That is the initial process — it takes months, however, for the bars of silver to be ready for shipping. The important thing to know, however, is that it takes *six* times the amount of mercury as there is silver in the ore."

"And where does the *mercurio* come from?"

"From the mother country — principally from the Almadén mine. That is why we sometimes run short. We don't have the element easily available

here, so it must be imported. This is where Your Excellency could aid the
king. Bring your power to bear on those in España who are in charge of the
mercury and its transport. The court in Madrid has the exclusive right to
sell the mercury, and the bureaucracy has a stranglehold on it. Delays keep
us from producing as much as would be possible. Alert the king to the problem. Ask him to facilitate the export of mercury to us."

The viceroy turned to his secretary. "Did you make a note of that?"

"*Sí, Excelencia.*"

"*Muy bien.* And what is the second item of importance?" the Duque asked.

"The second are the highwaymen and savages who prey on the silver
trains." Don Rodrigo sat forward, his nervousness now gone. "Excellency,
the insecurity of the roads seriously threatens to retard the mining industry.
You cannot imagine the number of men that are necessary to guard a train
of wagons filled with twenty thousand marks of silver. It would take an army
to guard the train properly."

"Make a note to study the problem of the roads—two-pronged: one, deal-
ing with *bandidos* and *indios salvajes,* and two, proper royal escort." The viceroy
turned back to Salvatierra. "Three?"

"The third thing Your Excellency knows better than I. Once the silver
gets to the port at Veracruz, if it cannot get to the mother country, it does
Don Felipe no good for his European wars."

"And that is one of the major things I would like to accomplish as viceroy—clean the *Caribe* of these damnable Dutch and English pirates who prey
on the Atlantic fleet. The *flota* must be able to travel regularly—without fail."

Although winters in the viceregal capital could be cool, they were mildness
itself compared to what Augustín had known as a child. Freezing, snow-
laden wind often battered the exposed village on the mesa top as the people
huddled in their dwellings, eyes burning from the smoke of the hearth fires
that were only minimally successful in warming the interiors and their occupants. But in spite of the mildness of the winter in the Ciudad de México,
Augustín was delighted with the arrival of spring and the soft, warm air
perfumed with blooming flowers and trees.

If he wanted to see snow, all he had to do was gaze at the perpetually
snow-covered peaks of Popocatépetl, or "smoking mountain" to the Aztecs,
and his White Lady, Ixtaccíhuatl, who slept nearby.

As Augustín neared the Colegio Máximo, he saw a crowd gather, pushing
to get one of the *hojas volantes* from a young man who was handing out
broadsides with news from the *navío de aviso,* the ship that sailed ahead of
the Spanish fleet bringing the report of its arrival or perhaps other important
news from Europe.

When Augustín glimpsed the headline on a broadside that a man had
managed to secure, he, too, pushed his way into the crowd, vying for one of
the news sheets.

"Portugal and Catalonia have revolted!" people exclaimed. "The Duke of Bragança is on the throne of Portugal as King Dom João IV!"

Augustín's height allowed him to reach above the crowd and grab one of the *hojas*. He pushed his way out of the mass of people and when he was clear of them, stopped to read the incredible news.

For sixty years Portugal had chafed under the yoke of Spain. Now they were once more claiming themselves an independent nation as they had been before King Sebastian led them to ruin in 1578 at Alcácer-Quibir in northern Africa.

With revolt on both his eastern and western boundaries, the King of Spain had his hands full, and it appeared that if he had to lose one, he would lose Portugal and not Catalonia.

Augustín turned from the Colegio Máximo and hurried toward the Casa Profesa. Undoubtedly Padre de la Cruz had already heard the news, but his mentor might know more now that he was so often at the viceregal palace.

Augustín found him in the sacristy, folding his stole.

The old priest nodded at the *hoja*. "I see you've heard."

"Yes. What a shock. How did the Duque take the news?" Augustín asked.

"With a laugh. 'My cousin is a timid soul,' were his words. He said Bragança is neither a man of courage nor decision. They say he didn't even want the throne but his wife forced him to take it because she wanted to be a queen!" Padre de la Cruz motioned to a chair. "Let me sit a minute. I'm afraid saying Mass exhausts me these days."

"Here," Augustín said, moving the chair closer and pulling up one for himself. "Did the viceroy have anything else to say?"

"Not much. He's concerned that this is a sign of the mother country's weakness after its long years of European wars, and he said he believes Don Felipe needs to rethink his priorities. He's afraid the king is becoming beleaguered with the attacks on all sides—he even sent the Duque a note concerning the Portuguese who reside here in New Spain. Seems to think that, given the example of their compatriots, they might try a revolt of their own since they are, for the most part, wealthy merchants who might think trade would be better if they were rid of the restrictions of the Spanish crown."

"That's ludicrous."

"The Duque's own words!" Padre de la Cruz said with a laugh.

The news from the *navio de aviso* was like a brief wildfire that swept through the city and was shortly extinguished. The affairs of Europe made little impact on the inhabitants of New Spain. Although life on the northern frontiers was rough and difficult and the land uninhabitable except by the most sturdy souls, the viceregal capital lived a pleasant life of its own, gaily celebrating *máscaras*, bullfights, innumerable feast days, and the arrival of the Philippine fleet with its lavish cargoes of silks, satins, and porcelains. Myriad other entertainments, both public and private, filled the days of the inhabitants of the City in the Lake in which the great Moctezuma had once amused himself with even more fantastical entertainments.

The Duque gave sumptuous *meriendas* and lavish balls while at the same time he appointed a well-respected officer as governor of the fort at San Juan de Ulloa whose job was to see that the coast was kept free of pirates. In the meetings with the *oidores* of the Audiencia, he discussed the problem of the security of the roads along with other matters that affected the country he governed for the King of Spain.

María Luisa hired another seamstress in order to have the finest gowns for the balls at the viceregal palace to which they were now invited, and Don Rodrigo supplied the horse-loving viceroy with one of the finest stallions in Mexico, along with enormous silver spurs and a Puebla saddle lavishly encrusted with the same metal about which he gave mining advice to the Duque. Life in the Salvatierra house was a whirlwind of activity, and Augustín seldom saw the parents when he came to tutor the children.

But on the morning of June 10, 1642, all of Mexico City awakened to shock and disbelief. Rumors flew like wind-fanned flames through the city's streets.

Chapter 11

"No!" Rodrigo de Salvatierra shouted. "No! It cannot be!" He pounded his desk with his fist, rattling the cup of hot *chocolatl* sitting on it.

"I deeply regret to say that it is true," Augustín said. "I just spoke with Padre de la Cruz, and he confirmed it."

Salvatierra slumped into his chair and wiped his hand across his face. "Taken prisoner?"

"In the early hours of this morning." Augustín took a chair opposite Salvatierra. "At ten o'clock last night Bishop Palafox called the members of the Audiencia to his place of lodging and showed them the letter he had just received from the king. He asked them to summon the *maestre de campo* Antonio de Vergara and to gather troops. At 4:00 A.M. they burst in on the viceroy, who was sleeping peacefully, and informed him he was under arrest for treason. They wouldn't even allow him to dress completely, prodded him out the door, and allowing only one page to accompany him, they put him in a mule-drawn carriage and took him to the *convento* of the discalced Franciscans at Churubusco to await the first ship back to Spain."

"Oh, God, no. All my plans ruined!" Salvatierra gulped and pinched his eyes with his fingers to stop the unexpected tears. "How could this have happened to me? Just two more years and Luís would have been old enough to travel with Escalona back to Spain. With his ducal patronage and protection, Luís would have risen to a high position, without a doubt. The boy is intelligent and good-looking—the Duque would have seen to it that he found a worthy wife among the nobility. And then Luís could have returned to New Spain and assumed a position of the highest order." Salvatierra's shoulders shook but he made no sound.

"Don Rodrigo, perhaps if you thought on the Duque's misfortune, it might ease your own pain and disappointment," Augustín said quietly.

Salvatierra took a deep breath, wiped his hand across his eyes, and looked up. "I'm sorry, but I don't have your nobility of spirit, Augustín. My son is the most important thing in my life, and I will do whatever is necessary to assure his success. This is a mortal blow. I had pinned all my hopes on the Duque."

"Don Rodrigo, you yourself said Luís is intelligent. He is a fine, hard-working boy. He will assure his own success, I can guarantee you."

"I'm sorry, Augustín, but as a religious with no ambition other than to serve God, you don't understand that in New Spain you must have a title in the family or you will never reach the highest level of society."

"God is gracious, Sir. We must always remember to thank him for the blessings we do have and to remember that he has a plan for us even though we may not yet know what it is."

"*Treason?*" Salvatierra had not been listening to the seminarian. "Where did the charge of *treason* come from?"

"As I understand it, Bishop Palafox wrote the king a secret letter and dispatched it on a swift *navío de aviso*. He gave credence to wild rumors he had supposedly heard that the Duque was setting in motion a conspiracy to seize power here in New Spain, declare himself king and align himself with Portugal. The idea of the plot, according to the bishop, involved the Portuguese in Veracruz arming themselves, rising up and taking the city. They in turn would be supported by the governor of the fort at San Juan de Ulloa—the viceroy's own appointee who by chance also happened to be Portuguese. In addition the bishop claimed the Duque had taken over 60,000 pesos from the royal treasury and had been loaned another 350,000 to help the revolt in Portugal and that he had sent the money to Lisbon on pirate ships."

"That would be laughable if it weren't such sheer stupidity. Who in his right mind could believe that a few Portuguese merchants in Veracruz could seize Mexico! Whatever could have persuaded the bishop to believe that nonsense?"

"Palafox had in his possession another letter from the king, which he also showed the *oidores* of the Audiencia. Not only did it name him archbishop of New Spain, it authorized him to take over the reins of the government—as the new viceroy."

"God damn that son of a bitch to Hell!"

For days the city buzzed with the news. The Jesuits looked upon the change in leadership with great concern. In the Duque they had found amicable support; the bishop, they knew, harbored distrust, dislike, and dissatisfaction with the rich, powerful semi-autonomous order that owed its allegiance only to the Pope. Augustín cared nothing for the politics involved in the power struggles between the orders and the secular clergy, and he hoped he would not be affected by them. His sole interest was in the intellectual realm of study and teaching.

He wanted nothing to do with any of the corridors of power. He had enjoyed the company of the Duque de Escalona but recognized, too, that he had been flattered by the attention. Its influence on Rodrigo de Salvatierra had not been beneficial either.

But even worse than the personal effect of power on himself and on Luís's and Antonia's father was the ugly demon of power wielded against innocent people.

Scarcely had the Duque been jerked from his bed in the viceregal palace than the all-powerful Inquisition brought its vengeful arm down on the unsuspecting Portuguese inhabitants of New Spain. Scores of those with Lusitanian backgrounds were suddenly denounced before the Tribunal as Judaizers. Many were women — even grandmothers — who were dragged to the dank, infamous cells of the so-called "House on the Corner." All their worldly goods were immediately sold, the proceeds filling the Inquisition's coffers, allowing the Lord Inquisitors to live like royalty. A portion of the ill-gotten gain, however, was sent to Don Felipe as an example of the great service the Holy Office could render the king.

Augustín was overcome with revulsion at the power of the Church being perverted in this way.

Letters arrived from *Nuevo México*. It had been over a year and a half since he had sent his with Fray Manso and the last cart train.

In his room he opened the letters eagerly, glad to forget the unpleasant occurrences of the viceregal capital and anxious to hear the news from a distant place. But what he read plunged him even deeper into gloom. In Santa Fé the governor Luís de Rosas had beaten two priests with a stick, bloodying one of them, and when the new governor Flores died shortly after reaching the *villa*, the *cabildo* of the city seized power and incarcerated Rosas. The former governor fully expected to be killed, for he had written his last will and testament and had sent it to New Spain with the cart train that had just brought the letters from Áco.

Fray Ramírez reported that in the last year, over three thousand natives of the land had died of the *viruela*, their bodies ravaged by the virulent pox. But it was clear from the friar's letter that illness brought by the conquerors was not the only scourge they had transported to the land. The Indians at Taos who had futilely denounced their priest to Church authorities for violating village women took matters into their own hands and killed the unsaintly friar. And every cart train from *Nuevo México* carried papers destined for the Tribunal of the Inquisition, denouncing sorcery, bigamy, and a host of other transgressions.

What kind of Church was he dedicating himself to whose members violated women, denounced a viceroy for power, threw innocent people into jail, and confiscated their property for their own gain?

He sought Padre de la Cruz at the Casa Profesa.

＊   ＊   ＊

"Come in, come in," the old priest said with enthusiasm when he saw the seminarian at his door.

When Augustín took the straightbacked chair to which the *padre* motioned, the priest reached out, put his knotted hand on Augustín's knee, and patted him gently.

"Yes, my son?"

"I just received letters from my grandfather and Padre Ramírez."

"I pray they are well."

"Yes, thanks be to God," Augustín said, crossing himself. "But the friar's reports of conditions in *Nuevo México* are so disturbing—yearly they seem to grow worse. Why can man not live together in peace, *Padre*? Why is he continually attempting to exploit his fellow man? Even the religious, who above all should set an example of brotherly love, are not immune to sin. It's common knowledge that the Lord Inquisitor Higuera de Amarilla's negro slave is his mistress. How many children has she borne him—eight?. And what the Inquisition itself is doing in the name of Jesus Christ is an abomination!"

"That is true, but we are all men, my son, even we priests. The Church is made up of men, some good, some bad. Great goodness has been done by the Church as well as great iniquity. We can only hope that wrongs will eventually be righted. *Corruptio optimi pessima est.*"

"That is very apt. Corruption of the best truly *is* the worst. It makes us doubt what we place our faith in."

"None among us is immune to sin, and that includes the Church. We are all constantly—for the entire length of our life—dependent upon God's grace. No one, no matter how he tries to perfect himself, ever succeeds."

Augustín put the letters from *Nuevo México* in the small silver box and turned his energies and thoughts to his teaching. He had become even more a part of the Salvatierra family. Don Rodrigo and María Luisa were distraught for weeks, and Augustín had tried his best to raise their spirits and counsel them that their hopes had not been destroyed. He urged them to pray for the Duque in his hour of difficulty.

He had managed to convince the father of one thing, though, and that was to have the children tutored separately, to allow him to prepare their lessons for the interest of each. Don Rodrigo had said it was foolish to devote equal time to Antonia even though it had become obvious she was a very bright girl, but Augustín had prevailed. The lessons he gave the son were intense, and the boy was progressing so that he should be able to enter the University with ease when the time came. The lessons Augustín gave the daughter were just as carefully planned, but they were of a different quality. Little Antonia sat by his side and held his hand when they read. Many times the hour had long since passed before they realized it. Augustín searched always for things her quick mind would enjoy, and they had developed a close, private relationship in which the girl told all her special secrets to the seminarian. He was the only one who would listen to her thoughts without laughing.

The three years of Augustín's regency ended and he embarked on his final four years of preparation for the priesthood. Theological study would comprise the following three years and at the end of that, ordination, to be followed by a year of meditation. Then he would have achieved his goal — he would be a Jesuit.

He knew he had been given preferential treatment during his regency because of the money Don Rodrigo had given to the Casa Profesa. None of the other Jesuit seminarians enjoyed the freedom he had known. Had any aspect of his training and comportment been lacking, he would never have been allowed so much time outside the confines of the Jesuit discipline. He was still allowed to tutor the Salvatierra children because of the pressure Don Rodrigo had brought to bear on the Jesuit hierarchy.

It was not pressure in the regular sense of the word but rather the weight of a great deal more money if the seminarian were allowed to continue as tutor. The Jesuits had tried to talk the father into sending his son to one of the Jesuit schools, for with Augustín's tutoring, he could have easily passed the examinations for San Ildefonso, but the boy did not want to go to school; he wanted only a tutor, and it had to be the seminarian.

With the new change in Don Rodrigo's will that would benefit the Order immensely and with the immediate monetary gift that would be forthcoming if they allowed the tutor to continue, the pressure on the Jesuit hierarchy was too great. Money was power, even among the religious orders.

Augustín was allowed to take time from his schedule to teach the Salvatierra children, but he was admonished that he could not shirk his duties to the prisons, hospitals, and other charitable endeavors to which the Jesuits and Jesuit seminarians lent their physical and spiritual talents.

He was grateful to be allowed to continue with the tutoring because his friendship with the family had grown very important to him. As a result, he determined that he should spend even more time helping others so that his absences while teaching the children might not cause anyone to suffer.

Many late hours found him at the evil-smelling prisons tending, along with a Jesuit companion, the poor devils there confined or at the hospitals, keeping a night-long vigil over a deathbed. Except for his trips to the Salvatierra house to tutor, Augustín was always in the presence of another Jesuit if he went to do ministries of mercy. Their work was less lonely because of the habit of the Order to go in twos. Perhaps the basis of the usage was one of mutual surveillance; however, if that were not the reason, at least it gave mutual support.

Although the hours he kept were long and tiring, Augustín felt content whether he was studying with intensity or aiding the unfortunate. He enjoyed the friendship and camaraderie of the Jesuits and the different sort of friendship he had found in the Salvatierra family. The loneliness of his childhood lay deep within, a long-forgotten memory. He was content with himself. His strict self-discipline had made the well-known discipline of the Jesuits no burden to bear.

Only Padre de la Cruz seemed concerned about his actions. Old and feeble, the *padre* was still his mentor and confessor, constantly urging humility and self-knowledge.

"Remember, my son," he would say at confession, "pride may masquerade as good works and virtue. What you do should be done for the glory of God, not in the interest of self-perfection."

Augustín wanted the approval of the old *padre;* he wanted to be what the old man would have considered worthy. Although he never admitted it to himself, Augustín felt deeply the lack of praise he received from the *padre*. His old mentor commended him upon his successes, but he was not forthcoming with a more personal kind of praise that would have made Augustín so very happy. Still he sought to make his old mentor proud as he devoted himself to his studies and charitable works.

One warm April evening as he returned with Miguel de Oviedo, a fellow seminarian, from their work at the hospital, the other Jesuit turned to him.

"The night is still young, let us take our compassionate work to a house I know that is in the most desperate need of the Lord's grace."

"I am not that tired," Augustín replied. "I should welcome the chance to bring the Lord's grace to those in need of it."

The two walked farther on, Oviedo leading the way as they turned down various streets. At last they came to a house with an ornate façade. "Do you know the place?"

"I don't believe so," Augustín answered. "What is their necessity here?"

The other seminarian smiled. "You will be aware of it soon enough."

A liveried servant opened the door to them. *"Buenas noches, Padre* Miguel," the servant said, smiling broadly, "how kind of you to pay us a visit again. Doña Marta will be most pleased."

Augustín looked questioningly at Oviedo, who only smiled. The servant stepped back, opening the door farther as they entered the opulent marble foyer.

"This way, please," he said elegantly, showing them into a *sala* to the left.

The blood left Augustín's face. He put out his hand to touch Oviedo's arm to ask a desperate question, but a young woman came running to the other Jesuit and threw her arms around his neck.

"Oh, Miguelito, how happy I am to see you," she squealed and brazenly kissed him.

The girl dropped her arms from around Miguel's neck and laced one behind his waist as she turned to look at Augustín.

"Madre mía," she whispered. "I did not know the Jesuits had one as handsome as this! What a lucky girl—the one who gets *him* tonight! I've half a mind to see to it that he has a good time myself."

Oviedo pinched her on the rear and pulled her tight against his side. "Oh, no you don't, Marta, dear. You are mine, remember?" He finally looked over at his horrified companion and broke into a loud guffaw when he saw Augustín's face.

"Don't be so shocked, *hermano.* Surely you've been to similar places."

A look of disbelief crossed Oviedo's face. "Good God, you really haven't, have you? Well, as long as you're here, I guess there's always a first time."

Had Augustín been able, he would not have known what to say. He glanced around the room, mortified at the sight of the half dozen or so indecently clad women who were smiling broadly at him. The entire room seemed to find his shock amusing.

Oviedo motioned to the women. "It looks to me like you have your choice of any of them. Enjoy yourself!" he said over his shoulder as he walked out with the girl called Marta.

Augustín could get no signals from his brain to tell himself what to do.

A pretty brown-haired girl walked toward him. He stood frozen, unable to move. She had a kind smile on her face, and she touched his arm gently.

"Would you like to wait for Padre Miguel in another room?" she asked softly. Augustín nodded dumbly and followed her from the *sala.*

She led him a short distance down the hall and took a lamp from its holder on the wall. She opened the door to a small sitting room, and the lamp spread its soft light into the corners. She closed the door behind them, and Augustín stood there awkwardly.

Setting the lamp on the table, she turned and looked at him. She must have seen the agony on his face. She crossed to the door, looked at him again, and left, pulling the door quietly closed behind her.

Chapter 12

Augustín fell to his knees. "Help me," he whispered. For a long time he knelt there, murmuring, "Help me."

What was he to do? Should he return to the seminary, tell them what he had witnessed? How could he go back and inform on Miguel? What he did was on his own conscience. No, he must wait and talk to him. He must make him aware of the gravity of what he did, and he must somehow help him.

He did not hear the door open, so absorbed was he in his desperate thoughts.

"I thought you might be able to use a little of this," she said as she set the wine and glass on the table. She left as silently as she had entered.

Augustín prayed for guidance, but at length no more prayers came to his lips. He sank down onto the sofa, covering his eyes with his hand as if wanting to shut out any visions that might appear there. He reached out and poured some of the tawny port into the glass. The aged wine was warm and mellow in his mouth. He leaned back against the sofá, seeking for the moment to blank out all thoughts.

He was not aware of the amount of wine he drank; he was aware only of the easing warmth that was spreading through him, leaving his mind numb. Again he was not aware of the door opening. "I brought you more, Father," she said softly as she placed the new bottle near the almost empty one.

He opened his eyes slowly. "Thank you," he murmured huskily.

She dropped to her knees in front of him. "Bless me, Father," she said.

Augustín sat forward and placed his hand on her head, murmuring a blessing, although he was not yet the Father she called him.

It seemed as if he could not lift his hand, and it moved, softly touching her hair. She looked up at him, and his eyes were on her, a strange intensity in them. A shiver ran through her body. She closed her eyes and laid her head on his lap. He lifted her face in his hands, but she seemed unable to look at him, for his dark-lashed eyes burned into her. She turned her face in his hands and kissed them.

His hands dropped from her face, and she lowered her head to rest again on his lap and her hands came to rest intimately on his thighs. At first he sat totally immobile, but then tentatively, he touched her hair and caressed it once and then twice.

She rose and took his hand and the new bottle of wine. He made no protest as she led him to another room and closed the door behind them. His eyes never left her.

She went to the bedside table and turned up the lamp slightly so that it spread its flickering golden light across the turned-back bed. She faced him and began to undress. His eyes watched her every move, dwelling on the different parts of her body as they were revealed. When she was completely naked, she walked toward him, took his hand, kissed it, and put it to her breast. His fingers moved slightly, touching the soft flesh.

"Taste them, Father," she whispered, as she put her hand behind his head and brought it down to her breast. A shudder passed through his body.

Then she took his face in her hands and lifted it, covering his mouth quickly with her own in a deep kiss. She molded her body sensually to his, and her arms went round his waist, pulling him closer.

His arms found their way around her, and she responded to the strength of his embrace. Her hands slid between their bodies and she began to unbutton the many buttons of his cassock. She pulled it from his shoulders and let it drop to the floor and finished undressing him.

"*¡Madre de Dios!*" she whispered and smiled when she surveyed his naked body. "You are beautiful, Father."

She led him to the bed and put her arms around him and drew him down with her. She seemed to shiver with delight as his body pressed against hers, and she pulled his face toward hers, and her tongue slid into his mouth as his hands wound themselves in her long hair. He pulled away from her and for a second she seemed to think he was going to flee, but he did not. He sat looking at her naked body.

He reached out and touched her, his fingers gentle in their inquiry. He touched her breasts and fondled them and ran his hands down her sides and over her belly and down her legs.

He touched her again in response to her movement and elicited more. Her hips moved softly, and she closed her eyes, for his own were riveted on hers, burning into her. He continued softly in his caresses, aware of those that brought her more sensation. Her hips arched toward his fondling and her head rolled from side to side and her hands clutched the bed.

"Now, Father," she murmured, her voice a hoarse whisper.

She laced her arms around his neck and put her mouth hungrily on his, pulling him down on top of her, her hips thrusting against him. Her hand slid down to him, urging him, guiding him.

There was just a moment of hesitation before his body covered her, and she cried out with the pleasure he gave her. A deep, rumbling roar tore from his chest, and he crushed her to him in a viselike embrace. His body jerked in spasms.

At last he lay still, covering her, his body still a part of her. He clung to her, his heavy frame pressing her into the bed.

His shoulders began to tremble faintly, and he was crying. She stroked his hair.

"Oh, *mi amor*," she whispered compassionately as she pressed her lips into his hair and kissed him.

"Would that all my men were like you, Father." She took his face between her hands and covered it with kisses, whispering, "*Ay, mi amor*, what a wonderful lover you are. How you made my body long for you, how you made me want you."

She rolled him to his back beside her, reached for the wine bottle and slipped her arm under his head. "Have some more, Father, it will make you feel better."

Augustín came groggily awake as someone shook him. He felt as if he had been kicked in the stomach by a mule. He became aware of someone dressed in black, chuckling deeply, and a haze of reality reappeared. A woman's naked arms were pulling at him, trying to get him to an upright position.

He managed to sit up, but as he did so, waves of nausea overcame him. His Jesuit colleague grabbed a chamber pot from under the bedside table and the woman held Augustín's shoulders as he retched and heaved. The sour stench of wine-laden vomit filled his nostrils.

He was vaguely aware that his face was being wiped with a wet cloth and that he was being dressed. He was pulled to his feet.

"You've got to help me, Augustín," Oviedo said, "for I'll never be able to carry the likes of you." But Augustín was too drunk to help.

"I'll go get a litter," the woman said, pulling on her clothes. "You will never get him home in the shape he's in."

Later Augustín felt himself being half-lifted, half-carried out into the night. He was vaguely aware of Oviedo speaking to him.

"We will say you became ill on the way home from the hospital. No one will believe otherwise of you. Carolina has paid the litter carriers handsomely; they will say nothing."

He awakened again and with consciousness came a blinding, pounding headache and a wracking thirst. He heard someone speak.

"He has no fever, which is a good sign. Perhaps he merely ate tainted food."

Augustín did not open his eyes, for the stark horror of everything that had happened—last night?—came washing back over him in its most vile and repugnant detail. The guilt and humiliation he felt could not have been worse than the most inhuman torture employed by the Inquisition. He was so deeply ashamed and horrified by his actions that he could not even pray for forgiveness. He could not endure the thought of God looking upon him. How *Dios* must loathe him.

He kept his eyes closed and remained in bed the rest of the day unable to face anyone, certain that the shame and abomination of his act would be written in his features. As the afternoon wore on, the stark realization came to him that he was not fit to be a Jesuit nor a priest of the Mother Church of any kind.

He must renounce all that he had worked toward, all that he had dreamed of since coming to the viceregal capital. His whole life had been sundered in one night. How was it possible to make an irrevocable vow before one's God and then break it so wantonly? The enormity of his transgression was more than he felt he could bear. What would become of the rest of his life? What could he do now?

Late that afternoon he heard someone enter his small room. He could not bring himself to open his eyes. He heard the soft, rustly voice of his old mentor, and his shame was excruciating.

"I heard you were ill," Padre de la Cruz said. Augustín was able only to nod, afraid to speak. The old priest continued, "I was quite worried when I heard, for I don't recall you being sick since that terrible first summer you arrived in the city and the floods left sickness and death in their wake."

Still Augustín did not respond. The *padre* took his hand. Augustín was no longer able to keep his eyes closed. When he opened them his mentor saw instantly the anguish there.

"Your sickness is more of the spirit than of the body, is it not, my son?" the old man asked.

Augustín nodded dumbly and shut his eyes. In spite of his efforts, tears spilled down his cheeks, and his shoulders shook.

Padre de la Cruz took him in his arms. "Do not despair, my son, do not despair."

Augustín lifted his head. "I must leave the Order, Father."

"Do not be rash, Augustín. Perhaps you would like to come to confession?"

"My sin cannot be forgiven," he whispered.

Padre de la Cruz's voice was as cold and sharp as a bitter wind from North Mountain. "Do not blaspheme. There is no sin that the Lord cannot forgive. Get dressed. I will be waiting for you at the church." With that he left.

For long moments Augustín remained motionless but at length he pulled on his clothing and trudged to the church. He entered the confessional, his hands trembling, and barely managed the formula of contrition before the tears began anew. When he had conquered them, the story poured forth from his lips in all its detail. He spared nothing.

When he had finished, he said, "Now you understand why I am not fit to be a Jesuit."

"I understand no such thing," Padre de la Cruz said. "Your carnal act does not make you unfit to be a Jesuit, but your lack of faith does."

Augustín was taken aback.

The priest continued, his voice sharp and stern. "Is your faith so lacking that you believe God has not the power to forgive the sin of one of his children? Your sin, Augustín, is not so much the sin of carnal knowledge as it is the sin of pride! Do you think you are so important that even God cannot forgive one of your transgressions? That you are too good for the Lord's mercy?"

There was a long, heavy silence before his mentor continued. "You should thank God for his graciousness in allowing you this sin of the flesh, for you were perhaps more the sinner before it. Pride is an insidious transgression. Before, perhaps you felt you alone were strong enough to order your life, that by yourself you could achieve perfection. Perhaps God allowed this to happen to show you that you, too, are human, that you are as miserable a sinner as the rest of us. Augustín, we cannot always depend on ourselves alone; we *need* the Lord. Perhaps now, my son, you will understand people a little better, perhaps you will have more compassion for man's weaknesses. Perhaps you will be a better priest because of this, and you will know that whatever happens, you will always need *Dios* and know that His mercy is always to be had."

"You are right, Father," Augustín said quietly. "I am no better than anyone else in spite of everything I have tried to do. I have been a great sinner. What you say is true. I have committed the deadly sin of pride, but if I am so weak, how can I ever do God's work?"

"*Dios* has a purpose for you, Augustín, and I think that purpose is what you have been working toward. This has been a trial. Can you prevail or are you going to succumb when God puts you to the first test?"

"I don't know, I don't know," Augustín said with anguish. "I want to be a Jesuit but I feel I am not fit."

"We are all sinners, my son. I am a sinner, all priests are sinners — all sons of Adam. But you must make your decision. Just remember that *Dios* loves us in spite of our frailties."

"I don't know what to do," Augustín said wearily. He paused for long moments.

"May I have permission to do a thirty-day spiritual exercise to seek God's help?"

"Of course, my son," Padre de la Cruz replied. The old mentor pronounced the words of absolution, and Augustín did not know until that moment what forgiveness really meant.

For a month he followed the strict rigors of Loyola's spiritual exercise, praying and meditating on forgiveness. At the end, he made his difficult decision.

It was a beautiful, cloudless, sun-filled day of the kind that the valley of Mexico could be rightly proud. As he walked toward the Salvatierra house, he was fully appreciative of the beauty God had lent the day. His spirit was cloudless and sun-filled, also. He did not deceive himself that his spirit would not have its moments of darkness as would the day, but he felt certain that he would now be better able to deal with the shadows that might obscure the sunlight to his soul.

The thirty days had been agonizing, stripping his most interior being bare and forcing him to face things about himself he would rather not have had to admit.

He was quite certain that his attempt to be perfect in every way was nothing more than a mask he had constructed. Was he such an abomination that a mask was necessary? His wise grandfather loved him yet knew the circumstances of his birth. Padre Ramírez had not rejected him when he had learned the truth but had, rather, given him the gift of learning by making it possible for him to come to Mexico City. Padre de la Cruz, whom he respected beyond words, had accepted him completely, knowing from the first the secret of his past. And God, whom he professed to believe was a loving God, had seen proper to give life to a baby whose mother and father were half-brother and sister. Did that not prove that God had a use for him?

Those were some of the many thoughts that pounded through his head during the agonizing thirty days. And there were other thoughts, too, that tortured him.

As a youth when the desires of the flesh began to blossom, he fought to deny them by plunging himself into study—reading, memorizing, reciting—until he collapsed from physical exhaustion. Or he would strain his body to the limits of its physical endurance at the *casa de campo* by running or wrestling or practicing the athletic pursuits performed by the ancient Greeks. He had been mostly successful and had in the past year or so achieved more control over the thoughts that had tormented him so painfully. The acute distress he sometimes felt when the physical desires came upon him had begun to diminish slightly, but one nagging question had always lurked near the surface in spite of his best efforts to obliterate it: What was it like to do with a woman what his body urged?

Now he knew. Now he knew the full excruciating pleasure of it, the all-consuming, irresistible force that impelled the body. Now he knew the wonder, the ecstasy.

Now he knew. And he would know forever. It had been torment not knowing; now it was torment knowing. At first he had felt filthy, vile, execrable, saw himself as an abomination in the sight of God. But when he meditated on what Padre de la Cruz had said, that perhaps God had allowed this sin to happen to show him a far greater transgression he was committing, Augustín had finally thanked his creator. He had not been motivated to achieve what he did for the glory of God but rather, for himself, so that he might tell himself that he was worthy of God's love, that he deserved to have life. How very blind he had been.

He thanked *Dios* for opening his eyes. He now knew what the vow of celibacy meant. By knowing a woman, he was now aware of the full extent of that which he was giving up. When he took his solemn vows upon ordination, if God granted him the achievement of that, he would understand fully that to which he pledged himself. He would be renouncing something of inexplicable pleasure, but he would be doing it in order to do God's work, not for his own self-righteousness.

When he entered the Salvatierra house, she came running toward him as if she had been camped in the foyer awaiting him. She was all arms and legs at barely twelve years old. How quickly the children were growing. He scooped her up in his arms, and she kissed him on both cheeks. Then she leaned back and looked at him, smiling her young girl smile. Her face became serious as she looked at him.

"You have changed," she said in a whisper.

"Yes, Little One," he answered quietly, astounded that her young eyes saw it, "yes, I have changed."

The smile returned to her face. "I like it, I think."

He laughed quietly and tweaked her nose affectionately. "I'm glad you approve; so do I. But you're changing, too. You're getting much too heavy for me to lift!"

"Next time, though," she scolded as he put her down, "don't take so long!"

He laughed, happy to be back.

Chapter 13

The remaining two years of theological study passed rapidly, and the day he had always envisioned in his dreams finally became reality. There was not a vacant place in the church. Before the start of the service, Augustín kept his hands clasped tightly together, not so much in prayer as in an effort to keep them from trembling. The ceremony took forever and yet was over in an instant — or so it seemed — and his ordination was more like a dream looked upon from afar. He thought of his grandfather and Juan Ramírez and wished they could have shared in his accomplishment.

He choked back an unexpected sob. He had always taken for granted that Padre de la Cruz would witness this day, had always wanted this day to be a gift to his mentor. But the man who had been everything to him as he had grown to be man in the viceregal capital had succumbed the previous winter to a chest congestion that took his strength and then his very breath from him. Augustín felt as if the *timón* of his life was gone; the rudder that had given him direction now navigated somewhere in heavenly spheres.

Later at the reception held in the patio of the Colegio Máximo, he had talked and accepted the congratulations and well-wishes of many people, still as if it were all an irreality. The tears of Antonia and the scarcely contained ones of Luís brought him awareness that the ceremony had changed his life.

"I am going to miss you," Antonia said softly, holding onto his hand.

"I, too," whispered Luís, trying manfully not to cry.

Augustín smiled at them. He lifted Antonia's tearful face. "It is only for a year, Little One. When I return, I will be a full-fledged Jesuit *padre*, and I will not have to leave again. And when I return," he smiled at her, "you will be a beautiful grown-up young lady."

"I don't want to be a beautiful lady," she replied stiffly.

Augustín laughed and patted her cheek. "God has already made that decision for you."

She continued to hold his hand but the tears ceased. Augustín turned and put his other hand on her brother's shoulder. Luís was no longer able to swallow his tears, and he hugged Augustín tightly.

"Apply yourself well to your studies, Luís. When I return I want you to show me how much you have learned in the year I was gone."

There was hurt and disappointment in Antonia's voice. "Don't you want me to show you how much I have learned, too?" she asked.

"Of course I do, Little One. In fact, I have a list of books for each of you that I expect you to have read by next year."

Brother and sister looked up, smiles on their faces. "You are both very dear to me," Augustín said, and they hugged him again tightly.

Don Rodrigo and María Luisa looked on fondly as the children hugged their tutor of the past six years. How the time had flown. It was difficult to believe Luís would soon be sixteen and his sister fourteen. The boy would be entering the University and the girl already had far more education than a woman of her station would ever need. Yet she had begged them to allow her to study during the upcoming year that Augustín would spend in contemplation at the Jesuit house in Tepotzotlán.

Don Rodrigo would miss the seminarian, the new *padre*, for he enjoyed the company of the intelligent young man, but he was glad nevertheless that Augustín would be away for a year. Perhaps during his absence, Antonia would lose interest in her books and begin to pay attention to those things that should be a woman's concern.

He recognized that his daughter was on the threshold of womanhood. During the past year she had shot up like a skinny weed, but she had the indications of real beauty that would blossom shortly. It was time to begin thinking about a suitable match for her. She had made one passing mention that perhaps she might like to be a nun so that she could continue her studious ways, but they had quickly put that out of her mind.

Now that Augustín would not be around to distract her thoughts with books, Don Rodrigo knew that he and his wife must begin immediately to assure the success of their daughter. He must talk to María Luisa and see that the girl was outfitted beautifully with new clothes. This next year Antonia would turn fifteen and they would celebrate her *quinceañera* spectacularly to introduce her to society as of marriageable age. He would spare no money.

Until now he had indulged her and had not insisted that she wear the elegant dresses appropriate for a daughter of his, but now it was time she begin to appear frequently in society, richly dressed, as testimony to his wealth and position. He would see to it that she made a splendid match. Of course a titled peninsular was preferable for her, for such a marriage in the family would benefit Luís more than any amount of education would.

Don Rodrigo and María Luisa approached Augustín as their children hugged him. Don Rodrigo put out his hand.

"Congratulations, Augustín, and our very best wishes," he said with a genuine smile. "We will miss your presence at home. Both María Luisa and I want you to know that when you return, our house is yours as it has been, and we hope to see you there as frequently as your duties will allow."

"Yes," María Luisa added, "you have become a part of our family, and you will remain so."

"I have enjoyed being treated as a family member although I did not deserve such kind consideration. I only hope you are pleased with my work."

"Pleased? That word is insufficient to describe my gratitude," Don Rodrigo said. "The education you have given Luís is the best he could possibly have received. And to make him enjoy studying in the bargain—that is not short of miraculous!"

He put his hand on his son's shoulder. "Yes," he said, "we expect great things from this boy."

He said nothing about his daughter. Only Augustín was aware of her hurt.

The mission supply caravan that brought the new governor Guzmán y Figuera to Santa Fé also brought the letters that contained the news of Augustín's ordination to the priesthood.

Juan Ramírez offered a Mass in honor and thanksgiving for the wonderful event. Rohona attended the Mass and offered his own thanks for the well-being and achievement of his grandson, but when the Mass was over, he walked down the Camino del Padre as they now called the pathway. On his arm was a basket of prayer sticks he had made with infinite care. When he reached the valley floor, he sent the prayer sticks to Wenimats, and offered cornmeal for the K'atsina. Hobbling along slowly, he crossed the valley floor. He did not go to the stone pinnacle very often anymore. With difficulty he climbed the sheer rock. The three weathered crosses were still wedged among the stones. He knelt at the middle grave.

"You would be proud, Mia," he said aloud. "Your beautiful grandson is a priest now. He has worked hard and done well. I am lonely, but my heart is content that he has succeeded in his desire. You, too, children, may be proud of your son," he said turning to the stone cairns on either side of the center one.

It was late when Rohona returned to the village. That night he would begin a letter. He would not tell his beautiful grandson that the rains had been scarce that year. He would not tell him that their stores of corn were low. He would not tell him that the attacks by the Apache were increasing with alarming frequency. He would not tell him how the governors and soldiers made the people carry heavy loads of piñon nuts and salt on their backs like pack animals to the banks of the big river to await the carts that would take them to Mexico to be sold for profit. He would not tell him of the weaving sweatshop maintained in the quarters of the governors' palace in Santa Fé where for no more pay than a handful of parched corn, and against their will, the natives labored long grueling hours. He would not tell his newly ordained grandson of the priest who beat villagers and violated village women. Áco was truly fortunate to have Juan Ramírez. *That* he would tell his grandson, and he would tell him that he still read Marcus Aurelius and found much there to consider.

Augustín's year of tertianship was over by the time he received the two letters from *Nuevo México*. Juan Ramírez spoke of the deteriorating conditions in the province, but his grandfather mentioned not a word of the bleak state of affairs the priest described. Augustín was disturbed for several days after the receipt of the letters, but he could do nothing save pray for the distant land of his birth.

He had received his long awaited status. He was now a solemnly professed Jesuit and had been given the status of professor at the Colegio Máximo. Had he been able to choose, that would have been his preference. Everything he had ever dreamed had come to pass. His happiness was limitless as he walked toward the Salvatierra house. He might have been sent anywhere to preach the Word, and he would have gone gladly, but he would also have suffered the loss of the close friendship he so enjoyed with the family. He thanked God profoundly for the blessings he had been granted.

The old servant woman opened the door, and when she saw him, her wrinkled face broke into a smile.

"How good it is to see you, *Padre*," she said, taking his arm and pulling him into the house. "They are all out, all except for Señorita Antonia, and she is in the patio. I will go tell her you are here."

Augustín placed his hand on her arm. "Let me surprise her."

"As you wish," the old servant said. "The *señorita* does not laugh as much as she used to, *Padre*. I think it will be good for her to see you."

A fleeting look of worry crossed Augustín's face. Quietly he descended the two marble steps to the sun-drenched, flower-filled patio. He peered around a leafy potted shrub and there she was, seated under an orange tree in full bloom.

The sweet heavy fragrance of the tiny white blossoms perfumed the entire patio and enveloped him. A book lay on her lap on the voluminous folds of the pale gold silk of her skirt. Her head was bent forward as she read, causing her hair to fall forward over her shoulders. Her hair was darker than he remembered, rather like old Campeche honey.

He had not succeeded in crossing half the patio before she looked up. He stopped in his tracks, stunned at the beauty of her face. She had always been a very pretty little girl, but in one short year she had become a beautiful young woman. For a fraction of a second, she sat there looking at him. Then she was on her feet, the book falling forgotten to the tiles, and she was running toward him.

"Augustín!" she said exuberantly, not realizing she had used his given name. She threw her arms around his neck and kissed him on the cheek as she had done when she was a child.

He was aware of how much she had grown in one scarce year, for she was now a tall young lady and no longer had need of being lifted to kiss his cheek.

She dropped her arms, backed away and her cheeks flamed with her embarrassment. "I'm sorry, *Padre*," she said in a stammer, "I, I forgot myself." She tried to wipe away the unexpected tears that had sprung to her eyes.

"Don't be sorry for a lovely greeting." Augustín smiled and reached forward, taking her face in his hands, and kissed her on the forehead as he had done when she was young.

The tears became more profuse, and Augustín took her hand and led her back to the bench under the orange tree. He reached down and picked up the book she had dropped and held it on his lap.

"You have become the beautiful woman I said you would."

Her light hazel eyes flashed like topazes in sunlight. "Not you, too," she said bitterly.

"I had not meant to give offense."

She looked down. "I'm sorry, but the only things people ever say to me anymore are inanities about beauty. I hate the way I look — maybe if I were a hag, people would leave me alone."

Augustín laid the book aside on the bench and took her hands. "Little One," he said, using the name he had called her when she was young, "what you say is an affront to your Creator. He gave you the gift of beauty."

"Forgive me," she whispered as the tears began anew. "It's just that I wish someone would appreciate me for something else."

She covered her face with her hands and wept bitterly. Augustín pulled her close and laid her head against his shoulder and smoothed her hair as he had done when she was a child.

"Little One," he said gently, "beauty is something God gives his children for a pleasure. It makes people happy to gaze upon an object of beauty. It makes me happy to look at your beautiful face, but that does not mean that is the only way you give me happiness. It was joy to me when you learned something difficult as a child; I delighted in your cleverness and intelligence. Those are merely other facets of your beauty. Your face would not be nearly so beautiful were it not for your soul, which spreads its beauty across your features."

"They want me to give up my books, but worst of all, they want me to marry a man I despise!"

Shock rippled through him. The little girl he had tutored — she could be no more than fifteen — she was too young for marriage! But as he remembered that first moment when she looked up at him, and now as he felt her head leaning against his shoulder, he knew that she was indeed old enough to be married. She was of the age that most girls in the viceregal capital wed. He had always thought of her as the intelligent little girl he had been given to teach, but he realized now that, foolishly, he had expected everything to be as before.

A profound sadness overcame him. The past was gone; it would never return. He no longer had the right to be the recipient of a child's adoration and affection. She was a woman now, she must be a wife and give her affection to her husband and to the children she would bear by him.

She seemed to sense his withdrawal. "No, please," she begged, looking up at him with tearstained, swollen eyes, "don't desert me, please. You are the only one I have ever been able to talk to. You are the only one who has ever listened to me."

He took her hands. "I will never desert you, Little One. You wrapped yourself around my heart when you were just a little girl; *Dios* will not let anything ever happen to that."

It felt good to express how much he cared for her. She, a little girl, had been the only one who had ever opened up the window in his heart and touched him deeply. He thanked *Dios* for her affection and promised Him silently that he would do everything in his power to see that she might be happy in her life.

Her face lit up with her joy upon hearing his words. She slid off the bench and went to her knees in front of him. "May I have your blessing, Father?"

As he made the sign of the cross on her forehead, the vision of another blessing he had given returned, and for a moment the face of the girl kneeling before him took the place of the one who had lain naked on the bed in that room.

He closed his eyes and swallowed. *Let my love for this woman be pure, O Lord,* he prayed silently, *let me see to her well-being as You would wish it.*

Chapter 14

Augustín was once again a frequent visitor at the Salvatierra house. He no longer came as tutor but as family friend and confidante, of not only the daughter but of the father, mother, and son. In his position as friend, he had sought to help Antonia.

"Don Rodrigo," he found the opportunity to say when her father spoke privately of his daughter's obstinacy, "the *señorita* is a woman now. You must not treat her like a child. You hope that by taking her books away that her interest will turn to marriage. Don't we all fight to keep those things that are dear to us? You yourself know how passionately she loves to read. When you deny her that, she thinks only of books. If her reading is not threatened, don't you think it is possible that she might not look upon marriage so unfavorably?"

"But what man is going to want a wife who spends her time reading?"

"Is that not better than spending one's time in idle gossip or something worse?" Augustín countered. "God saw fit to give your daughter a quick and keen mind. You must accept it as God's will; you cannot change it."

Don Rodrigo sighed. "Unfortunately I am afraid you are right."

Augustín met the man Antonia's father hoped for her to marry. He would have wished for someone more worthy of her, but he recognized why Don Rodrigo was taken with Raúl López Pacheco. That the man was a peninsular from the minor nobility blinded her father to the other fact that López Pacheco was an uneducated boor and a penniless, but money-conscious, sycophant.

After meeting the man, Augustín discreetly attempted to alert Don Rodrigo to some of López Pacheco's poorer traits, but his words fell on deaf ears. It seemed Salvatierra was willing to overlook any fault because of the man's place of birth. That was scarce recommendation for any man, much less one destined to be a daughter's husband.

If Augustín did not care for Raúl López Pacheco, the latter liked the priest even less. From the first meeting of the Salvatierra family, the peninsular heard nothing but the virtues of the brilliant, athletic Jesuit who was completing his final year of the rigorous training for the priesthood. That Don Rodrigo, his wife, and son extolled the wonder of the priest ad infinitum was bad enough, but the girl's obvious adulation of the Jesuit was more than a prospective suitor wanted to endure.

López Pacheco was not so dense that he did not recognize that many of the girl's innocent-sounding questions concerning the books he liked to read were a means to point out his lack of schooling. Nor did he miss her point when she talked about topics she and the priest had discussed. He would not have wasted his time on the pedigreeless Creole family had not the father's wealth been so substantial, and the girl herself, in spite of her penchant for learning, more beautiful than he had ever seen. She was perhaps too tall, but that was her only flaw, save the air of superiority about her, which he would relish snuffing out on their wedding night.

The first meeting of the priest and the peninsular was icily cordial, each one's opinion of the other quickly reinforced. What López Pacheco had not expected, despite the terms such as "athletic" that had been used, was the priest's stature and his magnetically good looks. No wonder the girl was smitten. What woman wouldn't be over the handsome face with its gray eyes, the thick, dark auburn hair, the tall, broad-shouldered, narrow-waisted physique?

The priest was no doubt aware of how the simple, tightly fitting black cassock showed off his physical form. Women always had secret passions for priests, anyway. It was undoubtedly because of the challenge their vow of celibacy offered. López Pacheco sneered inwardly. The priest probably enjoyed leading women on but, in reality, preferred his own kind.

Augustín was more charitable in his thoughts about the peninsular, but the thought did occur to him that not even the man's looks were apt to attract Antonia nor any other girl for that matter.

He was correct, for one afternoon Antonia vented her disgust of López Pacheco in vivid language.

"His white pudgy hands with their long, dirty fingernails revolt me, and his mouth is horrible. His lips are too full and are always flecked with a bit of spittle at the corners. He truly makes me sick." She shuddered with revulsion before she continued.

"That long, greasy hair of his soils those wide collars that have obviously known better days, and his prominent stomach along with his thick thighs make him look ridiculous in those tight pants he wears. I loathe everything about him. Have you ever seen such a repugnant man?"

Augustín laughed, and she was obviously not pleased. "I'm sorry, Little

One, but your description is so truly revolting I just can't help myself." He became serious. "Have you spoken to your *mamá*? Told her how you really feel? Perhaps if you enlisted her help . . ."

"Help?" Antonia said derisively. "My mother does not find that horrible man as offensive as I do—she, of course, looks at him from a different perspective. She had no choice in her marriage, so it would never occur to her that her daughter should. What she doesn't realize is that although my father was much older than she, he was still a fine figure of a man when they were married. Their wedding portrait is evidence of that, but if I mention how unattractive and revolting that *gachupín* is, *Mamá* always dismisses it, saying that a good wife could do wonders for him by seeing to it that he had his nails trimmed and cleaned, his clothes properly washed and ironed, his hair washed and perfumed."

Antonia imitated her mother's voice, "Why he wouldn't be half bad-looking if a proper wife saw to his grooming." She groaned and looked at Augustín. "The last thing on this earth I want to do is see to the grooming of a revoltingly unclean, ugly bore!"

López Pacheco was an uneducated man but not stupid. He was aware of the daughter's patent antipathy, and he was wise enough to realize that his avenue of success lay not in winning over the beautiful, too-intelligent Antonia but rather her parents.

It had not taken him long upon landing on the shores of the New World to recognize the value of peninsular birth and of his noble heritage, albeit he was the third son of a poor *hidalgo* of the minor nobility. He had come expressly to silver-rich Mexico with the purpose of finding a wealthy wife. As a peninsular, he had secured an unimportant, miserly bureaucratic job that paid him scarcely enough to eat, and he kept his place of lodging a secret. Little did he want the *alta sociedad* to know that he slept in a small shabby room in a fleabag boardinghouse.

He was rather astute at securing invitations to dinner so that he did not starve. The money that he made from his job he sank into a fine horse and Puebla saddle, for he had also been quick to recognize the value the Creoles placed on good horses and the ability to ride.

Unfortunately, he was a poor horseman, and the animal he bought was too spirited, with the result that he suffered any number of falls, bruising his dignity more than his body. Thankfully, none of the Salvatierra family had witnessed any of his unseatings.

As time went on and he could accumulate more wages, or if he could talk himself into more credit, he would improve his wardrobe. Little had he expected the clothes worn in the New World would surpass in finery that of Madrid. Everyone in the viceregal capital of Mexico was swathed in silks and satins from the Philippine trade and covered with jewels and gold. If he were going to convince the Creoles of his "genteel" birth, he must try to look the part.

Upon arriving in the capital, he began accumulating information on the richest families with marriageable-age daughters. It had not taken him long to find the Salvatierras, and that their daughter was young and beautiful quickly made them the object of his pursuit. He made a valiant attempt to impress her, but he soon gave up those efforts, for her dislike seemed to be increasing the more he tried. Although she made him burn with desire, he determined not to seek her company and turn her still more violently against him.

Success lay in courting the father and mother and in playing upon their desire for a Spaniard of noble background in the family. He quickly saw that the success of their son was paramount to them, and if he played his cards right, he would get them to sacrifice their honey-colored little dove to him never knowing that they had. If he were smart, no protest by the girl would be sufficient to stand in the way of the achievement of his desire.

He would not sell his peninsular birth cheaply; he would see that a healthy portion of Don Rodrigo's wealth would be his to enjoy along with the ripe, succulent daughter. López Pacheco laid his plans carefully. He would court the father and mother assiduously, determining just what pleased them and how far he could go. He would prefer simply to talk Don Rodrigo into permission to marry his daughter, but if the father required a title, López Pacheco would secure the money from Don Rodrigo by some means and return to Spain where he would buy a patent of nobility.

The kings of Spain, needing money to fight their endless European wars, had taken to selling grants of nobility to increase the royal coffers. With sufficient New World gold or silver, López Pacheco could buy himself the title of count, and *that* he knew would be irresistible to Salvatierra. The subject of money, however, would never cross López Pacheco's lips.

Around Don Rodrigo, he spoke intimately of his hunts with the king and other nobles. He spoke of the affairs of government in the mother country as if he were well versed in the subject and enjoyed the confidence of those close to the throne. He did not fear that Don Rodrigo would seek to corroborate his words, for he was careful to speak in generalities that would be difficult to prove.

He painted a picture of court life that was vivid and heroic, never losing the opportunity to mention "my father, the nobleman," or "my family and its ancient lineage," or "the vast holdings my eldest brother will inherit, land that has descended through the family because of the aid an ancestor gave King Ferdinand in expelling the Moors from Spanish soil." When he described his ancestral home, he did not describe the hot, arid, unproductive piece of land in Castile with its mouldering stone house that was falling to ruin, crumbling because there had not been enough money in even the last two generations to repair it.

To Doña María Luisa, he talked of similar things, but aimed at a woman's interest.

López Pacheco's voice purred, "The queen wears exquisite clothes and jewels but is such a warm person. I know you would enjoy the intimate conversations that she and my mother have as they embroider garments for their works of piety. Her Majesty does my mother honor by requesting her to accompany her to daily Mass because the queen well knows the virtue and piety of my dear *mamá*." He smoothed his hair and tried to keep his tone from sounding boastful. "My sweet sisters are often at court and you should see the number of the marriage requests made to my father by high-placed noblemen, wishing to join their own lineage to such an illustrious one as that of my own family." He laughed lightly.

The peninsular was astute enough not to spend all his time in the glorification of his family and the mother country. He was an adept flatterer, admiring the beauty of the valley of Mexico, its horses and its women comparable with any in Spain. He listened with rapt attention when Don Rodrigo or his wife talked, as if vitally interested in what they had to say, and he would comment on the correctness of their remarks or observations, always flattering, always insinuating himself into their lives. Cleverly he would ask them for their advice, Don Rodrigo on business matters or horses or entertainment in the viceregal capital, Doña María Luisa on customs in the New World, gifts to send his mother and sisters, her favorite charities so that he might give to the needy also.

Antonia found his constant presence with the family annoying but was pleased he did not try to force his attentions upon her. In her relief, she did not recognize the increasing admiration of her mother and father for the repugnant suitor. Luís, the brother for whom the parents did everything, did not like the peninsular much more than did his sister, but he was involved in his own pursuits and had little awareness that his parents were sustaining their relationship with the man for his possible benefit.

The real threat, as López Pacheco saw it, was the Jesuit priest who enjoyed the intimacy and admiration of the family. It was obvious that in the eyes of the Salvatierras he was just below the Creator and Jesus Christ in their esteem. The peninsular decided that he must discredit the priest and undermine his influence with the family.

But everything that he attempted to say that might have been derogatory in the slightest implication brought every member of the family to the priest's instant defense. Much to López Pacheco's disappointment, he decided that the priest was untouchable. Therefore, he must not attack the Jesuit in any way. In fact, he would be so patronizing to that paragon of virtue and intelligence that it would redound to his credit, and the family could only look upon his esteem for the priest of whom they thought so highly as evidence of the peninsular's good judgment.

López Pacheco had no doubt that the Jesuit fully understood that the aim of his friendship with the family was money through marriage to the daughter, but once he realized the Jesuit was untouchable, the Spaniard was even more convinced of his success if he were patient. He would do nothing to give the steely-eyed ecclesiastic any basis for the accusation of wanting to get his hands on Don Rodrigo's money. He would weave his honeyed web carefully. The mention of money would never cross his lips. He would never, under any circumstances, ask Salvatierra for anything. If the priest could be a paragon of virtue, so could he.

He would be a patient man. He would attempt to insinuate himself more deeply into the family's life as a close friend. He would not set himself up as a suitor for the daughter; he would play upon and feed the parents' ambition. He would strew their path with rose petals until they were firmly caught on the thorns of his own desires, and at the appropriate time, he would receive the money to buy his patent of nobility — if that were the price for the daughter's hand — and Don Rodrigo would think that giving López Pacheco the money had been his own idea. In that manner, if the priest pointed to the money for a patent of nobility as an example of the designs of the man, Salvatierra could respond, "But no, Augustín, you misjudge the good López Pacheco; it was my idea to loan him the necessary cash."

Augustín was forced to admit to himself that the Spaniard was indeed astute. Not for a moment did he change his view that the man had designs on the girl and her father's money. His discreet warnings had fallen on deaf ears, and the peninsular had done nothing that could be interpreted as proof of Augustín's misgivings. He could not even bring himself to tell Antonia of López Pacheco's cleverness. The girl was so relieved to be free of his attentions, thinking she had effectively discouraged him, that Augustín had not the heart to tell her that the man, far from being discouraged, was more determined and now followed a more clever path to achieve his goal. All Augustín could do was pray that López Pacheco's true colors would be revealed or that a more worthy suitor would appear.

He tried to tell Antonia that she should become more interested in young men and begin to think about marriage, but her hazel-gold eyes became dark, and she looked down at her hands in her lap.

"I do not want to become interested in stupid young men; I do not want to think about marriage." She paused and added softly, "I think I want to be a nun."

"Antonia," Augustín said gently, taking her hands, "you must have a vocation to be a nun — not wanting to think about marriage is not sufficient reason to take the veil."

"I could teach," she countered, "I am educated."

"Yes," Augustín said, "you are well educated, but that is not all that is required to be a nun. You must be willing to devote your entire life to God. You must give up the love of a man, which can be a joyous thing. You must give up the wonderful right to nurture a child in your body and then hold it in your arms and suckle it and love it and raise it to love the Lord."

"What about you, Father?" she asked as she looked up at him, her eyes unreadable. "Didn't you give up your right to be the father of a child?"

"Yes, I did. I shall never know that joy. It is a decision not to be made lightly. I had to renounce the love of a wife to serve God."

She looked back down at her hands, which he still held. "I, too, must renounce the love of a man," she whispered so quietly he had to lean forward to hear the last words.

"You are too young to make that decision, Little One," he whispered and kissed her on the forehead.

She looked up at him, her eyes bright with tears, and there was bitterness in her words. "It was not I who made the decision." She put her hand to her mouth to stop the sob within her, then leaped up and fled.

He sat in the patio by himself, his own sadness deepening. He could not bear the thought of her beautiful dark honey-colored hair shorn, nor the veil and habit hiding the beauty of her youthful body, nor the thought of her lively mind imprisoned behind the bars of the cloister. But most of all he could not bear never seeing her again once the iron doors of the convent clanged shut. She was made to be a wife, mother, companion — not the bride of Christ hidden behind bars. She would make a wonderful wife for a man she loved and admired, and that man would be immeasurably fortunate to have someone whose beauty was matched by her goodness and intelligence.

In the weeks that passed, she did not speak more of her desire to become a nun. When he would visit, they would talk of the things that had always delighted them, and she would lament that she could not attend the University as her brother did, and he would promise to teach her things that she wanted to learn.

They would simply not tell her parents that he was once more tutoring her. It was a secret they enjoyed.

Chapter 15

What López Pacheco desired and Augustín dreaded became reality in the spring. After a year and a half of assiduous effort, the peninsular succeeded in planting the idea in Don Rodrigo's mind to underwrite the cost of the purchase of a patent of nobility.

Don Rodrigo had come to view the laws of primogeniture as patently unfair—just as López Pacheco wanted him to. Why should a son's birth order deny him a right to honor and nobility when he was a product of the same lineage as the eldest son? Was he not of the same mother and father, of the same flesh and blood as his eldest brother who would accede to the title of nobility? Was not a second son or a third or a fourth just as noble as the first? The unfairness of the laws of primogeniture that gave the first-born everything—title, land, money—destroyed any onus attached to the "buying" of nobility as far as Don Rodrigo was concerned. It also destroyed any argument Augustín might have made about the absurdity, the vanity, the worthlessness, and the superficiality of a bought title of nobility.

Even the discussion of following false idols made no impression on Don Rodrigo. His response was that undoubtedly in the eyes of God a third son was just as noble as the first. He did not realize that the point of the comment had been his own obsession with a title. Don Rodrigo was a pious man who attended church regularly and gave more than lavishly to the religious institutions of the city. It did not occur to him that there was anything lacking in the practice of his faith.

Everyone except Augustín was overjoyed to see the peninsular off, bound as he was for the mother country by way of Puebla and San Juan de Ulloa. Mother and father were delighted at the prospect of the title that would return. Brother and sister were more than content to see the boor gone from their household. Augustín could think only with foreboding about the man's return and prayed fervently that the coming year would offer some solution to the terrible prospect of Antonia being forced to marry a man she could not stand — a clever, scheming, money-hungry one. To think that the beautiful, intelligent girl would be forced to submit her body unwillingly to such a man! The thought brought a black rage to his mind, and he spent a nightlong vigil of prayer trying to eradicate it. He was successful only in submerging it by praying for a solution to present itself within the year.

His visits to the Salvatierra house were as frequent as his busy schedule would allow, and he had begun taking note of suitable prospects as husband for the girl in the hope that she might find someone before the year was out, but any comments he made to her about the virtues of marriage were met with disdain or ridicule, and she resumed saying she would rather be a nun.

"At least then I could continue to read and live my life in peace not being made the chattel of some overbearing, stupid man," she said with anger.

"But not all men are like that," Augustín replied. "I know there is some man, somewhere who could match your intelligence and whom you could love." She only laughed bitterly and changed the subject.

Her parents were also adamant that she would not take the veil. In a family of many daughters, it was oftentimes preferable that some of them profess, for the dowry necessary to enter a convent was much less than the dowry required to marry a daughter well, but the Salvatierras had only one daughter and felt no lack of finances. They would see her married and married well.

On the advice of her mother and López Pacheco, Don Rodrigo had not told his daughter of his talk with the peninsular on the eve of the latter's departure.

"Let's not upset her, for she might do something foolish," her mother had said.

"Let me surprise her with the title," López Pacheco added. "What young girl does not want to be a countess?" And so nothing was said to the girl to hint that her future had already been decided for her.

Antonia lived her days in peace, filling them with reading and whenever possible with the company of her former, but now clandestine, tutor. He had been able to spend a weekend with the family at their country house, and it was wonderful to pass the entire day with him.

They rose early, packed a lunch and had their horses saddled. They started off riding with wild abandon and then let their mounts slow to a walk, resting, as they reined the horses close so they could talk. Augustín clowned by sitting backward in the saddle and riding standing up like a circus performer, scaring her that he might fall. They found a spring by which they ate their lunch, and removed their boots to dangle their feet in the icy water and laugh. They lay back on the grassy bank and recited Latin poetry, each trying to outdo the other. A slip of the tongue brought on the parody of famous lyrics, and they ended laughing until their sides ached.

"I surrender," Augustín said, out of breath. "You win, I can take no more."

"It will be a draw," she offered magnanimously as she rolled onto her side to face him. She smiled and pulled some grass and sprinkled it on his hair. "I will crown you poet laureate, if you will crown me poetess laureate." She touched his cheek softly and brushed away a blade of grass that had fallen there.

To her surprise he did not reciprocate with the sprinkling of grass but rose and took her hand, pulling her to her feet. "I confer poetess laureate on you," he said with mock gravity, but he made no symbolic crowning. They rode in silence back to the house.

"Don't you think they spend a great deal of time together?" Don Rodrigo remarked to his wife. He had no misgivings whatever of impropriety; his worry was other. "Do you think he will try to talk her into becoming a nun?"

María Luisa laughed. "No," she said, "I had wondered that myself until I overheard one of their conversations in the patio. Augustín was praising the married state for women. He seemed very convinced she should not think about becoming a nun. He is very much on our side and should be helpful when the time comes."

"I don't want to go," Antonia said with distaste. "I think it is horrible. It is no more than a carnival spectacle."

"But the Church is giving plenary indulgences to all those who view the *auto de fé*," her mother said. "Everyone will be there, and as our daughter you must go so that we may be seen as a family of piety. Besides, your father has the honor of being one of the *familiares* of the Holy Office. He will march in the parade. An absence such as this would be noted certainly, and it would appear as an offense to the Lord Inquisitors."

"People have been pouring into the city for days to watch the 'show'," Antonia said scornfully. "My presence will not be missed."

"Padre Augustín has consented to join us in our coach," her mother said, knowing that her daughter would not be so reluctant to attend the *auto de fé* if the good *padre* were there to occupy her time.

María Luisa worried about her daughter's penchant for being by herself. It seemed she enjoyed only the Jesuit's company. What was going to happen when they broke the news to her of her arranged wedding when López Pacheco returned? They would have to count on Augustín to make her see reason, and once she was married to the nobleman, she would have to give up her private ways. There would be much entertaining she would have to organize, there would be a palatial home to supervise, and then there would be the children. López Pacheco had mentioned he adored children and wanted many of his own. María Luisa herself looked forward to numerous grandchildren, for she had always lamented that she had been able to have only two children of her own.

In the end Antonia had agreed to attend the Inquisition's Act of Faith.

Carriages lined the streets through which the procession would pass. They were lucky to get a good location, for the streets were mobbed. The horses were unhitched so that the bodies of the carriages could be moved closer together, allowing more places along the street. The occupants would spend the night in their vehicles awaiting the procession that would begin at dawn.

The street vendors were numerous, hawking their tidbits, delicacies, and drinks so that the spectators might not go hungry during their nightlong vigil. People wore their best finery and left their carriages to promenade, exchanging pleasantries with their acquaintances. It was not possible to walk at more than a snail's pace due to the congestion of the streets. It seemed all the inhabitants of the viceregal capital as well as those of the neighboring villages filled the crowded thoroughfares. The city had the atmosphere of a huge party. Excitement was high; people laughed and joked. An outsider might have thought it was the celebration of a great holiday in the city rather than the eve of a great penitential rite of the Church that would culminate in heretics being burned at the stake on the morrow. The dreaded Inquisition would, the following day, give example of its holy work in the more than one hundred condemned who would march forth in procession from the dark, dank cells of the Inquisition's jail where they had been held, some for over six years.

Wearing a yellow *sambenito*, the long tunic on which were painted the flames of Hell and other demonic artifices, a *caroza* — the infamous miter of the guilty — and with a green penitential candle or a green cross in their hand, the condemned, along with their jailers and their confessors, would form a lugubrious cortege from the jail of the Inquisition to the expensive, velvet-draped outdoor stage that had been erected in the Plaza del Volador at an exorbitant cost. There the condemned would receive their sentences from the Holy Judges, the most excellent Inquisitors Don Francisco de Estrada y Escobedo, Don Bernabé de la Higuera y Amarilla, and Don Juan Saenz de Mañozca.

The stage was an architectural and decorative triumph. The architect Bartholomé Vernal had been in charge of the project, constructed of massive wooden beams, the cupola of which, with all its furbelows, filials, and figures, was of ebony and marble. Huge beams, chained and nailed, supported the stages of which the principal one was one hundred and twenty-three feet long, seventy-eight wide, and over ten feet high. Four other stages were erected at the four corners, two of which were one hundred and sixty feet long, the others somewhat smaller. In addition another immense stage, taller than the other, was erected in the plaza for seating the Tribunal. In the middle of this stage were seven arches twenty feet high with a drape of black velvet upon which was richly embroidered in gold the royal coat of arms of the king of Spain. The sides had two doors for entrance and exit that led to a passage one hundred and sixty feet long and ten feet wide leading to the School of Porto Coeli.

A gold-green cross of the Dominican Order would occupy the highest, most sumptuous position on the entire stage, and in front of the cupola on the principal stage was built an altar, sixteen by seven feet in size. A gallery on the principal stage was constructed for the prisoners and they would mount a staircase to hear their sentences.

The stages in their vastness contained compartments for the onlookers of social standing as well as rooms for resting if such were necessary during the long proceedings. In all, the stages could accommodate more than sixteen thousand people. Precious velvet hangings, rich carpets, hundreds of candles, exquisite paintings, and chairs of black velvet with golden tacks adorned the stages.

By Saturday, April 10, 1649, all was ready despite the fact that there had been only three months for the preparations — the Lord Inquisitors had threatened the workers with excommunication if the project were not completed on time.

At three-thirty on the afternoon of that Saturday preceding the *auto de fé*, the bells of the Cathedral and those of all the churches of the city began to toll, marking the start of the procession of the priests and nobles that would carry the Green Cross to the stages set for the Act of Faith on the morrow. The noblemen were richly adorned in black satins embossed with gold and wearing chains of gold, diamond-studded hatbands and jeweled pins that caught up one side of their soft, wide-brimmed black hats and secured white plumes there.

Following the nobles came the most exalted leaders of the religious Orders in procession, interspersed and mixed according to the form given to them by the Holy Tribunal as a symbol that, although they might be divided in Order and in the manner of defending the faith, they were as one when it came to opposing heresy. The different religious communities followed in bodies as the church bells continued to reverberate through the city. The many officials of the Inquisition were next in order, the insignia of the Holy Office over their capes, and hard behind them came the white-robed Dominicans, lit candles in their hands. They preceded Fray Luís de Mérida, whose honor it was to carry the Green Cross, which was over eight feet in height. Black cloth hung from the nails signifying the sorrow of the Church because of the betrayal of her children and the capital punishment she must inflict on the following day.

The choir of the Cathedral sang the "Vexilla Regis" as it marched slowly behind, its music at times combating that of the many tolling bells whose clamor did not cease until the entire procession had reached the Plaza del Volador, which was not until after seven P.M. Night had fallen, but hundreds of candles illuminated the entire plaza with a flickering yellow light. The Green Cross was placed in its position of honor and the huge audience that filled the plaza fell to its knees when the Cathedral choir began to chant the anthem and the Versicle of the Cross. When the devotion ended, the Dominicans continued to kneel around the altar, where they would keep a night-long vigil of prayer along with many other religious and laypersons who recited the rosary in loud voices.

Antonia fingered the beads of the rosary in her hand as her lips formed the "Aves" and "Pater Nosters," but her prayers were offered for something different than were the majority that night. She prayed that the Church might recognize the barbarity of what it did in the name of righteousness. One need not be educated to know that the love Christ spoke of had nothing whatever to do with the inhuman torture and incarceration practiced by the Holy Office. She felt physically sick that she would have to be a witness to the proceedings of the following day. She would be required to watch the dawn procession of the prisoners with their confessors and lay escort of whom, much to her disgust, her father was one.

When she, her mother, and Luís returned to their coach where they would spend the night sheltered from the elements, Augustín was waiting there for them.

She wanted to run to him as she had when she was young and feel his protective arms pick her up. She would like to have been transported from there and to feel the happiness she had known as a child. Sparse sunshine lit her life now, and what little entered was almost exclusively brought by the Jesuit. She knew he enjoyed her company, too, for he laughed and smiled and talked of many things with her that she sensed he did not with others. But she felt a need for his presence that resembled torture, and she was not so blind that she did not recognize it—a desire both emotional and physical she would never be able to express to him in either words or actions. Sometimes she trembled with fear that she might show or tell him what burned within her, for that would be far worse than the pain she felt at keeping it hidden. It would mean she would no longer have even brief moments of his presence. He would certainly despise her and never more would he spend time alone with her. The thought of that she could not endure.

"How good to see you, *Padre*," María Luisa said. "It was so kind of you to accept our invitation. Antonia refused to attend these holy proceedings until she heard that you would be accompanying us through the night vigil."

Augustín smiled kindly at Antonia, who evidenced discomfort at her mother's words. He looked back at María Luisa. "It is my pleasure, *Señora*, but I must leave shortly before dawn to accompany my community in tomorrow morning's procession. Such an act of sorrow as tomorrow would be much less painful if one were in the company of dear friends."

"Yes," María Luisa replied. "How sad that the Church must punish its New Christian offenders, yet this Act is such a wonderful example of our faith."

Augustín saw the look of revulsion cross Antonia's face, and he would like to have said something to her, but at that moment, three servants from the Salvatierra household arrived with hampers of food for the evening's repast.

When they finished the meal of cold meats and fruit and the dessert of assorted sweet comfits and jellies, María Luisa suggested they take a stroll to see the devotions. Antonia declined, complaining of a headache, but Luís agreed to escort his mother because he did not particularly enjoy the confines of the coach. Augustín, of course, would keep the *señorita* company.

When mother and son had gone, Augustín looked at Antonia. "You are discontented, aren't you?"

"How can the Church do something so horrible as burn people at the stake?" she demanded angrily. "And then forgive the sins of the people who watch the inhumane act?"

"I don't know," Augustín said simply, making no excuses for the Church. "I feel the same as you, Little One, despite the fact that I have dedicated my life to defend and propagate the faith. But you and I are not alone; there are others who feel the same, but we dare not protest except in the cases of individuals we know are falsely accused. The power of the Holy Office has no restraints, and it has become a monster in the hands of those who have been in a position to abuse its powers."

He continued in a tone he seldom used. "But this year is one of its worst. Over one hundred prisoners will appear in the *auto de fé* and all but one of those is Portuguese. Can it be that our brethren of Portugal are the only heretics in this vast country? How coincidental that Portugal just a few short years ago took back its independence from us, and now only the Portuguese in New Spain are thrown in the jails of the Inquisition as heretics and have all their worldly goods confiscated and sold!"

"They accuse them of being Judaizers. Why do they claim everybody is secretly practicing Jewish rituals? It seems so absurd since all the Jews were expelled from the mother country by Fernando and Isabella in 1492. That's over a hundred and fifty years ago!" Antonia said.

"It is greed and a kind of primitive racial hatred that goes back even farther than that." Augustín's voice was hard. "It was well over two hundred years ago—sometime in the late 1300s—that a priest in Seville inflamed and incited lower-class mobs to overrun the city's Jewish quarter. Hundreds of Jews were massacred, their belongings seized, and the mob's ringleaders moved on to other Spanish cities, causing horrible atrocities to be committed there, too. But it was all covered over by a thin veneer as religious fervor, and you know the first thing the mobs always did? Break into the *escribanías* and destroy all the documents of who owed whom money. The violence and horror was so devastating, it's no wonder that hundreds of Jews converted in order to save their lives and the lives of their children."

"So that's why they were called 'New Christians.'"

He nodded. "What's so ironic about it is that, after the conversions, almost a hundred years passed before the Inquisition was instituted—how can you call someone a 'new' Christian whose parents, grandparents, great-grandparents, and great-great-grandparents were Christians?"

The question was rhetorical, but Antonia said, "Obviously it's because they are descendants of Jews and are therefore considered tainted."

"That was the excuse for the creation of the Inquisition in the first place. They claimed the New Christians were heretics who still continued Jewish practices even though their family had been Christians for a hundred years. In reality they just coveted the New Christians' wealth, and this was a way to get it legally and 'morally.' They say our Lord Inquisitors in just the last two years have lined their pockets with three million pesos from the rigged auctions of the goods and property of the accused."

"It makes you sick to be a Christian if this is what your Church does." Disgust filled her voice.

Augustín nodded. "The Inquisition shakes my faith more profoundly than anything else."

Antonia was shocked by the frankness with which he spoke and glanced quickly out the windows of the coach to see if anyone stood close by in the darkness. She, too, knew the power of the Holy Office and feared it.

"*Padre*, be careful," she whispered as she moved to sit next to him, "I fear I should not have expressed my disagreement with the Church."

Augustín took her hand. "Perhaps you are right, and we should have a care with what and where we speak, but, Little One, you know that you may say to me anything you think, as I feel free to say to you things I dare not speak to others. It is a great contentment to me to be able to share my thoughts with you."

As they sat beside each other in the coach, Antonia looked sideways through the darkness at him, unable to see his face, wishing that she could read there the same thing she knew was on her own face. But she knew her feelings were not mirrored by his face despite the shadows.

"I, too," she whispered, a faint tremble in her voice.

At length María Luisa and Luís returned, and after drinking a cup of hot chocolate, which the servants prepared, the four occupants of the coach decided to try to sleep for a few hours. The following day would be a long and tiring one. It seemed the streets would never become quiet, and at midnight they heard the Dominicans sing matins. María Luisa relaxed in sleep, her head on her son's shoulder. Augustín felt Antonia's head come to rest against his own shoulder. Carefully he moved closer to the side of the coach, taking her gently by the shoulders and laying her down on the seat where she could sleep more comfortably, his lap serving as her pillow.

He was sometimes amazed at the closeness he felt toward the little girl he had tutored and who was now almost grown. Thoughts he could not share with others, he expressed to her. In the tenderness he felt for her, he put his hand on her hair and smoothed it softly as he leaned his head back against the cushion of the carriage seat and closed his eyes. She moved slightly in her sleep, snuggling closer toward him, sighing softly.

She awoke sometime later being shaken gently by the shoulder. "It is close to dawn," he whispered, leaning down near her ear, "I must be going now."

She turned toward him, their faces so close in the predawn darkness, she felt his breath fan her face. She touched his cheek with her hand. "Don't go yet," she murmured.

"I must," he said softly and kissed her on the forehead.

She sat up and threw her arms around his neck. "I don't want to have to watch this horrible thing," she whispered with anguish.

He put his arms around her comfortingly, whispering softly, "Dearest Little One, your mother requires it. Pray for the poor prisoners and for the Church. Do not think on the horrors of it, think only that God loves mankind in spite of some of the terrible things we do."

She hugged him tightly and kissed his cheek. "Thank you, *Padre*, I will try."

He kissed her on the forehead again and slipped out of the carriage. She lay back down on the seat and hugged herself tightly, wishing, in spite of herself, that his arms were around her and that his kiss had been on her lips and not chastely on her forehead.

Her skin crawled with horror as she watched. First came the effigies of those who had died in the Inquisition's jail, next the bound prisoners, garbed in the degrading, monstrous costumes of the condemned. Many were women, some young, others obviously grandmothers with gray hair. Whispers in the crowds preceded loud jeers and taunts, and Antonia wondered what it was that caused such a violent response from the crowd.

"It's him!" she heard someone remark. "The devil has eaten his soul, so they say."

"No!" another answered incredulously.

"But it is true. They say he speaks to the devil with strange words and signs and that near him one can smell the sulfurous odors of Hell."

"They say he commits abominations too terrible to repeat. He will go to the stake for sure."

"But he has proclaimed his innocence. He says he won't confess to something he has not done. He says it is a sin to lie."

"That proves he is the devil incarnate! He must confess! He must humble himself and beg for mercy. Only the devil would proclaim his innocence!"

Within moments, Antonia saw the man of whom they spoke. He was bound and gagged and trussed to a mangy burro led by an Indian. His hair was gray, matted and filthy, and he appeared to be somewhere over fifty. He jerked and twisted on the back of the burro as if in desperation. His eyeballs bulged and rolled and stared at the thousands who jeered at him. Children threw rocks at him.

Although she knew it was prohibited to show pity and that she could suffer severe penalties for doing so, Antonia covered her face in horror, unable to look at him, fearful she might be sick. *"Virgen María*, have mercy on this man," she whispered.

"That's him," people shouted, "that's Tomás Treviño de Sobremonte. The wickedest one of all!"

She somehow managed to endure the long, horrible process of the interminable reading and imposing of the sentences, and late that afternoon it ended. Because the streets were packed with people, she and her mother and brother could not take their carriage from the Plaza del Volador and had to make their way on foot with the rest of the spectators to the wide open space in the Alameda where the pyres had been erected. She was not sure she could be a witness to the hellfires that would be lit that day.

Church towers, rooftops, and windows were crammed with people. Even the branches of the Alameda's trees were festooned with morbidly curious humanity. The Spanish fleet was in port and sailors as well as officers had come overland from the coast to the capital to enjoy the spectacle and to revel drunkenly on solid soil.

The bells of all the city's many churches tolled lugubriously as the cortege of the accused and their accusers wended their way toward the awaiting pyres. Those who were spared the death sentence would receive their punishments on the following day, tied on the back of a burro and stripped naked to the waist—whether man or woman—as they were paraded through the streets and whipped. But first they would have to bear witness to the fate that awaited them if they were later found to have relapsed into their heretical ways.

They watched as sixty-seven effigies of those who had died from torture or sickness in the Inquisition's jail were paraded across the bridge over the moat that surrounded the Alameda and into the *plazuela* of San Diego where the *quemadero* was located. Boxes of the bones of the deceased had been placed behind the effigies that represented them. The Inquisition was not content to see anyone escape its holy wrath before the Tribunal had a chance to mete out its punishment—including those who had been fortunate enough to die first. Even the bones must burn.

Following the effigies came the thirteen yellow *sambenito*-clad prisoners who would go to the stake. Each had two confessors who exhorted them to repent their sins as they mounted a large platform. The crowds yelled and jeered and offered their own exhortations. Six of the condemned were women, five of them grandmothers.

"I am Ana de León Carvajal," one of the women sentenced to die cried out. "I am sixty-seven years old and I have loved the Lord all my life! Let God be my *testigo*. I am innocent of these charges!"

Like a giant venomous snake, the crowd's voice rose in one deafening hiss. Rocks and rotted fruit flew out of the crowd, pelting the woman as she stood unflinching.

"*¡Puta judía!*" people chanted.

Some of the prisoners stood stoically; tears bathed the faces of others. Tomás Treviño de Sobremonte thrashed and jerked, his screams silenced by the gag that bound his mouth.

A Dominican priest holding a large gold-green cross stepped forward toward the doomed prisoners while another shouted in order to be heard above the crowd.

"Repent! Kiss the cross and be reconciled with our Lord Jesus Christ. Kiss the holy cross and earn the privilege of a merciful death!"

The confessors each turned to their condemned and spoke.

One by one twelve of the prisoners were led forward, knelt before the cross, leaned forward and kissed the symbol of their death sentence. Only Tomás Treviño refused.

The twelve were led to the center of the platform and made to kneel once more facing the crowd. Most of the twelve closed their eyes as their lips moved in silent prayer.

A black-hooded executioner, a wire cord in his hands, stepped from the back of the platform and approached the kneeling penitents. A hush fell over the boisterous crowd and the only sound was a priest's voice intoning a doleful prayer.

In one catlike movement the executioner slipped the wire over the first victim's head, twisted the handles, and jerked upward. He released the wire and the lifeless body crumpled to the platform as a roar of approval went up from the crowd. In only moments twelve bodies lay inert on the rough planks.

As they removed the bodies from the platform, Treviño stood still and ramrod straight as if in salute of the dead.

The effigies, boxes of bones, and bodies of those who had been mercifully killed with the garrote were stacked on an enormous pile of wood and set afire. Treviño was dragged to an individual pyre, lifted up onto a small platform above a pile of wood, and tied to the tall stake. More firewood was placed at his feet and his gag was removed so that if he begged for mercy, he could be heard.

The crowd was once more strangely quiet and stared in silence as Treviño tried with his foot to pull the firewood closer to him.

"Throw on more!" he shouted in defiance. "I paid for it with my own money!"

"Satan!" someone shouted and the crowd exploded in rage, hurling curses, stones, and anything they could get their hands on at the man who would not beg for mercy.

"*Te saludo,* Tomás Treviño de Sobremonte," Antonia whispered. "You have more honor than any of us."

Chapter 16

A year had passed. Antonia shouted hysterically, as she pounded on the door, "You can't do this to me! Let me out!"

Only silence greeted her from the other side, and finally hoarse and weak from screaming, she crumpled to a heap on the floor and lay sobbing at her locked door. Even though she closed her eyes and covered them with her hands, she could not keep the vision of López Pacheco's loathsome, gloating face from her mind. He had stood there behind her parents, a crude condescending smile on his repugnant lips, as they told her she would soon be the Countess of Maralba.

"I will never marry that swine of a man," she said with cold vehemence. Her father looked at her with shock.

"I will enter a convent before I will marry such an uneducated boor." Her tone was filled with loathing and contempt. She had never spoken that way to her parents before, but she could no longer be proper when they intended to marry her to a man the very thought of whom filled her with revulsion.

She had an inkling of her mistake the moment before the words exploded from her father's lips. Vivid crimson spread across his features, and for an instant she thought he was going to slap her. His hand did not touch her, but the virulence of his words had much the same effect. She reeled at the violence of his tone.

"No daughter of mine shall *ever* speak to me that way!" he shouted. "You have been spoiled, coddled, and indulged too long. No longer! You will obey as a woman should obey, never questioning. First, you will obey me, then you will obey your husband! You have wasted your time reading your precious books, and what's more, they have made you think you need not do those things that are a woman's duty."

Don Rodrigo lowered his voice, but it filled her with even more fear. "You will *not* become a nun! *I forbid it!* You will marry Don Raúl López Pacheco, the Count of Maralba, and you will be obedient to him as a wife should be."

She stood for a moment in stunned silence and saw the revolting look of triumph on the gloating face of the peninsular.

"No," she said, "no!" and whirled toward the door to flee.

Her father grabbed her arm and jerked her back, but she twisted away in desperation. He reached for her again as she hit and kicked at him wildly. She could hear her mother sobbing.

She fought with all the strength she had, but it was not enough. She went limp and began to cry. Her father let go of her, and María Luisa ran to embrace her.

"Please, *Mamá*," Antonia begged, tears coursing down her face. "Please, I cannot marry that man!"

"Oh, *mi hija*, you are just upset. We should have told you you were to marry Don Raúl before he left. Then you would have had a year to become accustomed to the idea."

María Luisa patted her daughter gently. "It was my fault. I thought it would be better to wait to tell you until you knew that you would be a countess. *Mi hija*, you are just upset now. After you are calm and have a chance to think about it, you will see that the thought of marriage will not be so bad. You will be a countess. Isn't that wonderful?"

Sobs wracked Antonia, and she was unable to control them. "Come, dear," her mother said, "let's go lie down for a little while." Obediently Antonia went with her from the *sala*, but when they reached the entry hall, she pushed her mother away and ran for the door, fumbling for a moment before she succeeded in opening it.

Her mother screamed and Antonia, over her shoulder, saw the shocked faces of her father and López Pacheco as she ran out the door and down the steps. López Pacheco was the first one out the door after her but his corpulence did not permit speed, and her father quickly overtook him, although her father was a good twenty years the peninsular's senior.

Had she not been encumbered by the voluminous skirts of her dress, she might have escaped. As it was, she was ignominiously dragged back to the house and to her room. Don Rodrigo yelled for the chambermaid who came scurrying, frightened. He held Antonia by the arm, his grip viselike.

"Remove all her clothes from the armoire!" he demanded. When the quaking servant hesitated, he stamped his foot and shouted at her, "Do it, this instant!"

The maid ran to the wardrobe. Antonia stared aghast as the *criada* removed all her clothing from the room. "Leave her only a gown and a robe," her father said.

He dropped Antonia's arm. It throbbed painfully from the force of his grip. His face was cold and hard. "I'm going to wait outside while you remove the dress you are wearing. Then give it to the maid. You will remain in your room. There is no way you can flee; the door will remain locked and guarded, and you may save yourself the trouble of trying to bribe a servant, for they shall pay with their lives if they allow you to escape. You will learn respect for your parents' wishes if I have to beat it into you. You *will* marry the Count of Maralba, and there is nothing you can do about it."

She was left in her room alone, wearing only a thin white gown and its matching robe. The door being closed and locked sounded like a death knell to her.

López Pacheco had wished to stay, fearful that the parents might relent in view of their daughter's anguished screams, which could be heard from above, but astutely, he knew that he should leave, not only as if out of politeness but also, perhaps leaving the impression that he might be reconsidering marrying a girl who behaved in such a manner. He knew how desperately Salvatierra wanted a title in the family, and if he departed now, leaving her father in doubt as to his willingness to marry his daughter, it should act to keep the man's resolve strong so that he would not weaken in the face of her pleas.

Don Rodrigo offered the new count a glass of port. "No, thank you," López Pacheco replied smoothly. "In view of the circumstances, I think it would be best if I left now."

He pulled on the expensive perfumed kidskin gloves he had bought in Spain with Don Rodrigo's money. The peninsular dressed very well now. He had been foresighted enough to tell Salvatierra that the cost of the patent was considerably higher than he had known to be the case with the result that his wardrobe was now worthy of his new title.

"It's not necessary to go," Don Rodrigo said, trying to smile. He put his hand on the count's shoulder. "Forgive me for the scene my daughter caused. I know she will come to her senses shortly, and everything will be as we have planned it."

"I hope you are right," López Pacheco said, allowing a bit of doubt to tinge his words, "but don't feel you have not raised your daughter properly. The blame is not yours; it is the books, surely."

Salvatierra was not comforted by the words. "Wouldn't you like to dine with us this evening?" he asked expectantly.

"Thank you, but I'm afraid I have another engagement for this evening. Convey my regrets to your lovely wife, please."

The peninsular was reluctant to decline, for the food at the Salvatierra house was as delicious as it was abundant, but he would see his hand played well and the game won. He would have to be content with a cheap meal in a poor tavern that night, for with the purchase of his new wardrobe, there was little money left from that his benefactor had given him.

Don Rodrigo slumped into one of the chairs in the *sala* after López Pacheco left. He pounded his thigh. "That girl is going to marry the count if I have to carry her down the aisle screaming! I will not let this title slip through my fingers!"

✳   ✳   ✳

Much later Antonia leaped to her feet when she heard the lock on her door click. A tray was hurriedly placed inside and the door reclosed. She heard the lock turn, and she sank back down onto the bed. She had no appetite; she did not even bother to see what had been brought. She lay back on the bed, trying to think, but she could not make her mind form any coherent thought. She felt hollow inside, as if burned out by one of the Inquisition's fires. As she lay on the bed, she heard the rain begin. Thunder boomed deeply, and she knew it was likely to be a downpour as was so common in August in the viceregal capital.

"Padre Augustín will help me as soon as I can see him," she whispered to herself, but as she said the words a cold sensation swept over her.

"They won't *let* me see him! *Dios mío,* what am I going to do?" A crack of thunder rent the air.

"I must get to him!" she whispered, sitting up with a start. "He can get me to a convent! That is the only way I can keep from having to marry that man!"

She looked around the room. How on earth was she going to be able to get out? She tried the doorknob carefully but it did not budge. She went to the long, shuttered French windows and opened them. The rain beat in on her. She shook the bars in frustration, then bent to peer more closely at one. It felt as if it gave slightly as she shook it. She pushed against it with all her might. It moved! Where it had been welded to the crossbar, it had rusted.

Quickly she shut the windows. She pulled a pillowcase off one of the pillows and mopped up the water where it had rained in. With the other pillowcase, she dried herself as best she could. Then she went to the tray of food and gobbled some of it quickly so that it would appear as if she had been willing to eat. She blew out the light and crawled into bed. Now she must wait until everyone was asleep. Then she would make her escape. Someone would undoubtedly check on her before they went to bed. Although the desire to flee immediately almost overwhelmed her, she *must* wait.

The minutes were like black, heavy shackles holding her there. She had no idea what time it was. When she finally heard the lock click, she jumped in terror but lay still, pretending sleep. Light from the open door fell across her, but she did not open her eyes.

"Thank God," she heard her mother whisper, "she has gone to sleep, and it appears she ate her supper. Perhaps you were right, Rodrigo, to do what you did."

The door closed, and she heard the lock turn. She must still wait, wait until sleep had overtaken the household. She hoped her parents would sleep soundly, relieved, thinking everything was going as they wished.

Finally when she thought it was safe, she arose and went to the window.

The rain still beat down. She prayed its sound would muffle her own. She pushed the bar with all her might. It moved but not enough to allow her passage, for it was welded also at the crosspieces of the top and bottom. She sat down on the floor in the puddle the rain had made, and holding onto the bars on either side with her hands, she put her feet against the loose bar and pushed again and again.

At length she sobbed with defeat. Then she took on new determination and tried again. Finally one forceful kick caused the weld to snap, and she managed to push the bar out far enough so that she could slip her body through, clutching desperately to the other bars. She prayed their welds were strong and would not break with her weight, sending her plummeting down two stories to the ground. Because the rain had caused her fingers to become slippery on the iron bars, she was afraid of losing her grip.

Carefully she hooked one arm around a bar and turned slowly to see if she could reach a branch of the huge *aguacate* tree that grew close to her window. She felt the glossy leaves and then the branch but knew she would have to let go of the iron bar before she could get a secure hold on the branch with the other arm.

She was going to have to let go and swing around the branch at the same time and pray she caught it securely. She took a deep breath, crossed herself, and let go. She felt the leaves and small branches scratch her face and arms, but she clutched at the larger branch wrapping her limbs around it in desperation. She struggled to secure a hold on the tree, her lips moving in constant prayer. Slowly and carefully, her feet searching for footholds, she backed down the tree. She could feel the branches tearing her gown and robe as they were caught and she pulled them free. The soles of her feet felt lacerated.

Rain ran in rivulets down her face, and even if she had wanted to look where she was going, she could have seen nothing. She groped like a blind person, going inch by slow inch, fearful she might lose her footing or grasp on the rain-slick tree. She trembled from the cold, pelting droplets and from the fear gnawing her insides that they might discover her absence before she had a chance to get away.

At last she reached the main crotch of the tree. Somewhere below was the ground. She knew she must jump into the blackness and hope she landed without killing herself or breaking anything. She would prefer to die from the fall rather than be hurt and unable to flee further. She crossed herself. "Santa María, help me," she prayed, then leaped into the black nothingness.

Blinding pain shot through her feet and up her legs as she hit the ground. She felt the palms of her hands stinging from the abrasion as she sought to break her fall. She pushed herself to her feet and whispered, "Thank you, Holy Mother," and began to run.

It did not matter that in the rain and darkness she could see nothing. She ran blindly in the direction she knew would take her to the Jesuit and safety. Twice she fell headlong on the rain-slick stones of the streets but at length realized she must be nearing the main plaza. She slowed to a walk, her chest heaving from her exertion and peered into the inky wet blackness of the street, unable to see a thing. Suddenly she had the sensation she was in the open. She tried to rub the rain and hair from her eyes. Either she was seeing things or there were a few winks of light in the distance.

It had to be the the *zócalo* with its hundreds of stalls where the entire city came to shop by day for its meat, vegetables, flowers, cooking pots, and the like. At night many of the shops served as rude lodgings for their proprietors. Those were undoubtedly the source of the faint flickers.

She would have to make her way across the square. Surely everyone would have found some shelter from the downpour and there would be no ruffians about. She shuddered involuntarily at the thought of the men who were accustomed to prowling the streets after all good citizens were safely at home.

Her heart pounded as she came closer to the lights. She must pass by them to reach the Jesuit.

She was staring at the lights as she tiptoed by. Her toe came down in mud, and off balance, she fell noisily.

"*¿Qué fué?*" She heard someone say and looked up to see a man with a lamp in his hand staring out at her from the entrance to one of the stalls.

"Well, well, well," he said in a grating voice, "what do we have here, boys?"

Chapter 17

She came to her feet and stood frozen for a moment. The man took a step toward her and she screamed as she lurched forward toward him, her feet caught momentarily by the sticky mud. To her amazement, he stepped backward, a look of terror on his face.

"¡La Llorona!" he hissed between rotted teeth. "Dios mío, have mercy on me!" He stumbled backward, and the lamp dropped from his hand, enveloping the shack in blackness.

Antonia ran headlong in fear, oblivious of the rain as it continued to fall, her teeth chattering. She knew why the man was terrified of her. La Llorona — the phantom lady dressed in a long white gown who prowled the city at night, crying mournfully for her dead infant. The wailing woman was a legend everyone had been told as a child.

She began to run again; she must get to Augustín — he would be her salvation. She might reach the Colegio Máximo, but how would she reach him? She stopped suddenly. She could not go in there in her condition — she would raise the whole place, and she would be recognized. Her father would be summoned immediately. Her shoulders began to shake with sobs and she fell to her knees.

"Help me, Sweet Virgin," she cried despondently as the rain poured down. In a strange way, the answer to her prayer appeared to her. She rose and started back toward the stalls of the plaza; it was the only way.

She could see nothing in the first two stalls and went on to the third. She peered through a crack and in the faint illumination of an oil lamp saw an old man sitting with a pulque bottle at his elbow and worn cards in front of him. She walked silently around to the stall's entrance.

She let out a small moan, and then another a little louder. She heard rustling from inside.

"*Señor, Señor,*" she called eerily, "*por el amor de Dios,* come outside." Again the rustling. "Come outside," she called, allowing her voice to rise.

The flickering light came from the back of the stall, and she stepped aside where the light would not touch her. "Come to me, come to me," she called hauntingly.

The old man came out of the stall, peering into the darkness, protecting the lamp with his hand. "*¿Quién vive?*" he asked tremulously.

She slipped behind him. "It is I," she whispered, "*La Llorona.*"

The old man whirled around and the lamp's light gave life to her as if by magic. She was a dripping, white apparition that might have stepped out of the depths of a lake. The old man gasped. He, too, knew and believed the legend of the woman dressed in white. He wanted to flee to the relative safety of his meager lodging, but she stood in the way. He glanced over his shoulder, as if contemplating taking his chances in the blackness beyond.

"If you value your soul," she hissed, "you will not run, for I will find you and take you to my dwelling place in the lake." The old man trembled visibly, shaking his head that he would not run.

"Come, dear man," she said gently, this time. "I have an errand for you to perform this night. Come."

She put out her hand, but he took a step backward in fear. "Do not be afraid, dear one," she cooed, stepping forward. She grasped his trembling hand in her cold, wet one. The man shook. Slowly she began to lead him away. The lamp fell from his hand and sputtered out.

"Do not worry," she whispered, "nothing will happen to you if you obey *La Llorona.*"

The several blocks to the Colegio Máximo seemed miles, but finally they reached the ornate façade. "We are here," she said. "Now you must listen very carefully to your instructions." They stood close to the stone wall of the building, and she pulled him near so that he would hear everything.

"You must go inside and ask for Padre Augustín. You must say that you have a confession to make—it is a matter of life and death. But it *must* be to Padre Augustín and only him. You cannot make your confession to anyone else, otherwise you will fail in your mission. Be *certain* that it is Padre Augustín. He is very tall with gray eyes and dark auburn hair. You must tell him the confession concerns his 'Little One.' Do you understand?"

"*Sí,*" the old man whispered, his voice shaking.

"Whom does the confession concern?"

"His . . . his Little One," the old man stammered.

"Good," she said softly. "Now you must tell him nothing more until you are in the confessional. If he asks what it is all about, tell him you can only reveal it in the confessional. Once you are inside, tell him this: that his Little One is in desperate need of him, that his Little One is waiting outside the church and he is to go out to her." She paused. "Do you understand *everything*?"

"*Sí, sí,*" he whispered.

She let a tiny moan escape her lips. "If you value your immortal soul, *viejo,* you will do exactly as I have told you. If not, yours will be a watery grave like my *own!* Now go!" She gave him a push toward the door, and pressed herself back against the wall.

The man rang the bell and presently the heavy wooden door creaked open, and he whispered his message. He was taken inside and the door closed behind him. She sighed and crossed herself, praying fervently that her ruse would work. Then carefully she made her way down the long wall to the church. She found a small bit of protection from the rain between the columns that adorned the entrance to the sanctuary. Now she must wait.

Silently she began to recite the rosary using her fingers as the beads. "Santa María, have pity on me," she prayed. She was unable to quiet the trembling that shook her body.

The porter raised Augustín, and he threw on his cassock and grabbed up his stole, wondering what on earth the late visitor wanted. When he reached the entrance hall and held up the lamp he carried to better see the man, he was shocked by the look of terror on the wet and trembling *viejo*'s face.

"I must confess," the old man rasped in a quavering voice. "It concerns the *padre*'s 'Little One.' " Augustín was scarcely able to smother his gasp.

"I can say no more until I am in the confessional," the old man said, trembling more visibly.

Augustín turned to the porter. He tried to make his voice level. "Everything is all right. You may go back to bed. I shall take this poor soul to the church where he wishes the sacrament of confession. Good night."

Augustín turned and led the way to the church. Votive candles flickered on the main altar and in the various niches. He indicated the door to a confessional and the old man entered. Augustín went to his own door and seated himself on his side of the grate and put the stole around his neck.

The old man spoke the ritual words and began to babble something about *La Llorona* and the "Little One." A cold, hard knot of fear tightened in Augustín's belly. What was wrong? What did this crazy man's story have to do with Antonia, if anything?

Augustín spoke harshly. "Slow down. Repeat carefully what you have said."

The old man's voice quaked. "*La Llorona* — she told me to tell you that your 'Little One' is in desperate need of you. You are to go out to her. She is waiting outside for you."

"Stay here," Augustín ordered harshly, "do not leave this stall before I return. Under pain of excommunication, meditate on your sins, *viejo.*"

Augustín tore out of the confessional and ran to the heavy front door of the church. He ran out into the pouring rain. "Antonia!" he shouted, "Antonia!"

Suddenly she was in his arms, clinging to him, sobbing.

"My God," he whispered, "what has happened, Antonia?" He pulled her back against the church trying to protect her as best he could from the rain.

In a torrent, the words came from her lips of what had happened that afternoon and night.

"Oh, my God," he said, clutching her to him tightly. "Oh, my God. Come, we must get you out of this rain." He pulled her with him into the church, making sure the old man had not come out of the confessional. They eased along the wall to a corner, glancing about furtively to make sure there was no one else around. Antonia slid down to a sitting position, and Augustín crouched beside her.

"You must get me to a convent," she implored. "I would *die* before I would marry that man!"

"Of course, of course, Little One," he replied, his mind racing. "I will see you safe from that man." But he knew that the first place her parents would look for her would be in all the convents of the city and any in the nearby villages.

There was no mother superior, who, faced with the huge amount of money Don Rodrigo would offer in exchange for his daughter, could resist such a wealth for her convent. They would give the girl back without batting an eye, and once she was outside the convent walls, Don Rodrigo would again have absolute control over her. And Augustín was convinced that she *would* die before she would marry López Pacheco. How could he help her? What could he do if even the convents were not safe? She could not flee. As soon as they found she was missing, they would be searching everywhere, and a lone girl would attract attention no matter where she went.

An idea came to him. Perhaps it would work. If he could disguise her and hide her somewhere until the fury of the first days were past, and her father had had a chance to search all the convents for her — then perhaps Augustín could smuggle her into one and by the time her parents found out, it would be too late. He would have to charge the mother superior with mortal sin if she betrayed the girl. He would need some time to make the arrangements — and that was just as well for it would allow her father time to exhaust all the possibilities of her location.

"Little One," he whispered, brushing the hair out of her face, "it would not be safe for you to go to a convent now. You know that is the first place your father will look. He would bribe the mother superior and have you back in moments." Her shoulders started to shake.

"Do not cry. Here is a plan I have thought of. I will hide you somewhere — there is an inn I know. After your father has had a chance to search all the convents of Mexico City to prove to himself that you are not there, I will smuggle you into one, and by the time your father finds out where you are — if he does — it will be too late."

Antonia threw her arms around his neck, covering his face with kisses. "Thank you, thank you."

"Now," Augustín said, "I must reassure that poor old man you nearly scared out of his mind. Maybe there is something more he can do, though. We need mounts to take us to the inn. Time is dear." He pulled her close.

"Wait here for just a minute more. As soon as the old man leaves, go immediately into a confessional and stay there until I return."

Within moments the old man left the church, hurrying fearfully, and as instructed she slipped into the confessional. She sat there shaking uncontrollably with cold. She could not stop the chattering of her teeth, and she was terrified someone might come into the church and hear her.

She jumped with fright when the door to the confessional finally opened, but it was Augustín carrying clothes for her to wear. He had changed into dry clothing and now wore a long wool cloak with a hood to protect him against the rain.

"Put them on quickly," he whispered and closed the door. Moments later he spoke to her through the grate. "Tie your hair back with the piece of cord. You are going to be a monk."

She tied back her wet hair and slipped a woolen shirt over her head and over the wet rags of her gown. The shirt came almost to her knees. She pulled on another woolen garment that was longer still. Finally she pulled on the rough wool, hooded habit. It was too long by several inches, but by knotting the rope around her waist she managed to keep it off the ground.

"I am going to wait at the door of the church—you wait here until I come for you."

Gradually she began to warm as she waited in the narrow confessional. She heard the church door open and then some moments later, Augustín whispered at the door of the confessional, "Everything's ready."

Outside, he helped her mount the mule and draped a hooded wool cloak over her habit, tucking it in around her legs. He mounted another mule, the best the old man said he could find, and they started out. The pace was slow because of the rain, and she could scarcely control her terror that they were being followed.

After what seemed like hours, they came to a roadside inn well out of the city in a small village suburb of the capital.

Augustín helped her dismount. "I stayed here once or twice when I was a seminarian. The owner is a very discreet, honest woman, but it is best she think you are a monk. I shall make up some story. Do not speak if you can keep from it."

At length he managed to rouse someone. "Get Doña Rosilda," he said. "Tell her it is the seminarian Augustín."

Shortly the door was pulled open. "Come in, come in," the silver-haired woman said holding a lamp aloft. "What a terrible night. Is it really you, Augustín?"

"None other."

"Are you a *padre* now, eh?"

"Yes, for three years."

"Why you bad boy," Doña Rosilda scolded good-naturedly. "All that time and you haven't been to see me once to tell me the good news!"

"Forgive me, Doña Rosilda, but I am here now."

"Yes, so you are but what is this with you?" she asked, looking at the bundled form who stood timidly next to the priest, head bowed, face hidden.

"I have a favor to ask of you, Doña Rosilda," Augustín said. "The boy has promised a week long vigil of silence—that he shall not speak a word during an entire week so that he may listen only to God and may know which path he should take. He wanted to get away from the city and its influences. I remembered your place. Unfortunately we lost our way and were thus late in arriving. I hope you have a room."

"There is always room for you, *Padre*," Doña Rosilda answered with a smile. "Come." She led them up some stairs and down a hall.

"Is this satisfactory?" she asked as she entered a room and lit a lamp.

"Yes, quite," he said and placed a hand on the shoulder of the figure. "Do not worry, Antonio. I shall return. I know Doña Rosilda will see that all is taken care of, won't you, *Señora*?"

"*Claro*," Doña Rosilda assured him.

"If you could have the meals placed outside the door, then the boy could retrieve them and not have to worry about perhaps unthinkingly saying something to a servant and thereby breaking his vow of silence."

"It shall be done just as you wish."

When Doña Rosilda departed, Antonia dropped weakly onto the edge of the bed. Augustín came and sat down next to her, lifting her hoods away from her face, white with fatigue. There was unquenched fear in her eyes. Gently he took her face between his hands and kissed her on the forehead.

"Little One," he said softly, "you are safe now; do not worry."

"You are not going to stay?" she asked tremulously. "I will be here alone?"

"Dearest Antonia, I *must* go back. Who is the first person your father will seek? He will come to me to see if I know where you are. Won't his first thought be that you came running to your old tutor?"

She nodded weakly, and he continued. "I must go back and act as if completely shocked by your disappearance. I must pretend to help look for you. If they suspect that I have aided you . . ."

He did not complete the sentence. She began to weep, and he took her in his arms and held her comfortingly, whispering as he rocked gently back and forth with her. "You must be strong. God will aid us in this plan if we are strong. You are precious to Him, and He will help you if you only ask. I, too, shall pray with all my strength. God is loving, He will not desert us."

She cuddled close to him, her body trembling. "I will be strong, I promise."

"You are freezing," he said as he took her cold, bloodless hand. "Come, you must get out of those wet clothes."

He pulled her to her feet and lifted the cloak from her shoulders. He untied the rope belt and removed the hooded habit as she stood unmoving, except for the quivering of her body. She made no move to help and did not resist when he pulled the long wool tuniclike shirts from her.

The tatters of her once-white gown and robe were plastered to her body. Her trembling became more violent, and she looked up at him, her eyes wide and solemn, but she did not move. She saw him swallow and look away as he pulled the ragged gown from her.

"Get into bed," he said. "A bath will have to wait until tomorrow." He pulled the covers back, his eyes averted.

Obediently, she crawled in, never taking her eyes from him. He tucked the covers closely about her and began to rub them vigorously to warm her. There was a small knock at the door, and her eyes widened in terror.

Augustín crossed to the door, opened it, and stood so that his form blocked the view.

"I thought you and the boy might like a cup of hot chocolate after being out in such a night," Doña Rosilda said.

"Yes, thank you," he replied, taking the two mugs. "This is very kind of you. I will be leaving shortly; I must get back for early Mass. I won't be returning until late tomorrow evening. Would it be too much trouble to bring hot water for a bath for the boy tomorrow morning? He is caked with mud from the ride."

"Cómo no," Doña Rosilda replied, "I shall bring it myself."

He carried the hot chocolate to the bed. Antonia lay unmoving, her eyes fixed on him.

"Doña Rosilda brought us hot chocolate," he said with a smile. "This will warm you. In the morning she will bring you bathwater. Be sure you put the habit with the hood on and do not speak."

He sat next to her, helping her to sit up and drink as if she were a child, his hands covering hers to steady them. When she had finished the hot, frothy liquid, he tucked her back into the covers.

"I must go now," he said.

Her eyes still watched him solemnly. Her hand came out from under the covers and reached toward him. He grasped her hand and sat down on the edge of the bed.

"Go with God," she whispered as she brought his hand to her cheek and then kissed it.

Chapter 18

"*Señora*, do not cry," Augustín said with compassion. "God is gracious. He will allow no harm to come to your daughter, our dear Antonia. Come, let us pray," he said as he took her hand and knelt with her on the rich carpet. Don Rodrigo went to his knees, also, followed by López Pacheco, who heaved his bulk noisily out of his chair to kneel with the others.

"Dearest Lord," Augustín prayed, "give us strength in this hour of our travail. Do not let us once waiver in our faith in Your great mercy. Guide and protect and show Your love to our dear Antonia wherever she may be. Keep her safe, *Dios*, and give her understanding so that she may realize what You wish of her here on earth. Let her know that we all here love her deeply and want only for her well-being and happiness. Grant us relief from our fears and knowledge to do Your will in whatever You may ask of us. Give us our Antonia in safety we ask of You, please. Amen."

All took their seats again. Don Rodrigo's face was taut. "How could a mere girl have gotten so far in just one night?" he asked angrily. "I have been to all the convents within the *traza* today. How could she have gone to one outside the city limits? But, if she thinks she can hide for long, she's mistaken. I will search all the convents for a hundred leagues around the capital!"

"But what if she is not in a convent?" her mother wailed. "What if she is lying somewhere hurt?"

Augustín patted her arm. "Luís is still looking. He will not give up easily— he loves his sister dearly. If she is lying somewhere hurt, he will find her."

The peninsular was unusually silent.

At length Augustín rose. "I must go now, for my duties call, but I will pray tonight for Antonia's safety. Tomorrow I will return, *Señora*," he said to María Luisa. "Remember that God is merciful. If you hear anything, *anything,*" he said to Don Rodrigo, "send word to me at the Colegio."

"Of course, of course," Salvatierra said absently, adding wearily, "it's too dark or I would go now to the outlying villages. I have men watching the roads, however, so if she is not in a convent yet, there are many who will be looking for a young girl alone. The offer of a substantial reward for anything draws people like a cow's carcass draws vultures."

His wife began to wail at his choice of words when she pictured her daughter lying hurt or dead somewhere. Augustín comforted her, for her husband was so involved in his own thoughts that he seemed not to notice his wife's grief.

As Augustín made his good-byes a second time, López Pacheco spoke up. "I must be going also. I must look for my darling wife-to-be; I cannot bear this painful waiting for my heart's mate." He took María Luisa's hand and bent over it. "I promise you I will get her back." He straightened and stared at the Jesuit, as if awaiting some response.

Augustín looked levelly at the peninsular. "Perhaps we could enjoy each other's company if you are going in the same direction, Don Raúl," he said with feigned politeness, but not once had he called the peninsular by his newly purchased title.

"Yes," López Pacheco answered, drawing the word out as if there was special weight attached to it.

Only a small bit of light remained of the day as the two men walked from the Salvatierra house. They had gone scarcely a block when López Pacheco spoke. His tone was conversational, but there was a steely edge to it.

"What have you done with her, *Padre?*" he asked bluntly.

Augustín did not miss a step. "With whom?"

"With the girl, who else?"

"Why, she's in my cell at the Colegio," Augustín said derisively. "Would you like to see her?"

López Pacheco turned red and spluttered. "I know a sham when I see one," he said menacingly.

"I, too, *Conde,*" Augustín replied pleasantly, emphasizing the title with heavy sarcasm as he looked directly at the newly purchased count.

The peninsular's face seemed to bloat even more. "If you think you can get away with this, you are wrong! I am going to marry Don Rodrigo's daughter. It matters not where you may have hidden her!"

Augustín voice was controlled. "I have no idea where the clever Señorita Antonia is, but I say, more power to her in her escape from her revolting fate."

Augustín met López Pacheco's hate-filled eyes. "My dear *Count,*" he said, stressing the word unpleasantly, "haven't you realized yet that the *señorita* is an unusually intelligent woman? Don't you think that she would know that the very first person her parents would turn to would be her longtime tutor in whom she has always confided? If she truly wished to escape from you, do you think she would risk it by coming to me?" He smiled amiably. "I wish I knew where the girl was, for I would wish to know that she were safe, but I can tell you one thing, I am delighted she has had the intelligence and good judgment to escape from you."

"I am going to report what you just said to Don Rodrigo," López Pacheco threatened furiously.

"Shall we return there now?" Augustín's voice sliced like a razor. "I would welcome the opportunity to tell him exactly how I feel about this situation. Perhaps the time has come that he will realize that his daughter is more important than the mockery of a purchased title. He can buy a thousand more titles. Can he buy another daughter?"

"I have not lost yet!" López Pacheco said shrilly.

"Nor have you won yet," Augustín replied coldly, turning on his heel and striding away from the crimson-faced man whose fists clenched and unclenched at his sides.

Late that night, a cloak around his shoulders, Augustín slipped out the servants' entrance to the Colegio. He pressed himself against the wall and stayed there long moments motionlessly listening for any sounds, praying that if the peninsular were keeping an eye on the Colegio he was watching another door. When he heard no sounds in the darkness, he moved slowly and carefully along the wall keeping to the darkest shadows. When he was some distance from the Colegio, he picked up his pace and hurried quickly several blocks to where a mule that a small boy had rented for him stood tied.

When he arrived at the inn and left the mule in the stable, anxiety wound his nerves taut. He prayed that Antonia was safe and that she had not succumbed to the terrors of the previous day.

Doña Rosilda opened the door for him. She saw the concern on his face. "The boy is fine," she reassured him. "He must be quite young, no?" Augustín nodded. "Pobrecito," she said, "he cried most of the day, so the servants said."

"He is indeed a poor child, undergoing more travail than anyone his tender age should have to endure. I will go see him now."

"Perhaps you would like to take up a bit of food. The poor boy has scarcely touched any of his meals today."

"Yes, thank you."

Within moments Doña Rosilda returned with a cloth-covered tray for him. He was glad she did not accompany him upstairs.

The lamp on the bedside table flickered softly when he entered the room. Antonia lay in bed, her honey-colored hair in disarray on the pillow, her face turned toward the lamp. She was asleep, breathing softly, her lips slightly parted.

Augustín set the tray of food down and quietly moved a chair near. He sat looking at her, happy to see her face relaxed in sleep, showing none of the anguish he had seen on it the previous day. It was a beautiful face, finely boned, her skin like tawny velvet in the soft yellow lamplight. He drank in her beauty as if it were rich, old sherry—to be savored slowly. He felt himself relax and contentment envelop him.

He became aware of her smiling at him and whispering, "Augustín."

She lifted her head from the pillow, and he came to his feet and moved to sit on the edge of the bed beside her.

"Oh, Augustín," she said as she threw her arms around his waist and laid her head on his chest.

His arms encircled her. One hand went to her hair, stroking it gently, and the other touched her waist. He felt the softness and heat of her naked skin under his hand. They sat that way for long moments holding each other. He felt her breathing become deeper and uneven.

They sat apart and looked at one another. She clutched the covers to her. He tried to smile, but she was looking at him in that odd way she had the night before, her eyes wide and solemn. She took his hand and brought it to her cheek as she also had the night before and kissed it.

Her eyes searched his face and she swallowed. "I love you so much, Augustín. Please—I want to know what it is to be a woman."

There was a pause. Her voice trembled when she spoke again, and he could scarcely hear her. "Be my husband for tonight. Please, show me what it is to be a woman."

A strange look passed over his face, but he was perfectly still. "I love you more than life itself, Little One," he said, his voice low and husky.

She feared for an agonizing moment he was going to refuse her.

He pulled her toward him and covered her mouth with his own. The kiss was gentle at first, tasting, savoring, but then his tongue entered her parted lips, and the kiss became passionate, and his arms encircled her, pressing her body to him. She felt his hands caress her back and slip below her waist, and she shuddered with the sensation of it.

He pulled his lips from hers and looked at her, the passion in his eyes unmistakable. It was a look she had wanted to see for such an excruciating length of time. It was a look she never thought she would see.

"I have loved you for so long, Augustín, so long," she whispered, "and I have wanted to be yours—only yours."

"And you shall be," he said softly.

He pulled the covers away from her body and looked at her, his eyes smouldering with desire. She did not shrink from his gaze, but she could not keep the color from rising to her cheeks.

"*Dios mío*, you are beautiful," he murmured, "so very beautiful."

He had loved her since she was a child but had known that he desired her as a woman when he saw her for the first time after his year of solitude. He had missed her so that year—her happiness, her cleverness, her companionship—and then he returned and saw she had become a woman, beautiful beyond a poet's words.

He knew then that he desired her from somewhere deep within where the mind can never touch nor rule, but he had kept that desire hidden from all of himself save that most interior part of his soul that knew the truth. He continued to love her as he always had; she was the most cherished thing in his life, but he did not allow his desire any expression. Instead, he encapsulated it within him like a treasured, safely hidden jewel.

But somehow even the night before, he had known this was going to happen. He had known when he talked to López Pacheco that the peninsular would never be the one to possess the body of the lovely Antonia. He had known *he* would be the one.

It was meant to be. She was his just as surely as if she were his wife, and he was meant to be the man to show her what it meant to be a woman, to show her what the love of a man was, to show her how much he loved *her*. He reached out and touched her breasts, caressing them.

She touched his hand. "I want you so much I hurt inside," she whispered.

"And I, you," he murmured. "It has been the most exquisite torture I have ever known."

He pulled her into his arms and bent his head and let his mouth taste her hard-tipped breasts, tugging gently at them. Tiny sounds of pleasure came from her throat, and her body arched. His hand moved down over her belly, and she shivered with the caress.

"*Dios* how I want you!" He came to his feet, cradling her naked body in his arms, kissing her on the mouth as if he could not get enough of her. Then he laid her on the bed and stood looking down at her. For a brief, horrible moment she thought he had recanted.

But his fingers descended the long row of buttons of his cassock, and within moments he stood before her, naked.

"*You* are beautiful," she murmured as he came to her. "You are my Huitzilopochtli of whom I have dreamed since I was little. Oh, Augustín," she whispered softly, embracing him, her hands moving gently over the skin of his shoulders and down his back as her body pressed against him, "make me yours."

He took her face in his hands and lightly covered it with kisses, and his lips and hands discovered every inch of her body. And then something happened. It began in her belly, a red sun sending its fiery particles along her nerves to every corner of her being, feeling as if it illuminated her entire body with its fire. Her breathing came in small ragged gasps, and he lowered his mouth to hers in a tender kiss.

"Please," she begged, "please," as she clutched at him. "I want you so much, Augustín. I can endure no more."

His eyes burned with passion. Slowly he lowered himself over her, covering her mouth with his to stifle the cry she might make. Carefully, gently, he wanted to love her but could no longer control himself, and although he had wanted to be gentle with her, he was unable, and later he felt the wetness of her tears.

"I am so sorry, *amor*," he whispered, "I did not mean to hurt you."

"I do not cry from pain but from the love I feel for you," she said. "It was wonderful, more wonderful than anything I had ever imagined. To know your love is a joy that makes me cry."

As he urged the mule to a trot in the cool predawn air, Augustín could still feel the warmth of her body as if she were there with him.

"Thank you, Lord," he prayed, as the mule trotted through the cobble-stone-paved streets, "thank you for allowing me to love the woman Antonia. You knew our souls had been joined for a long time, did you not? And now we have known the joy of the union of our bodies. What a beautiful gift you have given your children, *Dios*, the love between a man and a woman."

He felt no guilt, no sin. As he had lain there in bed with her cradled in his arms, he had told her what he fully believed. "God in his graciousness has given us this love, Antonia. Something so beautiful could only be a gift from Our Creator. He has loved us enough to give us each other so that we might truly know the extent of *his* love."

"Oh, *mi amor*," Antonia had whispered to him, touching his cheek. "Every day in my prayers I shall thank him for the joy he granted me through you. For the rest of my life I will remember the love we shared, and I will never be lonely knowing that *Dios* let you be my husband."

He kissed her then. "For a week we will be husband and wife," he murmured. "It is a few mere days, but it shall be our eternity."

"Yes." She turned and offered herself to him, and he was a husband to her once more.

Augustín's sole worry was whether Don Rodrigo's agents might find her, but that evening when he visited the Salvatierra house, he was relieved to find that they had not the slightest shred of information concerning their daughter's whereabouts. He prayed fervently with them for her well-being, but the moments passed agonizingly for him because the only thing he could think of was returning to her.

He felt like a bridegroom, euphoric in his knowledge of himself as a man and in the knowledge that he was loved by a woman. Concealing his joy was one of the most difficult tasks he had ever faced.

He was coldly polite to López Pacheco, keeping his contempt in check.

The peninsular sensed there was something different about the Jesuit, although he could not determine what it was. There was a kind of absolute self-assurance about him; he seemed to wear a cloak of invincibility. He hated him more intensely than he had previously—hated the handsomeness of the Jesuit's face and the perfection of his physical person, which was accentuated by the simple form-fitting black cassock he wore. He hated his erudition and education, his aloof superiority—hated the fact that the girl obviously worshiped him and that the rest of the family were not far behind. But most of all, he hated that intangible something about the Jesuit that said he was a man in every sense of the word.

He did not want to believe that the Jesuit did not know where the girl was, but the *padre* was right, it would have been foolish for her to have gone to him. López Pacheco did believe, however, that the priest knew somehow she was safe. But how could both be true? He decided to be patient. Time would certainly unravel the mystery, and he would not miss another good dinner trying to get information out of the clever Jesuit. Eventually the *padre* would have to play his hand if he had a hand to play.

Augustín was relieved that he could depart the Salvatierra house alone. He did not wish to have to engage in conversation with the peninsular. The phony "count" might have been uneducated but he was a scheming, clever man. Augustín was quite certain that López Pacheco believed the former tutor knew the whereabouts of the girl.

Augustín wanted to rush immediately to Antonia so that they might have a few more precious hours together, but he knew he must exercise caution. When he could wait no longer, he slipped out the servants' entrance. He took a much more circuitous route through the city than he had taken before, seeking to discover if he were being followed. He tried to remember some of the things his grandfather had taught him about stealth. At no point did he have any evidence that he was being followed, but nonetheless he waited for half an hour listening and watching before he led the mule into the stable of the inn.

Again it was Doña Rosilda who opened the door for him. "Good evening, *Padre*," she said as he stepped inside.

"Good evening, *Señora*. How have things been?"

"The girl is fine," she whispered. "They did not find her."

Augustín steeled himself so that he would not tremble with the fear that congealed his blood. He tried to control his voice, but his words came out in a harsh whisper.

"What did you say?"

Doña Rosilda put her hand on his arm and with the other she clutched the crucifix that hung around her neck. "By the Almighty and the Sweet Virgin, I swear that I told them nothing and that they do not know she is here. As the Lord is my witness, I swear that no word will ever cross my lips of anything that has happened here."

She brought the crucifix to her lips and kissed it, sealing the vow she had made. She saw the anxiety on Augustín's face.

"Come, *Padre*," she said, "sit down a minute, have a cup of chocolate and let me explain."

Augustín nodded weakly and walked to the chair to which she made a motion with her hand. He sank down on it, covering his eyes with his hand as she went to get the hot chocolate. Within moments she returned.

She pulled a chair close. "They came this morning, two men, looking for a young girl with honey-colored hair. I saw them ride up, and I knew what they had come for. I rushed upstairs and told the girl. She was terror stricken. I hid her in a closet in case they insisted on looking in the rooms. Then I went back down to entertain them so they might not talk too much to any of the servants and hear about a young 'boy' who had appeared here the night the girl disappeared. They had a meal with plenty of wine, but they wanted to check the rooms anyway. I was afraid, but I was also afraid not to let them.

"Once they were satisfied the rooms held no girl, they left, but not before giving me a notice to post offering a substantial reward for her. I threw the thing in the fire after they had gone. I am quite certain they will not be back. I waited until they were well away before I went upstairs to her."

She paused. "I'm sorry, Father, and yet I'm not," she said, putting her hand on his arm. "But I knew that first night that it was not a young boy you had brought here. I knew by the look on your face it was a woman and that you loved her. I do not judge, Father. Priests are men just like other men — taking the cloth does not take their manhood away."

Augustín nodded weakly, and Doña Rosilda continued. "I was afraid the servants might suspect, also, so I have been the only one to see to her needs. Besides, a woman needs another woman to talk to, particularly after her first time." She smiled slyly.

She paused and her face became serious. "The girl loves you deeply, *Padre*. She told me the whole terrible story of what has happened to her and that you are going to slip her into a convent when it is safe to do so." She put her hand on his arm. "This place is at your disposal for however long you may want it."

"Thank you, Doña Rosilda," Augustín said, his gratitude apparent in his eyes.

"Come," she said, "do not waste any more time here. Your young wife awaits you upstairs."

Antonia was kneeling beside the bed praying when he opened the door.

Her head flew up at the faint sound, and her face was bathed in joy at seeing him. His chest constricted with the love he felt for her and the horror of the possibility that she might have been found that day.

She ran to him, and he saw that her long, free-flowing hair had been freshly brushed and that she wore a simple, embroidered nightgown, undoubtedly loaned to her by Doña Rosilda. When she reached him, he scooped her up into his arms, cradling her, and he covered her mouth with a passionate kiss.

"Oh, *mi amor*," he breathed, "how I have missed you today."

Her words rushed out, "Doña Rosilda knows about us, Augustín, and two men were here today looking for me."

He kissed her on the forehead. "Yes, I know," he answered. "She told me everything down below. It seems she has become our protectress."

The smile returned to Antonia's face. "She has taken it upon herself to see we have a proper honeymoon." She motioned to her gown. "She gave me this to wear, saying a partially clad woman is more enticing to a man than a naked one."

Augustín laughed. "I'm not sure I agree. When I remember how you looked last night, I cannot imagine anything ever exciting more desire in me than the sight of your naked body."

Color rose to her cheeks, but she was filled with a deep happiness at hearing him express his desire for her. "Look," she said, pointing to the bed, "she even brought new embroidered sheets for us, and a bottle of wine, and look at the flowers."

Doña Rosilda had indeed made the room look like a honeymoon bower. A new brightly colored bedspread graced the bed, a tray of sweetmeats sat by the bottle of wine, a lovely candelabra had replaced the serviceable bed lamp, and bright cerise and white flowers perfumed the room.

"She has been so good to me," Antonia whispered, her arms around his neck, "I almost feel like a cherished daughter."

He saw the sadness in her eyes and knew she was thinking of her own parents whom she felt could not possibly love her after what they had done.

"I am grateful that Doña Rosilda has been so kind to you, *querida*," he said, setting her on the bed and sitting down next to her, "but I want you to know that your parents do love you in spite of what has happened."

"Yes, I think they do—in their way. But they no longer have any meaning for me. I love them because they are my parents."

She looked at Augustín straightforwardly. "They have simply died for me. I have accepted it, and it has given me the future I wanted and that I welcome. It is best this way, really, for now I am free to carry on and live what life has in store for me."

She touched his cheek. "At some point, a child must break away from its parents—that is all I have done, but I choose to retain only the memory of them—the happy memories of my childhood. I care no more about the past. I feel an enormous sense of freedom. Augustín, I welcome the cloister and the taking of the veil. I can now devote my life to study, and I will truly have more freedom inside a convent than out."

He kissed her tenderly on the lips. "My heart has been relieved of a great burden hearing your words. I am glad that the unhappiness of this awful situation is not making you suffer unbearably. My deepest desire is for your happiness."

She touched his cheek again. "Last night you gave me everything I have ever wanted. I am content. I shall never want for more, for I have had the most precious thing in the world and that is your love."

"You want no more?" he asked with a smile.

She laughed lightly and lay back on the bed. "Yes, I want more. Do you?"

"*Dios*," he laughed, "it is the only thing I have been able to think about today."

Chapter 19

Two weeks passed. "I think it is safe now. Everything is arranged." Augustín's eyes were full of anguish and passion. He pulled her against him fiercely, kissing her voraciously, and then he pulled her gown from her and ripped off his own clothes. He took her wildly, and she responded with the same intensity. When he lay quiet, he clutched her tightly.

"I cannot get enough of you," he whispered hoarsely. "How can I bear to lose you?"

"You will never lose me, for I am yours. You have my heart and soul; they will always be with you. We can never be separated, Augustín. During the day when you are gone, I am not alone, for I know you are with me just as surely as you are with me now."

"That is true," Augustín replied quietly as he rolled to the side, pulling her tightly against him. "But I want your physical body. I need your physical body—it has been like sustenance to me."

"This love has been a gift of *Dios*, Augustín, you yourself said it."

He kissed her on the mouth.

He held her against his chest, and she heard his voice catch as he spoke. "I've made arrangements for you at Santa Catalina de Sena."

She fought a sob that threatened to burst forth but managed to whisper, "I know I shall be happy there."

They were silent for long moments.

"It is one of the best convents," he said, and she was aware that he was trying to make his voice sound enthusiastic, "not as harshly rigid as some, such as the Descalzas, and not as lax as Jesús María, with all its servants. You will be able to have your own small room with all the books you desire, and a dowry shall not be necessary. If a girl has mathematical or other skills, they waive the dowry because she will be an asset to the convent. You are well prepared in mathematics and *contadera* of the convent should prove very easy for you. The bookkeeping might even turn out to be rather interesting. The convent has many assets and varied property that bring in revenue; it could prove to be interesting to deal with it all."

She nodded and he continued. "The Mother Superior took a solemn vow that she will never, under any circumstances whatever, give you back to your father or let it be known that you are at the convent. Eventually perhaps, your parents may find that you are there, but then it will be too late. You will be known simply as María, a penniless but intelligent girl from a small town to the north. The Mother Superior did not think that you would know any of the novices, and the older nuns who have been cloistered for some years, even if they knew you as a child will probably not recognize you as a woman.

"I am fully confident, Little One," he went on, "that no amount of money will sway the Mother Superior, for she took a vow that she would suffer perpetual excommunication and eternal damnation if she ever released you to your parents." He paused and looked at her, and she saw the torment in his eyes.

"I am also a confessor for the convent," he said, caressing her cheek with his fingers. "At least I will be able to talk with you occasionally."

"*Gracias a Diós,*" she murmured.

"There is one other thing that I think shall make your life at Santa Catalina more pleasant. There is a young woman there, Sister Sophía, the *portera*, whom I think you will truly enjoy as a sister. She is extremely bright and shares your love of books. I told her about you—although she thinks you are penniless María—and she is joyful to have you coming and to have someone who shares her interests. She will be a good friend to you, I know, and you should not feel so lonely at first."

Antonia's face shone with happiness. "I would love to have a sister who likes the things that I like."

"As the *portera*, she holds the keys to the doors, so she will be the one to let you in, the one you will meet first."

She put her arms around his neck and kissed him on the lips. "Thank you, *mi amor*," she whispered, "thank you for making these arrangements for me. You have truly saved my life."

She kissed him again, long and lovingly. "And thank you for making me a woman, for loving me and showing me the joy that is possible between a man and a woman. I am content; I am more than content. I have such happiness that it will last me for as long as I am of this world and will surely follow me into the next where our souls will once more be together, joined as husband and wife."

She laid her head on his chest as he held her tightly against him. "When do we leave?"

His voice was ragged when he spoke. "Within an hour or two."

No more words were spoken, and afterward they lay weak and trembling in each other's arms, and their tears bathed their faces.

She dressed in the simple garment Doña Rosilda had secured for her. When they were ready to go, he pulled her fiercely into his arms and kissed her, his mouth bruising hers. She felt the hardness as he pressed her hips tightly against him.

She did not want him to stop, but she could not bear the thought of him wanting her so much, and for a fleeting, horrible second she thought she could not endure never again knowing his lovemaking.

She pushed herself from his arms and ran out the door and down the stairs, her tears blinding her, for she knew that had she stayed longer, she would never have been able to leave. She would have begged him to set her up as his mistress and come to her each day. That was what she wanted, but she would never do that to him. She could not let him ruin his life over her, just to satisfy the craving of her own body and soul.

He caught up with her outside and pulled her into his arms. This time he held her gently.

"Don't cry. I cannot bear to witness your unhappiness. Forgive me, please. We will go to the convent now."

She dried her eyes, unable to speak. He brought the mules from the stable and before he lifted her onto hers, he kissed her tenderly on the lips. "How very much I love you," he whispered.

"Augustín," she said and could manage no more.

They rode in silence through the dark streets, the clopping of the mule's hooves sounding loud and hollow in their ears, making their nerves taut, renewing the fear that they had known the night of their flight. The minutes passed with agony. Time was like a black tunnel that knew no end, and she was unable to stop her trembling. Terror held her in its ravening claws, and any noise made her want to scream as she envisioned the ugly, white, bloated face of López Pacheco ready to leap out of the blackness at her. She tried to will the fear to leave, but it would not. She jerked with fright when Augustín whispered to her.

"There it is, up ahead."

In the darkness she could faintly make out the façade. They had reached the convent safely. She sighed audibly with relief, feeling the tension that had wound her body in a coil relax its twisting grip.

Augustín dismounted and lifted her off her mule. He took the crucifix from around his neck and slipped it over her head. "It is my wedding gift to you, Little One."

She kissed the cross. "Thank you, Augustín. I shall cherish it always."

She fumbled in the pocket of her dress. "I, too, have a gift for you."

She placed something smooth and satiny in his hand, and he fingered it, not knowing in the darkness what it was. "I asked Doña Rosilda for a piece of silk—I had nothing to give you—it is a bookmark I embroidered for you so that when you read, you will remember me."

He kissed her on the lips. "You will never be out of my thoughts, *ever*."

The key turned in the lock and there were whispers, and then the door was relocked. It had only taken a few moments, but her life was irrevocably changed.

This is my path, she thought to herself when the door closed, shutting out everything of her past, including the previous two weeks. *I shall tread the path of my life with contentment. I am ready to accept whatever you have willed for me, Dios.*

The days passed and Augustín tried to renew his life. Teaching, however, no longer held the joy for him it once had. He no longer went to the Salvatierra house; he could not endure the memories it rekindled nor the emotion it caused in him. López Pacheco no longer frequented the house.

When it became clear as the weeks passed that the girl would not be found, the peninsular moved on. Augustín had heard he was now courting the daughter of another wealthy Creole family.

María Luisa wore black in mourning for the daughter she thought was dead. Don Rodrigo suddenly seemed like an old man. Remorse gnawed away at his ambition, and he was filled with bitterness. They both asked Augustín to visit them as often as he could because his presence was comforting, but he could not bring himself to go there more than once or twice. He asked Antonia if he could now tell her parents where she was.

"No," she whispered softly through the grate of the confessional, "not yet, not until I have said my final vows."

He lived for the weekly visits he made to the convent. He found himself scarcely listening to the confessions, impatient to hear the one soft voice he waited for.

They would touch their lips to the grate that separated them, and they would call each other "husband" and "wife," and they would whisper their love, but that night he would kneel in his small room at the Colegio, tears would trickle down his cheeks, and he would rise only when the light of dawn appeared, his legs stiff and sore. His prayers throughout the entire night were simple and always the same.

I love her, Dios. *Please help me. I don't know how to carry on without her. Show me what you want of me, and let me do your will, whatever it is.*

He was grateful for the contentment she had found in the convent. He thanked God that she was safe and that she had found happiness with the sisters of Santa Catalina. He could have talked to her for hours in the confessional, but they had only a very few minutes. She would tell him of her friendship with Sister Sophía, that she had time to devote to reading, that life away from the cares of the world eased one's spirit, that she was very happy. Augustín's only happiness was the knowledge of hers.

The weeks became a month, then two. The message one night from Sister Sophía to come to the convent startled Augustín and filled him with a heart-stopping terror. The note said it concerned "María," but it said nothing more. He ran the entire distance from the Colegio to the convent.

He tried to quiet his breathing when Sister Sophía opened the door.

"What is the matter?" he asked in a raspy whisper.

She put her hand gently on his arm in reassurance and led him to a secluded corner. "Father, I promised her I would not tell you, but I decided I must. María," she corrected herself, "Antonia is with child."

He leaned back against the cold stone wall as shockwaves coursed through his body. His immediate reaction of horror was quickly suffocated by one of pride. She had his baby within her.

He felt Sister Sophía's hand on his arm and became aware she was speaking. "Antonia became so pale and ate so little, I was becoming worried. Twice I found her losing her breakfast. I began to watch her more carefully and suddenly I knew what the matter was. When I confronted her with the knowledge, she broke down and cried and told me everything. She spared nothing, Father.

"She told me that for two weeks you were husband and wife and that she has loved you since she was a little girl. She also said that the entire blame was hers because she had begged you to make her a woman, and because the blame was hers, the consequences were hers and that you should not be told. She said she could not ruin your life with this knowledge.

"She is preparing to leave the convent and to go to some village where she is not known to raise the child there in secret. But, Father, I am so worried," Sister Sophía whispered. "A young woman alone, penniless, and pregnant, traveling roads filled with all manner of society's dregs. She has no money to buy food nor lodging—she said she would never take a penny from her parents, much less let them know she was alive. I had to break my promise, Father, I could not let her do this. She said you loved her too much to be told, but if you do love her, Father, then I thought you *must* know."

"I love her more than anything in this world," Augustín said in a hoarse whisper.

"Then stop her, Father."

Sister Sophía put her hand on his arm again. "Antonia said your love was a gift of God. Perhaps the child is a gift of God, also."

Suddenly Augustín knew what he would do. "Yes," he whispered, "the child *is* a gift of God. He gave Antonia to me as my wife, and now he gives me a child." He crossed himself. "Sister, I will take Antonia from the convent and care for her and our child."

"I don't think she will go with you," the sister said. "It would mean the ruin of your career—you could no longer be a priest, you would be an outcast. She would not allow that."

"But I love her. I want her as my wife, and I want my child. It is clear that *Dios* does not want me as a priest. His plans are other. Surely the love I feel for her comes from God—it could come from no one else. Sister, please, help me."

There was a silence before she spoke. "Perhaps you are right. I have seen the love on Antonia's face when she speaks of you, and it is beautiful. God works in ways man cannot sometimes understand. The love between you and the woman obviously should not be, but is. I do not understand, but perhaps it is right."

"How can I convince her to come with me?" Augustín asked. "How can I convince her that I was not meant to be a priest?"

"I think the decision must not be hers," she said. "I could allow her to slip out of the convent as she wishes, not knowing, however, that you are waiting for her. Once together, I think she could not leave you." Sister Sophía paused. "Father, do you fully realize what this means?"

"It means that I can never set foot in Mexico City again. It means that should the Inquisition ever learn what I have done, I shall be brought before the Tribunal and no mercy will be shown. It means that the rest of my life will have to be led in secrecy and lies. But it does not matter. God is gracious. If this is his will, then he will provide."

"I will tell her I will help her slip out of the convent," Sister Sophía said. "I am sure she will want to talk to you one last time at confession. That night I will open the door for her. May God be with you."

Chapter 20

He heard the door as it creaked open, and then a hooded figure emerged onto the street. He grabbed her quickly, covering her mouth with his hand to stifle her cry of fear, and then he kissed her with passion.

"No," she sobbed, "no. For the love of God, no, Augustín."

"Yes," he said forcefully. "Yes."

He picked her up in his arms and carried her to where the mules were waiting in an alley, and he covered her face with kisses and ran his hand lovingly over her still flat belly. She clung to him.

"You are my wife," he said, "you are carrying my child. That is all that matters. We are going away together."

She did not protest as he helped her mount. They rode in silence all night and at dawn she knew they were going north. They had a little bread and cheese for breakfast as they traveled, but it was not until they stopped later for lunch that they finally talked.

"I could not let you go alone," he said. "Sister Sophía feared for you and told me of your plan. You carry our child—I could not let you go alone. You are my wife; I love you. It is clear *Dios* has sanctioned this union and given us a great blessing. His will is that we love each other."

"I do love you, Augustín, and my greatest joy is that you are taking me away and that we will be together. But I am not deserving of your sacrifice."

"There is no sacrifice," he said as he took her face in his hands. "When I put you in the convent, all joy drained from my life, leaving me completely hollow. I asked *Dios* to help me, to show me his will, and he has shown me a village perched on a high rock. We go to Áco, where I was born, to live as man and wife."

❖　　❖　　❖

They traveled north toward Querétaro, paralleling the main route but staying well away from the road so that they would not be seen by whatever travelers might be headed in either direction. The greater the distance they could place between themselves and the viceregal capital, the safer they would be from the authorities, but the farther north they went, the more other dangers would lie in wait for them.

Augustín had secured three mules, two to ride and one on which he had packed what necessities he could: several woolen blankets, a large piece of frieze, which would offer a little protection from the rain, some extra clothing, a bag of parched corn ground into meal, some hard cheese, jerked meat, dry beans and tortillas, a couple of wineskins that could carry water, several knives, a hatchet and a small iron pot, along with a few other items. The two sacks of provisions Sister Sophía had managed to obtain for Antonia they tied onto the mule she rode.

They would seek no lodging or food until their own provisions gave out, for he feared the possibility that they might be hunted. Although his absence would be noted at the Colegio Máximo and the Casa Profesa, for the first few days no one would make serious inquiries, assuming someone else's emergency was keeping him occupied. It would be a week before the Mother Superior of the convent knew he was gone, when he did not appear for confession, and that the tentacles of the Inquisition had wound their way into all the nooks and crannies of the land.

He had no fear Sister Sophía would betray them, but what would the Mother Superior do when she found that the girl she had sworn to keep safe was gone — and then learned that the very man who brought her there had also disappeared? Augustín assumed she would guess the truth and hoped she would say nothing. She was a kind, saintly woman; he prayed she would not voice any suspicions she might have and deliver them into the clutches of the Inquisition, but nonetheless he took every care that they would not be noticed.

They made Querétaro in a little over a week, but they would skirt the city that had been founded by Otomí Indians and that now was a headquarters for Franciscan missionary efforts. They looked down at the city lying in the valley and could make out the dome of the Iglesia de San Francisco. Antonia slipped her hand into his and he squeezed it. There would not be many more such sights of civilization.

They pushed on north and found some thermal springs where they stopped for a day to rest and bathe in the healing waters and to allow the mules a day of rest and grazing.

Antonia washed their clothing and laid it out to dry, and naked, they made love in the warm water.

He caressed her breasts and touched her wet hair. "I thought I would surely perish when you entered the convent and the door closed behind you.

I had no idea how inextricably a part of me you had become. I could not think, I could scarcely act. I could have been of service to no one. It was as if you were my vital force, the spark that gave me breath."

She took his hand and kissed it. "Since I was young the only thing I ever remember looking forward to was being with you. This past week has been the most exciting of my life." She sat up and spread her arms at their surroundings. "This is an adventure—like we are on a quest. We travel through fascinating countryside, sleep under the stars, share our food. It is as if we are living the pages of a book." She laughed. "You are Don Quijote and I may be Dulcinea for now, but before long I will be Sancho Panza!" She made a motion with her hand to indicate an enormous stomach.

He smiled, trying to hide his concern. So far their flight had been much easier than he had expected, but he knew that with every league they traveled farther from the capital, the journey would become more difficult. The closer they got to the silver mines of the north, the more they were in danger of encountering the brigands who preyed mercilessly on whoever might cross their path. And just last year the Tarahumara had risen and killed two Franciscan missionaries, a Jesuit and some soldiers. The governor of Durango was ordered to establish a presidio at Papigochi to try to put a stop to the depredations.

She may have sensed his worry because she became serious. "I know we face grave difficulties ahead—and months of travel. We have all the wastes of New Spain to cross before we even reach the province of *Nuevo México*. I know, too, that we will be lucky to reach Áco before the baby is born, and I would not be honest if I told you that I am not terrified of that eventuality. But I am strong. I promise you, Augustín, I am strong. Don't keep your worries from me. I need to know what to expect so I *can* be strong."

"I knew you had strength when you were only eight years old." He pulled her to him. "When we leave the *bajío* and start climbing toward the *meseta central* and the Sierra Madre, travel is going to get much more difficult. The wastelands at San Luís Potosí and Zacatecas are steep and bare and studded with cactus, agave, and thorny *huisaches*. The land was formidable to me as a boy, even though I came from the desert of *Nuevo México*."

"Then it sounds as if we must be careful with our water," she said.

South of Potosí they saw a long silver train weaving its way down the main road like a segmented snake heading for the capital. The heavily laden *carretas* squealed and groaned, the strident sounds carrying across the countryside for miles. A large mounted escort of soldiers rode flanking the wooden carts with their precious cargo.

Augustín and Antonia had been traveling for six weeks. The terrain became much more difficult and some days they were able to make only half or as little as a third the distance they had in the *bajío*.

They had run short of water at one point and the only thing that had saved them from perishing from thirst was an agave plant whose heart Augustín had pierced with a knife, creating a spring of honey water that they drank greedily. The sweet-sour juice was nourishing as well as thirst quenching and helped give them a little added strength.

They were filthy, covered with a gray dust from head to toe, the thermal springs where they had bathed earlier in their trip a distant memory.

He saw that Antonia's face was growing thin and drawn and when he lifted her hand to place a kiss in the palm, his lips felt the rough calluses that holding reins all day, day after day, had raised on what had once been soft skin. She had never complained, but she made no more mention of their journey being an adventure, and he tried to submerge the growing guilt he felt for putting her through this.

When they passed near a village of natives, Augustín insisted they stop to see if they could not buy a little food. He found a person who understood Nahuatl and they were able to purchase a few provisions with a little of the money Sister Sophía had taken from the coffers of the convent to give Antonia. She had not wanted to take the money for fear Sister Sophía could get in trouble, but the *portera* had insisted.

"Ask my father for a donation then," Antonia had said. "He is generous. I know he will give you enough to cover what you have given me. If you have to, tell him you had a dream about me and that I am happy. I am sure he will give you a donation to pray for me. I can't bear the thought that you might suffer on my account if they find out about this."

Their provisions were dwindling again and the November nights were getting colder as the elevation rose. Each morning they were both shivering beneath all the blankets they had. Augustín wrapped her in his arms, trying to share his warmth, but he knew it was not enough. Their only remaining food was parched ground corn that they stirred into boiling water to make a kind of mush.

"I think we must begin to seek night lodging," he said.

Alarm crossed her face. "But it's dangerous, isn't it, to take a chance on people seeing us?"

"No one in Mexico City knows in which direction we have gone. It's unlikely anyone even knows that we are together. We are climbing higher and higher and it is going to get even colder as winter approaches.

"We will seek outlying *haciendas*. A priest can always find food and lodging in any home, especially one far from city or village. News is a scarce commodity—that's why I think we will be safe—and every *hacienda* gives freely of its hospitality for any scrap of information from the outside world. Priests are especially welcome for they can hear confessions, baptize children, and say Mass for a family that may have been without the sacrament for months."

"Don't you think they will question what you are doing in this remote region?"

"I will tell them I'm on my way north to work among the Tarahumara since I speak their language. And for you, we will employ the same guise we used with Doña Rosilda. You will be my *donado* traveling with me. Priests often have servant boys who accompany and assist them—no one will think your presence unusual." He nodded at the pack mule. "I brought a habit for you, thinking it might prove useful."

A frown crossed her face, but he continued. "When we see an *hacienda,* we will wait until dark to approach. Then I will get you to a room as quickly as possible, saying you are not feeling well, and you can stay secluded there until we leave. In that way they will not know you are a woman."

"What if they see through it as doña Rosilda did?" she asked.

"Do not worry, *querida,*" he reassured her, "they will be more gullible away from civilization."

They were somewhere in the environs of Zacatecas. The rough terrain dictated that they had to travel closer to the road. It was more risky taking a chance on one of the mules coming up lame in the mountains than meeting someone on the road. In the early afternoon they heard a bell peal.

"Where is that coming from?" Antonia asked.

"If we are lucky, we may be near an *hacienda*. Rich *hacendados* always ring a bell at mealtime inviting any traveler on the road to eat with them. They say that when Don Juan de Oñate lived in Zacatecas—before he conquered *Nuevo México*—he always had the most lavishly spread table and treated every traveler as if they did him great honor by partaking food with him. If we are near an *hacienda,* I think it best we wait until dark to approach."

They came to the top of a rise and saw the compound down below.

"Let's rest in those rocks until the sun goes down," Augustín said, pointing to an outcropping.

He took one of the bedrolls from the mule and spread it on the ground. Antonia was going through one of the packs on the mule.

"Come," he said. "Let's rest a while."

"I'll be back in a minute," she said. "I need to make a nature call." She walked between the rocks until she was out of sight.

After a while when she had not returned, he began to worry and called out, "Antonia?"

"I'm coming."

She stepped around a boulder and he gasped. "No!"

The long, dark honey-colored hair he loved to sink his fingers in was gone, and all that remained was a short cap of ragged curls. She might have been a young Greek boy from the Hellenic age.

"Antonia!" he whispered sorrowfully and took her in his arms.

She smiled at him. "It will grow back."

She put the knife she had used to cut her hair back in the pack on the mule. "Where is the habit you brought for me?" she asked as she took off her outer clothing and then ripped a wide strip of fabric from the bottom of an under petticoat. She wound the strip of cloth around her chest, flattening her breasts. Her waist had begun to thicken with the baby, but the loose habit would hide evidence of her pregnancy.

He handed her the habit and she smiled at him again because he looked so sorrowful.

"Let's not wait," she said. "Maybe there will be some food left. I'm starving."

Augustín put on his cassock, which he had not worn since Mexico City, and they started toward the *hacienda*.

They were spotted by a servant, and by the time they reached the walled compound, several people had come out to greet them, including a distinguished-looking silver-haired man.

"Don Bernardo de Ibarra at your service," he said. "You do us honor, *Padre*, to visit our humble home."

"*Gracias*, Señor Ibarra, but it is we who are honored," Augustín said, dismounting from the mule. Antonia did likewise.

Ibarra snapped his fingers and two servants immediately came forward, took the mules by the bridles and led them away.

"I am Padre Juan Sánchez," Augustín said, "and this is my *donado* Antonio. We are on our way north to minister among the Tarahumara."

The look on the *hacendado*'s face gave clear evidence that he did not think that was a wise idea, but he said, "Welcome, please come in. I hope that you will be our guests for as long as you like. You have a difficult journey ahead of you."

They entered the thick-walled compound, crossed a large open space and were ushered through heavy doors into the *hacienda*'s main house.

"A servant will show you to your room," Ibarra said, "and when you have had a chance to rest and freshen up, please join me later for dinner in the dining room. I will have a *criada* bring you something to eat in the meantime."

"Thank you for your kindness," Augustín said, and Antonia murmured a soft *gracias*.

They were led across an interior patio that had several fruit trees growing in it along with plants and herbs.

Servants with trays of food, pitchers of water, and one with an iron pot of steaming water scurried into the room in front of them.

Antonia's eyes widened when she stepped into the large bedroom. An ornately carved bed with an embroidered coverlet dominated the center and woven rugs covered most of the floor. A servant knelt at a fireplace in the corner of the room, lighting the kindling beneath several logs.

Once the fire was going and the servants had left the room, closing the door behind them, Augustín pulled Antonia into his arms. "Now aren't you glad I said we should stop?"

"I admit, it will be wonderful to sleep in a real bed. But what will they think about us sleeping together?"

"Nothing, I imagine. In many travelers' inns people who don't even know each other have to sleep together in the same bed—as long as they are of the same sex." He ran his hand down her back. "And here they don't know we aren't!"

They bathed with the warm water, hungrily ate the food left for them, crawled under the warm covers, and later fell asleep in each other's arms.

"I feel very refreshed after my long siesta this afternoon, Don Bernardo," Augustín said as they sat at the long dining table, eating supper. "I would gladly hear confession this evening for anyone on the *hacienda* who would like it, and tomorrow I will say Mass."

"That is generous of you, Father, we have been without the sacraments for nearly a year. But I warn you, you may be up late—there are many workers and I imagine most will have committed some *pecado* for which they wish to be forgiven."

"Are there any other sacraments that I could offer? Baptism, perhaps?" Augustín asked.

"*Sí, Padre,* there have been a couple of babies born to servant women. They will certainly wish for Holy Baptism for their infants. I, personally, would like for you to offer a Mass for the soul of my dear wife who died last year and for my only child who died quite some time ago." The *hacendado* looked at Antonia, and his eyes misted. "He was not much older than your *donado* when the horse threw him."

Like most isolated *haciendas,* this one had its own small chapel, and during dinner Ibarra sent a servant to tell all the workers that the new guest would hear confession in the *capilla.*

A long line had formed at the door of the chapel by the time Augustín, Ibarra, and Antonia arrived. Antonia entered the back pew and knelt while Augustín went to the front of the chapel where there was a chair placed on one side of a small screen. Don Bernardo knelt on the other side, the first to offer his confession. When he was finished, he rose and went to kneel in one of the front pews while the next person knelt at the screen to receive absolution for whatever transgression he might confess.

After praying, Don Bernardo rose and left the chapel, and as the pews began to fill with the people praying their penances, Antonia also rose, deciding to wait for Augustín in their room.

As she walked down the hall, Don Bernardo stepped out of the *sala.*

"Antonito," he said to her, "would you do me the honor of joining me for a few moments of conversation while the *padre* finishes with the confessions?"

She looked down at the floor. She had scarcely spoken since they arrived. How was she going to carry on a conversation without giving herself away?

"Please," he said, motioning to the room, "join me for just a moment. Do an old man a kindness. There are no young people about. My son has been dead for twenty years and yet it might be yesterday for the pain I still feel. Please."

She nodded and reluctantly entered the room.

He motioned to a chair. "Would you like a cup of hot chocolate, some *atole* perhaps?"

She shook her head and Don Bernardo took a chair as she sat down on the edge of hers, eyes downcast.

"Tell me about yourself," he said pleasantly. "Where were you born? How did you come to serve the *padre*?"

She thought madly for what to say. "I was born in the capital," she said hesitantly, her voice scarcely more than a whisper. "My parents died. I was an orphan and the Jesuits took me in." She swallowed. "Padre . . . Padre Juan was kind to me so I asked to be his helper to repay his kindness."

"Are you studying to become a priest like the *padre*?" Don Bernardo asked.

She shook her head. "I just want to be of assistance to him."

"You remind me of my son," the man said. "The color of your hair is somewhat similar, although his was a little darker, and you're about the same height." He laughed. "But he was not nearly so quiet! The house was filled with noise when he was alive."

There was a long pause as she sat with her eyes staring at her hands, which rested in her lap. She heard a slight noise and looked up.

The *hacendado* wiped his eyes. "Forgive me, you have brought back the memory of him. Please forgive me."

"I am so sorry for your loss, Don Bernardo," she said with compassion.

"Thank you," he said, composing himself. "Please forgive me for burdening you with my own sorrow. I'm afraid I am not being a very good host." He rose. "Thank you, Antonio, for your company."

Some time later Augustín returned to the room, and she woke as he slipped into bed. She rolled toward him and he pulled her into his arms and kissed her on the temple.

"I hope God forgives me for pretending to still be a priest," he said.

"You *are* a priest. God is undoubtedly grateful you have given a lot of people comfort today. I feel sorry for Don Bernardo—he seems so lonely."

"Losing a wife and child must be exceedingly painful when one lives in such an isolated place as this. God grant him peace." He stroked her hair. "Don Bernardo certainly welcomes guests with enthusiasm. I am thankful because I think it would be wise to stay here several days to rest and regain our strength with the abundant food he shares so generously."

She pressed up against him. "I have enough strength now, do you?"

He laughed. "Absolutely."

Exhausted from their weeks of travel, they slept late, not waking until the sun was nearly overhead. Servants brought warm water, trays with hot chocolate, stewed fruits with a dusting of cinnamon, fresh butter and quince preserves and leavened wheat flour bread—a luxury in a land where corn had been the staple for a thousand years.

"Disculpe," a servant said to Augustín, "but *el patrón* asked if you would care to go riding this afternoon. The weather is beautiful, but he said he would understand if you preferred to remain in the house since you have been traveling for days and may wish to rest."

"Thank you," Augustín said and turned to Antonia. "I will ride with Don Bernardo but you may stay here, Antonio, if you prefer."

"I feel rested. I would like to go."

"Muy bien," the servant said. She stepped out the door and returned with a stack of clothing in her arms. "These are some of the *patrón's* son's clothes. If anything can be useful to you, he said that it would give him great pleasure for you to avail yourself of it." The servant left and closed the door.

Antonia looked through the clothing and found a pair of trousers that she pulled on under the habit she would have to continue to wear. She must have indeed been fairly similar in size to the *hacendado's* son because the trousers were only a shade too long. Among the clothing was a beautiful pair of little-used Cordovan boots that with a couple of pairs of socks fit quite well.

None of the clothing came close to fitting Augustín, so he made do with what he had worn since Mexico City.

"I hope you do not think you must accompany me if you are tired from your long journey," Ibarra said when they came out into the patio, "but I thought perhaps you might enjoy a little ride since the weather is so nice."

"It is a beautiful day," Augustín said, as he felt the crisp, cool air and warm sun. "It will be our pleasure to accompany you."

Ibarra glanced at the boots Antonia wore. "I am so glad you can get some use from Crispín's things."

"I am honored to wear your son's apparel, Don Bernardo," she said.

They followed the *hacendado* out to where some servants held the reins of three beautiful dish-faced Arabians with alert, intelligent eyes.

"¡Qué lindos!" Antonia said with admiration. She ran her hand down the neck of a silver-gray animal and turned to Augustín. "This one reminds me of . . ." She stopped abruptly and looked down, horrified by what she almost revealed about their past and the Arabian her father had given Augustín when he was a seminarian.

"I agree," Augustín said quickly. "It does look like that Arabian near the Jesuit's *casa de campo* that we used to see when we went there."

"So you like horses, Antonio?" the *hacendado* asked.

"Sí, Don Bernardo."

"Then let's mount, and you can see if you like these."

They rode out of the compound and to the west up a steep rise and then along the ridge.

"My, but your *donado* rides well," Ibarra said to Augustín. "I would not have expected an orphan to have learned how to ride with such confidence."

"Isn't that magnificent," Augustín said, motioning at the vista they had from the ridge, giving himself a moment to consider how he should respond.

Then he continued. "Antonio said he learned to ride quite young—before his parents died—and he came to us when he was about ten or eleven." He tried to make his voice sound light. "But he loves horses and every opportunity he had at the *casa de campo* he was on the back of one, riding."

"Such a fine boy," Don Bernardo said. "So polite."

They began to join the *hacendado* at all meals, and he was solicitous of their wants, always inquiring what he could do or get for them. He and Augustín conversed late into the night, and Antonia excused herself early, fearing further scrutiny and that she might inadvertently say something that would reveal their deception.

She was starting to feel rested from their arduous travel, but she became aware of the *hacendado* looking often at her and she was becoming more nervous to be in his presence. Although she would have liked to, she felt she could not decline meals in the dining room and ask to have her food brought to her room where she could avoid his eyes.

The first day when they had slept late, Augustín said Mass in the evening, but following that, their routine had become rising early and Augustín saying Mass after which they breakfasted with Ibarra.

They had been there not quite a week when the *hacendado* looked at her over breakfast, smiled, and turned to Augustín. "I do believe the food is doing your *donado* some good. Look how his color has improved and how his cheeks have lost their hollows. He is starting to fill out."

Horror crossed her face and she lowered her eyes.

Augustín turned and looked at her, his face expressing his joy that she had plenty of food and had gained back some of the weight she had lost. He had not seen her look. "You are right, Don Bernardo. Antonio is thriving at your abundant table."

A servant came in and addressed Ibarra. "*Con permiso, Patrón*, but old Gertrudis was not feeling well enough this morning to come to Mass and she wanted me to ask if the *padre* could bring her communion. She said she's afraid she may not have many more opportunities to *comulgar* once the *padre* leaves."

"Of course I'll take communion to her," Augustín said, wiping his mouth on his napkin and rising. "I am finished."

Antonia came to her feet, but Ibarra said, "*Padre*, it's not necessary for Antonio to accompany you, is it?"

"No, you may stay, Antonio. Have some more *atole* with Don Bernardo."

Augustín left and Ibarra rose from his place at the head of the table, came and took a chair next to her. She did not look at him and knew her hands were trembling.

"I have watched you this past week, and I know that you are not what you seem."

Chapter 21

Her hands turned white as she clenched them together in her lap to keep them from shaking.

Ibarra went on. "Stay here. Stay with me. There is a servant boy here on the *hacienda* who is very conscientious and intelligent. I know his mother would welcome the opportunity for him to serve the *padre* because when the boy was a baby he came down with a terrible fever and she dedicated him to God if he should recover. The boy could go with Padre Juan to work among the Tarahumara and the *padre* could give him instruction."

Ibarra reached out and took her hands. "Stay with me. I will take care of you. I know you are not what you appear."

Antonia thought she might faint and battled the terror that threatened to overcome her.

Ibarra squeezed her hands. "I know you will think me foolish, but in one week I have come to love you."

"Don Bernardo, no," she managed to whisper.

"No, don't say anything yet, let me speak first." He released her hands. "You may be an orphan and have no money, but you grew up among wealth. You are no rude child from lowly parents. Your manners, your speech, the way you ride a horse give you away. You were raised in wealthy circumstances; you are obviously educated. If you don't want to tell me your background, that is fine. I do not need to know. All I need to know is what I have seen this past week and that I have come to love you and love your sweet temperament."

He sat forward. "All my wealth can be yours. Since my wife and child died, my money means nothing to me—absolutely nothing." He spread his hands. "All of this is yours if you want it."

He took her hands again. "Antonio, I love you like my son. Be my son, be my heir. Let me give you back whatever you lost. Let me live the rest of my life knowing that I have a son who can inherit his father's hard-won wealth."

Her eyes flew up. He had not seen through her deception. He still thought she was a boy.

"Antonio, be my son."

"Oh, Don Bernardo." She took a deep breath and he released her hands. "I am deeply honored and truly touched that you would wish me to be your heir, but it is not possible. I have dedicated my life to Padre Juan. He saved me from certain death—I am sorry that I cannot tell you the details—but I swore an oath to God that I would never leave his side."

Tears slipped down the *hacendado*'s cheeks. "Then you must honor your oath."

She was the one who took his hands this time. "Don Bernardo, you just told me about the intelligent little servant boy who lives here on the *hacienda*. Take him under your wing. Teach him to read and write and ride your beautiful Arabians. And then if he grows into the kind of young man who would make you proud and to whom you could entrust the *hacienda*, make him your heir even though he is only the son of a lowly servant woman. He undoubtedly loves the land where he was born, and you will be able to teach him all he needs to know."

Ibarra bowed his head and covered his eyes. Antonia rose and put her hand on his shoulder. "God is merciful, Don Bernardo. May he bless you for all the goodness you do."

When Augustín returned from taking communion to the old servant, Antonia told him everything that had happened.

"Although it has been wonderful to have an abundance of food and a soft bed in which to sleep, I think we must go now," she said.

"You are right. I will tell Don Bernardo that we shall leave tomorrow morning."

A short while later he returned to their room. "He will have the mules saddled and ready and we can depart after breakfast. I also asked to buy some provisions."

The *hacendado* appeared in good spirits at the table the next morning, his sorrow of the previous day not evident as he gave them advice on their route.

"You will have to spend many nights *al raso*, contending with the elements as you already have, but in a few places between here and Durango, you will find *tambos* for travelers. They are quite rude—sometimes only an empty shack, but they do offer protection from the elements. You will want to watch your belongings carefully. Try always to secure a corner in which to sleep. That way you will be protected on at least two sides from someone who might wish to help himself to your possessions. Stack your things in the corner, cover them as best you can, then lie down on the outside of them. I have instructed a servant to put a number of tiny bells with strings in your mule pack. After you have stacked your belongings in the corner, but before you have covered them, quietly tie the bells onto the items on top. In this way, if someone tries to reach over you and take something while you sleep, the bells will wake you and any other travelers in the room."

"Thank you for that piece of advice, Don Bernardo," Augustín said.

"But when you get to Durango, you must go to the home of my dear friend Don Pascual de Uriarte. I have written him a letter for you to take and he will welcome you delightedly."

They finished breakfast and when they walked out into the open area in front of the main house, there were four mules standing there, two loaded with packs, the other two with new saddles and bridles.

"Don Bernardo," Augustín said with shock. "I do not have enough money to pay for another mule and new saddles. I only wished for a little food."

Ibarra laughed. "I want no money. Your company has given me more pleasure than any amount of gold could." Augustín walked toward the mules.

"I have taken the liberty of adding a few more provisions and items I thought might be useful," the *hacendado* said. "You have a difficult journey ahead of you."

Augustín looked at the packs on the mules and turned to Ibarra. "I don't know what to say, Don Bernardo. Your generosity overwhelms me."

"It is my pleasure, *Padre*. I only wish I could do more for you and your *donado*."

Antonia walked toward the *hacendado*. She took his hand and kissed it. "*Gracias por todo*, Don Bernardo. I consider it a great honor that you asked me to be your son. I cannot imagine having a father I would love or respect more than you. I will carry you in my heart as my father if you will consent."

Ibarra smiled and took her hand. "That would make me very happy, and I will pray for you as my child wherever you go. I have taken your suggestion, Antonio. I have asked Ignacio's mother to send him to my study tomorrow morning."

"God will grant you much happiness in the years to come, of that I am certain," she said.

Antonia and Augustín mounted their mules.

"Oh, just a moment, *Padre*," Ibarra said as he motioned to a servant who stood nearby with a leather saddlebag in his hands. The servant brought what he held to Ibarra.

"There is a wheel lock pistol and some ammunition in this pack." A look crossed Augustín's face and the *hacendado* added quietly, "*Padre*, I know you are not supposed to take a human life, but for the life of your *donado* you may have need of the gun."

Ibarra stepped closer, put his hand on Augustín's thigh, and lowered his voice more. "I didn't want to alarm Antonio at the breakfast table, but the mountains between here and Durango are filled with *bandoleros*. Keep the gun handy; sleep with it—and that even includes when you are in a *tambo* for travelers. Do you know how to use a wheel lock?"

Augustín nodded but hoped Ibarra would not ask how since it was not a skill taught in instruction for the priesthood. He had learned at Don Rodrigo's estate, shooting at a target with Luís, but Ibarra said nothing more as he strapped the leather case behind the saddle of Augustín's mule.

"*Vayan con Dios*," the *hacendado* said, "and remember, my home is yours whenever you might need or want it."

"Thank you, Don Bernardo," Augustín said. "I shall always be indebted to you for your kindness."

Antonia urged her mule forward, leaned down and kissed Ibarra on the cheek this time.

"*Dios te bendiga*," she said.

Ibarra smiled and patted her leg.

They rode out of the compound, turned back and the *hacendado* lifted his hand in a good-bye.

That evening when they found a sheltered spot to stop for the night, they looked at what Ibarra had packed on the mules. In addition to abundant foodstuffs, they found new clothing, leather gloves, a few candles, a small tent of frieze that would give them more protection from the elements than their old piece, and a pair of boots that the *hacendado* had obviously ordered quickly made for Augustín because they fit him perfectly.

"My God," Augustín said as he pulled a leather bag from the bottom of one of the packs and looked at its contents.

"What is it?" Antonia leaned forward as he held open the bag. "Silver pesos. It is full of silver pesos," she said with amazement. "What a kind and generous man Don Bernardo is."

After they ate supper and prepared their bed, Augustín took the wheel lock from its case and loaded it. "Don Bernardo did not want to frighten you, but he gave me this gun with the admonition to sleep with it because of the bandits who roam these mountains preying on the silver trains. So if you hear anything in the night, do not hesitate to wake me."

"Perhaps you should show me how to load and fire it. My father would never have allowed me to learn because a girl would never need to know such things." She laughed but without bitterness. "He never expected me to be sleeping in the wild with the threat of *bandoleros*, either."

Augustín showed her how to load the gun, use the key to tighten the spring in the lock, and how to aim and fire, although they did not because they did not want to waste ammunition nor call attention to themselves if anyone were within hearing distance.

"You must try to support the gun on something because of its weight," Augustín said. "If you have nothing, sit down and use your knees as a support, and wait as long as you can before you fire. These weapons are not accurate at a very great distance."

They traveled for several days and saw no one. The weather grew cold and unpleasant and on the fourth day they rose to find a dusting of snow covering the ground as well as their little frieze tent. The snow had stopped but the mules trudged head-down into a cold north wind that day, and Antonia and Augustín wrapped the corner of their hooded woolen cloaks across their nose and mouth. Their fingers and toes were numb from the cold, and they stopped to put on another pair of woolen socks and to put a second pair, like mittens, over their leather gloves.

They traveled the road now for speed and so as not to miss a travelers' *tambo* in which they might spend the night. But they found none on that day's journey and were forced to make a miserable little camp. Augustín gathered some dead mesquite, managed to start a fire, and they heated one of their wineskins enough to thaw their frozen water, sufficient for a drink for themselves and a little for the mules.

Augustín seemed quiet that evening as they lay in their little tent and Antonia tried to lighten his spirits, asking him questions about Áco and his grandfather.

"I cannot wait to meet him and your aunt and Padre Ramírez," she said.

"And they will love you as I do," he said with a smile, and she snuggled next to him.

"Perhaps you could use a little of that love to warm me up if you can find me under all this clothing and bedding."

"Are you sure?"

"*Con certeza.*"

The next day was again gray and cold, but in the early afternoon, they spotted a small grouping of what might better have been called shacks than houses, but it was habitation and if there wasn't a *tambo*, they might at least be able to pay someone to share the roof over their head.

As they approached, they saw that there was a rude hovel that served for travelers.

They were able to take Ibarra's suggestion because the dirt-floored structure was empty when they arrived. They had everything stacked and secured in a corner, their mules' food, water, and care, as well as their own food and water, arranged with an inhabitant of one of the nearby shacks.

They had finished their beans and tortillas before another traveler appeared. Three soldiers with a dispatch for the governor of Nueva Galicia stopped first. They purchased kindling from one of the neighboring habitations and built a fire in the hearth in the center of the travelers' structure. A kind of chimneylike hole in the roof allowed a portion of the smoke to exit that way, but the warmth and light from the fire outweighed any discomfort they might have felt from the smoky interior.

Augustín and Antonia would have preferred to have kept to themselves, but the soldiers were friendly and initiated conversation.

"Where are you headed?" one asked.

"Although I don't have my cassock on, I am a priest," Augustín said. "This is my *donado* and we are going to minister among the Tarahumara."

"Pardon me, Father, but why the hell are you doing that? We're on our way south to Guadalajara with a dispatch for the governor to send us a contingent of men to try to put a stop to those savages' raids."

"We are well aware of the dangers, *Capitán*, but we are hoping that by bringing *Jesús Cristo* to the natives, they may embrace peace through Our Lord."

The soldiers snorted.

Darkness had fallen and two ill-kempt miners arrived to share the rude shelter. They offered a few monosyllabic responses to the gregarious soldiers' questions and then conversation lapsed.

The fire died down to embers, and everyone slept. Antonia grew chilly without Augustín's warmth since they slept foot to foot in a lopsided V to guard the exposed sides of their belongings. She pulled up her legs, trying to get warmer, but she heard a slight noise and stretched out her legs again, not wanting to leave a space through which a person could creep.

She must have dozed because the sudden tinkling of a bell near her head brought her to a sitting position as she bumped into something.

She grabbed for whatever she had hit and shouted, "*¡Ladrón!,*" doubling over in pain as she was kicked in the stomach by a foot that was forcefully yanked from her grasping hands.

Her shout brought everyone awake, and the *tambo* was at once a confusion of noise and grappling bodies. One of the soldiers threw a handful of quick-lighting kindling on the fire and as it flamed up, the inhabitants of the room were able to distinguish between thief and not. Augustín and one of the soldiers subdued one *ladrón*, the two miners and a soldier grabbed a second who fought to get past the soldier who had stationed himself at the door.

Augustín saw Antonia doubled over in pain, gasping for breath and ran to her.

"What happened?" he whispered with alarm but she was unable to speak. He wanted to take her in his arms but knew he must not give them away. He patted her helplessly as she suffered to breathe.

One of the soldiers put more wood on the fire to increase the light in the shack and asked of Augustín, "*¿Qué pasó?*"

Augustín shook his head. "I can't tell yet. He's having a hard time speaking."

"You miserable son of a bitch!" one of the soldiers yelled as the fire spread more light in the room and he made out the identity of one of the thieves. "You sold us the goddamned wood! You got a little business here, stealing from the travelers who happen to stop in your piss-pot village?" He back-handed the man across the face.

"Fucking *putos*!" a miner cursed.

"And what's this, your son?" another soldier asked when he saw the second robber was only a teenager.

"Look!" the soldier by the door said, stepping aside, and the fire cast its light out the door so that they could see a stack of their belongings outside.

"We'll show you what we do with thieves!"

The soldiers dragged the two men from the *tambo* and the miners followed.

"Antonia," Augustín said with anxiety and started to pick her up.

"No," she finally managed. "Don't."

"What happened?" he asked again, reaching out to stroke her hair.

"I got kicked in the stomach."

"Oh, my God," Augustín said and helped her as she tried to sit up. "Do you think the baby is okay?"

They heard cursing and pleading and commotion outside.

"I don't know." She felt gingerly around on her upper and lower abdomen. "It hurts up here, sort of in the middle but my ribs hurt, too, on the right side."

"Let me take a look."

She grabbed his hands. "No! I'm okay."

A strangled scream from outside made her jerk. "What are they doing?" she whispered.

"May God have mercy on me. I don't know and I don't want to know."

She lifted one blanket that was twisted around her. "No wonder I was so cold. They took two *mantas* off me while I slept!"

"Antonia, *querida* . . ." Unquenched worry covered Augustín's face.

"I'm okay, I'm okay. There is nothing we can do tonight."

"¡*Santa María, no!*" a woman's voice shrieked. "Murderers! You are nothing but murderers!" The woman's voice wailed and others joined in.

"And this is nothing but a pighole of thieves! They got what they deserved! Maybe from now on you will learn not to prey on travelers. Leave our work as a salutary example for the rest of the inhabitants of this *escualidez*. If these are gone in the morning, we will burn your *chozas* to the ground!"

The screaming and cursing outside died down and the soldiers and miners came back into the structure, carrying in the things the thieves had stacked outside the door. One soldier's hands were bloody and he carried a bloody sword. Dark splotches on the other soldiers' trousers were obviously *sangre*, too.

She turned her face away. "Please get my blankets," she whispered.

"How is the boy?" one of the soldiers asked as Augustín approached them.

"I think he'll be okay. He got kicked in the stomach and the wind knocked out of him."

They heard the soldiers rise before dawn and leave, and shortly after that the miners picked up their belongings and were on their way.

As a little light began to filter into the room, Antonia sat up and winced when she touched the spot where she had been kicked. She pulled up the habit and woolen shirts she had slept in and saw the discolored purple bruise puffed out along the edge of her ribcage. She ran her fingers over the bruise and along its edges trying to assess what damage had been done.

"Oh, *querida*," Augustín said with horror as he sat up and saw the ugly bruise and scrambled over to her.

"*No te preocupas*. Luckily, I don't think a rib is broken. It is just a bruise." She ran her hand over her slightly rounded abdomen. "*Gracias a Dios*, the blow was as high as it was. The baby is fine."

Augustín took her in his arms. "What have I gotten you into?"

"An adventure," she said trying to make a joke, but he did not laugh.

While she added some of the wood left over from the previous night and stirred up the embers in order to make a fire over which to cook their breakfast, Augustín folded up their bedding and started carrying their things to the door. He stepped outside the *tambo* and she heard him gasp, and as she looked up through the doorway, she saw him cross himself.

"God have mercy," he said.

He turned quickly away and went to get the mules.

When he returned from packing the mules, his face was drained of color. She handed him a bowl of *gachas*. "What is outside?" she asked quietly.

"You don't want to see it. Avert your eyes when we leave."

They ate breakfast in silence, cleaned up their things, banked the fire for whatever traveler might appreciate a few live coals, and carried their breakfast things to the door.

"Don't look."

But Antonia could not keep her eyes from turning to the side as she stepped out of the shack. She sucked in her breath in horror. The dead, glazed, open eyes of the thief and his son stared at her from where their heads stood, impaled on spikes. Black, coagulated gore hung in thin strings from the severed necks and at the base of the spikes the father's and son's lifeblood had watered the bare ground.

Her stomach spasmed and she covered her mouth with her hand to keep from being sick.

"Antonia, no," Augustín said and pulled her into his arms. "Come, let's be on our way. I have asked God to have mercy on their souls. There is nothing more we can do here."

The weather improved and travel was not as unpleasant as it had been a few days earlier. They were grateful for the warmer daytime temperatures, but at night they shivered in each other's arms. It had been two weeks since they left Don Bernardo's *hacienda*, but it might have been a lifetime. They would have lost complete track of time, each hard day of travel indistinguishable from the other, if Augustín had not noted the days in a journal.

It often seemed to Antonia that they might as well have been the only people on the face of the earth. Even if they passed people on the road, it did not make her feel better, for they all eyed each other with suspicion until they had passed the others and faded into the distance.

In the evenings when they stopped, she would chat lightly, trying to lift the gloom that had fallen over them since leaving the *tambo* and its revolting sight.

"I think it is remarkable that your grandfather reads." Admiration filled her voice. "You said your Spanish grandmother taught him. Why would he have wanted to learn? It seems so foreign to the culture he grew up in."

"He always said that the only way the Spaniards conquered the natives of the land was that the foreigners had more knowledge than they. And he came to realize that knowledge could be put in books — or as he calls them, 'the leaves with marks.'" Augustín smiled thinking about Rohona sitting cross-legged on their roof terrace bent over a precious *libro*. "But his favorite author by far is Marcus Aurelius."

"His *Meditations*?"

"Yes, my grandfather lives a simple, hard life. He *lives* stoicism, so the stoic philosopher's words he understands completely. It is his *Bible*. Always as a child, he exhorted me to heed the words of the Roman."

"I wish I had a copy," she said. "I think I, too, would like to learn from the stoics."

"When we get to Áco . . ." Augustín paused, and she was sure he was thinking *if we get to Áco*, but he repeated, "When we get to Áco, I know my grandfather would be honored to lend you his copy.

"There is one line — I think it is from Book IV — that my grandfather always quotes, 'Be like the promontory against which the waves continually break, but it stands firm and tames the fury of the water round about.' My grandfather sees the rock of Áco as the promontory."

"What a wonderful idea." She moved to sit next to him and leaned her head against his shoulder. "I cannot wait to meet this man. How lucky you are to have him for a grandfather."

"And I am lucky, also, to have you, Antonia." He turned and kissed her on the lips.

Something woke her. She didn't know whether it was the cold or some slight noise, but she was instantly alert. She heard nothing more but she shook Augustín by the arm and whispered next to his ear. "Be quiet — I think there is something outside."

She felt him nod and he slid his hand to reach the loaded wheel lock. She felt him place something cold in her hand and realized it was the handle of his steel-bladed knife. He slowly sat up and leveled the gun at the tent flap.

Chapter 22

The flap was snatched back.

"¡Ándale! On your feet!" a rough voice ordered. "Let's see what you have in there with you!"

As Augustín pulled the trigger, a deafening roar shattered the air, a flash of light blinded, and acrid smoke choked them.

"¡Hijos de puta!" a voice outside cursed venomously. "You almost blew him in two!"

"Give me the knife," Augustín said as their hands fumbled in the dark, smoke-filled tent. He grasped the knife from her fingers and came to a crouching position.

She grabbed the wheel lock, scrambled out of their bedding, and reached madly, trying to locate the powder and slugs, and at that moment Augustín let out a fierce bellow and sprang from the tent.

She heard the grunts and blows of grappling men as her fingers touched the *pólvera*. Like a blind man with only the sense of touch, she poured powder down the barrel, found the slugs, and finished loading. She fumbled, inserting the key to wind the spring but managed to bring it to tension.

She felt for the side of the tent and crawled under and in the faint moonlight saw the two men scrabbling on the ground among the coals of their fire, but she could not make out which was which. She rose and moved closer to the front of the tent, and remembering Augustín's admonition, dropped to a sitting position, pulling her knees up and resting the wheel lock on them. If her eyes became more accustomed to the dark and she could make out the *bandolero*, she would fire.

She heard a guttural scream and her eyes did make out one of the forms as it came to a sitting position and stabbed the body on the ground again and again.

"Oh, God. Oh, God," she gulped.

Then her eyes caught another movement. Something off to the right crept toward the man who sat astride the one on the ground. She swiveled her position, aimed as best she could, and squeezed the trigger with both hands.

A scream sliced the night air in jagged pieces, mules brayed and the recoil of the wheel lock knocked her backward.

"Antonia!" Augustín shouted, pushing himself up off the body beneath him.

She sat up. "There is another one," she yelled, "over there."

Augustín turned and made out the form writhing on the ground, attempting to rise.

"You better kill me you bastard," the man growled, "or I'll follow you to Hell."

Augustín saw the glint of a knife in the man's hand, rushed forward, gave him a vicious kick, which sent him sprawling on the ground and was instantly on top of him, stabbing his knife into the man's heart.

Antonia leaped to her feet and ran to Augustín. He stood and pulled her into his arms. "Oh, *mi amor*," he whispered and she sobbed against his chest.

One of the mules made an unpleasant squawk. "We must check if they are all still here," Augustín said and let her go.

They found the four mules and herded them closer to the tent. "It appears they were in the process of removing the hobbles," he said. "*Gracias a Dios*, they did not succeed."

Antonia walked over to some of the embers that still glowed. She found two sticks and began to scrape the coals into a pile. She entered the tent and brought out some of the kindling they had put there so that if it rained they would have at least a little dry wood.

She coaxed a flame and the kindling caught.

Augustín came, sat down by the fire, and stared into the flames. "I killed three men today," he said quietly, "and I enjoyed it. I had no thought but that I wanted them dead. Dead." His head dropped between his knees. "*Dios mío*, what am I coming to?"

She came and sat beside him. "I too wanted them dead—I am not sorry. When one lives in civilized society, one has luxuries of action and belief that are not possible where there is no law."

The next morning Augustín used one of the mules to drag the bodies behind a small thicket of bushes. He cut off several of the thorny branches and placed them over the bodies.

"If they have compatriots nearby, we don't want them finding the bodies any sooner than necessary," he said to her when he returned.

She nodded. "Let me see your shoulder," she said when she noticed a spot of new blood blossom through a dried stain from the fight the night before. He had told her he had not been hurt.

"It's nothing."

"I don't care. Let me see it."

He pulled off his shirts and she saw the wound on his left shoulder that had broken open and started to seep blood again.

"Don Bernardo put some kind of ointment in the mule packs. I will get it."

When she came back, she saw Augustín holding the knife blade in the fire. "I'm going to cauterize it first. Then you can put the ointment on." He touched the red hot blade to the wound. It made a brief, horrible sizzling sound and the stench of burning flesh made her turn away and gasp.

When she turned back, he had removed the knife from his shoulder, but his teeth were still clenched together and his face was drained of color.

"Should we wait to put the ointment on?" she asked. He shook his head, and even though she spread the pungent smelling salve on the angry red burn with the utmost care, he winced but made no sound.

Two weeks later on the eve of the Savior's birth, they reached Durango. They did not hesitate for a moment in finding the home of Pascual de Uriarte.

They were welcomed as warmly as they had been at Don Bernardo's, and when Uriarte read the letter from Ibarra, the family showered them with even greater warmth. A brass tub was brought to their room along with bucket after bucket of hot water. Their filthy clothes were whisked away, stacks of clean ones left, and they both took long baths and washed their hair with hard-milled, perfumed Castilian soap. They were invited to midnight Mass in the family chapel and to the sumptuous Christmas Eve feast that would follow.

After bathing they crawled under the covers and slept for several hours, awaking refreshed and in good spirits, feeling clean and rested.

Antonia looked with some trepidation through the stack of clothing, afraid she might not be able to find anything that would hide her shape, but she found a linen shirt she was able to tie around her breasts to flatten them. And donning several long tunics over some oversize leggings, she found her form indistinct, especially when she tied a belt around her waist and made a blouson effect that hung down around her waist.

"My biggest worry," Augustín said expressing his own, "is that the priest who is going to say Mass may know the same people I do in Mexico City. He may ask a lot of questions that will be difficult to answer, and if we can, we must try to avoid sitting by him at dinner. I will offer to assist at Mass because I feel I must."

But Augustín's worries were unfounded. The priest was an elderly Franciscan missionary, too feeble to maintain a missionary flock. He lived now at Pascual de Uriarte's house off the *hacendado's* largess, supplying the sacraments to the family. He had not been back to Mexico City in over thirty years and would undoubtedly never see the capital again.

They sat down to dinner long after midnight. The Christmas Eve feast was magnificent with a whole roasted *cabrito,* a roasted suckling pig, numerous roasted fowl, and dish after dish of accompaniment. Their fingers dripped with sticky sweetness when they ate the deep-fried *buñuelos* dipped in cinnamon honey.

"Although I would love to, I think we mustn't stay as long as we did at Don Bernardo's," Antonia said when they reached their room in the wee hours of the morning.

"Yes, we must push on, I'm afraid. It is much farther to Parral than from Zacatecas to Durango."

The family cajoled and tried their best to get their guests to stay for the *Dia de los Reyes Magos,* but they said they could not stay to celebrate Epiphany with them.

"But you must wait until next week," Uriarte said. "There is a *cuadrilla* going to Parral. You cannot risk traveling alone with the Tarahumara on the rampage."

"What exactly do you mean by a *cuadrilla,* Don Pascual?" Augustín asked.

"It is usually fifteen to twenty people who travel together with a large *carreta* made into a rolling fort. The cart is reinforced with heavy planks to stop arrows and has slits for gunports on all four sides. If the savages attack, you climb into the *carreta* and shoot from the safety of the interior. It's more effective than you might think. The group takes turns at night standing guard and sleeping inside the fortlike cart."

"Does the *cuadrilla* have enough room for us?" Augustín asked.

"Claro," Uriarte said. "My nephew is in charge; he will see to it. The governor has established some military outposts along the way, although they are quite far apart. I think my nephew has arranged a military escort, which is getting more common now that the Tarahumara have decided to come down out of their mountains to attack with such frequency."

They left the following week with the *cuadrilla,* feeling much more secure traveling in a group with military escort but worrying that living in such proximity might be a danger in its own right. Don Pascual had replenished their provisions as had Don Bernardo earlier, and both Augustín and Antonia said prayers each night for the generosity of strangers.

Antonia had begun to worry about her ever-rounding stomach becoming noticeable, so before they left Durango she cut up a thin *manta,* folded it, and stitched it together to make a kind of padding for her shoulders that she could wear under her habit to give her a bulkier appearance so that the girth of her stomach would not be as apparent.

❈   ❈   ❈

Three weeks out, a band of Indians attacked and the rolling fort worked admirably. And even if someone had glimpsed a protruding stomach, no one would have guessed she was a woman when they saw her load a wheel lock, rest it on the slit of the gunport, and fire. She had learned after that first time not to let the recoil knock her over.

After days of arduous and grueling travel, they reached the farthest outpost of northern New Spain. Beyond Parral, nothing existed except leagues and leagues of wasteland until one reached the native pueblo villages along the *Río Bravo del Norte* in the province of *Nuevo México*.

If they had thought water had been scarce and often hard to find on their journey so far, they would think it nonexistent until they reached the *Río Bravo*.

Augustín bought a large water barrel to strap on the side of one of the pack mules. They said good-bye to the people of the *cuadrilla*, who seemed convinced they were crazy and not long for this world.

Although they needed to travel due north to reach *Nuevo México*, they headed west so that anyone who watched them depart would not know the real direction they would pursue.

"If we can make it far enough away from Parral without being seen," Augustín said, "it will be as if we dropped off the face of the earth. If we are ever mentioned to any of the missionaries who have worked among the Tarahumara, they will never have heard of us, and everyone will assume we were killed before we ever made it there."

The second day they changed directions. They prayed that no Tarahumara would see their tiny mule train.

As they traveled north the land was austere and arid and the elevation not nearly as high as that of Zacatecas or Durango. Because of the diminishing altitude, the nights were not as cold as they traveled through the desolate wastes of northern New Spain, but they suffered from dust, glare, and thirst, guarding their water as if it were liquid gold.

It had been over a month since they left Parral and they knew they were still weeks from the *Río Bravo*. The wind was relentless and dust storms filled their eyes and noses and mouths with gritty residue, and in the evenings when they stopped, they had little strength to make camp. They often had only a miserable little fire because there was not sufficient fuel for more.

They awoke one morning to find one of the mules lying on its side, its breathing labored. Antonia knelt and stroked its head while Augustín tried to pour a little water into its mouth, but it gave a shuddering sigh and died as if it could simply endure no more.

"Rest in peace," Antonia whispered. "You were a good mule. Thank you for carrying our things this far."

"We must reorganize the packs," he said. "We cannot burden the other mule with more. We must choose what to take and what to leave behind."

They laid out all their meager belongings and looked at them.

"Of course the water barrel must go with us." He moved it to one side.

"We can get rid of clothing," Antonia said. "We should pick out the least worn and leave the rest."

They sorted through the things, changed some items they wore for others, and made a pile. Augustín slowly placed his Jesuit cassock on top. She looked at his face and placed her hand on his arm.

"Don't you think we have room for that?" she asked.

"No. It must be left behind."

They came to the sack of silver pesos Don Bernardo had given them. They had used very little.

"Silver is heavy," Augustín said.

"Then we will leave it. Maybe some other traveler will find it and thank God for it."

They kept back only the most essential of their other goods and utensils. Their food had dwindled more than they had imagined, and all that was left, they must take with them.

He packed the mule with the things they would keep. They mounted the other two mules and started once more north.

Antonia glanced back at the dead mule and their pile of belongings. It appeared as if they left behind two carcasses instead of one.

Augustín did not take one last look, his eyes were fixed in the distance ahead of them, his mouth a hard line.

He did not mind that he had frayed and patched clothes, rough places to sleep and not enough food to fill his stomach, but every time he looked at the woman he loved, it was as if a knife were being pushed a little deeper into his heart.

Her clothes were not much more than tatters, and her cheeks had developed hollows from the scarcity of their food. He knew that as the baby grew, it became more and more uncomfortable for her to sleep at night on whatever might serve as their bed, but not once had she complained.

She, the pampered daughter of a rich Creole family; she, who had always slept between silk sheets; she, who had had servants to do her bidding all her life; she, whose table was always filled to overflowing with succulent things to eat, never complained once during the long, hard journey.

If he were tortured with doubts about her safety and what they were doing, she would sense it when they would stop to rest, and she would sit down and say, "Come," and he would come to her and lie with his head in her lap, and she would stroke his hair and talk about something pleasant until he dropped into sleep.

He had grown afraid to make love to her for fear of hurting her or the child, but at night she would cuddle close to him, and her silklike movements would make him forget everything, and afterward when she lay in his arms, she would say as she drifted off to sleep, "I love you, dearest husband, and I love the way you love me."

The first time he felt the child move, he was overcome with a sensation he would never have been able to express. It was wonder, pride, awe, joy, amazement. He had never thought he would engender a child; he had never thought to own a tiny slice of immortality through a descendant of his own flesh and blood.

His old mentor had said it was a sacrifice to give up the privilege of having children. It was not until that moment that he fully understood what the old man had meant. Fathering a child gave him a feeling of pride and strength and joy unmatched by any sensation he had yet experienced. It was a creative power, a brief glimpse of what it was, perhaps, to be God.

But that small glimpse brought another awareness that had lain hidden through the years. The decision he made to become a priest, to forfeit his right to father children, had also been a means to bury the stain that marked his soul and body indelibly: the act of incest that gave him birth.

Never, as he poured forth his love and the life force into the body of the woman he loved, had the thought occurred to him that he might perpetuate the sin of his birth. Not once had the possibility occurred to him that he might father an unspeakable creature on whose countenance was written the sin of its forefathers.

A thick pall of dread and horror fell over him. How could he ever have allowed himself to plant his seed in the beautiful, intelligent Antonia knowing what he might engender? From time immemorial there had been taboos against incest, and the stories of man have contained countless examples of it—from the mudheads of the Zuñi that he remembered from his childhood, to the Greeks and Aztecs. Monsters were more often than not the result of that carnal sin. With good reason the Church had sanctions against it.

Antonia saw the haunted look in his eyes. He seldom touched her; now they rarely made love. She knew also that in the evening when he said he was going off to pray that he scourged himself in penance for something of which she knew not.

He was drawing more and more into himself. At first she thought he was feeling remorse for having broken his vow of celibacy, for having to leave the priesthood and his entire future, feeling remorse for having gotten her with child, for the hardships of the journey. She tried to ask him if it were any of those things that troubled him, but he denied that they caused him any pain.

At last her own grief at seeing him thus became more than she could bear. One morning when she arose after a night in which he had not come to her bed, she spoke straightforwardly to him.

"We are turning back. I will not go on. Augustín, dearest husband, dearest lover, I cannot go on. Your unhappiness leaves my heart in heavy mourning. I cannot live if you are so full of despair, and although you say it is nothing, I know that *I* am the cause of it. I did not want you to throw away your life for me; I love you too much to cause you pain. I cannot bear the thought that I have brought you so much grief. We must turn back; it is not too late. You can continue in the life for which you have worked so hard.

"I will stop at Don Bernardo's and beg his mercy. I know he will take me and our child in. I will tell him you died on the journey. You will be able to make your way back to Mexico City; you will be able to find some explanation for your unusual disappearance. Padre Juan will no longer exist.

"We are turning back."

Chapter 23

He had listened to her every word, his head bowed. He looked up at her. "I no longer wish to be a Jesuit; the last thing I want is to return to Mexico City. I swear by all that is holy, *you* are not the cause of my unhappiness. I love you so intensely that it sometimes feels as if my heart may burst. I need you as I need food and air and water in order to live. I cannot do without you—*you* could never be the source of my unhappiness."

Tears ran in rivulets down her face. *"Then tell me what it is!"* she cried. "I cannot continue with the pain your grief causes in me."

He saw the resoluteness in her eyes. There was a long pause, and when he finally spoke it was so quietly she scarcely heard the words.

"I will tell you."

And so he had begun. She knew that he had been born in the province of *Nuevo México* and about his grandfather, but that was all. He began from the beginning and recounted the story his grandfather had told him many years ago. He took the small silver-encrusted box from among the few possessions he had brought with him and showed her the locks of hair that were his mother's and father's.

"They were brother and sister. They committed incest, and I am the child born of their sinful love. I have scarce right to exist, much less to make love to a woman and take the chance of engendering children who may bear the onerous sin of their father."

She looked at him aghast. "You mean you are afraid our child will be defective?"

Augustín nodded and looked away.

"Oh, *mi amor*," she whispered as she put her arms around him and hugged him tightly. "What a terrible burden you have had to bear, but there will be nothing wrong with our child. This I know as surely as I know that God exists. Your mother and father were only *half*-brother and sister. You are perfect—there is absolutely nothing wrong with you."

She took his hands. "You are beautiful, Augustín. You are the most handsome man I have ever seen. I can still see you in my mind dressed as Huitzilopochtli. I was only a girl then, but I knew the man I married must look like that. Not only do you have physical perfection, *mi amor*, you are one of the most intelligent men in all of Mexico. You don't need *me* to verify that fact.

"How can you ever imagine that any child to whom you would give life would be less than perfect? Your mother and father had no knowledge of what they did—their love was blameless—and you, their child, carry no stain of sin upon your soul or body. Do not torture yourself, Augustín. I love you, I cherish you, I thank God that you were given life. You have enriched my life immeasurably; I would change nothing. I love the ground as my bed, rags as my clothing, and mush as my food because I am with *you*—nothing else truly matters."

They reached the *Río del Norte* and *Nuevo México* in the early spring in bitterly cold weather. Their progress had slowed, for Antonia was growing heavy with child and could not manage more than a few miles a day.

Because there was little large game and the wheel lock was not accurate at long distances, it was of little use for hunting. He fashioned a bow and arrows as he had remembered how his grandfather had taught him and as he had once taught Luís. After several attempts he became reaccustomed to the primitive weapon. He had no arrowheads, metal or stone, and had to be satisfied with hunting only rabbits or small birds that he could stun with the blunt arrow. He took the obsidian fetish from the silver box and rubbed his fingers over it, wishing he could remember the hunting prayers, but he did remember to feed the fetish when he made a kill as Rohona had taught him.

Antonia had watched his actions. "Is what you do an Ácoma ritual?"

"It is a prayer. You thank the animal you kill for giving you sustenance. The Ácoma believe they are a part of every living thing."

"Do they believe in a god, a creator of all life?"

"Not in the Christian sense. The Ácoma believe their creator is a woman."

"A woman?" Antonia asked and smiled. "I like the thought of that. What is she called?"

"Iyatiku."

"What a lovely name," she said and repeated it.

"Actually there were two sisters. Iyatiku who was dark and Nautsiti who had fair skin. A rainbow impregnated Nautsiti, who gave birth to twin sons. She took one and went away to the east and became the mother of all the people across the ocean. Iyatiku and Nautsiti's other son remained here and became the mother of all the native peoples of the land."

"I am a daughter of Nautsiti then," Antonia said.

Augustín pulled her into his arms. "So you are."

❈   ❈   ❈

When they reached *Nuevo México*, he wanted to be even more careful that they should not be seen, for he wanted no news of a strange Spanish couple wandering the province to spread among the inhabitants.

They followed the *Río Bravo* on its western bank because all travel between the province and New Spain used the eastern side. They had no carts, so they would not be forced to cross the deadly, waterless *Jornada del Muerto*. Travel would be difficult over the rough terrain on the west bank of the river but they would at least be near water.

They discarded the water barrel. It would save weight and not make footing as unwieldy for the pack mule. The only waterless expanse they had left to cross was when they left the banks of the *Río Bravo* and struck west toward Áco, but their wineskins filled with water should be sufficient for that.

Winter wasn't content to leave yet and blew one last, bitter cold breath down upon them. They huddled together in the small tent, shivering, their stomachs growling with hunger because they were rationing the last small portions of their precious food.

During the day they trudged head-down, often unable to ride the mules because of the rocky terrain. But at last the land evened out and they came to the marshes at San Marcial.

For a week they camped, hidden, near the *ciénega*. The warmth of spring could finally be felt during the day, and the marshy land teemed with waterfowl. They had more to eat than they had had in months, and they regained some of their strength.

Augustín would have liked to have stayed longer because of the abundance of food, but the baby would be born soon, in perhaps less than a month. They *must* reach Áco.

It had been over three years since he had had any word from his grandfather or Padre Ramírez. How old would his grandfather be now? He tried to calculate the old man's age and decided he must be close to seventy-five. Anything could have happened in three years. He prayed fervently that Rohona was alive.

The closer they had come to *Nuevo México*, the more anxious he became to see the grandfather he had left twenty years ago, the grandfather who had raised him, loved him enough to allow his only grandchild to go to the distant capital of New Spain, never to return again. But he was returning and he had the strange sensation that it was meant to be.

Desire and necessity to see the steep-walled sandstone mesa once more burned in his breast, and he prayed constantly, "Let my grandfather be alive."

That was the same prayer that was on his lips as he dropped to his knees to give thanks, and she knelt beside him, her hand in his.

There ahead of them it loomed. He had once thought he would never see it again. His last memory had been with the eyes of a child, looking back over his shoulder for one last glimpse of his home. But there it was—ivory-pink in the distance, its jagged, vertical cliffs as awe-inspiring to the man as they had been to the boy.

"It is incredibly beautiful," Antonia whispered. "What a magnificent rock on which to build a village."

"Áco," he said. His voice dropped in awe, "We have truly reached Áco." The memories of the past came flooding back over him, and he could not stop the tears that blurred his vision of the rugged rock citadel that rose sharply from the valley floor in front of him.

"Thank you, *Dios,*" he whispered, "thank you for allowing us to reach the White Rock." The high-perched village was like salvation to him.

He embraced her. "We have made it, Little One, we have made it!"

Riding toward them on a mule was a friar, his blue robe pulled up about his knees. Their presence in the valley must have been noticed by someone. Augustín began to run toward him, and the other put his heels into the mule's sides to urge it to go faster.

It was not until he was close enough to see the gray eyes of the running man that Juan Ramírez recognized who it was. He leaped off the mule before it stopped. The two threw their arms around each other.

"Augustín!" he cried, "Augustín!" Tears rolled down the cheeks of the priest. He looked toward the woman who stood at some distance from them.

Augustín spoke quietly, his eyes lowered in shame at having to disappoint the man who had had such great expectations of him.

"I have left the Jesuits, *Padre.* I love the woman, and she carries my child." It was all he said in explanation. At the moment it was all he was capable of saying.

The Franciscan put his arms around him again. "Welcome home, my son, welcome home."

The woman's face lit in a smile as she watched them. She was heavy with child, her dark, tawny hair had been chopped raggedly, her clothes were scarcely more than rags, her face thin, but Juan Ramírez was instantly aware of her beauty.

"My daughter," Juan Ramírez said, walking forward to greet her, "welcome."

"Father," Antonia said softly as she knelt and kissed his hand. Gently he pulled her to her feet.

"You are Antonia, are you not?" he asked.

She looked at him in shock as did Augustín who spoke. "How could you know that, *Padre?*"

The priest turned toward him. "From your letters, my son. It was clear you loved the little girl whom you tutored and who had become a woman.

You were not aware of your love, but that awareness was inevitable and it has brought you home."

Together they walked toward the mesa. "And Grandfather?" Augustín asked tentatively.

Juan Ramírez smiled. "He is well, as is your Aunt Siya."

"Gracias a Dios," Augustín whispered.

"The road," the friar said when they reached the path. "The *Camino del Padre,* as they call it."

"You have been successful here, *Padre,*" Augustín said with admiration. "I remember when you spoke, trying to persuade the Ácoma to build it. In the end you were successful."

"Yes, but I almost despaired before success came. I am anxious for you to see the church—it is the best in all of *Nuevo México. Dios* has been very good to me."

"He has been good to all of us," Augustín said.

The *padre* climbed the ladder first.

"I bring you a surprise," he said in Queres to the old man and woman who were seated on the rooftop.

They smiled, wondering about the priest's unusual words. Then an apparition appeared atop the ladder.

Siya gasped, but the old man sat totally still.

Augustín walked quickly toward him and knelt in front of him.

Tears rolled silently down the old man's wrinkled copper cheeks. "Mastya," he whispered.

Augustín embraced the old man, his own tears running freely down his face, and then embraced his aunt, who wept uncontrollably.

He kissed them both and rose, took Antonia's hand and brought her forward. "This is Antonia, Grandfather," he said. "She brings a great-grandchild to you."

Antonia fell to her knees in front of the old man, her eyes downcast. She was unable to speak.

"My granddaughter," the old man said in Castilian, his voice thin with age. "Welcome. My grandson has brought me a granddaughter for my old age, and she brings me a great-grandchild. The years vanish behind me, and I am young again."

She looked up at him, and he smiled gently at her. Tears once more clouded his eyes as the memory of another Spanish woman came back across the years to him, a woman with gray eyes and hair the color of wet pine bark, whom he had first gazed upon fifty years past.

"You must forgive an old man," he said. "The tears come foolishly now."

Antonia could not stop her own. "Mine are from joy, Grandfather," she said, "joy from finally seeing you and Áco. My blessings are as uncountable as the stars."

Rohona smiled. He liked the words, for they sounded Indian.

Antonia turned to Augustín's aunt. "You are Siya," she said with a smile.

"Yes," the old woman replied shyly.

"I have much to learn," Antonia said to her. "I hope that I may not be a burden to you and that you will teach me the things I need to know."

Antonia learned quickly. She would have worked to exhaustion had Siya allowed it, but she said the girl must save some of her strength for the baby that would surely be coming soon.

Antonia felt a deep contentment. She felt as if she herself had come home. She loved the companionship of Siya, who loved to laugh, and who worked feverishly to prepare for the baby's arrival.

From the first moment, her love for Rohona was finely forged, too, and she delighted in the stories he told. They had begun to talk together about the books they had read, and she was amazed to learn that the old man had almost the entirety of Marcus Aurelius memorized.

"He says many things that I understand," the old man said. "And these eyes are getting old. They will not see much longer, so I must have the words in my mind where I can see them."

"I will read to you, Grandfather," she said.

Augustín worked with a driving diligence. It was May, the planting time. As they descended the *Camino del Padre,* Augustín walked slowly beside his grandfather, whose pace lameness and age had impeded.

The old man laughed. "The *padre* told me once I would appreciate the road in my old age. Then I did not believe him—now I do."

Augustín was able to till the soil and plant more than his grandfather could have done in weeks.

"You returned just in time," Rohona said joyously. "Now we shall have abundant corn with a strong back to plant it." When his grandfather's words continued, Augustín felt a flicker of worry.

"I hope the K'atsina bring enough rain," the old man said.

They spent long hours working in the fields, but in spite of the time he spent at the labor, Augustín always found a few moments to go off alone to pray. The habits of the Jesuits did not die easily.

He managed to keep his dread hidden from Antonia, but when alone, it came back to haunt and torment him. He prayed fervently for the well-being of the child and did acts of penance in solitude. He took extreme care that Antonia would not know of his anxiety, for her happiness at Áco was a source of great relief to him. It seemed as if she had never lived in the viceregal capital, the daughter of a wealthy man. She worked alongside Siya, learning quickly the ways of Áco.

Padre Ramírez was the source of a good portion of her happiness. He confessed them both and asked if they would like for him to marry them in the church. That sacrament they had never dreamed of being able to receive, and Antonia cried with happiness.

Augustín, however, said, "*Padre*, it is not possible, you know that."

"God said to Peter," the friar replied, "that those things forgiven on earth will be forgiven in heaven. I have absolved you of your sins, and there is no impediment to your marriage."

Augustín did not argue further, for he wanted as much as Antonia that she might be his wife in the eyes of his Church and faith. She would no longer be living a life of sin, and the child would not be born a bastard. As for himself, he desired the sacrament as a seal for the love he felt for the woman who carried his child.

Juan Ramírez prayed deep into the night. "Whatever sins they may have, Lord, put them on my shoulders. The woman Antonia and the man Augustín were meant as husband and wife. Grant them peace, grant them happiness. Whatever may be a transgression, charge it to my soul, Lord. Let *me* at the Day of Judgment be accountable."

And so they were married.

The warmth of May softened the air, and the valley of Áco began to green. Tiny lavender flowers sprouted here and there on the valley floor when the baby was born.

"She brought the child forth like a woman of Áco," Siya said proudly. "She did not even whimper."

Siya pulled back the edge of the blanket so that Rohona could see his great-grandson. "A boy," Siya said, her voice full of pride. "He is beautiful— so big and strong—he will be like his father."

Rohona looked at the tiny, red face. "Yes, he will be a fine man. He shall know the ways of Áco and be proud. His home shall be this rock, as this rock shall be the home of his sons and their sons. My grandson has returned to Áco; his descendants shall not leave."

Part Four

EL REGRESO

The Return, 1651

Chapter 24

Over the east mesa the sun rose, its brilliance blinding, turning the tears on the old man's cheeks to drops of crystal. His frail arms trembled as he held the naked baby aloft. It was the fourth time he had performed the ritual.

"Behold the child Mokaitsh," he spoke to the sun.

He gathered the child to him protectively, wrapping its blanket about it. "You are named for the mighty hunter, little great-grandson," he whispered to the baby in his arms, whose face was dabbed with corn pollen.

"You shall be strong like Mokaitsh, fearless yet instilling fear in others, intelligent and of infinite patience whether you stalk man or beast. You will carry the color of Mokaitsh in your eyes. The soft gray color of Mokaitsh's fur will be reflected there, and when you are a man, the people will say you were well named—Mokaitsh, the mountain lion."

The old man turned and started back. The house rows glowed golden in the rising sun. He spoke again to the sleeping baby in his arms. "Your mother has given you a name to be proud of also, and she does me honor by the name.

"She wants to call you Marco Aurelio after the man who wrote the leaves that these old eyes have read so many times. Those leaves of the foreigners these eyes have understood. You, great-grandson, will read those leaves and profit by them as I have."

One month later Padre Ramírez baptized the child. "Marco Aurelio Mokaitsh, I baptize you in the name of the Father, Son, and Holy Spirit. May the blessings of God Almighty be upon you, now and always."

The year that followed was filled with contentment for Augustín. Every day he sought a few moments of solitude to thank God for granting him such happiness. From a secluded perch he had found, he gave expression of his gratitude. The craggy rocks that jutted up from the valley floor like misshapen pillars provided private vantage points from which a person might survey the starkly beautiful valley with its two larger, uplifted rock citadels: the one on which the village perched and the pink and ivory Katzimo to the east, the Enchanted Mesa, sacred to the Ácoma.

Farther to the west lay another rock pinnacle upon which rested the graves of his mother, father, and grandmother. He had visited it to pray on the occasion of his son's first birthday. The visceral fears that had haunted him before the birth of his child had been proven without base, and he was ashamed that he had let them gain control over him.

His son was strong and healthy, beautiful and alert. The sin of incest was nowhere evident as he had so feared. When he had knelt by the three piles of stones with their weathered crosses, he had finally been able to forgive his parents their sin, although he knew ultimately that that was God's domain. The anguish he had felt since he was a child, the deep-rooted self-deprecation that was the origin of his loneliness, vanished in that brief moment of forgiving. When he returned to the village that afternoon, the sense of freedom he carried in his breast was limitless. He was freed from the past, the present and the future lay unfettered before him.

"How truly ignorant I have been, *Dios*," he spoke aloud to the vast expanse of the valley. "You never cease to open my eyes — and I thank you profoundly for it. What next do you have in store for me? What next will you teach me?"

Siya and Antonia had prepared a feast for the first birthday celebration, although Padre Ramírez was the only guest. The baby, called alternately Aurelio or Mokaitsh, had recognized the extra hustle and bustle and toddled about excitedly as if he understood there was going to be a party. Antonia worked diligently grinding and regrinding, sifting and resifting, the wheat that Augustín had grown next to the corn, squash, melons, and chiles. At last she was satisfied with the texture of the flour. With honey the friar had given her, she made a sweet, sticky piñon nut cake that delighted everyone.

From his mother, Aurelio received a little stuffed horse with embroidered eyes, from his Auntie Siya a new shirt, from his grandfather a miniature bow and blunted arrows, and from his father a new pair of moccasins that Augustín had made under the tutelage of Rohona. But the gift that delighted the boy most was a small brass bell tied onto a satin ribbon that the priest had brought to him. Aurelio shook it with glee, and it was still clenched in his hand when his mother put him to bed that night.

Augustín was happier than he ever remembered being. Not a small measure of his contentment arose from Antonia's acceptance of life at Áco. Many were the times he wondered how she could adapt so uncomplainingly to such an alien existence. He, at least, had been born there and had spent his first ten years of life in the village. He marvelled that she so eagerly learned the chores that life there required. Never once had she spoken of discontent. He questioned her on several occasions about her real feelings, afraid that hiding them might eventually make her situation intolerable, but she assured him again and again that her happiness was genuine.

"My parents ceased to exist for me. They and the city of Mexico are but a vague, distant memory. It was as if I underwent a rebirth when we fled," she said. "When I realized I was carrying your child, I was filled with a joy that I could never begin to describe. In that moment I knew my life had changed. Nothing would ever be the same again; I had before me a future that was not connected in any way to the past. Then, when you came for me and I knew that my life was to be with you—what or where it was did not matter. It seemed to me that God had given me a gift more wonderful than I had ever dreamed of—and that was to be with you and have your child. In view of that, how could anything else matter?"

Aurelito, as he was called by his parents, filled his household with delight. His great-grandfather, who counted seventy-seven summers as nearly as the old man could reckon, seemed stooped and ancient scarcely a year before. Now there existed a new light in his eyes, a frequent smile at his lips, and a surprising quickness to his steps.

He composed beautiful songs as he made his prayer sticks for the K'atsina. Daily, in the early morning, he gave thanks to the K'atsina from the rooftop of their dwelling and then later there was great joy in his words when he knelt in the cool, quiet interior of the massive adobe church and thanked the Castilian god for the return of his grandson, for the presence of his Spanish granddaughter, and for the well-being of his great-grandson.

Sometimes he would laugh as he knelt in the church. "*Dios*, I will never understand you or your purpose." Then more seriously he would add, "I give you my prayers of thanksgiving, even so."

Siya, too, seemed much younger than her sixty-nine years. Antonia quickly became the daughter Siya had never had, and in the Indian woman, Antonia found a motherly loving and caring that filled a void in her life and effectively blocked sorrows from the past that might have crept unsuspecting into the present.

Siya taught her how to sing the grinding songs and to put a smudge of cornmeal on her cheeks as a prayer when they knelt at the grinding bins. They walked half a league to the west of Áco mesa, and Siya showed her where to find the clay for making pots.

"Áco has the best clay of all the villages," Siya said proudly. "Our pots are lighter and harder because our clay is more finely textured."

When they reached the spot Siya sought, she continued, "But before we dig the clay, we must ask its permission." She spoke quietly in Queres to the ground and then looked up at Antonia. "This clay wants to be a beautiful pot," she said to her with a smile.

They dug the clay with sharp sticks and put it in their baskets to carry home.

Siya showed her where to find the red ochre to color the pots as well as the fine, soft white clay to make the kaolin slip. They gathered green stems of the bee plant and boiled them down to make a gluey substance to which Siya added a black mineral.

"This," she said, motioning to the unpleasant looking mixture, "will make our black paint. Now all we lack are our brushes, and those we make from yucca leaves. We tear the leaves into strips of different widths, chew the ends to turn them into a fringe. You'll see it doesn't take long to learn to make good brushes."

Antonia smiled. Siya thought everything was easy, but for someone who had been raised in the viceregal capital with servants to do one's every bidding, making things with one's untrained hands was not an easy task. Growing up as she had, she never learned to watch a mother, an aunt, or a grandmother to gain a skill, with the exception of embroidery.

"One last thing," Siya said before they sat down to begin, "you must have scrapers and polishers." She went into one of the rooms where they kept their many tools and came back with several small leather bags. She dumped out the contents and showed them to Antonia.

"These smooth, round pebbles are for polishing the pot," she said. "Whenever you are near a streambed, always watch for good pebbles to bring home because different pots have different curves and you need to have just the right pebble for polishing." From another sack she took a large handful of hard pieces of gourd shell. "And these, daughter, are for scraping and shaping the pot. See how the edges all have different curves? These are what you use to give your pot the shape you want and to make it with nice thin walls — this is the most difficult part of learning to make a good pot."

Everything was laid out neatly and carefully. Lumps of grayish clay soaked in a large pottery vessel. They knelt in front of *metates*, and Siya sang a short prayer before they began. On each *metate* were broken potsherds.

"Now we grind," Siya said. "We grind the potsherds just like cornmeal until it is soft and fine. This makes the temper."

After they were finished, they brushed the temper off the *metate* and set it aside. Siya took several large, uneven lumps of clay from the soaking water and put them on her *metate* and on Antonia's. She dipped her fingers into the pot of water and sprinkled it on the clay.

"Now we knead. In this way we will be able to remove any pebbles or impurities."

Antonia watched Siya's rhythmical motions as she kneaded the clay and sought to copy them but knew her movements were as awkward as a child's. Siya had her clay ready long before Antonia did.

"Let me finish your clay this time, daughter," Siya said, "so we can get to making the pots—that, besides painting, of course, is the most fun." Siya wrapped her clay in a damp rag of old *manta* and quickly finished Antonia's.

"The next step is to add the temper. The old pots help make new pots. That's how we do it here at Áco, and they do the same at Zuñi, but when I lived in the *villa* of the *españoles,* I saw women from Santo Domingo use the volcanic sand they have near their pueblo as their temper. At Taos and Pucurís they don't have to use anything because their clay already has tiny specks of shiny rock that work just the same."

After the temper was added and the clay was finally ready, she dipped her hands in the pot of water to wet them, pinched off a piece of clay, and flattened it in her hand. She pressed it into the bottom of a shallow old bowl sitting in front of her and molded it in the bottom. Antonia did likewise. Again Siya dipped her hands in the water.

"Now we make the ropes," she said as she took more clay and deftly began to roll it into a sausagelike rope, which she placed on the base she had just made, pinching the clay together. Antonia followed her example, but it was necessary for Siya to help her occasionally in order to keep the curve somewhat regular as they built up the walls of the pots.

It looked so easy when Siya did it, but in spite of Antonia's best efforts, her little "child" was bent and crooked.

"Oh, Siya," she said dejectedly, "I don't know if I shall ever be able to make a proper pot."

Siya patted her hand. "Don't worry, daughter, you will make beautiful pots. It just takes a little practice." She helped Antonia straighten the pot so that the vertical sides of it were not quite so lopsided. She picked up a curved piece of gourd shell, handed it to Antonia and took one for herself. "Now we push out the walls and start the shaping. Put one hand on the inside of the bowl like this, now turn the bowl, pressing out with the hand inside while you use the gourd scraper on the outside, pressing and scraping."

At last the pots were finished, and Siya helped Antonia even the walls on hers.

"Now we put them in the shade to dry for a day or two. We don't want them to crack."

They made several more pots, and when they were all dry, Siya showed Antonia how to grind and prepare the paints and make the yucca brushes. After the pots were dry, they gave them several coats of white slip and when that was done polished them with the pebbles Siya had shown her. Siya began decorating her pot with intricate black and white geometric designs.

"May I put flowers on my pot?" Antonia asked. "I don't think I can draw designs like that yet."

"Surely, daughter, put whatever you wish. Your pot will tell you what it likes."

Late that afternoon, Antonia showed Siya her pot. On one side, perched on a stylized flower, was a fanciful bird with a curving beak and three rounded tail feathers. A wide red band encircled the bottom of the pot and curving lines bordered the top.

"It is beautiful, daughter!" Siya exclaimed. "What a lucky pot. Tomorrow we will fire them. Padre Ramírez always saves the dung from his sheep for me. It makes a very good, even, hot fire — very good for our purpose."

When the pots had been fired and had cooled, Antonia felt a similar sort of satisfaction as that she had felt upon giving birth. Her little pots, although misshapen and crooked, looked very beautiful to her, and when Rohona complimented her on her work, it was as if someone had told her her lame child was lovely.

"Oh, grandfather," she said with gratitude and surprised him by giving him a hug and a kiss on the cheek.

Just as the past was vanishing for Antonia, so, also, was it for Augustín. Life at Áco had a rhythm to it that now seemed a part of him, as if he might never have lived elsewhere. His happiness was profound, but there was one worry that was often present. Would there be enough rain for the crops? He had not remembered the land so dry when he was a child.

"That is true," Rohona said when questioned about the drought. "The K'atsina do not bring as much rain as they once did. There are many who say that it is because we give prayers to the foreign god and not to the K'atsina, but I have never forgotten to send prayer sticks to Wenimats."

"*Dios* sends rain when we pray to him, also," Augustín said, and from that time on his prayers on almost all occasions contained that petition.

As was the custom at Áco, care of grandchildren frequently devolved upon grandparents while the mothers and fathers worked in the fields, and during the summer Rohona was more than pleased to spend his time at the dwelling making leather and wooden toys for his great-grandson and teaching him the things one can teach even a toddler.

The winter after Aurelio's first birthday the entire family spent its days together as the fierce cold of the season precluded planting work, but no hands were ever idle. It was a time they all savored as Siya and Antonia embroidered the cloth that Rohona wove.

Embroidery was one thing at which Antonia excelled. That she had had to learn as a child. She made beautiful altar cloths and vestments for Padre Ramírez, and he told her that if she wished to make more, he would send them to Santa Fé where he was sure they would fetch a very good price. Antonia was hesitant, but Rohona urged her to do it.

"With the earnings, we might have the *padre* buy us some sheep or a burro. The wool is a very good fiber to weave, and if I had more of it, I could weave more, and now that my legs are not as strong as they once were, I can be useful by weaving."

"Then, of course, I shall make things to send to Santa Fé," she said, delighted she could do something of value for the household.

Augustín was busy with leatherwork and spent a great deal of time sitting beside his grandfather receiving instructions and profiting from the old man's experience and knowledge.

"In our villages working with skins is the work of men. I remember when I first lived with the *españoles* in their *villa* near Ohké that I went to Taos with an old man named Domingo to trade with the buffalo Indians that came from the plains." Rohona chuckled. "I say 'old man,' but I am much older than he was then. But at that time he seemed very old to me. Time does funny things to our minds, Grandson." He picked up the fresh, wet deerhide that lay near them, and Augustín helped him drape it over a log that leaned against a wall of their house. He continued, "On the plains it is the women who work the skins, but they do not have corn to grind like the women here."

"Perhaps there is no such thing as 'women's work' and 'men's work.' Maybe it's simply that *Dios* put us on the earth, and we must survive in the best way we can," Augustín said.

"Perhaps. But now," Rohona said as he picked up a curved scraper, "we must remove all the flesh. We soaked the skin in the stone pool like you saw, and now it is soft enough to work." He handed the scraper to Augustín. "Scrape with smooth downward strokes, and when this side is done we will turn it over and remove the hair and the grain."

The process took much longer than Augustín expected and the hide was nicked in numerous places, evidence of his lack of skill. After the skin was scraped, they put it back in the pool to soak again before starting the actual tanning process. When they were ready to begin that, Rohona had Augustín tie the hide to the top pole of a drying rack, stretch it, and peg it down.

"Now we use the deer brains we boiled," Rohona said, unwrapping the corn husks in which the brains had been kept. "We rub them into both sides of the skin, and when that is done, we wring the hide out until it is dry, and then we rub it with a piece of sandstone until the leather is very soft."

Again the process required much more time than Augustín would have thought, and he understood why the Ácoma were so careful with their belongings. When one bought a piece of cloth and had a tailor make a pair of breeches, one had no appreciation of the effort involved, but if you spent days preparing a piece of material sufficient for scarcely one garment, you were going to take good care of that article.

"I think this skin would make a nice tunic for your young wife," Rohona pronounced when the leather was ready.

Augustín smiled. "I know it is far from an expert tanning job, but I am proud of it, just as Antonia is proud of her pots. I promise you, Grandfather, one day neither of us will shame you with our work."

"Grandson, you give me pride, only pride. But let's see," Rohona said, "let's rub this hide with a thin wash of white clay to make it really white and fitting for such a fine wife as yours. I will get some of Siya's clay that she uses for the slip on her pots. That makes the leather very beautiful."

When Augustín presented Antonia with the garment, no elegant lady of the viceregal capital could have been happier, even if she had just received a new dress of the finest Philippine silk.

Although tiring, the work they did was interesting to them, but what they enjoyed most were the long conversations that accompanied their labors. Siya had only the rudiments of literacy, but she nevertheless enjoyed listening to the discussions that animated the other three. Rohona's reading was minuscule compared to his grandson's as well as to that of the girl who had been tutored by the beloved boy he had sent to Mexico so long ago, but both Augustín and Antonia never ceased to be amazed at the perspicacity of the unschooled old man.

And while the adults sat working and talking, the baby with the red-gold hair toddled busily among them amusing himself with bits of leather and tools, stopping occasionally for a loving hug given by one of the adults.

Padre Ramírez came often and spent the long, cold days of winter enjoying the companionship of the household.

"With the next mission caravan, I shall send to Mexico for books for the boy for his education," the priest said proudly. "Already you can see Aurelio's quick intelligence."

At last the sharp claws of winter were retracted, and although the early morning air carried a stringent chill, the earth and rocks absorbed the brilliant rays of the sun, which was on its way north bringing the renewal of life to the land.

Augustín had prepared the ground for planting, but Rohona said the moon was not good and they should wait before punching the seeds into the ground with the planting stick. Augustín took advantage of the brief respite from work and sought the rock outcropping that had become his place of prayer and meditation. As always his prayers, as he knelt on the ledge of rocks some eight or so feet above a small sandy arroyo, began with an outpouring of his thanks for the gifts God had given him.

"How unworthy I am to receive your multitude of mercies, Lord," he would say, "but I shall ever strive to do your will. Ask of me whatever you wish, and I shall do it with great joy."

He did not feel the roughness of the pale sandstone on which he knelt. He thought only of the stark beauty of that land that God had created. Near where he knelt a tiny white flower grew valiantly out of a small fissure in the bare rock. What courage that small blossom had in the face of its harsh surroundings, but it gave unmistakable evidence of the renewal of life God brought.

The sun beat warmly down on his shoulders, and the rocks around him soaked up the warmth of the strengthening rays of the sun as it moved on its path north for summer. A pair of sharpshinned hawks circled overhead, their acute eyesight taking in the earth below and any movement that might mean food.

And there *was* a movement below that caught Augustín's eye. A writhing ball of intertwined rattlers fell from a crevice in the rocks well below him onto the sandy bottom of the small arroyo that ran between the high rocks on which he knelt and between the interspersed boulders on the other side. The rays of the returning sun had brought the sleeping nest of snakes from its winter habitat. Life was returning to the valley of Áco.

He closed his eyes and prayed. *Please, Lord, bring rain to this valley for the crops of summer.*

A small noise that should not have been in that isolated place sent a shiver of fear through him.

His blood chilled when he saw the source of it. A small child squatted on the edge of the narrow, sandy arroyo waving a stick at the writhing mass of snakes. The sound had been one of childish delight. He had heard Aurelito make that sound many times, and the child below him could not have been much older than his own son.

"No!" Augustín shouted to the boy in Queres as he leaped to his feet. "Get back! Get away from the snakes!"

Where on earth had the child come from? There must be a parent or grandparent somewhere near.

"Get back!" he shouted again, waving his arms, but the child just stood and smiled at him, waving the stick in its hands.

Augustín saw a small bit of sand slide down the side of the arroyo like a miniature avalanche. The edge was going to crumble away and send the boy down into the snakes.

"Get back!"

More sand slid into the arroyo. The child wavered on the edge.

"Thank You, *Dios*, for the great joys You have given me," Augustín shouted at the sky, then leaped from the ledge down into the shallow arroyo. As he landed in the deadly pit, he shoved the child backward from the edge. He felt a sharp pain in his thigh and another in his chest, then another. He knew he would die quickly and was thankful. The poison would be potent after the long winter. He crossed himself as best he could and began the Act of Contrition. Somewhere in the distance he heard a voice. He turned his head and saw an old grandmother embracing the child. Near her lay the bundle of firewood she had been gathering.

"Please," he managed to speak in Queres, "go tell the old man Rohona what has happened. Please bring the *padre.*"

It was all he could manage, and he felt the sand against his face.

Chapter 25

Grief rent the air.

Tears he could not stop rolled down Juan Ramírez's cheeks as he said the last rites over the inert body of the boy he had sent to Mexico some twenty-odd years before. The boy whom he had loved as a son, the man whose return had filled him with such great joy, lay dead.

Rohona keened his grief in a high chant, and the boy's aunt wailed her sorrow. Quiet sobs shook Antonia's shoulders as she rocked back and forth clutching her son, who understood nothing of what was happening. The toddler pushed himself out of his mother's arms and scrambled down into the arroyo where his father lay so still and unmoving.

By the time they had reached the arroyo to which the old grandmother led them, the snakes had all slithered away. The boy who was scarcely a month from his second birthday crawled on his father's chest not comprehending why his father did not hug him and wrestle with him playfully. Juan Ramírez picked the boy up and hugged him in place of the man who could not.

His job finished, the priest climbed out of the arroyo. It was now the turn of the snake medicine man who stepped down into the arroyo with his medicine pouch.

"*Padre*," Rohona said to Ramírez when the medicine man had finished. "I have a favor to ask."

"Anything."

"My grandson should rest with his parents, but I no longer have the strength to take him alone."

They put the body on Juan Ramírez's mule and transported it to the pinnacle. Neither man was young and it took the rest of the day, using ropes the priest brought from the *convento*, to get the body to the top.

When Ramírez reached the flat top of the pinnacle and saw the three stone cairns with their weathered crosses, he stood in amazement. "You made these?"

Rohona nodded.

Nothing more was said until the fourth grave was finished.

The priest made the sign of the cross over each cairn and spoke the words his god would understand.

Rohona sprinkled cornmeal to the cardinal directions, his prayers in the language his gods comprehended.

"Our boy . . ." Juan Ramírez started, but his words caught in his throat and he was unable to continue.

"Oh, Mia," Rohona whispered, "how many pieces of my heart lie under these stones."

"Grandfather," Antonia said respectfully as she stood in front of him. He sat stooped and quiet on the house rooftop. "It has been a month since my husband, your grandson, died. May I speak to you about something very important?"

Rohona looked up at her and nodded. In scarcely a month he seemed to have aged twenty years. She knelt in front of him.

"Please forgive me if I am forward. I do not wish to be disrespectful, but I want to discuss something that affects me deeply."

"Please, speak openly, Granddaughter."

Antonia looked down at her hands folded in her lap, looked up, and began. "You know that I loved your grandson more than life itself. I need your help, Grandfather. I have drunk the herb of forgetfulness, and it has helped me, although I know I shall never forget Augustín. But now I must put all my efforts toward raising his son as he would have wanted."

Rohona said nothing and she continued.

"Grandfather, I desperately need your help to raise Aurelito so that he may learn all that he needs to know to live among the Ácoma."

There was a long silence. Rohona sat with his eyes closed, and she knew not whether he slept or even heard. She had seen the transformation wrought in the old man upon the return of the grandson he had sent to Mexico long years previously. Rohona seemed ancient when they arrived, but within days the cloak of age had fallen away from him, and although he limped because of his maimed foot, he seemed full of vigor and a renewed love of life.

Now, the cloak of age again enveloped him. He sat with his shoulders stooped, his eyes on the ground or often closed, he scarcely rose to walk; he refused most food.

Antonia was terrified. How could she raise the boy alone there at Áco with only Siya's help? She had none of the skills of life that would be vital to the boy's existence there. Would she have to seek the Spanish settlement? What would happen if the truth were learned by the Spanish authorities and by the Church with its powerful, vengeful judicial arm—the feared Inquisition? She sat quietly, calling on every strength she possessed to keep her courage alive.

Rohona opened his eyes and looked directly at her. His face was solemn. "You are filled with wisdom, Granddaughter," he said. "I, too, drank the herb of forgetfulness, but it did little good. I have let my sorrow wrap me in its robe of self-pity, and it has blinded me to the thing of most importance." He touched her hand again.

"You will have my help, Granddaughter. As long as this body draws breath, I will help you raise the son of my grandson, your husband. Together we will raise up a fine man who would have made his father proud. In my sorrow for a death, I have forgotten the joy of a precious life."

"And yet the death, too, should give us joy," Antonia said, tears rimming her eyes. "What greater knowledge could we have of the true worth of a person whom we loved than that he should give his life for another? Did not the family of the child say as much? Is that not what *Dios* wishes of us? Does he not sometimes have a purpose for us that we are too blind to see?"

"Sometimes I do not like your *Dios*. I cannot see his purposes," Rohona said.

Antonia started to come to the defense of the God she and Augustín loved, but Rohona threw his arms up to the sky and shouted heavenward.

"Finally *You* have made an old man see!" he said to the sky. He sat there for long moments, and Antonia wondered whether the old man's grief had affected his mind, but when he looked back at her and smiled, she saw perfect lucidity in his face.

"An understanding of your god's purpose has come to me." He closed his eyes and paused before he spoke again.

"A long time ago a woman I loved spoke also of your god's purpose and said that one day I would know what that purpose was. She said her death had a purpose. Now you say that my grandson's death has a purpose. I *now* know what that purpose is."

A tentative smile trembled at the corners of Antonia's lips, and her eyes were filled with questions and incomprehension as she looked at the old man's smiling face.

Rohona closed his eyes again. He sat that way for some moments as if absorbing the full impact of his new knowledge. Then he looked up.

"Many years ago my son Alejandro came to live at Áco. Because he had the blood of Spaniards, he was never accepted. It was a source of deep pain for me, for I loved him and wanted my people to accept him. But they would not. And then his son, my grandson Augustín, who was born here on the rock of Áco, he, too, was rejected by my people. No children would be his friends. He was a lonely little boy whose only companions were the books that had been his grandmother's. To send him away to the far city of Mexico made me feel that my heart had been torn from my chest, but to read his letters and know of his happiness gave me contentment. His son—your son, my little great-grandson—who was likewise born here on the rock of Áco, would also have been rejected by my people. He would never have been accepted; he would always have been a friendless, lonely outcast among the Ácoma."

Tears of pride came to Rohona's eyes. "But his father has given him a gift that no one else could ever have given. With his death, his father has given him the gift of life—a life of acceptance among the people of Áco."

Rohona looked at the sky again. "Why did I not see it?"

He touched Antonia's hand. "It took my granddaughter's words to this foolish old man to make me understand. The answer to the purpose of my grandson's death has been in front of me for days and yet only now do I recognize it. Has not the mother of the child he saved made a set of clothes for your son?" She nodded, though still uncomprehending.

"To make a set of clothes for a child, Granddaughter, is to say that that child is like a son to you. Has not the father made the boy a beautiful pair of moccasins and a bow with beautifully feathered blunt arrows? Has not the family brought us many succulent dishes? Has not the family brought their little boy Gyatyu to play with Mokaitsh, the son of the man who gave his life for their son?"

Rohona sat up straight and threw back his shoulders. He suddenly looked much younger than his many years. "Yes," he said with satisfaction, "my grandson's child will be accepted by my people. I shall teach my little great-grandson the ways of Áco, and he shall truly be a person of the White Rock."

Life was not easy for them without the strong back of a man to plant and harvest and hunt, but they survived. Antonia helped in the fields, as did all women. Siya, too, would help while Aurelito stayed in the village and played with Gyatyu, bobcat, who was his best friend, while the boy's grandmother watched over them.

Padre Ramírez helped them, sharing from the church's goods. They had no one to hunt for them, but Gyatyu's father brought them venison several times a year, and there were rabbits and small game at regular intervals.

Since before the Spaniards came, the Ácoma had domesticated turkeys, which they kept for their feathers. Antonia took great pains to increase their flock, and the animals served them as a source of food, also. But *shiwana*, the clouds, did not bring sufficient rain, and all the Ácoma suffered when their crops suffered.

They were not alone. None of the fields in *Nuevo México* saw enough of the life-giving moisture. Some of the villages were suffering more than Áco.

Drought brought another scourge to the pueblos besides withered crops. The village dwellers did not have enough to eat, nor did the nomadic peoples. Navajo and Apache raids were increasing with alarming frequency. Never was the *Camino del Padre* without its sentries.

❖   ❖   ❖

The months, which then turned into years, were blurred and without distinction for Antonia, save for the development of her son. He now spoke Queres fluently, preferring it over the Spanish his mother had taught him. He was beginning the rudimentaries of reading under the tutelage of his mother and Juan Ramírez. He shot his small bow with amazing accuracy already, and he and his best friend Gyatyu were inseparable, running and playing games that imitated the warriors of the village.

When Aurelio was six there came a change in his home life. He knew something strange had happened but he did not understand fully what it was. All he knew was that a sixteen-year-old half-Indian boy with piercing black eyes had come to live with them—permanently, it seemed.

Aurelio sat, his gray eyes wide and with a touch of fear in them, as the strange teenaged boy gave Siya a stained letter written on the paper of the *españoles*. His auntie's nervousness and his great-grandfather's cold, hard features did nothing to put Aurelio or the other boy at ease, but there was nothing in the visitor's hawklike features that gave the slightest indication of fear.

Although Aurelio could never have articulated it, he saw the proud arrogance as well as perhaps a bit of cruelty in the boy who had come so unexpectedly from the *villa* of Santa Fé to their dwelling there on Áco mesa.

Siya took the letter gingerly and opened it. She looked at it for only a moment and handed it to Rohona, who likewise glanced at it.

"Granddaughter," he said to Antonia, "would you be so good as to read the letter to us. These old eyes do not see so well anymore."

Before she began, Antonia's eyes glimpsed the signature DOROTEA at the bottom of the hastily written page.

"Dearest Siya," the letter began. Antonia's voice was hushed but all could hear, for there was not a sound in the room.

I have no right to send Diego to you, but I could think of nothing else to do, for time was precious. I cannot expect you to understand, knowing how you suffered at the father's hands, but in my fear for the boy's well-being, sending him to you was the only thing I could think of.

After all these years, I am sure you are just as disbelieving as I that Isidro should have a son—those countless girls who suffered his abuse never giving him the son he so desired, the son that I also could not give him. In his sixty-fourth year God granted him his lifelong desire from a young Apache girl. But God's gift was also his retribution and punishment: Isidro's own son killed him.

Please do not look with horror on Diego for what he did. God will undoubtedly punish me, but there were times when I wished I had had the courage to kill Isidro. And you, Siya, as much as anyone, have a right to despise the memory of this brutal man.

In spite of the fact that he was engendered by a man I loathed, I love Diego as my son, and I hope that by you knowing that, you will be able to feel a small bit of kindness and pity toward him. He, too, suffered greatly at the hands of his father. To make the boy behave, Isidro would beat Diego's mother right before his eyes when he was small. You cannot believe the suffering he inflicted on this boy — the son he had waited so long for.

I loved the boy as mine even though he was not, and I tried as best I could to ease the abuse he received from his father, although what I could do was precious little. In the end, Diego was driven to kill his own father. I will not relate the circumstances other than to say Isidro was in a rage, and although he was an old man, he was whipping the boy cruelly. In self-protection, Diego drew a knife. Isidro laughed and said, "Come on. Kill your father." I will never forget the look on Isidro's face as Diego stepped forward and plunged the knife into his heart.

The Spanish authorities are hunting Diego, and although I believe he was justified in his act, he would surely hang here if he were found. I will understand fully if you cannot take the boy in, but if you could give him shelter until he is rested and perhaps a little food, he might be able to continue on to the distant Hopi villages and there perhaps find a refuge.

For anything you can do for him, I will be eternally grateful. I miss you, Siya, and so wish I had news of you. I send you my prayers that God grant you all his many mercies. Your faithful friend, Dorotea.

Siya glanced at Rohona, and although no one else saw it, there was a question in the look. A slight movement of the old man's head indicated approval.

"Welcome, my son," Siya said in Spanish to Diego. A smile lit her face, and she embraced the surprised boy.

For a moment Antonia saw the boy's defenses drop and realized he had been frightened despite his proud, fierce look.

Antonia turned to the boy. "Welcome," she said warmly, "I am glad my son shall have a brother."

Diego looked at her and there was surprise again and gratitude in his eyes. Aurelio did not quite comprehend what had happened, but he was glad to see the tension in the room disappear, and he liked the thought of a big brother. He walked over to Diego.

"You are my brother now?" he asked tentatively.

The boy smiled at him and then glanced at the adults in the room. "Yes," he said, putting his hand on Aurelio's shoulder, "I am your brother now."

Chapter 26

"He was an evil man," Siya said. "When the *padres* in the *villa* of Santa Fé used to talk about *el diablo, his* face was always the one that appeared in my mind."

Siya told her the story of Isidro Inojosa, and Antonia felt sick with revulsion and filled with pity for the women who had been subjected to his cruelty.

"How could Dorotea have endured so long?" Antonia asked.

"She is a *santa,*" Siya said. "It was she with whom Augustín stayed in the *villa* before the cart train took him to Mexico. She was his grandmother's closest friend."

"She knows nothing of what has happened since we returned, does she?"

"No," Siya said. "I do not think so. Padre Ramírez has not been to the *villa* since you have been at Áco. The journey is too hard on him with the painfulness he has in his bones now."

"I think he suffers much more than he ever allows anyone to see," Antonia said, "but just looking at his hands one is aware immediately of the extent of his trouble. His hands and fingers have become so bent that he has much difficulty in removing the lid from the silver wafer box and even in turning the pages of the missal when he says Mass."

"He is a *santo,* also," Siya said.

"Yes, God will have a special place in Heaven waiting for this *padre.*"

Returning to their earlier conversation, Antonia continued. "I would like to write Doña Dorotea a letter and tell her all that has happened. I think she would like to know. I could also tell her that Diego is now living with us and will be safe here at Áco. Would there be any danger in sending such a letter?"

"Not if it were taken by the right person," Siya said. "I know Doña

Dorotea would be grateful for a letter. Go ahead and write it, and I will tell Rohona so that when someone is going to San Felipe or Santo Domingo, they can deliver it into the *villa* to Doña Dorotea."

Antonia had never seen Dorotea, but as she wrote the letter, it seemed to her that she was writing to a friend.

Diego is like a member of the family, but he works harder than is necessary. He seems to think he must in order to justify his living here, but I cannot tell you what a boon he has been for us. It was difficult not having a strong man in the household, for neither Grandfather, nor Siya, nor I had the forces necessary for some tasks. Although he is only sixteen, he does the work of a man. I know you must miss him sorely, but I want you to know that he has a home here, and we have taken him to our hearts. He will not lack for love. My son, Aurelio, is de-lighted to have an older brother, and Diego is so good to him.

I am sorry that Diego hates the Spanish so, but considering the circumstances, it is understandable. It seems that you and I are the only ones of Castilian blood that he accepts. I have tried to tell him there are many Spaniards who are good, but he refuses to believe it and says that you and I are the only ones of that race who merit living. I hope he will learn to believe differently. Perhaps Father Ramírez will help change his mind, for he is certainly a good man and he is a Spaniard.

Diego suffers from nightmares, and many times I have risen to com-fort him, although I think he does not wake. He calls me "*mamacita Doro*," so obviously he misses you very much indeed. At those times he seems so young and vulnerable. Although I know I will never take your place, I hope that I may comfort him, for it tears my heart to see him trembling and crying while he clutches at me as if needing protection. In the morning he makes no mention of the disturbance to his sleep. I pray that as he begins to feel safe here the troubling dreams will go away.

Dearest friend, for you do truly seem a dear friend to me, now you know all that has occurred, past and present. Siya sends her love, and Diego in particular—he wanted me to reassure you that he is well. He also wanted me to tell you that he would sneak into the *villa* soon to see you, but I think—I pray—Grandfather has convinced him not to. Perhaps one day it will be possible, but the danger is much too great now. I told him that I knew with absolute certainty that no matter how much you would want to see him, you would never wish him to come to the *villa* and expose himself to such great danger. I send my love and prayers and assurance that I shall try to make this seem a real home to Diego. Your friend, Antonia.

The runner left that day for the *villa*, the letter securely tucked into the pouch he wore at his waist. When he returned, in less than a month, he brought with him a letter from Dorotea.

She expressed her deep sorrow over the death of Augustín but her joy at knowing he had a son who lived at Áco and with whom Diego now had a home. She could never repay their kindness and would be forever thankful for it. She also wrote forbidding Diego to come to the *villa* for several years at least. She included news of the *villa* that made Diego once again give vent to the expression of his hatred for Spaniards.

The governor, Juan Manso, was having an affair with Margarita Márquez de Carbajal, the wife of a captain, and she was pregnant with his child; the Hopis had come to Zia Pueblo to denounce their priest who had tarred and feathered their villagers; there were complaints from San Marcos that the priest had violated village women; the Navajo had ambushed Jemez Pueblo, killing nineteen and taking thirty-five prisoners; and a colonist by the name of Juan Domínguez had gone in retaliation with a force of Spanish soldiers and a contingent of Pueblo warriors.

Diego fumed. "Spanish dogs! They'll hump anything in sight! And so will the *padres*! If they did not steal the food of the pueblos, there would be no hunger in the land. If they did not make slave raids on the Apache and Navajo, there would be no attacks by them. Everything that is evil in this land is because of the *cochinos españoles*! Why don't you rise up and kill them all?" he demanded of Rohona. "There are enough of you."

"Sometimes killing serves a purpose; other times it does not." There was something in Rohona's tone of voice that made Diego refrain from saying more.

After that outburst, Diego did not express his hatred of Spaniards for a long time. Antonia did not know whether it was because of Rohona's words or because there had been no occasion, but she was quite certain that Diego's feelings were unchanged. As for his feelings toward her, it seemed they had been gradually undergoing a change. She felt he had transferred to her the love he had felt for Dorotea and perhaps, even that of his own mother, although he did not speak of her.

She could not have wished for a more conscientious or helpful son. He had indeed made her life easier, and she was sure that he would have taken over all her chores had she asked. If she were carrying something, he would take it from her and carry it; if she were at the fields hoeing weeds with the scratching stick, he would tell her to go sit under the thatched sun shelter and rest, he would finish. She would protest and keep hoeing, but eventually she would have to give in to his persistence.

Diego was not tall, but his strength belied his size and age. He was small and wiry and of tremendous endurance. He had obviously taken after his Apache mother much more than his father, for in native dress he looked every bit Indian, Antonia thought. There was in the bone structure of his face a hint of his Spanish heritage, but his skin was as dark as any Ácoma.

Antonia was always surprised that Diego was gentle and usually respectful at home, for there was an unquestionable arrogance about him and an unsettling intensity that spoke of violent emotions.

She had discussed Diego with Siya, and the latter had remarked that had it not been for the love Dorotea had given the child, he might have been very much like his father.

"But I like the boy," Siya said, "he is a good boy with us — with those he likes — and he is not far from worshiping you, daughter."

"I was granted only one child, perhaps Diego can be another," Antonia said. "He is so good to Aurelio, and I know Aurelio is delighted to have him as an older brother. I just hope the influence is always for good as I hope for Diego's sake that family life here will ease his spirit and that the nightmares will go away."

"They are still frequent?" Siya asked. "I am getting old and do not hear too well anymore. I am afraid attackers would be upon me before I awoke."

"He still has bad dreams but they do not come as often as they did at first. At those times, though, he is more like a child than a man almost grown. He is comforted by my arms around him rocking him or my stroking his hair while his head lies in my lap. I try to comfort him, thinking how terrible it would be if it were Aurelio who were so disturbed."

Life went on, and Diego strove to fit into the life at Áco. Rohona decided he would not tell the villagers that the boy's father was a Spaniard. Because Diego looked so much like a native, Rohona determined that he would say he had been taken on a slave raid and raised as a servant in a Spanish household and had run away to Áco. They had taken him in to help them since they had no able-bodied man in their house.

If the villagers were told that, it would make the boy's acceptance in the village easier and would, at the same time, explain Diego's Spanish habits and his lack of native skills. The latter, however, would not last long, for Diego applied himself with vengeance to the pursuits of all Áco's young men. Already his sinewy body could run as far and as long as any Ácoma his age. He practiced for hours with a bow, for there was no gunpowder available at Áco for the wheel lock pistol of his father's he had brought with him.

Rohona was pleased to see the boy's diligence at mastering the use of the bow, but he derived double satisfaction from it because wherever and whenever the boy went to practice, Aurelio was at his heels, his own bow grasped in his hand. Rohona could see the daily improvement of both, and he was glad for the Apache in their household. At times, however, Rohona worried about the boy's violent hatred of Spaniards, recognizing the danger and lack of wisdom in that volatile emotion.

Careful thought and dispassionate action were what was necessary for the achievement of success. Violence might bring the appearance of the immediate gain of one's objective, but first appearances were often fleeting. He must try to temper the boy's attitude — if not for the boy's sake, for the sake of his great-grandson, who would not be served by adopting the Apache's beliefs.

Augustín's death had taken a dimension away from the long conversations of winter, but Rohona and Antonia continued them. He talked frequently of the Roman, Marcus Aurelius, and of the stoicism that governed the emperor's life and informed his writings.

"The soul does violence to *itself* when it goes against any man with the intention of injuring him," Rohona said on occasion. He hoped that Diego would listen and profit by the wisdom from the printed leaves.

Antonia also talked frequently of Marcus Aurelius's philosophy, but it was not as benefit for the Apache boy but rather for her own circumstance. The stoic Roman's words, along with her belief in God, gave her the tools with which she wrought her happiness there on that stark, isolated sandstone rock.

Spanish was now scarcely spoken in their home. In the seven years that Antonia had lived there, she had mastered Queres, although her words still carried a distinct accent. When Diego came, they reverted to the language of the conquerors of *Nuevo México*, but he had aversion to it and quickly learned that spoken at Áco.

It was dusk when the news spread through the village, leaving in its wake palpable ripples of fear. Men returning from early spring work in the fields two leagues away ran into the village raising the alarm. Nomads had been seen in the distance by a sentry on a hilltop. They were on horseback, without a doubt Apache.

The pale Spanish strangers with their swift *caballos* had come into the land sixty years ago. At first the nomads of the land enjoyed the animals they captured as food — now they recognized their great value for swift attack and, more important, swift retreat. The horse was a prized possession of the Apaches, who ever sought to increase their own herds at the expense of the Spanish and to the profound detriment of the peaceful, village-dwelling pueblos.

The nomads' new mobility allowed them to make increasingly daring and profitable raids on the Pueblos' stores of grain. Not only had the advent of the Spaniards themselves brought harm to the villages, their horses, in the hands of the Apaches, brought greater destruction. Those villages farthest from the Spanish capital and least protected were suffering the most. Particularly those near the salines to the east of the Great River had felt the fierceness of the newly mobile nomads. Áco, too, had seen more raiding attempts than ever before, but their high rock served them well. The fields, however, were always vulnerable.

The men came running into the village, and instantly the *Camino del Padre* was under heavy guard. Ladders were pulled onto rooftops, quivers were snatched from their hooks, rocks were readied by the parapets of the rooftops.

"Get into the house," Antonia said to her son. "Stay inside."

"But where is Diego?" the boy asked. "He was at the fields."

A fleeting worry crossed Antonia's face when she realized that what Aurelio said was true, but she replied with assurance, "He is undoubtedly with the men guarding the *Camino*."

Her words seemed to satisfy Aurelio, but he said, "Let me stay out here. I can throw rocks, too, if they come."

"No!" Antonia said forcefully, "get into the house! You are too young to be out here." The boy obeyed her words reluctantly.

As darkness fell over the mesa, the tension in the village mounted. Siya, Antonia, and Rohona took turns sitting alert by the parapet while the others slept. Women and old men unable to fight were far from helpless if the village were attacked. From the safety of the rooftops they could rain down hundreds of stones on any attacker, and every rooftop was always well supplied with piles of the small missiles for just such a purpose.

There might have been a collective sigh of relief in the village when dawn came. There had been no attack in the hours just before the sun rose above East Mountain, and when the orb spread its bright light over the valley erasing the shadows of the night there was no trace of attackers to be seen. Men went down off the mesa to look for telltale tracks that might indicate there had been strangers down below in the night. Their report of none was received in the village with great relief.

"But where is Diego?" Aurelio pestered. "If there are no Apaches near, why hasn't he come home to eat by now?" Siya and Antonia were wondering the same thing. About that time, Gyatyu, Aurelio's inseparable friend, called the greeting to come up.

Aurelio was down the ladder before any response had been given to his friend below. It was not long, however, before they returned, out of breath, their eyes wide.

"No one has seen him since the fields," Aurelio said breathlessly, his young face filled with worry. The adults, too, could not hide their concern.

The rest of the day was filled with tension as the hours passed and the half-breed boy did not return. The men who had gone heavily armed to the fields that day reported no sight of Diego when they returned home that evening.

"Do you think the Apaches took him as a prisoner?" Aurelio asked that night.

"I don't know," his mother answered. She did not ask the other question in her mind—had he joined the Apaches to go live with them? She did not know that was also a question in Siya's mind.

On the fourth day, Diego reappeared and he had in tow two Apache ponies in addition to the one he rode. The village, filled with fear four days previously, was now filled with wonder.

In the days that passed, Aurelio never tired of hearing Diego's story of how he had crept up on the Apache camp and stolen the ponies.

"Will you take me with you some day when you go to steal Apache ponies?" Aurelio asked.

"When you are old enough," Diego promised.

Aurelio could scarcely control his excitement. Rohona, on the other hand, had difficulty concealing his own anxiety. What if the Apaches tracked Diego to Áco? What sort of retaliation could Áco expect if the ponies were found there? Was stealing ponies something he wanted his great-grandson to engage in? The answer to the last question he knew without a doubt. He must make Diego aware of the danger in which he had placed the village.

"If the Apaches track their ponies back to Áco, you have placed not just yourself but this whole village in peril. Do you stand ready to defend every life you have put in jeopardy here?

"A village is like a body. Both are made up of many parts, and each part is important and has its special function. Would you knowingly eat the deadly nightshade just because you thought it might taste good? No, you would put your whole body in peril. When one is a part of a village, one must consider others as if they were a part of one's own body and act accordingly. What you have done is to foolishly endanger many lives. That is why decisions must be made by a group with the welfare of the village in mind at all times."

Diego listened and grunted his acknowledgment of the truth of the old man's words, but Rohona was quite certain that the young man was not entirely convinced nor entirely willing not to repeat his daring deed.

"This is a matter for the war chiefs and elders to discuss," Rohona said, "for it is a matter that affects the whole village." Perhaps Diego did not have to obey Rohona, but he would have to obey a decision made by the tribe.

Rohona had not expected the discussion in the head *kiva* to last so long. He felt certain that the quick consensus would be that stealing ponies brought too much danger to the village. He had not counted on the many voices of the younger men to applaud the act; he had not expected that they would be in such awe of the deed. The consensus finally reached was that, for the moment, there would be no more pony stealing, but that did not mean that it would not be tolerated at some point in the near future.

"I am getting old," Rohona said to himself as he hobbled home that night. "I no longer know the hearts of the young men."

Chapter 27

Aurelio grew strong and tall and filled his family with much pride.

"He is a beautiful boy," Rohona would say as he watched the boy play at being a man.

His grandson's skin was tanned bronze by the sun of *Nuevo México,* his red-gold hair glinted in the same bright light, and his gray eyes were dark-lashed and filled with intelligence.

Padre Ramírez, who taught the boy reading and writing every day, commented many times on the aptitude of the son of the boy he had sent to Mexico for schooling.

"He is just as brilliant as his father was," the priest would say.

Not once, however, had it occurred to him to send this boy away from the village. He mentioned one day to the mother, however, that when Aurelio was just a few years older, he could be a great help to him in copying certain texts, as it was becoming increasingly more difficult to hold a pen.

"Padre," Antonia said, unable to keep from glancing at the knotted fingers of the priest, "I have a good hand, let me help you until Aurelio is old enough."

The friar accepted her offer without hesitation, and from that day on, every morning when early Mass was over, she would go into the *convento* where the priest had his living quarters and his small library in which he also kept the books and records of the church. She would enter and tally the number of bushels of corn produced on the Church's land, or she would note the number of spring lambs born, or she would enter births, deaths, baptisms, and marriages of villagers, or she would write some dispatch to Santo Domingo where the Custodia was located. She enjoyed the work and was grateful to be able to help the priest who had so added to her happiness at Áco. It was just as evident how grateful and how needful Juan Ramírez was of her help. She had not realized he was almost unable to write.

When he was eight, Aurelio made his first communion. It was an important day and one filled with pride for Antonia. She wished that Augustín could have lived to see this moment. He would have been so proud. The tears slid down her cheeks, and for the first time since the year of his death, she felt a deep, hollow loneliness that she could not dispel with willpower.

Diego would not attend daily Mass with them, although he was a baptized Christian, but on the occasion of Aurelio's first communion, she asked him to accompany them and he agreed.

Upon seeing her tears in church, he grasped her hand tentatively in a sign of comfort and support. She smiled through her tears at him, grateful for his caring. She had come to depend on Diego; they all needed each other there at Áco.

She and Siya prepared a feast for the occasion. Once the tears had been shed in church, her happiness returned by the time the ceremony was finished and they all gathered to enjoy the meal that had been prepared.

Aurelio's first communion was important to Antonia. There was another ceremony in the same year that was much more important to Aurelio's great-grandfather. Rohona had known the ceremony was coming. He had not expected what would happen.

The Hotcheni had gone through the village four days before, calling out what was to occur in Mauharots four days hence. A fleeting thought, a poignant wish, passed through Rohona's mind, but he did not dwell on it.

When Gyatyu's father appeared on the roof terrace after having called out the greeting to come up, he addressed Rohona as *Diumu,* or brother. Rohona thought his mind must surely be playing tricks on him. Perhaps he was dreaming. He was getting old; his mind seemed no longer to know the difference between reality and dream, but Kohaiya's words were very real.

"What I do is unusual. I hope that I do not offend you," the man said with solemnity, "but it would give me great pleasure if I might be your great-grandson's uncle. It is the place of a father or grandfather to choose the man to become his child's uncle for the ceremony, but I have learned you have asked no one. Your great-grandson is like a son to me; I would be honored to be his uncle. I do not wish to presume."

Rohona sought to control his voice. "Nor did I. I would not ask that of someone and place them in such an awkward position."

"Your great-grandson was born on Áco mesa," Kohaiya said. "He is being raised as an Ácoma. You have given the people of the White Rock much good counsel, and you have never forgotten the K'atsina. Neither should your great-grandson."

"Thank you," Rohona said with humility.

Gyatyu's father continued, "Your grandson gave me the life of my son. I wish to give the son of your grandson the life of the K'atsina."

The emotion that rose in Rohona threatened to overpower him. He did not know whether his aged body could endure it. It was a desire so deep yet so unattainable that the sudden fulfillment of it struck him as if sharp, jagged lightning had split *lanye*, the tallest of pine trees. For a moment he could not speak.

More difficult than not crying out when they had cut off his foot was finding words to bring forth at that moment. His voice, when he finally spoke, was no more than a hoarse whisper.

"By giving my great-grandson the life of the K'atsina, you give this old man life also. *Diumu,*" he said, "Brother, you do me great honor; it will be the great good fortune of my grandson to have you as an uncle."

Rohona summoned Aurelio. "Mokaitsh," he said, "your new uncle has come for you. He will take you to Mauharots. You are to be initiated into the K'atsina Society tonight."

Aurelio looked at his great-grandfather with incredulity. Rohona had already told him that he would not be able to participate in that secret, very important society into which all the children of Áco were initiated because there was no one to sponsor him. Aurelio had not understood the reasons his grandfather gave him. Would his best friend Gyatyu still be his best friend after Gyatyu had gone through the initiation and he had not? Aurelio's disbelief at his great-grandfather's words was clearly etched on his face.

"Yes," Rohona replied to his unasked question, "it is true. You are to be initiated into the K'atsina Society, and Gyatyu's father will be your sponsor, your new uncle."

Although Aurelio could not hide his happiness, he quickly recovered and spoke to Kohaiya in a serious voice more adult than his eight years. "I am proud to be your nephew, Uncle."

Rohona could not suppress the tears as he watched Kohaiya put Aurelio on his back to carry him to the *kiva* as all sponsors carried their children. Seventy years evaporated as Rohona remembered himself as a boy.

It was hot and stuffy in the *kiva* that night long ago when he had been carried to Mauharots. He knew he would not be afraid, for his prayer arrow had reached the narrow, inaccessible cleft in the ivory-pink sandstone. There his fear now lay. Tsitsunits made a terrible noise as he rushed down the ladder with his back to the rungs. He brandished his yucca whips, and his huge teeth seemed to sneer menacingly at the children as he ran and danced among them, but Rohona had not been afraid. He knew Aurelio would not be afraid.

All that night Rohona would chant his prayers and on the morrow he would make prayer sticks to send to Wenimats.

Rohona knew that there would be those who would disapprove of what Kohaiya had done; he knew that there would be those who would never accept his great-grandson as Ácoma, but that did not matter to him now. His great-grandson would be able to dance for the K'atsina—that would make him Ácoma.

Rohona could not keep the tears from misting his eyes when he saw the *wabani* tied in Aurelio's red-gold hair as Gyatyu's father led him onto the rooftop terrace much later that night.

Antonia could never have fully understood the depth of the importance of the ceremony through which her son had just gone, but she understood enough from Rohona's and Siya's faces to know that what had occurred was of tremendous significance.

The following morning at Mass, she said a special prayer of thanksgiving for the ceremony she did not understand. Afterward she told Padre Ramírez about the occurrence of the previous evening.

He smiled and took her hand, led her to the altar rail and knelt. She went to her knees beside him.

"I, too, wish to say a prayer of thanksgiving. This is a momentous day," he said. He crossed himself. "Thank you, *Dios*, for this wonderful sign. A child is rejected, a child is taken back, and with him goes the knowledge of You."

When they went into the *convento*, Antonia asked, "What does it really mean, *Padre*?"

"I cannot tell you for sure," he said truthfully, "but to the best of my understanding it means your son is now an Ácoma."

Antonia's eyes were luminous with tears. "I think that may be his salvation here."

"Who knows," the priest said, "perhaps it is all the work of *Dios*."

"You may be right," she said, "and Augustín is smiling, too."

Padre Ramírez patted her on the shoulder as he turned away. She watched him walk slowly and painfully to the desk where the ledgers were kept, and she prayed silently that the Lord would have mercy on the saintly friar and ease his pain. The *padre*'s difficulty in walking was daily becoming more apparent, and his acolyte had to assist him during the Mass to rise from a kneeling position.

Four days after the K'atsina initiation, Gyatyu's mother came for her new child. She took Aurelio home with her, removed the *wabani* from his hair and then shampooed his hair with yucca suds. She bathed him and dressed him in a beautiful outfit of new clothes. For his breakfast she made him many delicious things, and afterward she gave him the basket of gifts the K'atsina had sent for him. He was delighted.

Rohona, Siya, and Antonia stood on the roof terrace and watched as Gyatyu's mother brought Aurelio home. He stood tall and proud as he carried in a blanket of corn the K'atsina had given him. That corn he must plant in the spring by himself. It was sacred corn — corn whose growth would mean long life and good fortune. Gyatyu's mother carried the basket containing the other gifts from the K'atsina.

Aurelio would now begin the early morning runs on the valley floor with the older boys. It would not matter whether there was ice on water left outside, it would not matter if there was a dusting of snow on the ground or if it were the depth of his ankle or knee. Each morning before dawn he would arise, and wearing only a breechclout and rabbit fur–lined moccasins, he would descend the steep rock to run on the valley floor. He would go to the *kiva* with the other boys, he would learn to dance for the K'atsina, he would learn to sing prayers for them, he would learn to make prayer sticks, and he would learn the ancient story of Iyatiku.

By the time he was eleven, he was proficient in them all. He stood a head taller than other boys his age, and one could already glimpse the man who would emerge from the boy with the red-gold hair. He made his family and his new uncle very proud, and as well, Padre Ramírez.

This made the decision the priest had to make easier and yet more difficult at the same time. The boy danced beautifully for the K'atsina and made his prayer sticks as he should, but he also attended Mass and had a clearer view of *Dios*'s love than many adults Padre Ramírez had known in the viceregal capital of Mexico City.

The boy was a fine reader, and the priest knew he had little left to teach him, for the boy's pursuits should be those of the Ácoma. His knowledge of reading, writing, and literature were abundant for self-enjoyment and the pleasure he might derive within the vast expanses of his intelligence. One day his literacy might be valuable to the people of the White Rock should any civil or ecclesiastical authority attempt to undermine the life of the village.

Padre Ramírez's work was done. It filled him with great sadness. He had converted the Ácoma. He had brought them the message of the Gospel; he had built the *Camino del Padre*, which had made their life on the rock easier; he had brought them new animals, and they now enjoyed the warmth of wool and the sustenance of mutton; he had brought them new plants, and they now benefited from the fruits and vegetables in their diet. And he had seen the son of the boy he loved like a son accepted into the tribe, and with him went also the spark of *Dios*.

Yes, his work was done and he wanted to end his days on the Rock. He wanted his bones interred in the burial ground in front of the church, in the dirt that he and the villagers had laboriously carried in baskets on their backs up from the valley floor. It was a hard decision he had had to make, but he made it during a pain-filled nightlong vigil.

When morning came, he could not rise from his kneeling position and fell to the floor. The sacristan had to help him to his feet. Yes, he had come to the only decision possible, but he must tell them — tell one man, in particular, first. That would be more difficult than the decision itself.

"No, you cannot," Rohona said with agitation. "It would *not* be in the best interests of the village. That you have difficulty in walking does not hurt the people. *I* have difficulty in walking; many have difficulty in walking. No, you *must not go!*"

"Yes, I must. I can no longer carry out my duties. I must go and allow a younger priest to take my place so that the Ácoma may be served. It was my fervent desire to end my days here on the White Rock, but it is not to be."

Rohona heard the resolution in the priest's voice. "Then ask for a younger priest to come," he said, "but stay here with him. Stay among the Ácoma. End your days here as you desire."

Although he would dearly love to take Rohona's suggestion, Padre Ramírez said resolutely, "No, I cannot. The new priest would not be able to make the Ácoma his flock. They would come to me and not to him. His work would be undermined by my presence here. I know I must leave, for I would only be a crutch or a stumbling block. My purpose has been served and served well, I hope. It is God's will that I not end my days here on the White Rock."

Rohona said no more, but that night he prayed to the Castilian god as well as to the K'atsina.

The farewell was tearful. The entire village came down off the rock to bid its good-bye to the priest who had lived among them for over thirty years. They had not realized he had become as much a part of Áco as the massive church he built there.

Rohona had not been the only Ácoma man to ask the priest to stay, but no one succeeded in changing the friar's mind.

Antonia wrote the letter, which the *padre* dictated to the Father Custodian at Santo Domingo. She was devastated. The thought of losing the man who had been an important source of her happiness at Áco left her with a feeling of desolation. Padre Ramírez tried to comfort her but did not succeed.

The runner took the letter to Santo Domingo, and two months later, a cart and a small escort of soldiers arrived at the base of the mesa to take Padre Ramírez back to civilization — first to Santo Domingo and then to Mexico City in the next cart train.

No priest came, much to the relief of the Ácoma, but the Spanish soldiers assured them that one would be sent out soon. The soldiers did not realize that their words were not reassuring.

Rohona looked upon the departure of the old priest with great foreboding. He was very troubled. What would a new priest at Áco bring? Would he allow them to dance for the K'atsina as the *padre* had? Would he allow them to keep the sacred masks that, when worn, became the K'atsina themselves? Would he allow the medicine men to perform their healing?

Rohona had heard what happened in other pueblos, and anger filled him with its violent, roiling heat. The priests in many villages forbade any dancing whatsoever; they took out the K'atsina masks, heaped them in a pile, and burned them; they flogged villagers on any pretext; they forced the people like slaves to plant corn and wheat for the church, not allowing them time to plant their own fields for the sustenance of their families; they made villagers weave hundreds of *mantas*, tan hundreds of hides, so that the *padre* might export them and make his church the richest in the province.

It had been a long time since Rohona had experienced the emotion of hate. That was the feeling he had harbored in his breast when he made the woman with gray eyes and hair the color of wet pine bark his in the golden leaves. But now he must not hate; he must not let anger rule him. The conviction did not ease the worry that gnawed at him, however.

Diego must have sensed the worry, but he had not understood it. "Grandfather," he said, "do not worry about the priest leaving. It is better that he has gone. Now Áco can return to the way it used to be before the Spanish dogs came into the land."

Would the boy never learn? Would he never see? Rohona had to control his words. "The worry is not the priest leaving. The worry is who comes in his place."

"But Áco should not allow another to come. If one comes, they should drive him out."

"Then another one will be sent."

"Drive him away."

"Eventually there would be a confrontation. Áco would be the one to suffer most."

Diego had not learned Indian manners. He had not learned that young people do not argue with their elders out of respect and politeness.

"Why do you take their abuse?" he demanded. "Why don't you stand up to them? If all the pueblos united, you could push them out of the land tomorrow. They are few; you are many. Why don't you act like men?!"

Rohona ignored the boy's incredible rudeness. "It is easy for a man to die," he said. "The difficult task is to live."

Again there was something in the old man's voice that made Diego refrain from saying more.

Juan Ramírez had gone. It did little good to worry—worry would change nothing, Rohona knew. The *padre* was no longer there to give Aurelio his daily lessons. Rohona would take the priest's place, but his lessons would not be the same.

He would teach his great-grandson about the man for whom the boy was named. He would impart to him the wisdom of Marcus Aurelius; he would teach him so that he might profit from the words of the Roman. The old Ácoma man would not be Zeno in Athens teaching from the Stoa, but he would be Rohona teaching from a roof terrace of Áco.

His grandson would be influenced by men like Diego, and the boy would be well served to know and heed the words of the philosopher-emperor. And so Rohona had begun the lessons.

They would sit on the roof terrace in the early morning after Aurelio's daily run. The boy would read, and Rohona would ask him to explain what the Roman meant. If he understood, Rohona would expand on what the philosopher was saying, adding examples from life at Áco that were apropos. If he did not understand, Rohona would explain, again employing native metaphors and examples.

To live as Marcus Aurelius counseled was not difficult at Áco. For a bed, the philosopher had a plank and a skin; at Áco a hard mud floor and a skin sufficed. Aurelio needed no admonition to dress simply, for a breechclout and moccasins were his daily attire. He already worked with his own hands in the fields — he had followed that tenet of the Roman's advice since he was old enough to hold a digging stick. He wanted little, for there was little at Áco to want; he lived frugally because life at Áco was a life of frugality. He lived comfortably close to nature as the philosopher-emperor taught, but it was in the realm of human nature and human will that Rohona wished the boy to understand the Roman's counsel.

To Aurelio, Rohona admonished in the philosopher's words, "Begin the morning by saying to yourself, I shall meet with the busybody, the ungrateful, arrogant, deceitful, envious, unsocial. All these things happen to them by reason of their ignorance of what is good and bad. But I who have seen that the good is beautiful and that the bad is ugly, and that the nature of him who does wrong is like me, I can neither be injured by any of them, for no one can place on me what is ugly, nor can I be angry with my clansman, nor hate him. For we are made for cooperation, like our feet, our hands, our eyelids, like the rows of our upper and lower teeth. To act against one another then is contrary to nature."

That was a profound lesson for an eleven-year-old — as were many of his grandfather's lessons — but the boy sat and listened respectfully, for he knew his grandfather was very wise.

Chapter 28

For nearly four years, Áco was without a priest. One had been sent out, but he did not remain. He was unnerved by the unfriendliness and the silent hostility he perceived in the village. Although he could have pointed to no evidence, he lived in constant fear that from some shadow would come a flint knife or an arrow. He was one friar who did not relish the thought of martyrdom.

The Church did not want to see the exceptional work of the *padre* Juan Ramírez disappear, and the Father Custodian did not want to see a native village slip back into paganism. Perhaps in numbers lay the solution.

Aurelio was scarcely fifteen when the two priests arrived in Áco. Fray Nicolás de Freitas had served in the *convento* at Santa Fé and at Cuarac, and Fray Diego de Santander had ministered at Abó, San Marcos, and Senecú. They knew *Nuevo México* well; they knew Áco not at all.

Unlike the Ácoma, Antonia welcomed the advent of the new priests, for she had missed the sacraments. She recognized they would never replace Padre Ramírez, but she was glad to have the resumption of the Mass. She was worried, however, about the explanation she would have to give about her presence there in the village. Although she wore native dress and spoke the language, her Spanish heritage would be instantly apparent to the newcomers.

When the first priest came, Rohona suggested that she say that when she was young she had lived on an isolated *hacienda* in northern Mexico, that Apaches had raided her father's livestock, killed her parents, and kidnapped her, taking her back north with them. For corn, deer hides, and *mantas*, she had been traded to an Ácoma who had no children. She had grown up at

Áco, married a half-breed Ácoma man who had since died, and had had a child. It was a complicated story, but any explanation of her presence in the village would have to be unusual.

Finding a Spanish woman in an isolated village like Áco would be strange indeed, and the new priests confirmed this when they saw her. She told them the story Rohona had fabricated, and it appeared they believed it, but she was terrified when they suggested enthusiastically that they search for some possible relative in Mexico with whom she could live.

"Oh, no," she said as her face paled, "that was over twenty years ago. I could not leave here. This is my home. I love the family I live with—they are like my own parents to me. No, I do not want to go back to Mexico—*this* is my home." Her words were plaintive and yet emphatic at the same time.

"Perhaps we could at least make a few inquiries," Nicolás de Freitas suggested.

"No," she breathed. She allowed tears to slide down her cheeks—perhaps that would make them realize how strongly she wished to remain at Áco.

"There, there," both priests said patronizingly, "do not worry, *hija*, if you really feel that way, then I suppose it's not necessary for you to have to leave here."

Antonia thought madly for something to say to change the subject. The less they thought about finding some imaginary relative of hers, the better. Perhaps if she could be of use to them, they would forget their suggestion that they try to find a distant relative in Mexico.

"If I could be of assistance to you, Fathers," she said, as she discreetly dabbed her tears away, "it would be my honor to do so. For a number of years I was Padre Ramírez's secretary and bookkeeper."

She saw the shock on both friars' faces and added a quick lie. "Padre Ramírez taught me to read, write, and do figures. Each morning after Mass I would go into the *convento* and help him. I derived a great deal of pleasure and satisfaction from the work. And, not wishing to boast, I do think that I rendered the good *padre* some service." She looked down, hoping to appear unassuming.

Diego de Santander smiled broadly and glanced at the other priest. Antonia missed the look that passed between them. Because of that, neither did she catch the significance of their words.

"Indeed I am sure you did render him a great service," de Freitas said, still smiling.

Santander smiled, also. "It is no wonder Padre Ramírez never wished to move from this pueblo and lose such a valuable helper."

Antonia smiled with a feeling of accomplishment.

De Freitas turned to Diego de Santander. "I am quite certain that we could use the services of this kind lady, aren't you, *Padre*?"

"Most assuredly," the other friar answered.

Antonia left, promising to be there after Mass the following day. When she returned home, she related what had happened.

"At first I was afraid," she said, "but now that I am going to help them, I think all is well."

"I do not like it," Diego said abruptly. "I do not like those two priests."

Antonia laughed. "You do not like any priests, do you, *hijito*."

Diego did not show his displeasure to her, but he did not like for her to act as if he were a child. He was twenty-five. He was a man and had been for numerous years. It did not matter that fifteen-year-old Aurelio was taller than he. He was the man of the household, for Grandfather was much too old, and Aurelio was yet a boy. The fifteen-year-old was a good hunter and would be a man soon, but he, Diego, had a right to speak.

"I have heard the stories from the other villages where those two priests have served," he said angrily. "They are not servants of the Lord! *They* are the lords, and the Indians are *their* servants!"

"You may be accusing them unjustly," Antonia said. "What you have heard are rumors. It is what they do *here* that will tell us whether or not they are good friars."

"I don't like it," Diego said. "I don't like you working for those two men."

"Nor do I," Rohona said quietly. It was the only time he had ever agreed with Diego.

Antonia looked at Rohona with surprise and dismay. She had always accepted the wisdom of the old man's words.

"But I promised them I would help tomorrow after Mass," she said.

"Then you must help," Rohona said, "but have a care, Granddaughter, and help as infrequently as possible."

Antonia felt a measure of relief, but Diego's face showed only his black hatred of Spaniards. Rohona continued. "Perhaps by helping them, you may hear them speak of the village. In that way we may learn what their thoughts and plans are."

"Of course, Grandfather," Antonia said. "If the priests have Áco's well-being in mind, I shall learn of it. If they do not—*Dios* forbid it—*that* I will try to learn."

The following morning after Mass, Antonia went to the *convento* as she had promised. She showed the friars the books she had kept for Juan Ramírez, and they were duly impressed. They were quick to realize that if she continued her previous work, it would lessen their own considerably. She was treated well if a little too solicitously.

When she came out of the church, Diego was waiting there for her. "Did they do anything?!"

Antonia put her hand on his arm. "No, *hijo*, what did you expect? The priests are just happy to have someone to help them."

"Of course," Diego said with sarcasm.

When they reached the house, Antonia related to Rohona everything that had been said in the *convento*. He nodded in approval.

"Would you like for me to ask them any questions?" she offered.

"No, Granddaughter," Rohona replied. "I think it best for you to sit very quietly and do your work. In that way, they are more apt to forget your presence and speak about those things that may concern the village."

Her occasional presence in the *convento* did not, however, serve the purpose Rohona had hoped when two weeks later they had occasion to witness the new friars' tactics. It was scarcely dawn when they were awakened by noise in the village. Diego was the first to inform the household what was happening.

"The friar dogs are driving the people to church like animals!" he shouted with rage.

Soon, they all verified Diego's words as they saw the priests, whips in hand, farther down the house rows, climbing the ladders to each house, forcing all the occupants into the street and toward the church.

"Por *Dios*, no," Antonia said with a shudder.

"Come," Rohona said, "let us go to the church before they drive us. This matter will be discussed later."

"No!" Diego snapped.

"We *will go* to the church," Rohona reiterated. There was absolute authority in his voice. Diego's piercing black eyes were like slits in his sharp-featured face, but he obeyed and followed the family down the ladder.

There was total incomprehension on Aurelio's face. "Why do they do this?" he kept asking of his mother as they hurried along with the others toward the church as if they were a herd of sheep.

It was some time later that Aurelio heard the answer from the priests themselves. Neither friar spoke Queres and they harangued in Spanish, a Queres translator they had brought with them from Santo Domingo rendering their words into the native language.

No one in Antonia's household needed the words of the translator to explain what the friars said.

"Everyone in the village will come to Mass on Sunday! Everyone! There are no exceptions! Not even for the sick! They must be carried if they cannot walk!"

The friars shouted other admonitions before Mass began, but Antonia scarcely heard when the intoning of the Latin words began, for she was praying earnestly.

Dios, *please*, she begged, *let them understand Áco. Please guide them, and preserve this village, I beseech you.*

That was essentially the same prayer the old man next to her was offering to the Castilian god. Rohona's lips moved silently.

"I ask the preservation of Áco, *Dios*."

Diego's lips did not move; they were fixed in a sneer. His eyes flashed, full of loathing.

That night Mauharots was filled. The word went quickly through the village for the men to meet. Antonia did not know when Rohona and Diego returned that night, but she went alone to early Mass the next day. She dreaded going to the *convento* but knew she must. The friars were in good spirits. She tried to hide her surprise by getting quickly to work, praying they would say nothing to her.

De Freitas laughed. "So these are the fierce Ácoma," he said to Santander, paying her no mind. "You saw how they all went to Mass on Sunday—no one attacked us. While we have them scared, we might as well get rid of the devil masks. I'm sure they have them."

"You know they do," Santander replied. "We will go to the *kiva* and take them out. How I enjoy seeing those vile things burn."

When Antonia left the *convento* she could scarcely keep from running.

On the roof terrace she knelt in front of Rohona. "They are planning to go to the *kiva*, take out the K'atsina masks, and burn them." The masks could never mean to her what they meant to the Ácoma, but she knew they were just as sacred to the villagers as the consecrated host was to her.

Rohona remained calm, but she knew better than to think he was unaffected by the news.

"Go quickly, Mokaitsh," he said softly to Aurelio, "ask Gyatyu's father to come."

"It must be done immediately," Rohona said as he finished relating to Kohaiya what Antonia had overheard. "The masks must be moved and hidden immediately."

"I go at once," Gyatyu's father said.

"The *padres* must not know," Rohona added. "Send at least two men to the church on the pretext that they need to confess. That will occupy the friars while the masks are removed."

"Your wisdom is good. It shall be done." Kohaiya spoke to Antonia before he descended the ladder from the roof terrace.

"Your skin may be light like the color of Nautsiti's and not dark as Iyatiku's, but you are a woman of Áco."

The following day when the Spanish priests violated the sanctity of Mauharots in search of the devil masks, as they called them, they found nothing save some drums, gourd rattles, and a few pottery dishes. They were livid as they came out of the *kiva* and down to the square. Furiously they had the war chiefs brought forward.

"Where are they?" de Freitas screamed. "Where are the devil masks?"

A man stepped forward. He spoke in heavily accented Spanish. "Padre Ramírez told us they were bad. We burn them many, many moons ago." De Freitas drew back his hand to slap the man, but the native went to his knees, groveling at the *padre*'s feet.

"Please," he begged, "I tell only truth."

The other war chiefs fell to their knees. "It is true," another said. "We burn them all for the *padre*, long ago."

"I should whip you all to see if you really are telling the truth!" de Freitas shouted. His face was bathed with his anger at being thwarted in his plan.

"You are nothing but heathen devils!" Santander boomed, his fury as great as that of de Freitas. "May your souls fry in Hell if you are lying!"

Both friars stood for a moment pondering whether or not they should flog the war chiefs as an example and a warning, but the prime moment of their fury had passed, destroyed by their hesitation. Santander looked at the war chiefs and then out at the people who witnessed the humiliation of their leaders.

"There will be public penance for the entire village tonight!" he shouted. "For three hours in the church you will kneel and contemplate your manifold sins!" The two priests strode angrily away toward the church.

When they were out of sight, the war chiefs rose. The looks on their faces were not ones of humility. Most were covered with a deadly anger. One chief, however, turned to the crowd, a broad smile on his face. He lifted his arms high and did a quick, gleeful dance, then he began to mimic the two friars. The women began to giggle behind their hands, and soon the other war chiefs joined in the mirth.

Later, when they sat in the *kiva*, anger had returned to the faces of the war chiefs. "I will not eat dirt at the feet of a *padre* ever again," one chief spoke as others nodded in agreement.

The chief who had begun the mimicking spoke. "They are fools. The *padres* are nothing but fools. Let us manipulate them, not they us. *Let* the *padres* think we are docile, like the sheep they brought into our land. If we act as if we are meek and they command us, then their own feeling of power will blind them."

"That is wise counsel," Rohona said.

All listened to the quiet, reedy voice of the old man, for they knew the value of his words. "Let us be clever like the coyote and sly like the fox. Let us outwit these *padres*; let us play games with them. Let us give them no satisfaction."

That was the view that prevailed in Mauharots that day, although there were many who were of a differing opinion. The young men desired vengeance and the violence of force; the older men knew the wisdom of slow persistence and patient endurance.

Chapter 29

"They should be killed!" Diego shouted. "Or drive them from the village if you don't have the courage to kill them."

"They are only two men," Rohona said. "We have nothing to fear from them. Let us be like the rock of Áco itself. The rain beats down upon it, the wind blasts against it, even the powerful lightning strikes at it. But those all go away, the sun comes out, and the rock is still here, just as it was before and just as it will always be. Let us be like the rock on which our village is built."

Diego did not argue with Rohona. He never did, but his opinion never changed.

After the *padres'* unsuccessful attempt to burn the K'atsina masks, life in the village returned to what it had been. Every Sunday there appeared for Mass an adequate number of villagers to satisfy the priests. Little did the friars know that families had been admonished to attend church on a rotating basis, so that the *padres* would think they had occasioned the increase of the faithful. They did not look at the Indian faces; all they counted were the bodies.

The translator from Santo Domingo was sent back, an Ácoma taking his place to translate sermons. This, too, the *padres* did not realize was the doing of the village and not the result of their own decision. Lest the translator learn of the village's plans, the leaders deemed it wise to get rid of him. This they had skillfully done by putting forward an Ácoma translator whom the priests readily accepted, believing it meant the Ácoma would be more inclined to accept the Word and themselves as preachers of it.

Antonia did not know, either, the full extent of the Ácoma's complicity. She was merely thankful for the peace of the village. Once a week or so she would go to the *convento* to help with the books, although Diego still registered his disapproval and was frequently waiting for her when she came out.

During the time in which she helped at the church, she took as a sincere compliment the *padres'* words praising the beauty of her script; she interpreted their holding her hand at great lengths as only an expression of their appreciation for her help. The fact that the village was at peace and the *padres* had done nothing more to the villagers made her look kindly at these men of God. They were not young men, so when they patted her on the cheek or put their arm around her shoulder or touched her hair and commented on its beauty, she looked at it as a paternal action.

When they spoke of the comfort she had given Padre Ramírez, she responded that she hoped she had been a small comfort to him because he had given her a great deal of happiness, to which they replied, "It would give us a great deal of happiness to give you pleasure." She had not noticed the transposition of the words. Nor, indeed, did she notice other remarks of a nature more suggestive than appropriate to a priest's language.

After time, the friars became impatient with her appearance of innocence. They could not lay it to dullness, for she was obviously intelligent. She gave no indication that she was being coy nor playing games.

"Perhaps she is just waiting for us to make the first move," de Freitas said.

Santander concurred. "Maybe Ramírez told her it was all right, and she believed him."

"It's been a long time," de Freitas said, "and each time she comes here, I think I can wait no longer. Even at my age, I still have dreams."

"Yes, I dream of that light, creamy skin — of having a Spanish woman — instead of that old, dark-skinned hag that supplied my needs at Senecú. Yes, we must take the business in hand."

Antonia finished the books and was preparing to leave when the priest took her lightly by the arm. "I am in need of comfort today, *hija,*" he said softly.

"Comfort?"

"Yes," he said with a sly smile, "I am in need of the kind of comfort you gave Juan Ramírez."

She looked at him with puzzlement but an inkling of comprehension seeped in when he moved closer and his other hand went to her cheek in a caress.

"No," she gasped as she stepped backward and pulled out of his grasp. "Oh, no, Father. It was not what you think."

De Freitas, who had until now said nothing, approached her. "We know the comfort you gave Padre Ramírez. As your priests we need and *want* it also."

He reached out and grasped her by the arm, but she pulled away, her eyes wide and filled with shock. "You can't believe that Padre Ramírez . . . ," she said hoarsely, but she did not finish the sentence, for both priests stepped toward her at the same time.

"Yes, little girl, we do," Santander said. "Don't try to play naive with us. Why else did you offer to 'help' us?"

"I only offered to *help*, nothing more!" There was a rising note of hysteria in her voice.

"Well, we want your 'help,'" de Freitas said, "in fact, we *require* your help." He grasped her roughly by the arm. "Yes," he said, "as your priests we demand it of you."

"You cannot demand *that*."

"We can demand that of you or denounce you to the Commissary of the Holy Office," de Freitas said. "A Spanish woman living in an isolated native village—that is strange, indeed. How difficult would it be to convince the Inquisition that you—and your son—had reverted to paganism and were devil worshipers? How difficult would it be to convince them that you were the concubine of their chief medicine man—a fornicator with the devil!"

Antonia gasped with horror, unable to speak. De Freitas smiled evilly. "Do you understand now how we can demand it of you? How do you like the thought of you and your son in chains taken in the cart train to Mexico and thrown into a filthy cell of the Inquisition's jail?"

"But Padre Ramírez is in Mexico City," Antonia said. "He would tell them the truth."

Santander threw back his head and laughed. "The good *padre* is dead. The news came in the last cart train—he died at the Franciscan *convento* there. The last words on his lips were of his love for the Ácoma. We, of course, know why!"

She dropped to her knees and crossed herself as tears slipped down her cheeks. "Oh, *Padre, Padre*," she whispered, her voice constricted in sorrow.

De Freitas and Santander took momentary pity on her. "You may go," de Freitas said. "You may have today to mourn your beloved priest, but tomorrow you must come to the *convento* after Mass, otherwise you know what will happen."

Antonia rose and fled from the room. As she ran from the church, Diego grabbed her.

"What happened? What did they do to you?" he demanded furiously.

She was sobbing and babbling incoherently. He shook her forcefully by the shoulders. She went limp and murmured, "Padre Ramírez is dead. He died in Mexico City."

Diego supported her and walked with her toward their house. When they reached the ladder, he helped her climb it. Once she reached the roof, she took control of herself and walked to where Rohona sat, dropped to her knees in front of him, and spoke the same words she had spoken to Diego.

Her head dropped forward, and she dissolved into tears again. Rohona took her hands and comforted her, hiding his own pain at the knowledge of the death of the friar who had been more than a friend to him for so many years.

That night Antonia spent on her knees praying. The household thought it was because of Juan Ramírez's death. They did not know she was praying for help and guidance. During the night she reached the only decision she felt was possible.

The next morning they went to Mass to pray for the soul of the man they had all admired. When the prayers ended, Antonia told Rohona she must go help the friars. He saw something in her eyes that disturbed him.

"Why today?" Diego demanded. "You just helped them yesterday!"

"I must go," she said, not looking at him. He took her by the arm, but she gently removed his hand. "I must go."

She would have preferred the dank cell in the Inquisition's jail to the hell she would shortly undergo, but for her son, she would endure anything. For his sake, she would pay the price the friars demanded of her. It would be for him, and it would be for Áco, too, because it would keep the Holy Office from prying into the practices of the village.

Her steps were heavy with dread, and she paused before opening the door that led to the quarters of the *convento*. She had not been able to take communion that morning because her revulsion was such she could not have taken the host from the hands of those priests. What a vilification of the Church those two men were. How could they call themselves priests? How could they make such a mockery of *Dios*? Antonia's eyes were on the floor when she entered the room, but she knew the unsaintly men were there.

"How kind and wise of you to come," de Freitas said.

"Such 'help' as this shall not go unrewarded," Santander added, as if that could possibly have influenced her decision.

"Come," de Freitas said, "into the patio. It is beautiful in the morning. The peach tree is heavy with fruit. It will be an idyllic setting."

Antonia did not lift her eyes as she walked into the patio enclosed by the *convento* on three sides and by the wall of the church on the other. She could not look at the peach tree Juan Ramírez had so long and lovingly nurtured. She flinched involuntarily when de Freitas touched her.

"Do not be afraid," he said soothingly. "We just want to admire your beauty."

She could not control her trembling as he took the woven cotton blanket from her shoulders and let it drop to the ground. He removed the soft deerskin gown she wore, and when she was naked before them, she heard their intakes of breath.

"Sweet Lord in Heaven," Diego de Santander breathed.

"No woman could be more beautiful," de Freitas said. "Juan Ramírez was truly fortunate. You are lovely still, *hija*. Just how old are you?"

Her words were scarcely audible. "Thirty-two."

"What a comfort you shall be for me in my old age," de Freitas, who was nearer her, said. He reached out to touch her.

"Your breasts put the beautiful peaches of this tree to shame." But his hand never reached her. There was a strangled sound and a gasp, and Antonia's eyes flew open.

"Don't move!" Diego spat at Santander. He held de Freitas around the neck, a knife poised at the friar's jugular vein.

Antonia's knees buckled, and she almost fell before she recovered. "Diego," she gasped. "No! For the love of God, don't kill him, Diego. For *my* sake, don't kill him."

Diego looked at her, but his arm did not move. She grabbed her deerskin gown and pulled it on. "Please, Diego," she pleaded. "For my sake, don't kill them. Don't place that on your immortal soul."

"No," Santander said weakly, "we can make it worth your while." Diego laughed in the priest's face.

"Please," Antonia begged. "Let them go."

Diego pulled his arm tighter around de Freitas's neck, cutting off the man's air. The friar's face reddened and he gasped for breath. Diego let him go.

"Go today, dogs," Diego hissed. "If you ever set foot on this rock again, you will be dead before you can say 'God have mercy.' I am Apache," he said proudly and threateningly. "I am not Ácoma, I will never bow and scrape to Spanish swine. If you ever breathe a word of anything that has happened here on this rock, *my* people will come for you, and you will be found with your throats slit from ear to ear no matter where you try to hide in *Nuevo México*."

Santander, who had served at Abó, one of the pueblos most menaced by the vicious Apaches, fully believed everything the wild-eyed heathen said.

"You have our word." His voice shook.

Diego's eyes narrowed. "That is not worth as much as coyote shit."

De Freitas's face had become a sickly ashen color, and he suddenly looked like a very old man. "By the Holy Cross," he said, kissing the crucifix he wore, "I swear nothing shall ever cross my lips."

Diego spat in the priest's face. "Get out of here. Be off this rock before the sun sets!" He took Antonia by the arm, and they left the patio, the two friars standing as if rooted in the ground.

As the sun began its descent toward the west mesa, the friars made their descent from the White Rock. The villagers watched them silently, their faces revealing no emotion.

The village was awake that night until the wee hours as the drums beat and they danced their good fortune to be rid of the hated friars. Word of what had happened that morning in the patio of the *convento* spread. That Diego acted singly and disassociated himself from the Ácoma by proclaiming himself Apache, exonerated him of tribal disapproval. His act was, in fact, met with admiration and appreciation. Among many in Mauharots he was regarded as not less than heroic.

The drums beating sounded in Antonia's ears, and she could not pray. She did not know how long she had knelt there trying to pray—for what, she was not sure. The household had gone to watch the dancing, and she was alone. She could not cope with the sordid occurrence of that morning. She was humiliated and bitterly angry and felt betrayed by her Church. She heard someone coming up the ladder, and from the slow, unevenness of the steps she knew it was Rohona. It was late; she hoped he had come home to sleep. She did not want to talk to him.

When Diego brought her home that morning, he had done the explaining, as she could not have. She felt unclean and debased. She could face no one and stayed alone for the entire day. She could still face no one, but Rohona hobbled into the room and came to sit by her.

"Granddaughter," he said softly in his rustling, old voice, "as the philosopher says in the printed leaves, things do not touch the soul, not in the least degree. What happened in the *convento* cannot touch your soul nor can it turn or move your soul. Your soul turns and moves itself alone. The friars cannot fix on you what is ugly, no one can. Remember what was said in the leaves: Pain is neither intolerable nor everlasting, if you bear in mind that it has its limits and if you add nothing to it in your imagination. Do not add to today anything in your imagination, Granddaughter."

Antonia no longer wanted to be alone. "Oh, Grandfather," she sobbed, and the old man cradled her against his withered chest as she cried with her pain.

"Your god has a purpose for things. We know that," Rohona said softly. "Perhaps he had a purpose for today. Perhaps it was his way of removing the bad priests from Áco without the village doing something dangerous or foolish."

She sat quietly for a few moments. "I have prayed for the preservation of Áco, Grandfather, perhaps *Dios* has merely answered my prayer."

"Perhaps," Rohona said.

Chapter 30

"I am going to follow the *padres*," Diego announced the morning after their departure. "I want to throw another scare into them so that they will not have second thoughts about denouncing Áco. I want them to be constantly looking over their shoulder, fearing all shadows. In that way they will not be tempted to make reprisals against this village."

"Be wise in your pursuit," Rohona said, giving his approval to the plan.

"Rest assured that I will, Grandfather," Diego said, glad to have the old man's sanction.

"Go with God," Antonia said to Diego as he prepared to leave. She did not want him to go. She would have preferred to have forgotten the horrible episode ever occurred, but she recognized the validity of what he intended to do. Once away from the pueblo, the friars might, indeed, have second thoughts. Their anger and wounded pride might make them bold. They might put into action the threat they had used against her.

"I will be back for harvest," Diego said as he left.

And he was. Aurelio had wanted to go with him, but both his mother and grandfather had forbidden it, and he had to be satisfied with the Apache's recounting of the tale.

"The first night when I caught up with the priests," Diego said, "I dipped my hand in ochre paint and left a bloodlike handprint on their mules. In the morning when the friar dogs saw the gory sign, they recoiled in fear and looked madly about them, trembling." His lips pulled back over his teeth in a mirthless smile. "They did not see me, however, because I watched them from behind a chamisa bush on the top of a small rise. It was not difficult to follow them, even though they were riding mules and I was on foot."

He had not ridden one of the ponies he had stolen from the Apaches because he would have been easier to spot. He could dogtrot for days without stopping, as could most young natives — hunting required it. When the Spaniards went out on retaliatory raids, a contingent of Pueblo warriors always accompanied them on foot, and although the Spaniards were mounted on horses, the natives, with their untiring dogtrot, had no difficulty in keeping up with the metal-clad riders.

"The second night," Diego told them, "I left the skinned carcass of a headless jackrabbit in their camp, impaled on an arrow. On the third, I howled eerily like a coyote off and on throughout the entire night, but I left nothing in their camp. The next morning they looked frantically about for something, sighing with relief when nothing was found, and likewise for another night I left nothing. I could see those friar dogs begin to relax, so on the following night, with its head attached, I stuffed the rabbit skin with rocks and whittled two sticks to appear as fangs and stained them with the juice of skunk berries to make them seem bloodied. I stuck them in the rabbit's mouth, and with the aid of another stick, I propped the animal in a sitting position near the friars' heads."

Diego smiled maliciously at the memory. "When they awoke the next morning, they were visibly shaken by the strange animal that seemed to have been watching during the night. You should have seen the cowards! They must have crossed themselves a hundred times throughout the day or made the cross of their thumb and index finger as a sign to ward off evil. Their lips moved in constant prayer as they glanced again and again over their shoulders. But they never saw me."

Aurelio's eyes were wide in astonishment, and he laughed to think about the frightened priests. "Go on, go on," he urged Diego when the Apache had stopped to get his breath. Diego's eyes glittered and he continued.

"I allowed several more days to pass without leaving any sign at night. Then when the friars were within a day of the *convento* of Sandia Pueblo — their first possible refuge — I used wicked cactus thorns and nailed a horned toad to a crude crucifix I had made. I planted it between the two sleeping friars and watched in the morning when they discovered it." He laughed at the memory.

"De Freitas's face turned to ashes when he looked at the thing. His hand went to his mouth, and — can you believe? — he vomited all over the ground. That day they exhausted their poor mules to reach Sandia. The friars stayed at the pueblo for a few days before they continued on to Santo Domingo, but I had one last thing to do."

Diego paused and Aurelio sat forward, eager to hear the rest.

"When the friars were feeling most secure at Santo Domingo, I wanted to breach their sanctuary for one last warning so that they would think there was no place where they could ever be entirely safe. It was easier than I thought to gain entrance to their sleeping quarters. I held a flint knife to Santander's throat. I should have killed him, but I didn't." He looked at

Antonia. "I just hissed and both friars were instantly awake in the blackness of the room. 'Remember and remember well what was spoken at Áco,' I said to them. 'You will be watched always, and if you value your life and do not wish a horrible death, your lips will remain sealed. There will always be someone in the shadows to slit your gullet open should you speak of Áco.' As quickly and as silently as I had come, I was gone."

It had not taken Diego as long to return as it had to go, for he dogtrotted back, scarcely stopping.

Antonia shuddered at Diego's tale, but her only hope was that the friars would not denounce her and her son's presence at Áco. If Diego had achieved that, she knew she could not fault his methods, for her son's life there at Áco was the most crucial thing that existed for her.

Aurelio laughed and laughed at Diego's tale as he pictured the two terrified, cowardly priests on their journey back to Santo Domingo. Rohona did not laugh, but his eyes gave evidence that he, too, found amusement with the story.

"I made another visit," Diego said softly. Everyone turned to look at him, surprised at his different tone.

"I continued on to the *villa*." No one spoke, the silence in the room taut.

"I went to *mamacita* Doro's house, but she no longer lives there — she rests now in the *campo santo*."

"Oh, no," Antonia said. She rose and went to embrace Diego. "I am so sorry. I know how much you loved her."

Tears slipped down Siya's face. "Doña Dorotea," she whispered with poignancy.

Rohona put his hand on Siya's arm in comfort. "She was a good woman."

The harvest that year was scarcely adequate. Siya and Rohona stayed in the village, impeded by age, but Diego, Antonia, and Aurelio went to the fields two leagues away, where they toiled side by side harvesting the corn. At midday they rested under the thatched sun shelter, thankful for the shade it offered.

Sun shelters, made necessary by the cloudless sky, the relentless sun, and the lack of trees, were a common sight near native fields there in arid *Nuevo México*. Four poles supported smaller saplings through which were woven odd branches or brush — anything that would provide shade. Although the sun might be murderous, the altitude and dry climate of those western reaches would cool a person if he had the merest spot of shade.

They all took a long drink of fresh water from the pottery water jar whose porosity allowed for evaporation, thus keeping its contents cool and sweet. They lay back and for an hour slept before they rose to continue with their work.

The ponies Diego had stolen from the Apaches were a boon for harvest. Rather than having to carry the large baskets of corn on their backs with the head strap cutting into their foreheads, they could attach the baskets to either side of the ponies and transport much more grain more rapidly and with less bone weariness at the end of the trek home.

Back in the village, the corn had to be shucked. The husks were pulled back, tied together, and strung. And then there was roasting, parching, soaking, grinding.

At the end of the day of harvesting, Antonia was not thinking of all the work that still remained. She was aware of the fatigue in her back from bending and stooping, aware that her hands hurt from the hairlike cuts made by the cornhusks, aware of the headache caused by the sun beating down incessantly. She was aware, but she did not think about them. She did not think about such things nor about the work awaiting in the village after harvest. Such thoughts were valueless. She greeted each day with equanimity.

"I am rising to the work of a human being," she would say in the words of the Roman philosopher, and then she would thank her god for that privilege.

Diego and Aurelio continued with the corn while Antonia prepared the supper they would eat there under the sun shelter that would serve also as their sleeping quarters that night. The fire had been made earlier and was now a bed of red-embered coals. Two rabbits Aurelio had killed roasted on sticks stuck in the ground at an angle over the fire. Antonia shoved ears of some of the younger corn, their husks wrapped tightly about them, into the coals to roast. She roasted chiles on the fire and quickly peeled them, and out of a pouch she took a thick roll of *guayave* Siya had made.

By that time Aurelio and Diego were finished with their work and were sitting waiting to wrap a chile in the gray-blue paper bread. The crispy rabbits were torn apart and eaten with the fingers along with the chile encased in the *guayave* bread. Antonia pulled the corn from the coals and after the husks were carefully pulled away, each one stuck a sharp stick through the ear to hold it securely for eating.

"I am starving," Aurelio said as he ate hungrily.

"You are always starving," Antonia laughed. "Will you never stop growing so that you don't require so much food?"

There was pride in her laughing words as she looked at her tall, handsome son. The firelight made his hair seem to flicker like the coals, and his eyes appeared darker than the gray they were. Nothing, however, could diminish the broad shoulders and the boy's stature, which was—even sitting—obviously much greater than that of his mother or Diego, ten years his senior, whom he thought of as his older brother.

Diego laughed, too. "Already the girls look at him with eyes that say he is a man. He will be making a set of beautiful clothes before we know it!" he said, referring to the way in which an Ácoma man made a marriage proposal.

The firelight did not totally hide Aurelio's blush. "Well, what about you?"

he said to Diego. "You are older than I am. Why haven't you made anyone a set of clothes?"

Antonia saw the Apache's unsmiling face. "Oh, Diego, I hope you do not think you cannot marry because of us," she said. "You should have a wife by now. Please, do not deny yourself the happiness of a wife and home on our account. I would be truly unhappy if that were the case."

"That is not the case," Diego said abruptly as he rose and walked away from the sun shelter into the darkness of the night that had fallen.

Antonia turned to her son. "I wonder why Diego acts this way?" she asked, perplexed.

Aurelio shook his head. "I don't know, *Mamá*, but I do think he is happy living with us."

Antonia smiled and touched the cheek of her handsome son. "One of these days, my son, you will find a woman with whom you will want very much to live, and you will love her as much as I was loved by your father."

Antonia glanced out at the darkness. "I think it is probably time that you go. I shall sleep soundly knowing that you are guarding tonight, my son."

Aurelio leaned forward and kissed her on the cheek. "Sleep well, *Mamá*."

Antonia watched as he disappeared into the darkness. She was sure Diego's words about the way the girls looked at him were true. His face had the look of youth, but his body was that of a man already. How much he looked like his father when Augustín had portrayed the Aztec sun god Huitzilopochtli.

She had looked at the mythical god with the eyes of a little girl, but even then she had known she wanted a husband who looked like that. She remembered, too, the Jesuit's year of solitude, the months that seemed an infinity. When he returned, she looked up at him across the patio of her house and saw the look in his eyes that said she had become a woman. She ran to him and threw her arms around his neck as she had when she was a child, but when he put his arms around her, she felt them as a woman would feel them. She felt her breasts against his broad chest; she felt his hard, lean body against hers, and she knew what it was to want a man to be a husband to her in that special way. When their arms dropped and they stepped apart, she saw that the look was either gone from or hidden in his eyes. She *wanted* him to look at her like she was a woman. She knew it was wrong for him to do so, but she also knew that she loved him irrevocably and that she could never love another man.

She sat for long moments, her forehead resting on her knees, her arms hugging them as the past swept through her mind. Her body trembled slightly when she remembered. As if it had been yesterday, she saw him standing beside her bed in the inn as he removed his cassock, and she saw his beautiful body, and he came to her and did that which she had so longed for him to do. A tiny sob came from her throat, and she threw back her head, squeezing her eyes shut as she hugged herself and rocked gently. She wiped away a tear from her cheek that had slid down from the corner of her eye. She straightened up and pushed back her hair. She must not think about the past.

She put away the supper things, pushed the dying coals into a smaller pile, added another piñon log to the fire, and unrolled their blankets and sheepskins. She spread the sheepskins on the ground beneath the thatched shelter. Aurelio would not be coming to sleep until much later after his watch. She did not know when Diego would return. She knelt beside her sheepskin bed and crossed herself.

"Thank you for the harvest, Lord," she prayed quietly, "bless us all, and take away my dreams tonight, please."

She wrapped herself in her blanket and lay down. Exhausted from the day's labor, sleep came quickly to her.

Diego had sat in the shadows and watched her. The faint firelight outlined her body, and he saw her sadness and her loneliness in her posture. The light glinted off her hair.

How many nights, without appearing to, he had watched her comb her long, wild, honey–colored hair, and he remembered how when he first came to live with them she had risen at night to comfort him when one of the hated dreams came. Long after the dreams had ceased, he continued to act as if they recurred. Her hands were so gentle when she smoothed his hair, and her soft, whispering words of comfort were like nectar sipped from a flower. Her gentleness was a balm that soothed the hatred and the desire for violence that were constantly within him.

More than he wanted to kill his father, he had wanted to kill those two priests for what they intended with her. Every night in his mind he saw her naked trembling body as she stood there in the patio of the *convento* while the two lecherous friar dogs drooled and panted at the sight of her breasts and thighs—her skin like a pearl in the morning light. And yet he, too, had felt the tightening in his groin—and felt it still, but he had made no sacred vow of celibacy.

He wanted to be a husband to the gentle woman. He was already the man of the household. He supplied the family with food, and he protected them, but he wanted to be a man for the woman, too. He wanted to feel his life force in her, give her pleasure and show her how he loved her.

The embers of the fire cast only the faintest light when Diego rose. His steps made no sound. He picked up his sheepskin and laid it next to the sleeping woman. Quietly he lay down facing her. She had said he should marry. He had seen her loneliness. That night she would know that he loved her.

Gently he pulled the blanket away from her. He touched her hair in the darkness, and he moved his body against the length of hers. He felt her soft breath fan his face as he brought his head down near hers, and his arm went around her, drawing her near. Suddenly she was awake, and he felt her fear.

"It is Diego," he whispered. "Do not be afraid."

"What is it?" she asked, her voice filled with perplexity. "What is the matter?"

Diego pulled her closer to him. "I love you," he whispered near her ear. "I want to be your husband."

She gasped and pushed against him.

"Do not be afraid," he whispered, not surrendering his hold on her. "I won't hurt you. I want only to give you pleasure. You are still young, you have not had a man give you pleasure for a long time. Let me be a man for you."

His mouth came down on hers in the darkness, but she struggled violently, twisting and trying to push away from him. She succeeded in freeing her mouth.

"No. Diego, no!" she said desperately. "Do not do this. Let me go!"

But Diego did not let go. He kissed her voraciously anywhere his mouth touched. His hands were all over her, pulling at the tunic she wore. His hands slid up her body to caress her breasts, then between her legs.

She struggled against him, pleading for him to stop.

"For the love of God, Diego," she begged, "don't!"

But still he did not stop. He continued his wild caresses and rolled his body onto hers. There was no way she could prevent what he was going to do. Her strength was no match for his hard, wiry body. She ceased fighting.

He felt the struggle leave her and thought it was acquiescence. His caresses became more gentle, but when he heard her sobbing, a ragged cry of anguish caught in his throat, and he rolled to the side, scarcely able to endure that she did not want him. He had never cried except during the bad dreams when he was young, but at that moment he cried again.

Antonia heard his anguish, sorrow filling her, knowing that he loved her in a way that she could never return. She sat up, reached out and touched him. He pulled away as if her fingers burned him, but she spoke, nonetheless.

"Diego, you are very dear," she said softly, "but I love you like a son. That is the way I will always love you. You must find a young girl to love who can love you in the way in which you so desire and in the way in which you deserve to be loved."

He made a guttural sound as he came to his feet.

"Diego!" she said, but he was gone.

Chapter 31

Sleep did not return to her. Sometime near dawn she heard Aurelio slip onto his sheepskin and wrap himself up in his blanket. Fresh guards would be posted for the hour of danger in the predawn when the Apaches frequently chose to attack. She heard Aurelio return but not Diego. She must try to sleep at least a little; the day that rapidly approached would be a long, hard one.

She was deeply troubled by what had happened that night. The fact that Diego loved her as a woman and wanted her as a wife came as a shock. She was horrified that he had seen her as a woman for a wife instead of as a mother, which was how she saw herself in relationship to him. She was touched that he loved her and did not think of her as an old woman, as she sometimes felt herself to be, but a poignant sadness overcame her at the thought of the rejection he had to suffer from her.

Diego had scarcely known love in his twenty-some years and she loathed the fact that she had been the one to cause him this pain and that she could not return his love. Now the love she could give him as a mother was impossible.

Since Augustín's death, she had lived only for the present, not allowing thoughts of the future to intrude in her mind, but now she could not prevent such thoughts. Would Diego leave Áco? Would he stay? Could they manage without him? She prayed that all would be well, but she had a dark sense of foreboding that wrapped itself around her and from which she could not extricate herself.

She knew the harvest would not last them through the winter. Would there be a piñon nut crop in spite of the lack of rain they had suffered? Would the nomads increase their attacks? As her thoughts darkened with gloom, the day lightened, but she had not noticed. Sleep had been a stranger to her that night, and neither the words of the philosopher she so often read nor the words of the prayers her lips so often spoke came to give her comfort.

Indigo faded to gray, then brightened to pink as it feathered along the eastern horizon. A dove called hauntingly in the still air, and she knew the night was over. She would have to work that day without the benefit of sleep, but she rose without recriminations and without self-pity; she rose to the work that awaited her. She said her prayers, rolled up her blankets and sheepskin, combed her hair quickly with the nettle comb and rebraided it, her fingers trembling slightly with the foreboding that would not leave. She took a handful of dry pine needles from a leather pouch and was poking the barely glowing embers of the fire when she heard the alarm.

Aurelio heard it, too, and was instantly on his feet, an arrow drawn like lightning from its quiver and readied in his bow. "To the arroyo, *Mamá*," he whispered with urgency, "get to the arroyo!"

Antonia did not hesitate. She grabbed up the skirt of her tunic and ran headlong for the nearby arroyo and the meager safety it might provide. In the distance she heard the wail of other women as they, too, ran to what they hoped would be safety.

Sand choked her, and she felt her hands abraded as she threw herself into the arroyo and slid down the side. She tried to scramble to her feet, but fell to her knees as the soft sand gave way beneath her. She managed to claw her way along on hands and feet until she got her balance on the sandy-bottomed ravine. She ran but with nightmarish slowness as the sand gave way with every step. Up ahead the arroyo bent where a jutting piece of clay had resisted the runoffs of summer cloudbursts. She threw herself behind the small wall and pressed up against it. She held perfectly still, trying desperately to quiet her breathing.

From her meager sanctuary she heard the terrible noises of the attack. Her lips moved in fervent, silent prayer, imploring that God protect her son and the others. She began the Act of Contrition, asking forgiveness of her sins. She heard the hideous yells of the attackers, the intermittent screams of Ácoma women farther upstream, the pounding of hooves, the dull sounds of combat, the whinny of a wounded horse. Her eyes were squeezed tightly shut.

Listening to the distant sounds, she did not hear the one close by. When she did, it was too late.

Flashing obsidian eyes, much like Diego's, glinted with evil satisfaction at her from a sun-hardened leather face daubed with paint. A scream caught in her throat as she came to her feet to flee from the mounted nomad, but he swooped down into the arroyo, his horse's hooves throwing up a wave of sand as he bent down, grabbed her around the waist, and yanked her up onto the horse with him. The pony leaped and pawed its way up the other side of the ravine as Antonia fought and kicked, trying to throw herself from the lunging animal.

From a distance Aurelio saw with horror the nomad and his captive. In the same instant, a bloodcurdling cry rent the air and Aurelio saw Diego, on horseback, coming full speed. He saw the arrow leave Diego's bow. What happened next was etched like terrible pictures in his mind. The arrow struck the Apache just under his chin and he was flung lifeless in the air in a shower of bright blood. Aurelio saw his mother pitched from the riderless horse as it stumbled and fell headlong into the sand, its leg snapped like a dry stick.

Before Aurelio could reach them, Diego had thrown himself from his horse and was standing over the dead Apache, blood dripping down his arm from the scalp he held aloft.

Aurelio saw the unmoving body of his mother near the writhing Indian pony, and he knew at once she was dead. Her face was oddly serene, but her chest was crushed to a welter of bloody bone and flesh by the horse's hooves. Aurelio drew the Spanish steel-bladed knife that had belonged to his grandfather Alejandro, and grasping the writhing horse's neck, slit its jugular vein.

At that moment Diego saw that the woman was dead. With a guttural, atavistic sound, more gruesome than the first, he plunged the bloody knife into the belly of the dead Apache, slitting him open chest to groin, spilling the steaming intestines onto the sandy ground. Another growl, another flash of the knife, and Diego flung the nomad's sexual organs into the dust.

Aurelio knelt beside his mother and lifted her head onto his lap. Tears streamed down his face as he made the sign of the cross on her forehead with his thumb and mumbled what he hoped was absolution. She looked so beautiful she might only have been sleeping. Together he and Diego carried her back to the sun shelter. A few Ácoma women gathered, keening the death of the Spanish woman who had lived among them and mourning their own grief.

The Apaches had made off with some of their meager harvest as well as two Ácoma women and two small children. The attack would have been worse had Diego not come riding at full speed out of nowhere, killing the leaders and scattering the others before they could take possession of all the corn harvested by the hard labor of the Ácoma.

The cortege that wound its slow way across the valley floor that day was, in all its aspects, funereal. A messenger was sent immediately to the village to warn of the attack that morning, but when it became clear that the nomads had fled from the valley and did not plan to attack the village, the people came down to the base of the mesa to await those who returned.

The effort was supreme, but Rohona managed to hobble down the *Camino del Padre* with the aid of two walking sticks and Siya's help, as feeble as that was. Whispers reached his ears before his old eyes dimly sighted the pony and its burden.

Tears coursed down his wrinkled copper cheeks, and he thought his heart would not endure. He had seen too many of the people he loved die. It was not right that the old should bury the young. Why had God not taken his life instead of the granddaughter he loved so much and who was of such a comfort to him?

He was somewhere over ninety growing seasons old; he was a useless old man. He could scarcely see, much less walk. His food was gruel because he no longer had enough teeth to chew. Why did God leave *him* upon the earth? Why must he witness the death of his children and grandchildren? Why must he see that the rains no longer came to water their crops as they once had? Why must he see the nomads attacking with more frequency to rob what little grain they could grow? Why was he left to water the earth with his own tears?

Aurelio embraced his great-grandfather, weeping.

"You must take her to the pinnacle," Rohona said, his voice raspy with age and the emotion he sought to control. "You must lay her to rest with her husband, your father. Get Diego to help you for I am too old to go there. You must make a cross for her and say the prayers of the Castilian god."

Aurelio nodded, unable to speak, but Diego, who had stood the entire time beside the body, heard the words of the old man and needed no request from Aurelio. Together they led the horse toward the west as the old man turned and started the torturous climb back to the village on the mesa top.

"This is the last time I will ever set foot off the White Rock," Rohona whispered to himself.

"They must die! They must *all* die!" Diego's black eyes flashed with hatred as he stood on the stone pinnacle and gestured violently. "She is dead because of them!"

The stillness of the vast expanses enveloped them.

"It is futile," Aurelio said as he knelt at the head of the newly stacked rocks that covered the body of his mother. "It would be impossible to find all the attackers. Who knows into which mountain valley they have gone? And the one who attacked her lies dead already, his guts spilled on the ground."

"I do not speak of the Apache!" Diego shouted. "The Spanish dogs are her real killers!"

Aurelio looked up at Diego, surprise and incomprehension covering his youthful face. Diego snorted contemptuously.

"Do you think the nomads would attack the Ácoma for their grain if the Spanish dogs had not come into the land, raped and pillaged it? They have taken farmland that belonged to the pueblos for generations without number; they make the Indians grow grain for the Spaniards' own consumption; they make raids on the Navajo and Apache, taking the nomads' children to be their slaves, and those they don't want for their own household, they send with the wagon trains to be sold in the mines of Mexico."

Diego's eyes blazed as he continued. "The land begs for water! The rain does not come, the plants turn brown and die, and we feel hunger in the pits of our stomachs, and we will die. And who has caused it all? The Spanish pigs! They brought their cruel god into the land, they forbid the dances, the prayers to the K'atsina, the healing ceremonies. They have made the villagers turn away from the gods who bring the rain. Instead of dancing with joy and beauty and sending song-prayers of thanksgiving to the gods who sustain them, the people must now grovel on their knees and beat their breasts in contrition, begging the god of the Castilians not to punish them for their sins. The rain will not return until the Spaniards are all gone from this land! They *all* must die!"

Aurelio's eyes were on the mound of stones before him. "My mother is dead," he said. "She was Spanish. Are you happy that *she* is dead?" There was a touch of bitterness in his voice as he continued. "For that matter, I, too, am Spanish. Aren't there those in the village who point that out when given the opportunity? You know there are people who seem to hate me just because I have the blood of Spaniards in my veins."

Had Aurelio been looking at Diego's face, he would not have understood the expression. He would not have known that the black, twisted hatred on the half-breed Apache's face was self-hatred. He would not have known Diego blamed himself for the woman's death — for he had left her unprotected. He had ridden back at breakneck speed when he saw the telltale tracks of the pony-mounted nomads, but he arrived too late, and it was his arrow that caused the attacker to drop the woman to her death beneath the sharp hooves of the horse.

But the self-hatred went deeper still. Had it been possible, Diego would have taken his knife and drained every drop of Spanish blood from his veins. For as long as he lived, Isidro Inojosa, the man he hated most in this world, would be a part of him. Half of him had been engendered by one of the Spanish swine, and he loathed the fact, turning his most virulent hatred toward all those of that race.

How was it, then, that he had loved the woman with the dark honey-colored hair? He watched her comb her hair at night, and that simple act had always filled him with desire. When he could secure a small article of her clothing, he would sleep with it, burying his face in it, savoring her own special smell. He had seen her bathing once or twice, and he had to gratify himself, so strong had been his desire for her. How could he love the woman when he hated the Spaniards and hated that part of himself that was of them?

But the woman had long ago ceased being Spanish for Diego. She had become Nautsiti, the fair-skinned sister of Iyatiku who took her son and went with him to the East where she raised the boy who later became her own husband. The honey-haired woman wore the clothes of Áco; she ground corn like the women of Áco, a smudge of cornmeal on her face as a prayer while she knelt grinding; she spoke the language of Áco; she slept on a pelt on the floor as did the Ácoma. She was not Spanish, but rather, the long-absent Nautsiti returned to live among the children of Iyatiku, and he was the son who became the husband. Or so he had dreamed and desired. But now she lay dead beneath a pile of stones, and he would wreak his vengeance on the nomads who were the immediate instrument of her death and eventually on the Spaniards, whom he saw as ultimately responsible for her death.

It was not lost on Diego that the very nomads who killed her were also of his own blood—Apache. A violent battle raged within him, and his body trembled with the violence of his emotion. He went to his knees beside Aurelio, who turned and looked with surprise at Diego's uncharacteristic action. Diego's eyes were riveted on the pile of stones in front of him.

"She was not Spanish," the half-breed said. Shock flashed across Aurelio's face.

"She was Nautsiti, but no one knew," Diego whispered.

Aurelio started to speak, but no words came out as he stared at the man ten years his senior whom he had considered his brother. It was as if he did not know him.

Diego turned his intense eyes on Aurelio. "You are not Spanish—you are the son of Nautsiti. Together we will avenge her death!"

Diego came to his feet like a snake striking. "We must go!" he shouted.

Aurelio crossed himself and rose.

Together they rode back to the village on the horse that had carried her body to the pinnacle. Aurelio rode behind the wild-eyed Apache.

His body felt strangely numb, but his mind was pierced by questions that seemed formed without words or sense. The only thing he understood clearly was that his life would never be the same again. That realization, however, he was not yet prepared to accept. He wanted to scream "No!" in defiance, but the word only reverberated in his brain and did not issue from his lips.

Siya had the herb brew of forgetfulness prepared when they returned. She offered it to Diego and Aurelio as she spoke softly, nodding toward Rohona.

"He said he will not drink it, for it does not work for the old—they cannot forget. Only the young are able to forget."

Diego pushed away the pottery bowl she offered. "I, too, will not drink," he said in a hard voice. "I do not wish to forget. This memory will be my food until they all are dead."

Siya took an involuntary step backward, her old face registering shock at the Apache's voice and words. Aurelio reached for the bowl.

"I will drink," he said softly, "I wish to forget."

He took a long gulp from the bowl. He descended the ladder and when he reached the corner of the house row, the emetic brew had its age-old effect, and he retched again and again.

Part Five

EL IMPEDIMENTO
The Obstacle, 1667

Chapter 32

The same day they returned from the pinnacle, Diego received permission from the Hotcheni. Two other Ácoma warriors went with him. Before Diego left, Aurelio questioned him about his actions.

"Why do you go to ask the help of the foreigners in hunting down the Apaches who attacked us? Aren't you the one who hates all Spaniards, the one who wants to see them all dead?"

Diego smiled knowingly. "Why not kill two snakes with one stick?"

The following days were difficult for Aurelio. The night before his mother died, he had told her he was a man. He now knew how hollow those words were. He looked to her for comfort and security; he had been a boy playing at being a man.

Now he must *be* a man — the luxury of youth was over. He watched Siya, her back stooped, her hands knotted, trying valiantly to prepare the corn from the harvest. All the work his mother had done now fell to the old woman, who hardly had the strength for the job that lay ahead. Aurelio began to help her parch the corn, although she protested feebly, but when he started to grind the corn she tried to prohibit him. That was women's work.

"Eating is everyone's work," Aurelio had replied. "*Mamá* is no longer here, and there is too much for you to do alone, Auntie. Food must be prepared for winter, and there is little of it. We must all work." Siya had not protested again.

Aurelio worked with diligence to aid his aunt, but he worried most about his great-grandfather, who sat the entire day, his almost sightless eyes staring into the distance. Numerous were the times during the day when Aurelio would glance at his great-grandfather and see tears rolling down the old man's wrinkled cheeks. In the evenings Aurelio would go sit by him and read from the leaves the old man's eyes could no longer decipher, but not even the words of the philosopher whom he had understood so well could lift the old man's spirit.

One night instead of reading, Aurelio spoke. "The words from this book, you have taught me, Grandfather. You have shown me their meaning and have made me understand their wisdom. How many times have you admonished me to put them in my heart, for there would come a time when they would serve me well?"

The old man nodded in affirmation of what the boy said. Aurelio continued. "Now is one of those times. The philosopher's words have served me; let them serve you, Grandfather.

" 'Nothing happens to any man which he is not formed by nature to bear,' " Aurelio quoted. "Is that not what you have said to me many times, Grandfather? How am I to believe these words if you who have taught me do not believe them?"

Rohona smiled, reached out and touched his great-grandson. He regretted that his eyes no longer allowed him to see the handsomeness of the boy's face.

"Ah, you are a clever one," the old man said. "There is truth in the philosopher's words. When I heard that your mother was dead, I thought that I could not endure it, but I did not die—here I sit. But as the Roman said, 'Even he who laments in silence is like the pig who kicks and squeals when it is sacrificed. What nature brings to each is for the good of each thing, and it is for its good at the time when nature brings it.' " Rohona's aged eyes looked heavenward and then turned toward Aurelio.

"The philosopher said that everything must die at its appointed time— that is nature—and nature is not evil. If the Castilian god is real, your mother has died only to this life on earth. As for myself, Grandson, I can tell you only that I shall no longer squeal like the pig."

Aurelio embraced his great-grandfather. "That is all I need to know."

He felt a great sense of relief after hearing his grandfather's words, and the old man no longer seemed quite so griefstricken, but at night Aurelio had to combat his own loneliness and the feeling of loss that would threaten to overwhelm him.

During the day, however, a nagging worry did prey at the corners of his mind. What ultimately were Diego's intentions? When the Apache said he was going to Juan Domínguez to get the Spaniards' help for a retaliatory raid on their attackers, Aurelio could not believe his ears. He knew the half-breed could not have had a change of heart toward the rulers of the province.

What did the burning-eyed Apache have in mind? That seemed to have been a worry of his great-grandfather, also, for when Diego and the two warriors appeared a number of days later with a small group of mounted Spaniards, the soldier-colonist Domínguez at their head, Rohona called to his great-grandson.

"Mokaitsh," he spoke to him, using his Queres name, "go with Diego to hunt the nomads but watch that he does not have a foolish plan."

"But I did not intend to go on the raid, Grandfather," Aurelio said. "I am staying in the village to help you and Auntie. *Mamá* is dead; her attacker is dead. Killing Apaches will not bring her back."

"That is true," Rohona said. "As the Roman affirmed, you must love peace, but you must also be a good warrior. The time may be coming when you will need to know not only how to hunt the deer but how to hunt a man. My eyes no longer see, but my mind sees many troubles coming. The safety of Áco must guide you. It is for this reason I ask you to go with Diego and the others. I fear Diego may have a plan that is not in the best interests of Áco. Stay close by him, Grandson. Learn what he has to teach if such is beneficial, but be always aware of that which may not be. Use the cleverness you possess and that your namesake *mokaitsh*, the mountain lion, imparts to you. Do not worry about Siya and me; it is more to our advantage that you go."

The Spaniards camped at the base of the mesa for two days while preparations were made and provisions gathered. Diego no longer worried that he might be recognized by the Spaniards. It had been ten years since he escaped to Áco. Dressed in native clothes no one would have guessed he was half-European. Even the aquiline nose and piercing black eyes so like his father's would not give him away. They served, instead, to intensify his feral appearance.

He was pleased Aurelio had asked to accompany him on the raid, but he worried briefly what the Spaniards would think of the tall, gray-eyed boy who was almost a man. His red-gold hair flowed down his broad, tawny shoulders, and he looked more like a deity than an Indian or a Spaniard.

There was no way he would not be noticed by the dozen or so leather- and metal-clad horsemen. To forestall questions, Diego decided to take Aurelio directly to Domínguez. He would even use the boy's unusual looks as a ruse.

The Spaniards' surprise at seeing someone of Aurelio's appearance was even greater than Diego had expected, and for a brief moment he thought it would be necessary to kill the pigs immediately, but as he began talking, it quickly appeared that most of the pale intruders were disarmed by his story.

When Diego began his wild fabrication, it took all of Aurelio's effort to remain expressionless as he stood scrutinized openly by the surprised Spaniards. Aurelio saw the surprise that also flashed in the eyes of some of the Ácoma who stood nearby, and he prayed the Spaniards would decipher nothing on their faces.

"Captain," Diego said with feigned respect, "I wanted you to meet Mokaitsh, a very unusual and very special member of our village. Is he not one of the most handsome warriors you have seen? Does his physique not speak of great abilities?" Aurelio would have been unable to keep from laughing had fear not taken it from him.

Domínguez nodded but his look was penetrating and mistrustful.

"You have heard, without a doubt, stories of the white *cíbola* to be found among the herds of the brown shaggy beasts," Diego continued. "To the nomads of the great flatlands to the east and north, the white *cíbola* is very rare and carries much importance. As with the shaggy beasts, sometimes there will be born a man with the white hair whose eyes are pale and sensitive to light. There was such a Hopi medicine man. He came to Hawikuh, and once when the Parrot clan went to Zuñi Salt Lake to gather the salt that forms there, he saw the girl, Yellow Feather Dancing, and said she was the one who had appeared in a dream of his and in whom he was to plant a seed.

"Of course her parents gave her to him, and he took her with him to his lodging. When she came out the next morning, she returned with her family to Áco. Her stomach grew very large, and nine months later she gave birth to a pale-skinned baby boy. The baby was very large and the mother had a difficult time with the birth. She called for Juan Ramírez, our saintly *padre* then, and told him to baptize her child and teach him his language, for she did not want the devil to take the baby since he was the child of a Hopi medicine man."

Aurelio could scarcely believe his ears as Diego fabricated the incredible tale, but almost as surprising as the story was Diego's manner. The Apache had never been one to speak many words, and yet now he gave the impression of a loquacious nature. Aurelio knew Diego spoke Castilian as well as any of the Spaniards there, but while he talked, he assumed an Indian accent, mispronouncing those consonants with which the natives had most difficulty, and occasionally he would use a Queres word, always begging their pardon before supplying the correct Spanish word—but what shocked Aurelio more than any of those things was the subservient manner of the Apache, so at odds with the virulence of his hatred for the people to whom he was speaking.

Aurelio had to admit Diego was clever. He had woven a wild story tinged with a bit of superstition to account for the strangeness of the events that supposedly had occurred, but he was careful to bring in a priest and the "true faith"—as the Spaniards saw it—to remove any hint of witchcraft or sorcery or whatever else might occur to them. .

"Yes," Diego continued, "Juan Ramírez baptized the boy, teaching him not only your language but also how to read and write."

Domínguez looked skeptical, but then he spoke to Aurelio in Spanish. "How old are you, boy?"

"I will be sixteen on my next birthday, sir," Aurelio answered politely, praying that the Spaniard would not ask him many more questions, for he did not know if he could keep up the charade Diego had begun.

"You are tall for your age," Domínguez said and turned back to Diego. "How many men do you have?"

"Sixty, *Capitán*. There are more, however, if you wish them."

"Sixty is fine," Domínguez said. "In which direction did the nomads flee? Where do you think best to search?"

"Although they attacked from out of the north, they were nomads of the south," Diego said. "They were able to take only a small amount of corn from us. Therefore I expect they will attack again, for they will want more for winter. They are in the mountains in the south, I am certain. If they do not attack Áco again, they will go for Teypana or Socorro, as you call it. Or perhaps they will cross the big river and attack the pueblos of the salines, the object of many of their plundering raids."

Domínguez seemed to have completely lost interest in the unusual, fair-skinned member of the tribe, and Aurelio stepped back, relieved to be out from under the scrutiny of the captain, although some of Domínguez's companions still looked at him with unconcealed interest.

Diego and Domínguez discussed the proposed raid for a few moments more and then parted, with plans made to leave at the first light of dawn the following morning.

When they reached the mesa top, Diego laughed with satisfaction and contempt.

"They believed it all. Their stupidity is matched only by their smell!" he said.

Diego's wild tale reached the mesa top before they did, and the entire village seemed to enjoy the mirth. Women and girls giggled behind their hands and men came up to Diego and complimented him on his storytelling ability.

Gyatyu saw Aurelio and trotted over. "Oh, Great White Buffalo," he said, unable to keep a straight face as he broke into laughter.

Aurelio was not amused. He did not enjoy being the butt of jokes. "You will no longer be my friend if you say another word concerning this matter," he said angrily.

"Oh, come, Mokaitsh," Gyatyu said good-naturedly, "the ones we are laughing at are the shiny-bodies who would believe such stories. No one is laughing at you." Gyatyu grinned. "We are all afraid to laugh at you—we all know you could whip any of us."

Aurelio's face relaxed into a smile. "I'm sorry, Gyatyu. I guess I took it all too seriously—it was a crazy story." Aurelio's face became more sober. "Did your father give you permission to go?" he asked quietly.

Gyatyu nodded. "After he talked to your great-grandfather, he gave his approval. He is going, too."

"I'm glad. I will feel more at ease knowing your father is there if I need his help."

"His help?"

"Yes, Grandfather has apprehensions about this raid."

Gyatyu was an intelligent boy and said only, "You know you can count on me." He trotted off and was lost in the crowd that had gathered to hear Diego's telling of the story. Aurelio managed to slip away and trotted home.

He told his great-grandfather everything, as best he could remember, of what Diego had told the Spaniards. The old man smiled at the tall tale.

"That reminds me of the story I had to fabricate for your mother's sake when those two priests came to the village." But the smile evaporated from the old man's face at the thought of the two godless *padres*. He went on: "Circumstances may sometimes require the invention of explanations for occurrences, but, although the stories may be necessary, they may bring their own harm. One must be ever vigilant to the dangers they may bring."

Examples of such flashed through Rohona's mind but he did not tell them to the boy.

He was glad Diego had been wise enough to add that the fair-skinned boy had been baptized and was now a *cristiano*. Superstition and gossip spread easily in the province in spite of distance and poor modes of travel. The last thing Rohona wished to see was some zealous priest sent to Áco to ferret out heathen practices. He had heard the stories coming from other pueblos about the increasing repression of native ceremonies and the growing enmity on the part of civil as well as ecclesiastical authorities toward the medicine men of the villages. For the people of the pueblos the shamans were not only healers of physical ills but also preservers and propagators of the religious customs, faith, and ceremonies labeled "heathen" by the Castilian conquerors of the province.

Aurelio recognized his great-grandfather's uneasiness and sought to reassure him. "Grandfather, you have taught me well to know the minds of men. Like the tracks of animals that lead us to game, so the diverse words and actions and the faint lines on a man's face—like tracks—lead us to his inner thoughts. Rest assured, Grandfather, I shall be alert."

The smile returned to Rohona's face, and he reached out and touched his great-grandson. "I have had many sorrows in my many years," he spoke in the rusty voice of old age, "but my joys have been many, also. *That* I must not forget, for that is the most important thing."

Before the sun crested on East Mountain, Aurelio and the other Ácoma stood poised at the base of the mesa. Captain Domínguez inspected them from horseback.

The Ácoma warriors looked fierce and physically hardened. The Spaniard well knew their reputation and believed it. Perhaps living as they did, isolated on their high-perched mesa, made them wilder in their nature than the natives of the pueblos that sat along the banks of the *Río Bravo del Norte*.

He spoke to Diego, who in turn translated for the Ácoma in Queres. Three groups of three warriors each stepped forward and at Domínguez's nod trotted off.

"We follow the center path," the captain said, issuing the order that had been agreed upon. The Spaniards on horseback and the remaining Ácoma, on foot, set out.

For several days they heard nothing from the scouts as they moved southward through the arid country and into the mountains. Game was hunted, and they all enjoyed fresh meat, the first they had had since leaving Áco.

Aurelio was proud that it had been his arrow that had brought down one of the deer they all ate voraciously, but he did not like Diego telling the Spaniards that he had uncanny hunting abilities.

Aurelio knew that he was becoming a good hunter, but he knew, also, that it was his namesake, the mountain lion, who aided his arrows in their paths. His great-grandfather had taught him the hunting prayers, and never once had he forgotten to feed the turquoise-eyed amulet he carried in his medicine pouch, and he always made his prayer sticks as beautifully as he could. It should not have been surprising, therefore, that his arrows were true.

He did not like Diego talking to the Spaniards about him; he would have preferred to have been forgotten by the metal-clad riders to whom by blood he was more related but from whom, by upbringing, he was a stranger. He knew that in his heart he was Ácoma and that he would remain Ácoma, always.

That some in the village still did not accept him because of his Spanish blood did not bother him greatly. He had a good, close friend in Gyatyu, and Gyatyu's father was to him like a real father: proud of his successes in hunting and in athletic endeavors, always there with help or advice if needed, but also present with an admonition should he do something that was better done differently — or not at all.

He had other friends, too, as well as his family whom he loved deeply. It did not bother him that he was not accepted by some of the villagers. When he was younger, occasionally he had to fight other boys who made fun of him or made disparaging remarks, but his size had always been a distinct advantage, enabling him to succeed even when those he fought were older than he.

Now, however, it was no longer necessary. Remarks were occasionally made sufficiently loud so he would be sure to hear them, but they were not of a nature provoking enough to bring the speaker to task for them. The lessons his grandfather had taught him served to enable him to tolerate words others might speak.

How many times had the old man admonished him in the words of the Roman philosopher, "Look carefully after the interests of friends, and tolerate ignorant persons and those who form opinions without consideration, and be easily disposed to be pacified and reconciled to those who have offended you by words or have done you wrong."

When he was younger he would fight, but now, no longer. In spite of his grandfather's teaching, however, he was quite certain that pushed too far he would indeed resort to physical measures, despite the Roman's admonitions. If the situation arose, it would arise, but for the meantime he was content with his place at Áco, and he intended to preserve it by whatever means necessary.

He looked at the Spaniards, and although he understood everything they spoke, they were foreign to him in spite of the fact that his own mother had been of their culture. Although he thought of his mother as Ácoma and knew within his heart he was Ácoma, he knew also in reality he would never be a true person of the White Rock. Natives from other Queres-speaking villages might live at Áco, but unless one were born of an Ácoma woman, one was not and would never be Ácoma.

Aurelio had not intended to go on the retaliatory raid, nonetheless to that point he had enjoyed it. He and Gyatyu trotted side by side, talking often during the day. He found the running exhilarating and was never tired at the end of the day's journey. From the time he was old enough to go on hunts, he had sought every opportunity to do so. He liked the pine forests, the mesas, and valleys and found the excursions, be they for game, piñon nuts, or the fruit of *ibitsha*, the broad-leafed cactus, more exciting than village life. He was learning to weave like his grandfather did, he liked K'atsina dancing, and planting was not unpleasant — but he lived for hunting.

They crossed through mountains and were again in flat, bare land — a stretching plain ringed by mountains in all the directions. It was a place liked by kits, the small, swift pronged-horn. That evening all would have enjoyed roasted antelope, but there would be no telltale fires lit, for the Apache could be in any narrow valley in the nearby mountains, and their sentries would see whatever small thread of smoke that might spiral upward from the plain.

They were wise to have no cooking fires that night, for at dawn the group of scouts sent to the east trotted into camp.

Chapter 33

"They have lodges in a small valley. They are the ones." The scout spoke in Queres with hand motions as Diego translated the words for Juan Domínguez.

"The Ácoma woman, Waastita, was seen. Only women and children are in the camp—the warriors, gone, save only a few."

Domínguez smiled with satisfaction, his black eyes hard and cruel—much like those of the half-breed who stood next to him translating.

"Mejor," the Spanish captain said, "this is even better. We take revenge on their families and our profit will be even greater."

Hatred flashed in the eyes of the heathen who stood next to him. Domínguez assumed it was for the Apache attackers. He did not know that the Indian next to him saw in his own mind a Spaniard named Isidro Inojosa grabbing a twelve-year-old Apache girl by the hair and yanking her onto his horse with him. Domínguez did not know that the man pictured the cruel rape, the subsequent birth of a male child, the vicious beatings, the mother sold and sent away to the mines in Mexico. Had Domínguez known those things, he might not have gone to bed that night with such a feeling of satisfaction.

"What good does it do to attack the nomads' camp if the warriors are not there?" Aurelio asked of Diego that night. "Surely a raid to rescue the women and children they stole would be sufficient."

"They killed your mother, Mokaitsh. She had done nothing; she did not deserve to die."

"My mother's attacker is dead," Aurelio said, trying to keep his own pain from surfacing. "It is not right to take indiscriminate lives."

Diego wanted nothing to interfere with his plan. "We go only to rescue the captured ones," he said smoothly, wishing to stop the conversation with the boy who was too tainted by the foreigners' god.

"I was afraid from the way the warriors spoke tonight that much killing was in store. They look to you, Diego," Aurelio said. "I am glad we go only to rescue."

Diego did not let his thoughts show on his face. The boy was too soft; he must learn.

Aurelio sought out Gyatyu's father that night. He wanted to hear his uncle's words. Like Diego, Kohaiya, too, understood the boy's weakness taught to him by the *padre* and his own mother. Kohaiya understood that the killing on the morrow was necessary. Destroying the attackers' camp gave Áco greater safety. To destroy food, the preparers of it and those who would grow up to attack Áco was a means of securing the safety of the village. Kohaiya was keenly aware of the dangerous increase in the nomads' attacks. They must be dealt with or Áco would suffer as the villages to the east of the big river were suffering. Kohaiya sought to warn Aurelio about what would really occur the next day, but he loved him like a son and thus tried to soften his words, lest their impact affect the boy so that he would not function safely the following day.

"There will be killing, Mokaitsh," Gyatyu's father said. "Rescue without it is impossible. Apache women know how to fight like men, and they will. You must be prepared."

Aurelio slept little that night. There were things that he understood but would have preferred not to, and at the same time there were things he did not understand but felt a driving need to. People would be killed on the morrow, that he knew with clarity, but what was going on in the mind of Diego?

His grandfather had sent him on this raid to see that Diego did not do anything foolish. How was he to know what that was?

Dawn came and his questions were still unanswered, but he rose, determined that his eyes would see with clarity during that day.

The sun was high when they reached the small sheltered mountain valley. The air had the crisp pungence of pine in it as they looked down at the unkempt assortment of lodges.

Silently they descended toward the lodges and encircled them. Once the Ácoma had a noose around the camp, the Spaniards, downwind, would gallop full speed, attacking the unsuspecting village simultaneously with the waiting Ácoma. The Apache sentries had already been dispatched, their throats slit.

Aurelio waited silent and motionless. Two mangy dogs near the edge of the camp fought over the leg bone of a deer. He hoped their interest in the bone would divert them lest they catch an unfamiliar scent. Women worked outside their lodges tanning deer hides. Naked children with matted hair ran and played. A few old grandfathers sat in the sun and dozed, and a handful of men left in camp sat repairing a horsehair bridle or tempering an arrow shaft.

Suddenly the peace was shattered as the signal to attack was given. Aurelio saw Diego enter the camp at a full run, a wild yell tearing from lips that were pulled back over his teeth like a snarling wolf. The other Ácoma followed, their yells piercing the air. From the opposite end of the camp came the Spaniards at a full gallop, metal clanging. As if in unison the surprised camp let out a wail of terror and pain, adding to the cacophony of the instant.

Panic filled the camp with confusion and was as palpable as the dust raised by the horses' hooves and the running, battling people. The Apache women sought their lodges and the weapons within as the few men in the village lay dead, the first casualties of the attacking Ácoma and Spaniards. Wheel lock pistols boomed, filling the air with acrid smoke. Arrows whizzed, flint-bladed hatchets thudded dully into human skulls and limbs. A child shrieked in terror. A horse whinnied shrilly. Aurelio stood there transfixed, the sounds crashing around him. Suddenly he saw a small boy, not more than four or five, crouching in terror beside a lodging. From the face he knew instantly it was an Ácoma child, one of those taken during the Apache raid.

He ran toward the boy, yelling in Queres, "Come! Come quickly, you will be safe now!"

At that same moment a snaggletoothed Apache woman turned and saw him and saw the child who cowered at the edge of the lodge. She lunged for the boy and grabbed him before he could flee. The flint knife in her hand flashed down and eviscerated the child.

A wild cry ripped from Aurelio's throat. He did not know his hand had let the arrow fly until he saw it thunk into the snaggletoothed woman's chest, and she crumpled, her life gurgling away, blood red.

He ran to the child, tears streaming down his face, and made the sign of the cross with his thumb on its forehead and mumbled the Christian words.

Some sound distinct from the terrible noises of the attack must have registered in his subconscious, because from his kneeling position he whirled around, his steel-bladed knife instantly in his hand.

He felt a sharp, biting pain in his shoulder at the same time his own knife thrust sickeningly into a human body and pulled upward. As the body fell onto him, he shoved it off. Warm blood spilled over his arm and chest.

The unseeing eyes of a young Apache woman stared at him, as her body jerked and a red-stained flint knife fell from her fingers.

Aurelio stumbled to his feet and was sick beside the filthy hovel that had been someone's home. Spasms jerked his body and when they were over, he trembled and walked staggeringly as if drunk.

The dust and melée of the attack swirled around him. It did not seem that it was his own eyes that saw the Spanish wheel lock pistol leveled at a sightless, tottering old Apache man who groped helplessly as the lead ball thudded into his face. It did not seem his own ears that heard the shrieks of a young Apache girl as a sword thrust impaled her on the steel blade; it did not seem his own arm that was taken in the arm of someone else as he was pulled away from the camp and into the pine trees from which they had come.

"It was ugly," Gyatyu said, as he scraped some sticky pine resin from the rough bark of a tree with his knife and smeared it on Aurelio's shoulder. Aurelio winced from the stinging pain and the pungent smell, but it seemed to clear his brain.

"Yes," he said in no more than a whisper, "truly ugly." There was a pause before he spoke again. "I killed two women. One of them was the age of Auntie Siya, the other no older than myself."

"We will never know whether it was you or I who killed the young one," Gyatyu said. "Your knife entered her chest; my arrow entered her spine."

Aurelio looked up, holding his shoulder. "Thank you, brother."

"We must join the others," Gyatyu said.

The sounds of battle had become the sounds of victory. A whimpering, cowering knot of captives was herded to the center of the camp. The Spaniards laughed and congratulated themselves as they inspected their spoils.

"This one will bring a good forty *pesos*," a chestnut-bearded Spaniard said as he took the arm of a stout young woman.

Another pulled back the head of a girl by her long black hair and leered into her frightened young face. "And this one will be a good bed-warmer," he laughed.

"My wife has wanted a boy to train for outside work," another said as he inspected a boy who could not have been over seven. "She should be pleased with this one."

The two Ácoma women taken captive by the Apaches cried as they were reunited with their kinsmen. Their arms were covered with burns where they had been prodded by the glowing ends of burning sticks, attesting to the treatment they had received at the hands of their captors.

To Aurelio's horror, the other Ácoma child had also met death during the raid.

How could a people be so barbaric as to kill children for no reason? And the Spaniards, weren't they equally barbaric, killing blind old men and women? And they themselves, the Ácoma, were they blameless?

The new captives were bound together, and the group set out quickly on the return journey. Victory celebrations would have to come later—once they had put a safe distance between themselves and the devastated Apache camp. With luck, the nomad warriors would not return to their pillaged lodging places for a number of days.

That night, however, there were individual celebrations as the Apache girls and women were divided among the men for their post-conquest pleasure. The Spaniards took the youngest, most attractive of the captives, leaving the remainder for the Ácoma to share, however they might determine among

themselves. Diego was given first choice for the success of the raid he had
led.

"She is yours when I am finished," Diego said to Aurelio. "You have gone
on a raid with the men; now you should enjoy it like a man." He clapped
the tall boy on the shoulder. "There are no *padres* here to turn everything
into a sin—you are a man now, you should begin to do the things that are
a man's to do."

Aurelio made no response, but that night as he lay wrapped in his blanket
and listened to the grunts of pleasure and the cries of pain that rippled
through the camp, he felt little desire to prove himself as a man. The visions
of the women he had killed, the dead child and the blind old man, a bullet
in his forehead, filled him with revulsion. It was not necessary for a *padre* to
be there to make him feel sin, for he felt as stained by it as was his clothing
stained by the blood of the women he had killed.

When he could no longer stand the visions nor the sounds, he rose and
crept silently away from the camp. The sounds faded, and he knelt behind
a clump of twisted juniper. His right hand tapped his chest, and he whispered
the words Padre Ramírez had taught him, the words his mother told him he
should continue to speak even after the saintly friar had left the village.

He had no idea how long he had knelt there when a tiny sound came to
his ears. His knife was instantly in his hand, and he moved silently from his
kneeling position to a poised, crouching one. The sound came nearer and he
knew someone approached stealthily. Had the Apache warriors returned
home so soon to find their homes destroyed and their families dead or gone?

Aurelio saw a faint movement at the edge of the juniper, and like his
namesake, the mountain lion, he leaped silently and swiftly. His arm whipped
around the shadow's neck, yanking it to the ground, and his knife was aimed
at its jugular vein. He knew at once it was not an Apache warrior, although
it began to fight desperately.

Aurelio dropped his knife and grasped the flailing arms, straddling the
small thrashing body and pinning it helplessly to the ground. The girl could
not have been more than ten or twelve, he judged. Her clothes were tatters.
She must have made her escape while her captor lay sleeping heavily,
drugged with the release of his passion.

Once or twice more she tried feebly to escape his grasp, but Aurelio held
her firmly. He moved his weight on her body to hold her more securely, and
she began to whimper. He realized what she must have thought.

He grasped both her hands in one of his as he reached into the pouch he
wore at his waist. From the pouch he withdrew some of the *guayave* paper
bread and a small piece of jerked meat Siya had sent with him. He put it in
her hand, and he could tell she did not know at first what it was or what he
meant by it. Slowly he eased his weight off of her and pulled her to a sitting
position. He took her other hand and put it on the hand with the food. He
spoke a word he had heard Diego use many times when he was a boy and
pestered him. He knew the word was neither Queres nor Castilian and hoped

it might be Apache. He didn't even know exactly what it meant. Diego had always used it as if it meant "don't bother me" or "get out of here" or perhaps worse, but he tried it.

The girl was silent. Aurelio pulled her to her feet and again spoke the word. She just stood there, trembling slightly. He turned her around and gave her a little push, speaking the word again. Perhaps she understood. She murmured something Aurelio did not understand and was gone, the food clutched in her hand. The next morning when the discovery was made that a captive was missing, Aurelio said nothing, his face expressionless as he had been taught by his great-grandfather.

The decision was made not to hunt for the escaped girl. The consensus was that it would be best not to delay in putting distance between themselves and the warriors who would be returning to their pillaged camp.

"Without food she will probably die anyway before she finds her people," Captain Domínguez said, dismissing the subject.

Aurelio said a silent prayer for the girl's well-being and felt a measure of expiation for his individual as well as their collective sins.

The long journey the next day as they dogtrotted through the rugged land gave Aurelio ample time to reflect on the many emotions that battled within him. The Apaches were barbarians, the Spaniards not much better, or perhaps they were worse—they, at least, should have a conscience. He could understand the Ácoma wishing to rescue their people taken captive, but they, too, had murdered women and old men.

I am not yet a man, he spoke silently to himself. *I have many things yet to learn.*

And he thought on the Roman's words, the words his grandfather had taught him. "A plant is bitter. Throw it away. There are briars in the road. Turn aside from them. This is enough. Do not add, And why were such things made in the world?" He looked straight ahead as he trotted. *I shall throw away the visions in my head. I will turn aside from them.*

Gyatyu, who had trotted silently alongside him for the entire journey, looked at him. "Your head is always filled with many words that rush like the big river in springtime, yes?"

"Sometimes I wish the words would run dry," Aurelio said.

That night in camp, Aurelio saw a kind of tautness in Diego that might have been excitement or expectancy. Rohona's words came back to him and he knew that he must be alert.

Diego was sitting with a group of men, talking. Suddenly Aurelio looked up, and he was no longer there. He could not have taken his eyes off Diego for more than a moment and yet he was gone.

An uneasiness prickled at the back of his neck. He walked to where Gyatyu sat and casually hunkered down beside him, speaking quietly. "Be prepared to warn the Spaniards of danger, should you hear the nighthawk cry."

A questioning look flitted across Gyatyu's face, but he nodded in assent.

"I go to look for Diego," Aurelio whispered as he rose.

At that moment he saw a man arise from a group and disappear into the darkness. Just as swiftly, Aurelio was no longer to be seen. With the silence of a stalking mountain cat, he followed the man. His stealth was rewarded when the man joined four others some distance from the camp. Among the four stood Diego.

The Apache spoke in low tones, and it was necessary for Aurelio to approach closer to hear. His proximity was such he could almost have reached out and touched them, and yet they were unaware of his presence.

"I found out from the Spaniards that they head for the big river tomorrow," Diego whispered. "When they are two days away we will strike. We must make it look like the work of Apache." The others nodded in approval. "I will give you more instructions later."

Aurelio slipped away, returning swiftly to camp where he sought out Gyatyu's father and told him what he had heard.

"I do not like the Spaniards," Kohaiya said, "but the plan is dangerous. Too many things might go wrong, leading the blame back to Áco. You may sleep peacefully tonight, my son," he said, placing his hand on Aurelio's shoulder. "I shall go to the Spaniards and encourage them to return to Áco with us so that we may thank them properly with a celebration in honor of the success of this journey."

He allowed a smile to show in his eyes. "I have yet to know a Spaniard who would refuse free food. You have done good work tonight, my son."

The next morning when the news spread that the Spaniards were returning to Áco with them, Aurelio saw the black rage that spread over Diego's features. He was glad the Apache did not know it had been he who had caused the change in their plans.

Chapter 34

The Spaniards returned to Áco, enjoyed the dances put on in celebration of the success of their undertaking, and ate heartily of the food prepared for the feast. They even carried away as "gifts" several baskets of corn from the Ácoma's meager harvest as well as a stack of cotton *mantas* and a few soft, tanned deerskins.

Aurelio felt a moment of bitter remorse for his actions when he saw the Spaniards leaving Áco with part of their precious harvest, but he knew he had done the right thing. As his great-grandfather always admonished him, the most important thing was the welfare of Áco. Better they allow the Spaniards to take a few baskets of grain than to take all of it in retaliation for an attack the Ácoma might have made.

Diego saw his chance to kill Spaniards slip through his fingers, and he was like a madman at home.

Rohona learned the details of the journey from Aurelio and Gyatyu's father. He was proud of his great-grandson, but he understood the Apache's hatred, for once he, too, had known the black, consuming emotion. He knew its danger, and yet he was sympathetic toward Diego because he had felt the voracious, gnawing fangs in his own entrails.

In the days that followed, Diego continued to rant and rave. Aurelio knew that several times the Apache had been out to the pinnacle where his mother lay beneath the pile of stones. At night he had even seen the Apache stroke a fragment of ribbon that had been hers.

Aurelio was speechless some days later when Diego brought home a wife. His great-grandfather and Siya were as shocked as he, although their faces did not show it.

Siya welcomed the woman Hishti affectionately and called her daughter. She took the basket with the four flours from her, and together the women prepared food. Like a good daughter-in-law, the woman scarcely spoke. Aurelio knew who she was, but he had had no idea that Diego had been interested in her.

She was rather plain, a few years older than Diego, and had a round, flat face, and her figure had lost any youthful curves it might once have had. She was not precisely stout, but she appeared to be strong of back and arm. She had never been married and until then had lived in her stepbrother's house. When she was a child, her stepbrother's father and mother had adopted her upon the death of her own parents.

Diego would not go to live in her house as was the usual custom. The Apache brought her to live with them. That night as they all slept in the same room, Aurelio heard the sounds of the wedding-night act but heard no soft laughter, no endearing words, no quiet muffled conversation lasting until the wee hours. He was filled with a kind of sadness; he knew at once that Diego did not love the woman he had made his wife that day. It took him only a moment to understand why Diego had married: They needed an able-bodied woman in the household. Now that his mother was dead, Siya was unable to handle all the work that was required. The woman Hishti was mature, accustomed to work and experienced in it.

Aurelio knew enough to appreciate what Diego had done for them but was sorry for the woman because she did not have the love of her husband. Although he could not remember him, he knew how his own father's love had sustained his mother. He knew the look in his mother's eyes when she spoke of his father. That look had been a definition for him of a woman's love for a man. He wanted someone sometime to look at him the same way.

The next morning Aurelio sought to find a glimmer of feeling between the two recently married people. He wanted to be wrong, but the woman's presence in their house affected Diego as much as a stick of wood might have. For her part, the woman scarcely spoke or looked up as she set immediately to work.

Everyone obviously knew why she was there, but Siya spoke affectionately to her and complimented her on her abilities and industry. Rohona spoke warmly to her and told her how happy he was to have a young, pretty daughter-in-law to comfort him in his old age.

Aurelio felt embarrassment, but he, too, told her how happy he was she had come to live with them.

Only Diego had no words for her. At night he would perform his obligations as a husband and she hers as a wife — but by day it seemed she scarcely existed for him.

Little by little, though, a smile came more readily to the woman's round, plain face, and it seemed she felt genuine affection for the two old ones. She appeared a little embarrassed when Aurelio attempted to make conversation with her, but he began to make her laugh with silly faces, and soon her shyness disappeared. Her seeming contentedness in their home removed the pity Aurelio had felt for her, and he thought her face less plain.

As winter came and bore down bitterly on them, the companionship of the household was the one small thing that made their misery more tolerable. All were hungry, but none complained. Diego had even ceased to rail at Spaniards, but no one suspected for a moment that his thoughts were elsewhere.

Game was scarce that winter, and Aurelio was one of the few in the village who found success with his arrows.

"The boy was well named," was a comment heard with some frequency.

Food was not abundant in their house, but not once did Aurelio return from hunting that he did not leave a portion of his catch with Gyatyu's mother. They were not the only ones who shared in his good fortune, however, for he would often leave a bit with a family to whom success had been a stranger.

The winter was bitterly cold, but there was only a little snow. Unless plentiful rains came in summer, it did not bode well for the rock cisterns on the mesa that held their precious drinking water. Nor did it bode well for their crops if they had to be planted in earth that had not seen winter moisture.

Summer came bringing its welcome warmth, but during the dry moon the water gauge was lower than even the oldest men could remember. Rohona could not see the water gauge, but when they told him where the water lay, he said that for all of his ninety-odd growing seasons never had it fallen so low.

Beautiful prayer sticks were made. K'atsina masks were carefully re-painted. Dancers practiced for days. The most sacred of the K'atsina ceremonies was performed with absolute adherence to ritual. Every household sought to follow every prescribed rule. No salt was used in any food for the specified number of days; husbands and wives refrained from sexual relations for the required length of time. Cleansing rituals were followed closely.

The wet moon came, but it brought no water. The K'atsina did not send the *shiwana*. The Ácoma saw their sparse, stunted corn turn brown and die from lack of moisture. All prayed for a piñon crop but few were deceived by the plentiful piñon cones. Even the *ibitsha* seemed to have fewer blooms that year.

Hishti worked unfailingly beside Diego and Aurelio in the fields, but their backbreaking effort produced such a meager crop, she could not hold back tears. When Aurelio saw them, she claimed sand had blown into her eyes. After harvest she took a stick and wandered for hours, digging edible roots.

That winter there were many holes opened in the walls of the houses in Áco as the villagers dipped into their stores of nuts. Three or four years of nut crops were stored in the walls of the homes for just such a purpose: famine. There was no nut crop that year, however, to replenish the mud-plastered holes, and they gaped open like hungry mouths staring at the hungry occupants of the dwellings.

When spring came that year, there were fewer Ácoma to greet the return of the longer days. Few babies born that year survived; their mothers' flaccid breasts were unable to produce enough nourishment for their tiny bodies. Many a grandmother and grandfather were buried with their grandchild, a sickness in the chest having taken its toll among the old.

Rohona, though, survived. "Why do *I* not die?" he would ask his great-grandson. His rusty voice had no reproach in it, only true questioning.

Aurelio would try to joke, although shards of ice stabbed his heart beneath his levity. "You have been here so long, Grandfather, the gods have forgotten about you," he would laugh lightly. "You shall live forever."

"I do not want to live forever."

Another summer passed, and Áco was again forgotten by the K'atsina. The Apaches renewed their attacks and all the village lived in dread. News reached them from the other pueblos. Drought and famine were sparing no one. Natives lay dead along the roads, and the Spaniards were burying their own with much more frequency. The *padres* opened up their coffers of stored grain, but if the rain did not return the following year, they would have nothing to give, either.

Hishti's plain face was no longer round. Her back was straight, but her body was no longer stout. Diego seemed made of sinew only; Siya was like a small wrinkled bird that had lost its feathers, and Rohona seemed no more than a fragile bundle of weathered bones. Only Aurelio appeared scarcely touched by the want they suffered. Perhaps it was only his size in relation to those with whom he lived.

He was tall and broad shouldered but without the merest hint of fat. The fine bone structure of his high-cheekboned face was accentuated by his leanness, and his face was that of a man now. The look of youth and the frequent smile were gone. His face was serious and intense, and his gray eyes could be hard, the color of his steel knife blade on a cold day of winter. His red-gold hair fell to the middle of his shoulders when it was not tied back with a thong of leather or a woven cord.

Rohona's eyes could not see the change that had taken place in the features of his great-grandson, but he sensed them. He had developed the habit of taking hold of the boy's arm, not for guidance for his sightless eyes, because he knew where everything was, but he took his grandson's arm to see if he could note any decrease in its size. Did the boy have enough to eat?

Rohona knew winter was coming by the sound of the wind. It blew from North Mountain with icy fingers. One day he called to Aurelio. "Take me up to the highest roof, Great-grandson."

Aurelio protested. "Whatever for, Grandfather? The wind is cold today."

"It does not matter," Rohona replied. "I wish to feel like the eagle today."

With great difficulty Aurelio helped the withered old man to the upper housetop. Rohona stood, trembling with age, his arms outstretched toward North Mountain. He chanted a prayer in a high, cracking voice. He turned to the west and the prayer was mixed with words of Castilian. He prayed in all directions, sprinkling cornmeal to the cardinal points. He sat down, and Aurelio put a buffalo robe around him, but Rohona pushed it away.

"I have decided," he said in his old rustly voice, "that today I will die."

"No!" Aurelio said with vehemence, "No!"

Rohona smiled, his sightless eyes, however, seeing many visions in his mind.

"Yes," he answered, "yes, but sit down, Grandson."

Aurelio complied with the old man's request but sought again to put the buffalo robe around his great-grandfather's shoulders.

"As best I can reckon," the old man began, "you now have twenty growing seasons. You are a man; there is nothing left for me to teach you. My work is done. I have raised you up; the work is yours now. You must raise up a son and teach him what I have taught you."

The old man's voice quavered, and he raised his hands, opening them wide.

"Heed the philosopher, Grandson: Be like the promontory, against which the waves continually break, but stand firm and tame the fury of the water round about you."

There was a moment of silence. "Go now," he said. "I am ready to die."

"No!" Aurelio shouted. Against the old man's protests, he lifted his great-grandfather in his arms and carried him down from the rooftop and into the dwelling.

"I am going to die today," Rohona said.

He was wrong. He lived for three more days. At dawn on the third day, Aurelio found him sitting by the fire, slumped forward. He thought his great-grandfather had only fallen asleep, but he had fallen asleep to life and sat now in death. Tears coursed down Aurelio's face as his lips formed Castilian words and his thumb traced a cross on the old man's wrinkled forehead.

Aurelio refused Diego's help and carried the withered body of his great-grandfather in his arms the entire distance across the valley floor and to the pinnacle. He placed the body on top of the pile of stones under which lay the Spanish woman called María Angélica. He covered the withered body of her husband with more stones.

Aurelio knelt and prayed both in Queres and Castilian. This pinnacle of rock that held the people he loved would not be his resting place.

"I want to be buried with your great-grandmother, but you must be buried in the churchyard," his great-grandfather had said to him. "You must be buried there with a water jug broken over your grave as is the Ácoma custom. When you die people will know you only as Ácoma."

When Aurelio rose, he felt the icy fingers of the wind from North Mountain wrap loneliness around him, reaching to his soul.

Like tiny feathers, he felt the first few flakes touch his skin. He turned his face upward and the snow melted on his face, mingling with his tears.

He stood, a solitary figure, etched in gray as the snow fell silently, covering the stone graves with a shroud of white.

Chapter 35

A glimmer of hope crept into their lives that spring before planting began. The ground had moisture in it. The experienced planters knew it would not be sufficient without summer rain, but at least the stalks might have enough of a start to better endure a lack of moisture later, but Aurelio did not allow hope to enter his breast. He had made all emotions strangers to himself that winter.

When he descended from the pinnacle after stacking the stones of his great-grandfather's grave, he willed his loneliness and pain to become numbness, and they had. He no longer laughed nor smiled nor joked. He was very solicitous of his auntie, who had taken the death of her brother quite hard. He would talk to her softly in the evenings and hold her withered, fragile hand. He was kind and considerate to Hishti, but he rarely stayed at home. He spent all his time in solitude, hunting. The game was of great necessity to them, and he was commended for his diligence. It was questionable, however, whether he would have done differently even if food had not been so desperately needed.

"I saw Aurelio coming down the house row. He has brought home a deer," Hishti shouted to Siya so that she might hear.

The old woman's lips curved in a wrinkled smile. "Have you ever known a finer hunter?" she said with pride.

"Never," Hishti replied, "he truly has the power of his namesake."

She went quickly to get the cornmeal and hurried out across the terrace and down the ladder to make the cornmeal road for the deer being brought to their house.

Hishti sprinkled the meal in Aurelio's path and up the ladder to the terrace, marveling at the strength of the tall young hunter who so easily ascended the ladder, the deer slung across his shoulders. Aurelio lay the deer with its head toward the fireplace as Hishti fetched beads of lignite that she placed on the deer's neck. She brought a bowl of cornmeal and set it near the deer's head.

"Would you ask Gyatyu's family to help share the hunt with us?" Aurelio said to Hishti.

She nodded and hurried to do his bidding. The diligence and skill of the Mountain Lion put food in the stomachs of many more than his own family there on the White Rock.

Shortly Gyatyu and his relatives arrived. Each one went to the deer, fed it a little cornmeal from the bowl placed near its head, touched the deer's face, and then rubbed their hands over their own faces, saying to the deer, "You are such a pretty deer and we know you are not lazy. Thank you for coming to our home and showing us that you are not ashamed of our people."

After the spirit of the deer had left, Gyatyu's relatives helped Aurelio skin the animal. Hishti and Gyatyu's mother prepared the head, placing it, with the horns still attached, into a large pot of boiling water.

"Here are your earrings, deer," Hishti said, dropping corn, pumpkin seeds, and piñon nuts into the pot.

While the head cooked, all hands helped prepare the meat, removing it from the bones and cutting it into thin strips that were hung on long poles suspended over the terrace roof. Most of the meat would go to Gyatyu's family because their household was larger than that of the hunter of the deer. Even the hide Aurelio gave to Gyatyu's father, for Aurelio already had more than enough buckskin to meet the needs of his household.

"You do me honor," Kohaiya said to him. "It makes me proud that you became my son at the K'atsina initiation. Your hunting ability shows the favor in which you are held by the K'atsina, and your generosity repays that favor. You are truly a man of Áco."

That spring Aurelio planted with care, but his spirits did not soar as did those of many of the Ácoma who were optimistic for that year's crop. The mood at the fields was one of general lightheartedness. The tasks of clearing, tilling, and planting were carried out with vigor and content.

Two daughters of Hishti's adoptive brother came to help in their fields as repayment for the game Aurelio had shared with them that winter. The two girls had come to their adoptive aunt's house upon a few occasions during the winter, but Aurelio had scarcely noticed them. Their presence in the fields attracted his attention even less.

One was older, in her teens, the other, a child yet, no more than eight or so. They laughed and giggled, and it was obvious their adoptive aunt loved them as much as if they had been the nieces of her own flesh. A smile always lit her face when the girls were near.

Hishti showered her love on her nieces. She had been married to Diego for more than three years but still her belly did not grow heavy with child. A baby would have given her much happiness despite the scarcity of food.

She felt, too, that she had failed Diego as a wife by not producing a child for him. He had said nothing, but he never said anything of a personal nature to her. She knew she was not pretty, but she had hoped that by giving him a son or a daughter he might find more pleasure with her.

What she lacked in beauty, however, her nieces enjoyed in abundance, but she was neither jealous nor resentful that fate had dealt its hand as it had. She took pride in their long, shiny black hair; in their lively, flashing eyes; in the white, even teeth of their smiles. Just having them around made her feel prettier. When the girls visited their house, Siya enjoyed their presence, too. It made her feel less old to hear their lively chatter. She would have given anything to have been able to join them at the planting fields. It was lonely in the village at planting time.

They had been at the fields for three days when Hishti spoke to the elder girl, Wiika, whose shiny black hair resembled the feathers of the oriole for which she had been named.

"Daughter," Hishti said, for at Áco a brother's daughters were considered one's own daughters, "trot back to the village and check on Auntie Siya. Make her a soft corn gruel, for she has not been eating too well of late. Spend the night with her; the company will lift her spirits while we are at the fields. Tomorrow you may come back here."

"Yes, Auntie," the girl replied.

"May I go, too? Please, please?" the younger girl asked with excitement.

Hishti patted her head, smiling kindly. "No, Daughter, you stay with Auntie Hishti. Wiika can trot faster alone. You are still young, and it is a good distance back to the village."

The little girl's face fell. "But I am already eight growing seasons. I can run fast," she protested.

Her older sister knelt beside her and stroked her hair. It was obvious the sisters loved each other very much. "Stay with Auntie Hishti, Gana. I will not be gone for long. Auntie Hishti needs your help because you *are* a big girl now. I promise, though, that tomorrow when I return we shall sneak off for a little adventure — just you and me."

Gana's eyes sparkled with mischief and delight, and she nodded in assent. She whirled around and flitted off like the snowbird for which she was named.

Wiika started at once for the village. The girls of Áco were just as good runners as were the boys, and many a boy had been acutely embarrassed at least once in his life by having been beaten in a race by a fleet-footed girl. Hishti smiled as she watched the lithe, slender sixteen-year-old girl disappear in the distance.

❋   ❋   ❋

By the time Wiika reached the village the sun was throwing long shadows across the house rows. She trotted to her own dwelling. No one was home, for they were all at the fields. By the time she had a small fire going, the water heated, and the gruel cooked, twilight had fallen. She carried the steaming, fragrant corn mush to Siya's dwelling. She mounted the ladder without calling up the greeting into the darkness, not wanting to wake the old woman if perchance she were napping, as the old frequently do. Her moccasin-clad feet made only a soft swishing noise as she crossed the roof terrace.

She heard nothing from within the house to warn her, but then she would not have, for he would have made no sound whatever. She did not scream when he grabbed her because she had been taught not to make precipitous noises. The only sound was her intake of breath. The bowl of steaming blue cornmeal mush as it crashed to the floor spilled on her hands and on the person who grabbed her.

An old, quavering voice from inside called out, startled, "What goes there?"

The person who held her knew instantly it was a woman he held and no Apache intruder. "Forgive me," he said as he let her go.

"It is me, Wiika," she spoke loudly so Siya could hear. Although she had recognized his voice the moment he spoke, her own trembled with her fright of moments before. "Please forgive me, I . . . I'm so sorry," she stammered, "I should have announced myself, but I did not want to wake Auntie if she were sleeping."

She knelt and began scraping up the spilled mush and the broken pottery shards with her hands.

Aurelio touched a pine-bundle torch to the embers that glowed faintly in the fire in the room. Instantly the resin-filled torch flamed to light, and he saw the shiny black hair that fell around the face of the kneeling girl.

"It's all right, Auntie," he said to Siya. "It is Wiika. We've had a small accident."

Aurelio placed the torch in a holder at the door and knelt to help the girl clean up the mess. "I'm sorry," he said, "I did not know you were returning to the village to bring food to Auntie Siya. Hishti did not mention it when I told her I was going to hunt a rabbit to bring to Auntie."

The girl's head was down, and she did not look up, but he heard a small noise. He lifted her chin. Tears were rolling down her face. He found himself looking into wide, black eyes that in the torchlight flickered brilliantly like obsidian in sunlight.

"Do not cry," he said. "It is my fault."

She tried to wipe away the tears with the backs of her hands but succeeded only in smudging her face with the blue cornmeal gruel.

Aurelio smiled, reached out and wiped the gruel from her cheek. Her skin was as smooth as the satin ribbon in the tarnished box. She smiled shyly at him in response. He saw her even, white teeth, and her dark lashes as she lowered her eyes again. He saw that she was very beautiful.

In silence they finished cleaning up the spilled gruel. They did not look at each other again. When they were done, they went in to Siya and seated themselves with her. There was an awkward moment of silence.

"I'm sorry, Auntie," the girl said with embarrassment. "I made you some blue cornmeal mush, but I spilled it all."

Siya patted her hand. "Thank you for thinking of an old woman," she said reassuringly. "Aurelio brought me a rabbit, so I have had a good meal, but your presence does me more good than food."

"I came to spend the night with you, also," Wiika said hesitantly, "but since your nephew is here, I will go to my dwelling."

"No, no," Siya said, patting the girl's hand again. "I would be less lonely if you stayed here as you had planned. Then I will have two young people to keep me company."

Wiika nodded shyly. Again there was an awkward silence.

"How is the planting?" Siya asked.

"It appears the ground has profited from the snow," Aurelio said. The conversation continued a while longer, then Siya began to stifle an occasional yawn. "I am afraid I am not good company. I cannot seem to stay awake. I sleep now, but don't mind me. It is early. You two do not have to sleep just because an old woman cannot keep her eyes open. Why don't you go out on the terrace, it is a lovely night." Neither of the young people protested.

Indeed the night was beautiful as they walked out onto the roof terrace. Aurelio put out the pine torch, and they stood in silence looking at the sky, scattered with the stars of late spring.

"Shall we sit?" he asked, breaking the silence. Quickly the silence returned as they seated themselves. At length he spoke again.

"The ancient people who lived across many waters to the east—to the east where Nautsiti went—they saw the stars as people and animals and gave them names. See the bright star, there," he pointed, "and see the one above it and the other one, and follow to that one and that one."

"Yes, I see," Wiika said.

"They call that Leo or the lion."

"You are called 'the lion,' " she said softly. "Are those your stars?"

"I shall call them mine. The water dipper they called the Big Bear. Look down from the water dipper over there. See the bright star there and the others there and there."

"Where?" she asked, "I do not know which ones you mean."

"There," he said, pointing, and with his other hand he brought her face to rest along his arm to sight the stars to which he pointed. He felt the warmth of her cheek against his skin. When he spoke again his voice, although more quiet, had a different quality to it. "That they called Virgo," he said.

"And what is a Virgo?" she asked. There was a pause.

"It is a virgin."

"May those stars be mine?"

"If you want."

Silence returned, but at length he spoke again. "There is much work to be done still in the fields. We should sleep now."

Together they rose. Inside, the old woman snored. Silently they entered the dwelling, and Aurelio found a rolled-up sheepskin and a woven blanket, which he gave Wiika. For a moment their hands touched. Then he moved away and she heard him spreading out his bed. She unrolled the sheepskin he had given her and lay down on it, wrapping the blanket around her.

"Good night," she said quietly into the darkness.

"Sleep well," came the soft reply.

In the morning he watched her as she prepared breakfast for the three of them. She was even more beautiful by daylight. Why had he never noticed before? She did not look at him that morning nor did she speak. When breakfast was over, Aurelio took Siya's hand.

"We must return to the fields. If the work delays, I will bring you another rabbit."

"Go, children," she said, "but I will miss you. You have made me feel younger by your visit. If you bring another rabbit," she said to Aurelio, smiling, "bring Wiika with you. She makes a very good breakfast."

She smiled at the girl, who sat with downcast eyes.

The two young people descended the twisting *Camino del Padre* and trotted across the valley toward the fields to the north. They did not stop once until they reached the other planters. Aurelio admired Wiika's endurance.

Hishti was smiling broadly as they approached. Gana went running to her older sister. "You are back," she shouted gaily, "do you remember your promise?"

Wiika laughed and tweaked her little sister's long braids. "Of course, I remember, but I must help with the work first. Tomorrow I promise we shall go on an adventure."

Through the rest of the day, Hishti constantly watched Aurelio and Wiika. The girl kept her head down, working diligently. Hishti smiled with satisfaction.

She had not seen Wiika so quiet, and she had never seen Aurelio glance at the girl before, and now he did so frequently. It was the same that evening as they all sat beneath the sun shade eating supper. The two girls usually chattered away happily; that night Wiika was unusually quiet. Only Gana babbled merrily. Hishti missed nothing, especially not Aurelio's frequent sidelong glances at the sixteen-year-old girl.

After they had eaten, Aurelio and Diego went to sit with the men to talk of the day's work and things pertaining to men. It gave Hishti the opportunity she had awaited to find out what had happened at the village.

Wiika's eyes sparkled as she talked and laughed. The new shyness had left her. She described the fiasco with the gruel and was able to laugh now. She told about sitting and watching the stars and about the many things Aurelio knew.

"And afterward?" Hishti asked with expectancy.

Wiika laughed and looked slyly at her aunt. "Of course you did not know Aurelio was taking a rabbit to Auntie."

Hishti giggled behind her hand. Wiika smiled.

"Unfortunately, nothing happened after we watched the stars. He gave me a sheepskin, took his own and laid it in a far corner of the room. I slept next to Auntie Siya, who snored all night long."

Gana had been just as interested in the story as was Hishti. "Did you want him to put his sheepskin next to yours?" the little girl asked innocently.

Wiika laughed and tweaked her braids. "Yes, I would not mind sharing a sheepskin with him."

"He is such a man," Hishti said. "He is so tall and his shoulders are so broad. And his hair when it is loose falls like red-gold rivers down his shoulders, and when he smiles, it would melt the snow off North Mountain in winter."

"Why, Hishti," Wiika teased, "I am going to tell Diego."

Hishti blushed. "But Aurelio is a beautiful man, Daughter, that you must admit."

"I admit it freely, Auntie," Wiika said with a smile. "I admit it freely."

Gana looked at her older sister, and she laughed in little chirps, like a small happy bird. "Is he going to make you a set of clothes?"

"I don't know, Gana," Wiika said.

"Do you want him to?"

Wiika smiled. "I would put them on, yes."

The next day Wiika took Gana on the adventure she had promised. They set out for a rocky area at a distance from the fields. Sometime later they came running back at full speed, hair flying out behind them as if chased by something terrible, Wiika in the lead. When she reached the sun shelter, she collapsed under it. Right behind her was Gana, who fell in a heap on top of her older sister.

Aurelio, having seen them, came running over, worried at what would cause such flight, but when he arrived, Wiika was laughing, pushing Gana off of her. Gana was flailing at her sister wildly.

Aurelio picked up the little girl, and she pounded on him for a moment before the tears came. She buried her face against his shoulder and threw her arms around his neck as she cried. Awkwardly he tried to comfort her as he looked questioningly at Wiika.

"I'm sorry, Gana," Wiika said contritely as she stood. She stepped closer and stroked her little sister's hair.

"Your eyes were so wide when I spoke jokingly about a rabbit with a snake's head, I just couldn't resist acting as if there were one there. I'm sorry."

Gana cried even louder. Aurelio understood her tears were from embarrassment and patted her gently.

"Do not worry, little Snowbird," he said reassuringly, "tricks like that make a person brave. Next time you will not run and be scared."

Her tears subsided. Aurelio smiled at Wiika over her little sister's head. Hishti was right. His smile could melt the snow off North Mountain. Aurelio sat down with Gana, and Wiika sat beside them. He lifted the little girl's chin and wiped away her tears. She smiled shyly at him.

"Forgive me, please, little Sister?" Wiika asked.

For a moment Gana looked petulant, but then she said, "Promise you won't do it again."

"Promise."

Gana looked at Aurelio and smiled. "My sister thinks you are a beautiful man."

"Gana!" Wiika gasped.

Aurelio blushed deeply, but managed to speak. "Your sister is beautiful, too."

Gana looked at him and smiled. "Am I pretty?"

"Of course you are. You are very beautiful, and you are sure to marry a handsome man some day."

"I hope so," she said emphatically. "I don't want to marry an old ugly one. That wouldn't be any fun."

She looked at him again. "The next time we go on an adventure, will you go with us?"

"I would like that," he said with seriousness, "but now we must plant more corn and pray the K'atsina send rain to our fields."

They returned to work, Gana using her digging stick with more application than she ever had. Two days later at the noon rest period, Aurelio found Gana.

"Little Snowbird," he said with a smile, "you have worked as hard as a little bird digging at the ground. Do you want to go on an adventure after our rest? You have earned it."

Gana smiled with delight. "Oh, yes. Yes!" she cried with excitement.

After they had slept, Aurelio, Gana, and Wiika started for the rocky outcroppings. They wound among the rocks, letting their imaginations run wild with stories and what-ifs. Upon agreement, they were to go their separate ways for a short while and bring back a "treasure."

Gana ran off without a backward glance, determined to find the best one. Wiika started to go her way, but Aurelio took her by the wrist. This time, her eyes did not fall from his. He led her between two small boulders.

"I need look no further for a treasure," he said quietly.

She blushed but did not look down. He rubbed his fingers on her cheeks in a caress and down her arms, and he taught her how the Spaniards taste their loved ones with their lips. And she learned quickly. His body pressed hers against the rock, and she was molded to him as they stood there, their lips joined for long moments. Aurelio lifted his head, listened and pulled Wiika away from the rock, as Gana came running back.

"Look what I have found! Look what I have found!" she shouted excitedly, waving the treasure she had discovered. In her hand was a perfect bluebird feather. "Look," she gasped, extending the feather for them to see.

Aurelio took it carefully and looked at it. "You have truly found a treasure, little Snowbird. This is a sign that you shall have much happiness in your life. Keep this feather and care for it. The bluebird left it there just for you." He smiled at her and returned the beautiful feather—true evidence of good luck and happiness, a gift any Ácoma would treasure.

"Did you find anything?" Gana asked them.

"Yes," Wiika answered. "I did not find a bluebird feather, but I found happiness, too."

"Good!" cried Gana as she ran off. "I want Auntie Hishti to see what I found."

Wiika smiled at Aurelio; they followed Gana out from the rocks and back to the sun shelter.

The next day at rest time when all had fallen asleep, Aurelio rose and picked up his sheepskin. He looked down at Wiika who also did not sleep. Without a word, she rose and followed him to the rocks.

On a soft sandy spot among the boulders, Aurelio laid the sheepskin. Wiika lifted the tunic of her dress and pulled it over her head. Never before had Aurelio seen such beauty. Her body quivered faintly. Her breasts were of shining copper in the sunlight, hard-tipped in dusty rose, and her legs were as sleek as her breasts. She lay down on the sheepskin, her eyes on him.

He removed his clothes, and she looked at him unashamedly. And then he was lying beside her, his hands caressing her, and he was on top of her, moving against her with all his strength as she moved her hips to meet him.

She stifled her cry as he entered her. Her arms clung to him, and she tasted his lips as he thrust again and again.

When they lay still, side by side, she put her hand on his chest. "The stars are no longer mine," she whispered. "I want them no more."

Aurelio ran his hand over her belly and touched her intimately. "This is the night sky filled with stars for me," he said. She smiled at him and moved against the caress of his hand.

That was one of the few times in his life that Aurelio's sense of hearing failed him. The small gasp made both of them turn to see Gana's surprised little face seconds before she whirled and ran away.

Chapter 36

Hishti was beside herself with happiness. Since she and the others of the village had returned from the fields, Aurelio had worked long into the nights. When he was finished making the articles, Hishti patted him on the shoulder but said nothing.

Aurelio smiled at her. "Is the fire ready for bread?" he asked.

"Yes, yes," she said as she gave him a little push. "Now go."

Aurelio left and bounded down the ladder. When he reached the dwelling, he called up the greeting. At the response, he started quickly up the ladder but slowed as he climbed the final rungs. When he entered the room off the roof terrace, he saw Wiika's father sitting there. His face showed nothing but he nodded and Aurelio seated himself.

"I have brought a set of clothes for your eldest daughter, Wiika," Aurelio said. His voice sounded oddly high to himself.

The father called to his daughter. Wiika entered the room, eyes downcast. There was something unusual in her face. She seated herself in front of Aurelio, and from the corner of his eye, he saw Gana peeking into the room. He picked up the bundle and placed it in front of Wiika.

"I have brought you a set of clothes," he said. "I hope you will find them to your liking."

Her hands trembled slightly as she took the bundle and rose. She went into the other room, and it seemed as if she were gone for hours. Aurelio heard whispering and commotion, but still she did not return.

At last she reentered the room.

She was not wearing the things he had made; the bundle lay in her arms. She knelt before him and laid the clothes in front of him.

He sat, stunned. "Why?"

She lifted her face. Two large tears caught on her lower lashes. Her words were no more than a whisper.

"The clothes were not made by an Ácoma." A small sob caught in her throat. She rose and ran from the room.

Dumbly, Aurelio picked up the bundle, stood, and walked slowly out of the room. He wanted to run. The clothes felt like burning piñon pitch in his arms as he walked back to his home, his steps measured and controlled only by willpower. He took the rungs of the ladder two at a time and was across the roof terrace in two strides. Viciously he poked up the embers of the outdoor summer fireplace. Hishti stepped from the dwelling in time to see him throw the bundle into the fire.

"No!" she gasped and ran to him, her face filled with disbelief. She put her hand on his arm. "What has happened?"

Aurelio brushed her hand away and turned to face her. She recoiled at the look in his eyes. She had never seen eyes so lethal.

"The clothes were not made by an Ácoma," he spat.

"Surely there has been some mistake," she said, horrified.

"There was no mistake."

His words were more bitter than the wind off North Mountain in the dead of winter. He whirled and entered the dwelling, returning moments later, his quiver slung across his shoulder, his bow in his hand. He was down the ladder and out of sight before Hishti could let out her breath. She descended the ladder and hurried to her brother's house, incomprehension written on her face.

When she arrived at her brother's dwelling, he did not even speak to her. Wiika was crying uncontrollably in another room. Gana sat in the room with her sister, her eyes wide and uncomprehending and filled with pain for the elder sister she loved. Occasionally she would put out her little hand and touch her sister, wanting to comfort her, but it did no good. Wiika's mother stood in the room helplessly, unable to ease the torment of her daughter.

Hishti spoke to her in whispers. "Why did she reject the boy? He is a good boy, a fine hunter; he would make a good husband. The boy truly held her in his heart."

"And she him," the mother answered, motioning to where Wiika lay, sobbing.

"Why?"

"Her father. The boy is not Ácoma. Her father said he would not have a Spanish dog as a son-in-law."

"But the Mountain Lion has been raised as a true person of the White Rock," Hishti protested. "His great-grandfather was the wise Rohona. He taught his great-grandson well the ways of Áco."

"I know," Wiika's mother said, "but it is useless. My husband will not be swayed."

Her shoulders fallen, Hishti returned home. She had so hoped to see the two young people together as man and wife.

Two weeks later, Wiika married another man. He was close to her own father's age, virulent in his hatred of Spaniards. His wife had died not long before, leaving two children who were only a few years younger than Wiika herself. Hishti saw the light go out of her niece's eyes. Overnight the girl had gone from being a lively, beautiful thing to a woman who never smiled. It cut Hishti to the heart.

Aurelio did not return for over a month. Hishti and Siya were sick with dread, imagining all manner of horrors that might have befallen him. Toward the end, even Diego had begun to worry and went looking for him, but he returned alone. Hishti's face fell but she said nothing.

When Aurelio finally walked into the village, he brought the pelts of a lynx, a mountain lion, numerous rabbit furs, and that of the prized jaguar of the south, his great-grandfather's namesake.

Hishti welcomed him warmly, but he acted as if she scarcely existed. His coldness frightened her, but nonetheless she had to tell him what had happened in his absence. That night she found the courage as he sat before the fire, staring blankly into it. She sat down beside him. A muscle twitched in his jaw, and his expression grew even more impenetrable as she spoke.

"I wanted you to know before someone else said anything. The girl Wiika has married Masanyi."

"Thank you for telling me," he said, his voice unfeeling.

"I am sorry," Hishti said.

"We will never speak of this again."

Two years passed. The crops were only a little better than the year Rohona died. Hunger still stalked Áco and the province of *Nuevo México*. The depredations of the Apaches increased as the pueblos' harvest of corn decreased. A runner arrived in the village with the shocking news that the pueblos of the Salines — Chililí, Abó, Humanos, and Tajique — had been abandoned en masse by their inhabitants. Most had fled their homes to go live among the pueblos closer to the *villa*, hoping to find protection from the ruthless nomads who preyed so mercilessly on their homes. Only Áco's impregnable location atop its mesa saved it from the repeated plunderings the eastern villages had experienced.

Unrest simmered in all the pueblos, but it was not due primarily to Apache attacks. The repression of native rituals by Spanish authorities grew more and more brutal. News from the rest of the province began to reach Áco regularly as each moon brought at least one person escaping from another pueblo, seeking on the craggy rock refuge from the Church or civil authority. When the rains did not come, the natives began to return in great numbers to the rituals of their ancestors. It was apparent that the god the Spaniards brought had little power, and more and more of the pueblo dwellers began to believe the gods of the people were angry.

The Spanish priests in some villages had once tolerated the native dances or looked the other way when rituals were performed, as long as the attendance at Mass did not sink too low, but in many places zealous priests ruled over their pueblo with an iron hand or a leather whip, exhibiting few of the traits of the man to whom they had vowed lifelong devotion. These emissaries of the Lord seemed intent on beating the love of God into their flocks. Some of the friars had met martyrdom in the Spaniards' seventy-odd years of domination. In Taos, Jemez, and Pecos priests had lost their lives. Only recently the prelate at Zuñi had been killed under questionable circumstances. It was said the Apaches had done it. The Ácoma heard a different story.

Since the conquest of *Nuevo México*, the question of authority between civil and ecclesiastical factions had been a bitter one, and in the middle were the natives. Each avaricious governor worked feverishly to insure that his tenure in the province be profitable monetarily, but lack of mineral wealth in the region precluded riches from that source. Goods produced by the natives were the only possible source of revenue. The priests, at the same time, wished to increase the wealth of their churches, and the only possible avenue for that was again at the expense of the labor of the pueblos. Both groups vied for this sweat from the natives' brows, and the consequences were multiple but similar. The governor would allow native rituals if it served his purpose. The friars acted according to their own dictates. Some used force, some used accommodation. The result was a lack of respect and growing contempt on the part of the pueblos for any Spanish authority—be it civil or ecclesiastical.

Unrest and discontent grew daily. Defiance of rules—Church or civil—was becoming more common. The divided authority of the conquerors could not cope with the increasing hostility of the natives. When cooperation between Church and state finally came about out of mutual necessity, it was too late.

Áco's isolation had spared it the heavy hand of Spanish repression throughout the years, but the sentiments of the dwellers of the White Rock were not softened toward their conquerors.

With the death of Rohona, the last visible evidence of Áco's original defiance of the Spaniards was gone. The memory of the massacre would never die, however.

The coming of a new priest to Áco brought a renewal of the old hatred and brought a desire for violence to many a breast. Would this priest be like many they had heard of? Would he be like de Freitas and Santander? No one expected he would be like Juan Ramírez.

That friar stood apart in their minds. He had become part of their tribal memory; he was woven into tribal mythology. That friar had earned his immortality.

Fray Lucas de Maldonado had chosen Áco just as had Juan Ramírez, as

a test of his faith. As with the arrival of Padre Ramírez, that of Fray Lucas
gave rise to discussion in the clan *kivas* as well as in Mauharots. Vociferous
outbursts urged removal of the foreigner by whatever means. Fewer voices
were raised urging peaceful, passive acceptance.

On one side Gyatyu's father's words were eloquent; those of Diego on
the other were among the most virulent. The hunter, Mokaitsh, did not
speak.

He feared nothing, even though he well knew there were those in the
village who looked upon him with as much scorn as they looked upon the
Spanish priest. Had Aurelio spoken, he would have urged passive acceptance—his great-grandfather's lessons had been well learned. Part of his
knowledge told him that to speak would be a detriment to his cause. So
speak in public he did not. His silence was not total, however. To those he
knew who held his view, he spoke in private. The clear reasoning of his
great-grandfather, the well-considered words of the Roman philosopher-
emperor, and his own well-worded rebuttals added to their own speech a
convincing strength.

In the *kiva* of Mauharots, Fray Lucas de Maldonado did not receive the
death penalty. He could not know, that first day he stood in the Church of
San Esteban and lifted the host in consecration, that his life had been spared.

Fray Lucas could not keep the shock from showing on his face as he
stepped in front of a kneeling Indian and looked into a pair of gray eyes as
he offered the host. Tawny but pale skin and red-gold hair made Fray Lucas
stumble on the Latin words that were as common to him as his own name.

Aurelio left Mass without speaking to the new priest. Later that day,
however, he returned to the church. Fray Lucas sought with little success to
control the questions that covered his face as Aurelio spoke.

"My mother was Spanish, my father part Spanish, part Ácoma. Both are
dead."

In those few words Aurelio answered the unasked questions but supplied
no curiosity-satisfying details. It was all Fray Lucas got but he was wise
enough to content himself with that.

"They taught you to speak Castilian well," he said upon hearing his own
language spoken without accent.

"I now speak only Queres," Aurelio said.

"Yes, of course. Perhaps, however, you might be willing to help me learn
your language."

"Perhaps," Aurelio said. He had little desire to have contact with the new
priest.

For reasons he could not fathom, Aurelio found himself spending time teaching the priest the language of Áco. Although he felt it was not wise to become
closely associated with the friar, for it would tend to separate him more from
his people, Aurelio enjoyed Lucas de Maldonado's company.

Fray Lucas was well educated, and thoughtful discussions of books and ideas, such as Aurelio had had with his great-grandfather, became more frequent.

The priest derived even more enjoyment from the discussions than Aurelio, for his loneliness was greater by far. One day, however, Aurelio spoke frankly to the friar and explained why their friendship could never deepen nor continue except at intervals.

"That the Ácoma dislike and distrust Spaniards is not news to you, *Padre*," Aurelio said. "Even I, who was born on this rock, whose grandfather was a revered member of this tribe; I, who speak their language and was raised in all their customs and traditions; I, who hunt and know the power of their gods as they do; I, who live and sweat as they do in the fields — even I am not exempt from the distrust of some, for Spanish blood is mingled in my veins with that of Áco. That is enough to separate me unconditionally from the acceptance of some. But I am a person of this rock. In my heart and in my being and in my soul, I am Ácoma. If I were to press a knife blade to my vein, no Ácoma on this rock could identify which part of my blood was that of the hated conquerors nor which the blood of Áco. I am Ácoma. The White Rock is my home; the White Rock will be my grave. It is for this reason that our friendship cannot be more. I cannot be Ácoma and Spanish at the same time. I have been raised as Ácoma, but it is of my own free will that I *choose* to be Ácoma."

"And what of *Jesús Cristo*?" Fray Lucas asked.

"My mother taught me to know the god of the Spaniards; my grandfather taught me to know the gods of Áco. I know them both, as I know that neither will ever desert me. Of that I have perfect knowledge."

"And of that, you are undoubtedly correct, my son," the priest said. "Thank you for telling me these things. You have given me an understanding, and I thank you for it, as I thank God for the privilege to be on this rock. Have no fear that I will ever jeopardize your life in this village."

From that time on, Aurelio and Fray Lucas saw each other infrequently other than at Mass, which Aurelio attended because he still knew the Castilian god. Upon a few occasions in the *convento*, they would have a long discussion. Each enjoyed the moment but sought no more than that, although Aurelio and Áco were always in the priest's prayers. The situation in *Nuevo México* was truly desperate, and Fray Lucas prayed fervently, begging his god to aid the Ácoma and the entire province.

"Give us a Moses," he would ask, "to lead us out of this wilderness and out of this famine."

Chapter 37

The decision to accompany Diego was made on the spur of the moment. Aurelio did not know he was going until he heard his own voice say so. Diego was pleased.

Aurelio darkened his hair by rubbing deer fat mixed with charcoal into it, and Hishti made a brew of tree barks that when applied to his skin effectively hid his ancestry.

As they trotted along the *cañada* that led through the mesas out to the river, called San José by the Spaniards, Aurelio wondered what had made him decide to go with Diego to the *villa* of the conquerors — the *villa* where his great-grandmother and great-grandfather had once lived. Perhaps that was it. Perhaps it was curiosity to see that part of his ancestry which he knew only as words his grandfather Rohona had spoken long ago.

As the tales reached Áco of the villages near the Big River, he began to wonder what life was like there. What was truly happening in those places? Áco was his world, and he had not thought past the confines of the mesas that surrounded it, save to think of tracking game or to wonder from whence might come an attack from the Apaches or the Apaches de Navajo. Suddenly he began to see all the villages of the land as one in their troubles and in their distress.

The newest visitor to Áco seeking refuge brought a worse tale than the previous. It was a tale few wished to believe but of which few had doubts. In spite of Áco's isolation, it struck dread and fear and fury into their hearts.

Forty-seven medicine men from various pueblos had been rounded up by the Spanish authorities and thrown into jail in the *villa* of Santa Fé. The new governor, Juan Francisco de Treviño, working in concert with the Church, was determined to ferret out and exterminate all native beliefs and practices.

To this end he had authorized the seizure of the native priests who would be tried in the capital for sorcery.

As Diego and Aurelio stood, unremarked by the Spaniards, in the plaza of the *Villa de Santa Fé* along with the huge crowd of natives, they watched the imposing of the sentences. Aurelio understood every hateful word spoken by the authorities; that he carried their blood in his veins was incomprehensible to him.

When he saw the three revered men sentenced to die hanging from ropes, their heads at grotesque angles to their bodies, he felt such revulsion as he had never experienced, not even in the raid on the Apache camp long ago. His anger and impotence blinded him, and he saw the subsequent beatings of the remaining medicine men as if he were looking through ghastly flames.

Every snap and thud of the whips made him wince as if the leather thongs were cutting into his own flesh. He understood, then, Diego's hatred of Spaniards. At that moment he could not have recalled one word his great-grandfather had taught him. The only thing he knew was an unquenchable desire for revenge.

Diego made a motion to him and they moved gradually away from the crowd. No one appeared to notice them as Diego led them to the deserted *campo santo* of the *villa*. The Apache walked slowly among the weathered crosses until he came to one and stopped. Aurelio read the name carved into the wood, *Dorotea de Inojosa*, and was surprised when Diego knelt and crossed himself. He saw tears slide down the Apache's face.

"I will kill them all," Diego whispered as he glanced at the cross of the grave beside the one at which he knelt. It bore the name *Isidro Inojosa*. "I will kill them in *his* name for what he made you suffer."

Diego rose and spat on the grave of Isidro Inojosa. "Let's get out of this accursed *villa*," he hissed.

They dogtrotted to Cochiti pueblo and stayed in the home of relatives of Gyatyu's father. At each village where they had chanced to stop, they were always given food, although drought and famine were at the doors like ravenous wolves. In Cochiti they heard, firsthand, the extent of the repression.

"They enter the *kivas* unrestrainedly, take out the sacred K'atsina masks and burn them in great fires. They have even destroyed the *kivas* themselves — never before in all the land have the *españoles* done this — until now. We cannot dance; we cannot pray. There are floggings in the village every day — even the women they strip naked and whip. Our children are herded to the church and told the K'atsina are evil; they are told not to obey us; they are told they will be whipped and their heads shaved if they do not tell the priests when we make prayer sticks. When our children are hungry, they are told it means the Castilian god is punishing them because their parents dance."

"Why don't you do something about it?" Diego snarled.

Kohaiya's uncle's son-in-law looked at the Apache and then at Aurelio and spoke to the latter. "I have heard good things about the Mountain Lion from my kinsman Kohaiya." Aurelio looked down and said nothing. There was a pause and the man seemed to make a decision. "There is to be a meeting in the kiva at San Ildefonso tomorrow evening."

Nothing more was said. Bowls of food were brought in and the men ate in silence.

The next morning the three left Cochiti early, trotting north along the *Río Bravo*.

Men sat shoulder to shoulder in the kiva of San Ildefonso. The first speaker was a Tegua and Aurelio could not understand his words, but there were a number of other Queres-speakers from other pueblos also in attendance and a translator was provided.

Man after man rose, recounted the acts of oppression that were taking place in their village, condemned the brutality inflicted in the *villa* on the medicine men, and harangued against their Spanish overlords.

But none spoke of action — until Diego rose.

"I am tired of talk. Give me fifty men, and I will lead them to the *villa* and we will free the medicine men."

First there was silence and then, like distant thunder, voices began to murmur and then reverberate in the ceremonial chamber as the storm of emotion grew.

The Tegua who was the first to speak that night rose and stood beside Diego, and silence fell over the *kiva*.

"What is your plan?" he asked of the Apache.

"The medicine men are being held in the storerooms of the governor's compound. Give me fifty well-armed men. We will approach the *villa* under darkness, and at first light, we will force ourselves into the governor's quarters and demand the release of the shamans. If he refuses, we will kill him and release them ourselves."

"And what if the *españoles* retaliate?" a man in the audience asked.

"What more can the Spanish dogs do that they haven't already? Are there enough pale strangers in this land to kill us all?" Diego's look was feral.

The Tegua standing next to Diego stepped forward. "Are there any who will go to the *villa* with this man?"

Almost the entirety of those present rose to their feet — including Aurelio. The Tegua nodded and motioned for them to sit.

"We will go to the *villa* and release the medicine men." Loud vocal approbation answered him and he continued. "We will send a contingent of warriors to secure the release, but in addition, we will conceal more men in the hills around the *villa* to support the warriors in their endeavor. We must move swiftly."

He detailed several men to plan the attack and he ordered runners to take the news to the surrounding pueblos to ask for men to come with haste to Santa Fé to act as backup for the warriors.

Diego, because he knew the *villa* well, drew pictures in sand with a stick and explained how the attack should be carried out and where the men waiting in the hills should be positioned.

With some ruse, he would bribe a servant in the governor's adobe-walled palace to leave a door open for him. Little would the *criada* know that she was leaving the door unbarred for an armed contingent of native warriors.

The next day Diego, Aurelio, and three other men trotted to Tesuque. They would scout the hills and Diego would go into the *villa* and make his arrangements.

Two days later, after trotting south without stopping, close to two hundred warriors from the Tegua pueblos of San Ildefonso, Santa Clara, San Juan, Tesuque, Nambé, and Pojoaque lay poised in the *cerrillos* around Santa Fé, while seventy men, instead of the fifty Diego asked for, descended quietly into the *villa*. Faint light etched a jagged line of the peaks of the Sangre de Cristo Mountains as Governor Juan Francisco Treviño slept.

Diego approached the door that was to have been left unbarred, gave it a light push, and it creaked open. He gave a hand sign and the warriors rushed from the shadows and poured into the patio and fanned out. Diego and a dozen men were in the governor's bedroom before any alarm had been given in the house.

"*¿Qué diablos?*" the governor sputtered as Diego woke him, rolling him roughly from his side onto his back and pressing a knife at his throat.

"I am the one who will dispatch you to the devil if you do not meet our demands," Diego said viciously.

The governor trembled and his facial muscles tightened in fear as he came fully awake and saw the native warriors who surrounded his bed.

"What, what do you want?" he asked weakly.

"Release the medicine men."

"I can't do that without consulting the *cabildo*," the governor said, having gained a little control over his voice. "The men were duly tried."

Diego pressed the knife closer against the governor's neck. "The *villa* is surrounded by two hundred warriors. I have seventy with me in and outside this building. Are you sure you need to consult with the *cabildo*?"

The governor nodded.

"You can consult with the *cabildo* in Hell!" Diego said, his lips pulled back over his teeth, and the knifepoint pricked the skin on the governor's neck, causing a bright drop of blood to blossom on the pale skin.

"Don't kill me. Don't kill me," Treviño begged, all pretense gone. "I'll let them go."

Diego yanked him up by his nightshirt, pulled him out of bed, and gave him a shove toward the door. "Go open the storerooms yourself," he ordered.

Aurelio had waited with the other warriors in the patio because Diego had said he should not get close to the governor so that he might not be identified later by his stature or his less than native looks.

In the early dawn light he watched with grim satisfaction as Diego prodded the governor across the patio to the storerooms. By that time the entire compound of the palace was awake but no one offered resistance when they saw the number of armed warriors and the nightshirted governor. Most of the servants in the governor's palace were natives from neighboring pueblos and may have felt little loyalty to the Spanish head of government in the province of *Nuevo México*.

The governor raised the bar and pulled open the heavy door to the storerooms.

"Tell them they are free to go to their homes," Diego said harshly to Treviño.

"You may come out," the governor shouted into the storeroom. "You are free to go."

One by one the filthy men, revered leaders in their villages, limped out. Their stench wafted through the patio and some people turned away at the sight of the oozing, crusted wounds on the men's backs.

"There are some inside who cannot walk on their own," one of the medicine men who hobbled out said, and several of the warriors went inside and brought out the rest.

The last to leave the storeroom came out under his own power, and although his wounds were as suppurating as any, with effort he stood straight, his black eyes burning.

"I have seen him!" he shouted. "He has come to me with a message!"

All turned to stare at the slight figure, but he said no more.

A day later Aurelio and Diego were back in San Ildefonso pueblo celebrating the success of the raid at the governor's palace. Diego was fêted for his courage and action, and many men from neighboring pueblos came to San Ildefonso to speak to him. He sat in the kiva as if holding court, as warrior after warrior came forward to greet him. Many brought him small gifts that they placed on the floor near him.

Aurelio sat in the back of the ceremonial chamber, watching. How the people hungered for a leader, someone who was willing to act. He admired Diego's initiative and courage but saw something in the Apache's manner that he had not seen before and it left him with a vague feeling of unease.

He felt no ambivalence, however, about what they had done. The raid on the governor's quarters was proper and well executed. The medicine men had been unjustly punished and the wrong needed to be righted. The raid itself harmed no one. In spite of the unbridled fury of some of the warriors, they had not allowed their passions and their strength in numbers to massacre Spaniards. It was clear in retrospect that had the men with Diego and those waiting in the hills been so inclined they could have easily stormed the sleeping *villa,* murdered many, and pillaged unrestrainedly. But they had not. They righted the wrong but did not exact retribution for it.

It was clear to Aurelio that the natives of the land must stand up for their rights. The province was in a miserable condition. The people had a right to practice their long-held beliefs and it could be done side by side with the god of the Spaniards who said, "Love thy neighbor." Would not both beliefs together be stronger than one alone?

They had a right to provide for their families first before they provided for Spaniards—either Church or civilian authorities. Would not the welfare of the province be improved for all inhabitants, including the pale ones, if each individual's needs were met before trying to enrich government officials or the Church? Native and foreigner *could* coexist.

But if they were to regain control of their lives from the dominion of the foreign intruders, the pueblos of the land must work together to secure the rights of each village and of its inhabitants. Spanish authorities would never accede to Pueblo demands unless the people acted in concert. The conquerors held control by piecemeal actions. Even their superior weapons could not match the overwhelming numbers of native peoples if the latter decided to work together.

Aurelio noticed another man climb down the kiva ladder, stand for a moment and survey the room before he gradually began to move toward where Diego sat. There was something about his body language that made Aurelio rise and move in Diego's direction. Had the authorities found someone to get rid of the leader of the raid that freed the medicine men?

By the time the man approached Diego, Aurelio was standing casually behind the Apache. The man bent forward, took Diego's hand, placed something in it, and closed the Apache's fingers around the object and then placed his own hands around the fist of Diego's hand. The man leaned forward and spoke quietly in Diego's ear.

"You are requested in the pueblo of Ohké as soon as is convenient for you. My master Po-pé awaits." The man turned and left.

Diego opened his hand. In his palm lay a small rust-red polished stone fetish with eagle-down feathers tied to it with a tiny rawhide thong.

The next day they left for San Juan Pueblo to find a man called Po-pé, one of the medicine men, they learned, who had been flogged in the plaza at Santa Fé.

When they arrived, they were quickly ushered to the upper story of a dwelling after Diego showed the fetish to a man who approached them in the plaza of the village. As they stepped inside the room in which sat half a dozen people, a slight figure rose and walked toward them.

He still had difficulty walking because of the many oozing, crusted wounds of his punishment, but he was not bent in pain. There was a light, a kind of visionary fire, burning in his eyes, and he obviously did not feel the pain. Before them stood the medicine man who had been the last to leave the storeroom at the governor's—the man who had shouted the strange words about a message.

He was not big, but there was something overwhelming about his presence, a dominating force, which Aurelio felt as if he could almost touch.

"Welcome, my son," the man said in Queres to Diego and breathed on his hand. "Your actions will be rewarded by Po-he-mu." Diego nodded, the man greeted Aurelio, and then said, "Please join us."

They seated themselves, were brought food and drink, and Po-pé began to speak. His eyes rolled back in his head and he shouted, "Po-he-mu! Po-he-mu!" His small body shook and his eyes flew open. "I am here, Caudi!" He looked to the left, staring through the people in his line of vision. "Tilini, it is I, Po-pé." And turning to the right he said, "Theume, I am ready."

He brought his hand close to a pottery bowl that sat in front of him and a burst of flame shot up from it and was immediately extinguished, leaving behind a pungent-smelling smoke that made them cough and their eyes water.

The medicine man intoned, "They come in fire. The figures come in fire. Fire gushes forth from all the extremities of their bodies! And from their mouths, and nostrils, and ears, and eyes! They come in fire, and they have given to me of their fire. It will end in fire and blood and the people *will* be free!" He shuddered and lifted his arms toward the ceiling. "Oh, great Po-he-mu, I thank you for your vision. I am your instrument!"

At one moment his black, piercing eyes seemed to see only into the future and dragged those near along with him into his vision. Then his eyes riveted on each individual sitting there, and his stare was like burning embers placed on one's eyelids, relief possible only by acceptance of his words, even though they might not be understood.

The medicine man's voice returned to a more normal tone. "A great deity who calls himself Po-he-mu has sent me a vision of all the land. He sends three figures who emit fire to give me of that fire, and with that holocaust we shall destroy our oppressors."

Aurelio glanced at Diego and the Apache's eyes seemed that they, too, burned with fire.

Po-pé's voice had lost all its strange zeal and he spoke matter-of-factly. "Others have tried to rise up against the intruders in our land. The Tiguas tried. Clemente of the pueblos of the Salines tried more recently, but the plot was discovered and he died at the end of a rope. We, however, shall conquer."

He looked at all the faces in the room. "We will rise up and slaughter all the foreigners in our land—all. We will return the land to the way it was before the hated intruders came, and life will be as it once was!"

All voices except Aurelio's rose in a fevered pitch of concordance. Po-pé lifted his hands for silence. "We need three things to achieve our goal: a plan, secrecy, and unity."

Instinctively and suddenly, Aurelio recognized that this man had the qualities necessary to lead a revolt against the oppressors. The realization struck him as if a sudden, cold wind had whipped his robe from him and left him sitting naked in winter on North Mountain. This man could achieve his goal. But was success really success?

Aurelio knew the visceral desire that was Diego's and the medicine man's. He had felt the hatred in his gut in the plaza of Santa Fé, had felt the desire to plunge his knife into all Spanish authorities responsible, but would the success of Po-pé's plan meet great-grandfather's criterion for true success?

Po-pé spoke of union, of one united purpose, of one united people. It was not an easily understood concept for the Pueblos; each village had always lived according to its own dictates. The task would not be easily accomplished but it was the only way. And if it succeeded, would it lead to security? Would it lead to the endurance of all they believed in? Would it assure the existence of Áco forever? Could Áco and all the villages survive if something were *not* done about the Spanish repression of all their ceremonies? If they could not dance, if they could not pray to the K'atsina, their life would crumble.

Aurelio and Diego stayed in San Juan for a number of days listening to Po-pé speak, but the Spanish *maestre de campo* in the village began to harass the medicine man, making his life difficult.

Po-pé decided to leave that pueblo and seek refuge with the Tigua-speaking natives of Taos in the north who had tried several times in the past to revolt against the foreign authority.

Aurelio and Diego accompanied the medicine man and the few trusted disciples who followed him. The people of Taos, like the Ácoma, were among the most hostile toward Spaniards, and Po-pé's vision was immediately embraced in Taos. The charismatic Tegua medicine man from Ohké began to set his vision in motion.

In Taos Aurelio began to find his nights peopled with unsettling dreams and would awake unrested. During the day he listened to the medicine man and offered his own suggestions for how the plan might best be implemented, but at night he would dream of carrion-eaters circling high overhead and of mutilated feet lying on the ground. Nearby a book fell open beside the feet and the wind blew the pages, and he thought he saw a phalanx of Greek warriors with overlapping shields. More pages blew open and he saw the sun glinting off the swords of a Roman legion, which then became the metal-clad soldiers of Cortés's conquering army. He heard his great-grandfather's frail voice whispering, but in the morning he could never recall what the aged man had said to him.

He began to experience a feeling of uneasiness and began to grow concerned about the welfare of those they had left in the village of the mesa top. Diego, however, still burned with enthusiasm and devotion to the vision, but it disturbed Aurelio that his great-grandfather spoke to him at night but he could not decipher what he was trying to tell him.

Finally one day he said to Diego, "I must return to Áco. The household is undoubtedly in much need of game."

From the look on Diego's face, Aurelio knew that the Apache had not thought once about his wife or his home.

"Yes," Diego said, contemplating for only a moment. "That is good. As for me, I will stay here and aid our cause. I will tell our master that you must depart."

As he saw the steep-walled mesa rise in the distance, Aurelio felt a surge of long-absent contentment. He was not aware of how much he had missed his home, how much a part of him the high-perched village was. He ran up the *Camino del Padre* and trotted quickly to his dwelling, nodding and speaking hello to those he saw in the streets, feeling contentment when he heard the words of "welcome home."

Hishti and Siya welcomed him with great joy, coming to greet him and pat his arm.

Gana, there visiting her aunt when he arrived, had grown taller in the several years since he had quieted her tears at the fields and she was growing prettier still. He smiled at her and started to speak, but she looked at him with loathing.

Why should she have such hatred of him? He had never harmed her. There at the fields her liveliness had captured his heart. He had delighted in the little sister of the girl he loved. Had her father's hatred become hers, too?

The sudden thought of Wiika was like a knife stabbing at his entrails. Wiika had a child now. He had seen her with a large belly and then later saw the infant on her back on a cradleboard. The child had the heavy features of its father and none of its mother's grace. An emotion he had not experienced before took hold of him. That should have been his child on the cradleboard; he was the first to know the body of the fair Wiika.

"I am going home now, Auntie," Gana spoke. "I do not like the smell in this room."

"Gana!" Hishti said with shock. "Never speak that way in this house again! You disgrace your parents by the wickedness of your tongue."

The girl lowered her eyes. "I'm sorry, Auntie," she said and ran from the room.

"Forgive her," Hishti said to Aurelio. "She is just a child. She does not know what she says. For me, I am filled with much contentment that you are back. Siya and I have missed you."

"Yes," Siya said in her reedy voice, frail with age, "you have brought back the sunshine to our house. This old woman no longer feels quite so old."

Hishti did not ask about her husband.

Chapter 38

Four years passed and still Diego did not return to Áco. Twice they received news of him from visitors to the village: He was at Taos with Po-pé. That told Aurelio everything.

Hishti never spoke of her husband. If she missed him, Aurelio was not aware of it. They had a simple existence and did not suffer to the same extent as some of the villagers. Their needs were few, and they gave of any extra food they might have. Out of pelts Aurelio brought home and tanned, Hishti made garments for Wiika's small children, who now numbered three, and for Gana, also. Aurelio never asked Hishti what she had done with the tanned skins.

Fray Lucas also gave of any assistance that he could. He worked alongside the natives in the fields at the planting time. He was not accepted as Padre Ramírez had finally been, but he was tolerated by the Ácoma and some were even favorably inclined toward him for his healing, upon several occasions, of sick children. Once or twice a year the friar and Aurelio would have a long discussion, enjoyable to both. Other than that, their contact was limited to Mass on Sundays and holy days and a brief "hello" in the village plaza.

A feeling of unease pervaded the village streets; it had been there so long it had become a part of their very existence. Food had been scarce for such a length of time that many had forgotten the meaning of abundance. Children of twelve or so had never known what it was like to have full bellies. That, too, was now a part of their existence.

Not once did a child return home that he did not carry a rock or two to add to the pile of missiles that lay ever ready on their roofs. Not one year had passed in the last several in which there was not at least one raid by the nomads who suffered, too, with the drought that seemed to have no end.

The past year the Navajo swooped down on their fields, destroying some of the crops and killing an Ácoma man. They then proceeded to the village, attempting to pillage it. Only its propitious location and the fierce fighting of Áco's warriors saved it from destruction.

Even those who had never accepted him as Ácoma were thankful for the Mountain Lion's presence among them. Red-gold hair flying behind him like flames and a yell more shrill and bloodcurdling than any Apache, the Mountain Lion would attack ferociously, inspiring courage in his own, instilling fear in the attackers. Word had filtered back to Áco that there had grown up among the nomads a legend of a firebird that swooped down to aid the Ácoma in battle. Few at Áco had any doubts as to its identity.

Aurelio became a tacit war leader, although he did not speak in Mauharots. In fact, no word was ever spoken conferring any authority upon him. But when an attack came, all followed his lead as if it had been vested in him.

Never again in her aunt's presence had the girl Gana said a word to the Mountain Lion, but if there were an occasion when no other ears would hear except his, words like snake venom would reach him. Never once had he looked at the speaker of them.

Many of the villagers had come to view the Mountain Lion with a degree of awe. In the village people stepped aside to let him pass. He was very much a part of the life of Áco and yet he was aloof from most people without being conscious of it. The only houses he frequented were that of Gyatyu and his wife and that of Gyatyu's father and mother.

Gyatyu had married a quiet, pretty girl four years ago, and they now had a two-year-old daughter and a four-month-old son. Aurelio did not begrudge his friend his happiness nor his two beautiful children. His friend's happiness was a source of happiness to him, and he delighted in Gyatyu's little daughter, who would hang on his neck and beg for him to tell her a story.

Aurelio did not notice that one or more friends of Gyatyu's wife would visit her when he was there. He was even less aware of the girls whose eyes followed him in the street. When Gyatyu was first married, he mentioned that Aurelio, too, should seek a wife. The comment was met with such a cold, vehement "no" that Gyatyu had never spoken of it again.

That summer the crops were no better than they had been for years. Hunger would still walk the streets of their village that winter, but the evidence pointed to a fair piñon crop that fall. The nights grew crisp and the dawns brittle, and all awaited the ripening of the cones, when they would burst open, dropping their small, sweet nuts to the ground. Perhaps that year would replenish their dwindling stores.

The day of gathering piñon dawned clear and bright, the sky the vibrant blue of fall. Household after household descended from the mesa, and even the smallest children had baskets, almost as big as they were, on their backs. Toward the west they started, toward the piñon forests with their blankets of brown nuts lying on the ground at the base of the short-needled, asymmetrical trees.

Aurelio breathed deeply the cold, clear air. It was the kind of day he loved the best. All camped near the spring that night, and early the next morning they arose, anxious to push on and reach the piñon forests. High, thin wisps of cloud marred the expanse of vivid blue that morning, and to the northwest a faint line of dark blue appeared, but few took notice of it. It would still be a beautiful day for gathering before the cold *shiwana* reached them.

Aurelio did not stop at the first trees in spite of their abundant crop. He pushed on higher; he loved the forest and its pungent scent of pine. Again he breathed deeply, bathing his lungs in the clear, cold, fragrant air. Toward noon he sat on a smooth rock and ate the gray-blue paper bread Hishti had prepared. He had always liked solitude. That was one of the pleasures of the hunt—to be away from voices, to hear only the sound of a small animal or a bird. Many enjoyed the conviviality of the piñon gathering. He preferred to be alone and sought, therefore, a small remote canyon, which in winter would be snow-filled but through which the rains of summer ran—if they would ever come again.

By afternoon, Aurelio's basket was filled and his stomach, also, with many sweet nuts. They were better roasted, but no gatherer had ever been able to wait. He leaned his full basket against the base of a tree, deciding he would hunt a squirrel or a rabbit to have for supper in addition to the roasted nuts. He glanced up at the sky. The weather was going to change, but he thought he had enough time before starting back. In spite of the cool fall air, he dropped his deerskin robe.

It did not take long to find a bushy-tail. The squirrels, too, were pleased with the piñon abundance that year. Upon returning to the spot where he had left his robe and basket, Aurelio stopped in midstride.

Instantly he was alert, an arrow, like lightning, poised in his bow as the squirrel he had just shot moments before was dropped to the ground. There sat his basket upside down, its contents scattered on the ground. No curious animal had done that. He approached cautiously and saw the footprints.

She hurried swiftly, unknowing that he was upon her. He yanked the girl around. At sixteen she was the image of her sister at the same age. The wide black eyes were filled with fear and surprise, which vanished instantly when they saw his face. Then contempt took the place of the fear.

"Spanish dog," she spat as she tried to push away from him. "Let me go!"

"What have I ever done to you?"

"It is not necessary to do anything. You are as contemptible as turkey dung without doing a thing."

His grip tightened on her arms. "You miserable she-coyote," he said. "You are going to pick up every last piñon nut you spilled from my basket."

He shoved her toward the spilled basket. She almost lost her balance, but when she saw she was free of his grasp, she turned and ran, darting through the trees, her robe of deerskin flying out behind her. He was upon her in seconds, knocking her to the ground. She kicked and flailed at him violently, her screams like that of a captive lion. He caught her arms and pinned her to the ground. Her chest was heaving, her eyes narrowed.

"You are not Ácoma," she taunted. "Any girl of Áco would die before she would ever allow a Spanish dog to put his despicable seed in her belly—and you thought my sister would let you."

She had misjudged the knifelike coldness in his gray eyes. Suddenly he was pulling at her tunic, pulling it above her hips.

"Die, then," he said bitterly, "because a Spanish dog is going to put his seed in the belly of an Ácoma bitch, and she will grow great with the hated thing in her body!"

With his knee he wrenched open her legs and with another violent thrust he entered her. She cried out with pain. Wildly he thrust again and again, his heavy weight crushing her. His mouth came down on hers, voracious, devouring, and his tongue thrust between her lips. He felt her body moving with his. She was locked to him, and his movements became more wild and frenzied until a roar burst from his chest.

His strength and anger flowed out of him as he lay heavily on top of her, feeling as if he could not move. He became aware of her sobbing and pushed himself up and withdrew from her. He pulled her tunic down as she cried softly, her eyes closed.

When he saw her bruised lips, remorse filled him. She was so young; a virgin still. With the scorn now gone from her face, he saw that her beauty had surpassed that of her sister's. He picked her up in his arms and cradled her, stroking her hair.

"I am so sorry, little Snowbird," he whispered. "I did not mean to hurt you. I have *never* wanted to harm you."

For a long time he held her against his chest, and she did not move.

He heard the sound of the wind rise in the trees. Suddenly he looked up and saw the darkness that was too early to be the end of day.

"Come, we must go," he said, rising and lifting her to her feet. "We must get back to the others; the weather is changing."

She smoothed her dress and he straightened his own clothes. He picked up the deerskin robe she had been wearing and put it around her shoulders. Obediently she followed him back to where his basket sat empty. He began quickly to scoop the nuts into the basket. She knelt beside him and helped. Then they started out at a quick pace.

The sky grew more and more ominous, and Aurelio knew what to expect. The first flakes fell gently, floating down among the trees like tiny, fluttering white petals, but he was not deceived, and they kept moving swiftly.

The first snow of fall could be treacherous. When he finally spoke, there was a dusting of it already on the ground.

"We must stop," he said. Gana looked at him with seriousness. "We must find shelter, for the night will be upon us before we can reach the others. The snow will not stop until the ground is white."

He put his basket down. "Stay here," he said. He trotted off, returning within a few minutes.

"Come," he said as he picked up the basket, "I have found a place for us."

They hurried along and climbed a small ridge. On the other side, facing south, an overhang of rock formed a natural shelter. Quickly he began to cut pine bows, which he laid on the rock floor of the overhang. When the floor was covered with a thick layer, he cut larger branches and leaned them at an angle against the jutting rock. At the base he secured them with a row of stones.

Gana watched him silently as he prepared the shelter, and she began to gather sticks and dead branches. At one end of the shelter there was a V-shaped cleft in the overhanging rock. A little behind and beneath that she put a ring of stones and began filling it with sticks she had gathered.

"Good," Aurelio said when he saw what she was doing. "The smoke will rise to the overhang and out along the rock to the cleft. It will make a perfect chimney."

Darkness fell quickly, and by the time the shelter was ready, the ground wore a thin white blanket of snow.

He spread his robe on the pine bough floor, and they brushed the snow from their clothes and crawled into their newly made protective arbor, Aurelio arranging the last pine boughs behind them.

The shelter was only tall enough to allow them to sit inside, but they were thankful for it nonetheless. At one end was the small fireplace Gana had built, and at the other sat the basket of piñon nuts. Aurelio struck flint and after a few attempts the fire started.

The rock cleft functioned perfectly as a chimney, sparing their eyes from the smoke. When he had skinned the squirrel as best he could in the cramped quarters, Gana placed the meat on sticks to cook over the fire. They had not spoken a word.

They heard the wind come up and saw the pine boughs protecting the opening move. For a moment Gana's eyes were fearful but it soon became obvious the boughs would hold, and she relaxed. When the pieces of squirrel were crispy, she handed one to Aurelio and they ate in silence. Roasted piñon nuts were their dessert; handfuls of snow gathered out the end of the shelter their drink. The fire died down to embers, and she added one of the larger pieces of wood so that it might burn slowly in the night to help keep them warm.

Aurelio's voice seemed unusually loud in the shelter when he broke the silence.

"I think it is possible to stretch out partway so that we might sleep more comfortably than sitting."

Gana nodded. The space was cramped but Aurelio moved, and she was able to lie down facing the rock wall at the back of their shelter. Aurelio lay down on his side beside her, facing her back. The shelter was not long enough for him to stretch out completely, and it was necessary to bend his knees against the back of hers.

They used her robe to cover them as best they could, but the chill of the night made her move against him for warmth, and they were cupped together. The curve of her body fit closely to him; he felt her buttocks against him, and the intimacy of their position worked its effect upon him, and he was unable to control its power over him. She did not move away.

He wanted her again, but he could not forgive himself for what he had done to her that afternoon in the piñon woods. Without knowing it, he found his arm across her, pulling her gently nearer, back toward him. It was only to share his warmth, he told himself.

Then he felt the soft movements of her body as she pressed back more closely against him, her hips moving against him.

His hand slid over her tunic, caressing the small hard mounds of her breasts beneath. Down her side the caress moved and back up along the curve of her hip as he lifted her tunic. Ever so softly his hand slid over her hip and caressed her in front. She made no protest. He heard her small intake of breath. He caressed her there and felt the gentle movement begin in her body, and then she shuddered slightly and made small noises in her throat. She moved her buttocks against him, arching her back, and he slid gently into her. He felt her wince momentarily but then she began to move and he tried to be gentle but could not. A heavy scent of crushed pine needles enveloped them, and her small noises of pleasure increased his desire. When at last the moment came, he crushed her into him, his pleasure unbearable.

He finally lay quiet, drained, as he held her cupped against him, and he caressed her cheek with his fingers. His hand played along her body and stroked her hair. He sought to memorize with his hands every detail of her. At some point they slept, nestled against each other, although he had no realization of it.

Sometime later he awoke and placed more wood on the dying embers. She snuggled against him in sleep, seeking his warmth, which he was glad to give.

Somewhere near dawn he awoke. A faint light crept into their shelter. She stirred and sighed softly, and his hands could not resist the softness of her flesh. He turned her to face him, although the darkness still hid her features. His hand found her, and she moved against the caress. He did to her what he had the night before, and the evidence of the pleasure she found in it filled him with a deep emotion he had not before felt.

Later they again slept, and when he awoke, he knew the snow had ceased, for a bright light shone outside their shelter. In the faint light within, he finally saw her features relaxed in sleep, and he was even more acutely aware of her beauty. Her eyes fluttered open, and she smiled sleepily at him.

Unable to keep his feelings hidden in his eyes, and so that she might not see their full depth, he turned and lifted away a pine bough. The sunlight was blinding to them both as it reflected off the new snow.

"It is beautiful," she whispered, as her eyes became accustomed to the light.

"It can never touch the beauty of the one with whom I lie," Aurelio said softly. His hand caressed her cheek, and he bent forward, placing a kiss on her lips. When he released her mouth, he saw her tears.

"Please," he said, "don't cry."

"I am so ashamed. I did not mean those terrible things I said to you." Words began to pour from her lips.

"When I was little, I loved you, too, as my sister loved you, but I did not envy her. She was my big sister, and I loved her, and I wanted her to be happy, and I knew that you made her happy. I saw you both that day lying on a robe together. I did not know then everything that a man and a woman do together, but I saw you doing something to my sister, and I saw you were making her happy so I knew it was good.

"When we returned to the village, my father learned Wiika liked you. Never had I heard such terrible things spoken. My father called you abominable names, and I was frightened more than I had ever been in my entire life. Wiika began to cry, and she could not stop. My father said she would no longer be his daughter if she accepted a set of clothes from you. He said she would be unmentionable filth, and he would pray that she would die, her eyes pecked out by crows if she put on clothes you had made. I could not understand what had happened.

"All I knew was that my sister was unhappy and somehow you were the cause. I began to hate you then. When Wiika married my father's old friend, and I saw the light go out of her eyes, I knew she would never have happiness again. I blamed you, and I hated you all the more. I could not stand it when the other girls in the village talked about you and how handsome you were, for I knew you had brought misery to my sister. I was filled with a desire for revenge. Had I been a man, I would probably have tried to kill you."

She paused for a moment. "Yesterday when you did to me with force what you had done to my sister with her consent, I felt something I had never felt before. At first you hurt me, but then . . . I wanted you. I no longer cared about what my father had said. Afterward you held me, and I knew you were sorry for what you had done, but I was not. I wanted your arms around me, rocking me as you had when I was a little girl. I knew then that I had always loved you."

"Oh, little Snowbird," Aurelio said softly, pulling her to him. "How your words ease my pain."

Chapter 39

Aurelio shot a rabbit that morning for their breakfast, and they both ate hungrily but dallied over the last few bites, not wishing to leave. At length he said, "I am afraid we must go. The others will fear for our safety."

Gana nodded, but when he reached for the basket of piñon nuts to hoist onto his back, she bent and picked up a handful of the new snow, quickly making a ball of it, and when Aurelio turned around, she threw it at him, her aim perfect, as the snow splatted in his face and he sputtered with its wetness.

He laughed as he set the basket of nuts onto the ground. Gana flitted off among the trees like her namesake, but Aurelio quickly caught her, sweeping her up into his arms.

"That shall not go unpunished," he spoke with mock seriousness, as he carried her back to the shelter and its bed of pine boughs.

"I like this kind of punishment," Gana whispered as he laid her down.

Later they both rose and started back in the direction of Áco, leaving their tracks in the virgin snow. In the afternoon they found where many villagers had weathered the night, all appearances indicating they had continued on that day.

They did not overtake the others before nightfall. Their shelter that night was similar to the one the night before. It would be cold but the weather was not inclement. They were in too much of a hurry to construct more than a quick shelter. Their desire for each other had not abated during the day. Both were relieved they had not overtaken the others, and they did not even bother to make supper.

Early the next day as they continued on, they were met by a search party headed by Gana's father. When he saw that she had not returned to the village on her own, he, along with several others, set out to find her.

When he saw her safe with the Mountain Lion, his first reaction was one of relief. His second, of anger. The Mountain Lion had tried to take one daughter, already. He would not take this one, either.

Gana's face showed nothing as they approached. She ran to her father and threw her arms around his neck. She wanted her joy to appear that of seeing him.

"You are safe, Daughter," her father said.

"Yes," she said, "I was on my way back to join the others as it began to snow. The Mountain Lion came upon me, and when it got dark and we had not overtaken you, he said we should seek shelter for the night, that it was safer than to continue when we could not see."

Her father grunted in assent. Aurelio said nothing. He held his face expressionless. Without further words, they returned to Áco.

That night Gyatyu came to visit him. He had seen something new in his friend's walk, something indefinable, and he was curious. He came directly to the point.

"What has happened?" he asked.

"I must learn to keep my secrets better hidden," Aurelio said with a smile.

Gyatyu pressed on. "Surely you intend to confide in your best friend," he said with a grin.

Aurelio told him what had happened. He did not relate all the details of the two nights, but he did tell his friend about the spilled nuts and the consequences of it. He said enough that Gyatyu understood fully what had occurred.

"Are you going to make a set of clothes?" Gyatyu asked.

"I don't know," Aurelio said. "I do not know what course to follow."

Hishti entered the room, and their voices dropped lower. "But don't you want a family, children?" Gyatyu asked.

"Yes," Aurelio said softly, "I would like a child very much. There is only one person, however, for whom I wish to make a set of clothes—and you know the obstacle there."

"Perhaps time will offer a solution," Gyatyu said.

The next day Gana came to visit her aunt.

Hishti glanced up from her grinding when her niece came in the door unannounced. "The Mountain Lion is in the village today," Hishti said quickly. "He has not gone hunting."

Her niece never visited if Aurelio were somewhere on the Rock. Hishti knew the girl's hatred and her free tongue; she had no desire to repeat the scene that had occurred previously, and so she had asked Gana not to visit unless Aurelio were hunting or at the fields. Hishti did not want the Mountain Lion displeased. He furnished abundant food for the house, and it appeared Diego would never return. Besides, she had great affection for Aurelio; he had become the son she had never had.

"It's all right," Gana said slyly. Although she was bursting to tell Hishti everything at once, she wanted to see her aunt's reaction when Aurelio returned. Gana spoke again, trying to keep the mischief from her eyes.

"Perhaps the Mountain Lion will be making another set of clothes soon?" she asked innocently.

She was going to tell Aurelio that day that if the right person made her a set of clothes, she would put them on no matter what her father said. After all, acceptance or refusal was an Ácoma woman's prerogative. Her father could state his opinion, he could even disown her, but he could not stop her from putting on the clothes.

Hishti shook her head in response to Gana's innocently asked question. "No," she said, "the Mountain Lion will not make another set of clothes. Wiika is still in his heart."

The smile slipped from Gana's face.

"Why just last night his best friend Gyatyu was here," Hishti said, reaching for the woven basket to sift the flour she had been grinding. "I overheard their conversation. Gyatyu asked the Mountain Lion if he didn't want children, and the Lion replied that, yes, he would like a child very much, but that there was only one person for whom he would make a set of clothes — and that was impossible. Even Gyatyu acknowledged the problem. Wiika is still in his heart. No," Hishti said with finality, "the Mountain Lion will never make a set of clothes for another woman. He himself said it."

What Hishti did not know was that Aurelio had been referring to Gana in the conversation she overheard. Had she seen the look of horror on her niece's face and known the mistake she had made, Hishti would have bitten her own tongue off.

Gana's face had a sickly pale look to it. "I must go now before he gets back," she said, her words strangled.

Hishti finally glanced at her niece. "What is it?" she asked, seeing the terrible look on Gana's face. "Are you ill?"

"He must not see me." She rose and ran from the room.

Moments later Aurelio entered.

"Was that Gana I saw scurrying down the ladder?" he asked.

Hishti looked quickly down at her flour. "Yes."

"Why was she leaving in such a hurry?"

"She did not want to be here when you returned," Hishti said quietly.

"She didn't?" Aurelio asked with surprise. "Why?"

"You know how the girl feels about you; she has not made a secret of it, I'm afraid." Hishti's words came painfully from her.

"Hasn't she changed her mind?" Aurelio asked, a strange note in his voice.

"No," Hishti whispered. "I'm sorry."

She trembled at the violence of his actions as he grabbed his bow and quiver from their hook. Instantly he was out the door. Why was he so upset? He had known for years how the girl felt. Why did it make him so angry now?

For over two weeks Aurelio did not return. When he did, the look he wore on his face never left it. It was a closed, hard, dangerous look. Even the villagers noticed it and gave wide berth to him when he was in the street.

Gyatyu's shock was perhaps the greatest, for he had known the happiness in his friend's heart. He saw it change suddenly, and he asked what happened.

"I was a fool," was all Aurelio would say.

Winter came that year, announced by a cold violent blast out of North Mountain, raising the dust in the streets and tearing at the robes of the Ácoma whenever they had to venture outside.

Few could remember a winter of such constant, bitter wind. The wind seemed to carry disease with it, for many of the Ácoma fell sick. The medicine men were exhausted by the healing ceremonies for which they were requested day and night. Fray Lucas, too, spent many a sleepless night at the bedside of a sick child, praying when all his other efforts had failed.

Hishti returned home one evening, her eyes red. Wiika's youngest child had died. The next morning the middle one succumbed.

Aurelio wanted to ask about another member of the household, but he had not, and when Wiika's father died, he became even more concerned. He was thankful when the days began to grow longer and fewer of the Ácoma were carried to the churchyard to have a pottery water jar broken over their resting place. He was thankful, too, that his old, frail Auntie Siya survived.

Game had been scarce that winter, and he had had to travel farther and farther from the valley to find it. Success had always been his, but that was not the case in many households. Some were desperate. He admonished Hishti to give what they could spare to those who might need it. He knew a good deal of it went to Wiika's house.

The weather turned warmer toward the end of March, and every household had at least one man in a hunting party that set out to seek the game that might have come out to feed. No one was surprised however when the warm day grew chill, and dark clouds gathered suddenly. How many times had they had one last snowstorm after the moon of March had changed?

What they had not expected was the storm's ferocity. The wind that had plagued their winter blew with anger and violence, drifting the snow and stealing their body heat.

Two hunters in one party who ranged too far from the group were found the next morning, frozen in the snow. A similar fate had taken the member of another party. Many suffered painfully in their fingers and toes. Some planters would be missing a finger that summer when they went to the fields to hoe the hard soil. It would be difficult for some to hold a bow securely.

Aurelio did not know that Wiika's husband was one of those so affected until he overheard Hishti talking to Siya in a loud voice so that the old lady might hear.

"It is both feet," Hishti said. "They are purple and swollen. The sickness has already entered his body. His fever rages, and he is delirious. It is only a matter of time."

There was a pause. "I don't know what will become of them," Hishti said with despondency.

Two days later Wiika's husband died. That day a deer was taken to their dwelling.

"Thank you," Wiika said to Aurelio with genuine gratitude. "The food can be well used in our house."

Wiika's mother looked at Aurelio. "I hope you will forgive my husband the enmity he carried for you. At times he could be a very stubborn man. He would not see that who one's parents are sometimes does not matter. I thank you for the deer."

"You are welcome," Aurelio said. "Your household shall not want."

Deep inside he had wanted to catch a glimpse of someone else; his disappointment was great when he did not.

He had not intended to, but that spring he found himself upon frequent occasions at the house where he had not before been welcome. His excuse was the game he brought, but often he sat for longer than necessary in conversation with mother and elder daughter. Twice he had seen the younger daughter slip quietly out of the room when he entered. He never saw her on the street.

Planting season came and all those who were able-bodied went to the fields. Even small children carried a digging stick. No one was exempt from work when it was a matter of life, and corn was life to the Ácoma.

Aurelio and Hishti worked, the sweat pouring from their brows. Both were strong and felt the need to feed more mouths than just their own. At the end of the week, Aurelio hunted. He left one rabbit with Hishti and trotted some distance to another arroyo where the fields of Wiika and her mother's household were located. He saw the three women and Wiika's only child in the distance.

When he came near and saw Gana—there was nowhere now to which she could escape—it felt as if a lightning bolt had struck him. He approached, but Gana turned her back on him and continued to hoe as if he were not there. But he had seen.

His hands suddenly became damp, and something began to swell inside his chest. The words he had spoken long months ago among the piñon trees had come to pass.

Gana's tunic could not hide the evidence of their two nights together. He had seen clearly from her figure the child that she now carried. He knew beyond all doubt that it was his. Wiika spoke to him, but he did not hear. His words were not in response to hers.

"I did not know," he said softly.

Wiika followed his gaze to Gana. "Yes," Wiika said, "she is with child." Aurelio's eyes, questioning, went to Wiika's face. "Yes," she answered in response to his unspoken words, "it is yours."

Gana's words came back to him—any woman of Áco would die before she would allow the seed of a Spanish dog to be put in her belly.

He wanted to feel the joy that had burst within him, yet his pain was too great, his torment more than he thought possible.

Wiika saw something of his emotion in his face. She put her hand on his arm gently. "You once said to her that she would marry a handsome man. That is still her desire, I think."

Aurelio looked at her, incomprehension in his eyes. A soft smile came to Wiika's lips. "You are a handsome man, Mokaitsh," she said.

Aurelio looked back at Gana, bent over her hoe. No words came to his lips. He handed Wiika the rabbits and turned to go, then stopped.

"Is what you speak the truth?"

Hishti witnessed the hours Aurelio spent working when they returned from planting. She felt great contentment. "At last," she whispered to herself, "at last."

He had asked her for the softest, whitest deerskins of those he had tanned and then given her for the household's use. She gave them up willingly, happy that he was finally making use of them for something this important. From the tarnished silver box she saw him take a purple satin ribbon, faded now to mauve. He looped it through the edge of a piece of the softest cotton blanket he had just woven. Hishti was filled with joy to watch him work. It bothered her, however, that she saw no joy, no excitement in him as he made the several things. She would have wished to see great happiness or at least contentment in him. What she saw instead appeared sadness.

Aurelio's steps were slow and heavy as he descended the ladder. It took every bit of willpower he possessed to approach the dwelling. He called the greeting softly; he could not force his voice louder.

Wiika, who must have been near the roof's edge, looked down. She motioned for Aurelio to ascend. Together they crossed the roof terrace and entered the dwelling. Gana and her mother knelt, grinding corn. When Gana looked up and saw the bundle Aurelio carried, a tiny sob caught in her throat. She pushed herself up and fled into the other room. Aurelio looked helplessly at Wiika.

"Give me the bundle," she said softly, and Aurelio handed it to her numbly.

Gana let out a sob when she saw Wiika enter, the bundle in her hands.

Wiika held the bundle out toward her. "These are for you, little Sister. They are for you."

Gana took a step backward, her hand at her mouth as if she wanted to stifle a cry. Wiika stepped toward her. "He brought them for you," she said gently. "I refused my happiness a long time ago, little Sister. Do not refuse yours now."

Again Wiika held out the bundle toward her. "Take them," she said.

Gana's hands trembled as she reached and took the bundle. She slipped to the floor on her knees and held the bundle against her chest. Her face dropped against it, and her tears fell onto the soft deerskin.

Wiika quietly left the room. Aurelio looked up at her when she returned, his face etched with worry and pain.

"Go to her, Mother," Wiika said softly to the other woman. Wiika sat down beside Aurelio and touched his arm. "We must wait now."

Each succeeding minute increased in agony for him. Would it never cease?

Gana finally stepped into the room. On her arm was a basket; covering her body was a soft, white deerskin tunic. In her other hand was a small bundle. Aurelio's chest constricted as she walked toward him, eyes downcast. She knelt in front of him, and her eyes still did not meet his.

"I have four flours," she said, her voice scarcely audible. "I should like to prepare you food with them."

"Oh, Gana," Aurelio said, taking her chin in his hand. Wiika and her mother slipped from the room.

Aurelio lifted Gana's face so she was looking at him. "Little Snowbird," he whispered, "I have missed you so. Why do you cry?"

She looked at him through her tears. "Because you bring me joy," she whispered.

Aurelio took her face in his hands and pulled her gently to him, covering her lips with his.

Hishti's eyes widened with shock. She had expected Wiika. She sputtered but was unable to speak when she saw Aurelio and Gana step onto the roof terrace.

Gana ran to her and hugged her. Still Hishti could not speak.

"Won't you help me prepare the food?" Gana asked her with a smile.

Hishti had known Gana was with child. She had had no idea it was Aurelio's.

She had heard the story of Gana seeking shelter with the Mountain Lion last fall, but it had never crossed her mind that anything might have happened. She was told Gana did not know who the father was; sexual relations before marriage were not uncommon nor were they highly disapproved of.

A glimmer of her conversation with the Mountain Lion the previous fall, when he had seen Gana scurry down the ladder, came back to her. He had seemed so happy when he returned from gathering piñon nuts, but when she had told him Gana hated him—that was when he had rushed angrily from the room. And she had thought it strange that Gana would visit when the Mountain Lion was in the village. A terrible look came over Hishti's face, and both Aurelio and Gana looked at her with incomprehension.

Tears came to Hishti's eyes. "Please forgive me. Please forgive me," she stammered.

She blurted out what she thought had happened. Gana and Aurelio looked at each other, and all their defenses fell away.

"Oh, Hishti," Gana said, "there was no way for you to know. It does not matter now."

Hishti's tears did not stop, knowing the pain that she had caused.

"Look," Gana said, not wishing for her aunt to cry, "look what else my husband made for me." She took the small bundle that had been with the set of clothes Aurelio had made. She opened it and held out for Hishti to see, a tiny doeskin shirt and a small, soft white cotton blanket trimmed with a mauve ribbon.

"Oh, Gana," Hishti said, "I can never tell you the happiness you have given me today."

That night as he lay with Gana on soft sheepskins, Aurelio, with a tender caress, ran his hand over her large belly. She covered his hand with her own.

"Do you feel your child?" she asked.

"Yes."

"The child will be Ácoma," Gana whispered, "just as its father is Ácoma."

Aurelio took her in his arms and stroked her hair. "Yes, my child will truly be Ácoma."

Part Six

EL LEVANTAMIENTO

The Uprising, 1679

Chapter 40

During the dry moon, Siya died. Her life simply fluttered away. She had not fully understood what had happened between Aurelio and Gana. All she knew was that they were now married and Gana was with child. As Siya lay in her final hour, Aurelio and Gana knelt at her side.

"Do not cry, little Gana," Siya said in a raspy voice. She reached out her frail, trembling hand and touched Gana's stomach.

"I go soon to join the others, but I am content. I shall bring them the wonderful news that the Mountain Lion will soon have a child. I have worried much that my nephew would have no descendants. You have given me a wonderful gift by giving him a child."

Her chest heaved with the exertion of her speech. "I die filled with happiness," she said moments before her breathing stopped.

Aurelio felt a deep sadness at the death of his great-aunt. His one last fragile tie to the past was gone. There was no one now who knew the story of the Indian Rohona and the Spanish woman María Angélica. All those who shared his blood were gone.

His child carried his blood, but the baby would come from the belly of an Ácoma woman. The child would be Ácoma—only Ácoma. The past was dead forever as if the Indian Rohona and the Spanish woman had never existed.

Only one thing, though, still endured—the lesson his great-grandfather had instilled in him. When he had returned to his mesa top village from Taos, he was able to make out what his great-grandfather spoke to him at night: Áco must exist always.

❉   ❉   ❉

By the next moon, Diego returned. The small, wiry Apache seemed made only of hardened sinew. In his black, piercing eyes burned a fire so intense it might have had its origin in Hell. No emotion showed on Hishti's face as the husband she had not seen for over four years appeared in her doorway. It was as if she had forgotten him, had never known him — which was nearer the truth than she herself knew.

She was no happier than was Aurelio to see Diego's return, and the Mountain Lion felt a dark apprehension spread over him. That night Diego spoke to them of Taos.

Aurelio knew what was coming before Diego said the words.

"The plans are laid. We shall not fail."

Later that night Diego went to Mauharots. Aurelio knew he must also go, although it was the last thing he wanted to do. Mauharots was hot and stuffy, the air charged with tension. There was scarcely anywhere to sit. The word had spread, and all wanted to hear the words the Apache brought from Taos.

"A runner will arrive," Diego began, his strident voice the only sound in Mauharots. "Around his waist will be a knotted yucca cord. That is our proof, our signal. Each day when a knot is untied we shall know how many days remain. When the cord no longer has a single knot, that will be the day to carry out the sacred plan. To every village a runner will go; every village will have a knotted cord. On the appointed day every village in this land will rise! In one thunderous voice, with one terrible arm, we will strike our oppressors. With the swift destruction of a lightning bolt, we will fall on our enemies, and our land will run red with their blood. Their blood shall water our crops, and the rain shall return with their deaths. No one will be spared. Neither man nor woman nor child nor priest — not one drop of Spanish blood will be left to taint this land!"

There was a moment of silence, then a deafening roar rose in the *kiva*. Gyatyu's father would not speak against it nor would his friends nor their friends. Neither would Aurelio speak. The die had been cast. There was no turning back. Like a red tide, the people would rise. And when the tide fell, it would leave its bloody mark across the land. What Po-pé had plotted would be successful. He had achieved the one thing necessary for success: unification.

Five years had passed since Aurelio witnessed the hangings and beatings in the plaza at the *villa* of Santa Fé — five years in which Po-pé had worked. The Tegua medicine man would not be Moses leading his children out of the wilderness and to the Promised Land. He would be the Avenging Angel falling on their oppressors and returning their land to the promise of the K'atsina.

The dancing in Mauharots lasted until dawn. A joyous excitement, long repressed, ran through the village. A heady sense of power filled the men, and they felt strong once again. Prayer sticks were made, clubs fashioned, and the warriors fasted ritually.

The day after Diego returned, Aurelio and Gana moved to the house of her mother. There was now a man in Hishti's household; there was none in Gana's mother's house. Tradition dictated that daughters return to their mothers' homes when they married.

Hishti was beside herself with grief, but she tried not to show it. She lived now with a total stranger. She knew there would never be a child to ease her pain — she accepted loneliness as her lot for the rest of her days.

Aurelio told Gana, her mother, and Wiika what had been spoken in Mauharots. "We await now the arrival of the knotted cord," he said.

Fear showed in the faces of all three women. Gana was heavy with child, and her mother had said the baby would not delay more than a few days. Instinctively Gana pressed her hands to her stomach as if protecting the child she carried there.

"There is nothing to fear," Aurelio said. "What will happen is going to happen, but this household will be safe."

He knew that with certainty, but he also knew that he had to be very cautious. Blood was a powerful intoxicant, and once a mob had a taste of it, the murderous throng frequently did not stop until its thirst was quenched many times over.

For several nights Gana did not sleep well, the weight of the baby precluding any comfortable position. Aurelio saw worry on her face and knew its source, although she had not spoken.

"I am Ácoma," Aurelio said to comfort her. "You know that I am Ácoma; the K'atsina know that I am Ácoma. They and the mountain lion, my namesake, will protect me. Do not be afraid."

Gana tried to smile but could not.

Aurelio hoped beyond hope that the knotted cord would not arrive, but early one morning he saw the runner enter the village, the rope tied around his waist. Only two knots remained. Áco was many days from Taos.

"It is done," Aurelio said to himself. "It is done."

A sudden dread filled his chest. He trotted home and went to the highest rooftop of his house to pray, first to the K'atsina and Iyatiku.

"Protect Áco," he asked of them. And then he prayed to the Castilian god — to the god whose children would soon be lying dead.

He waited until nightfall. It would not have been safe earlier. Silently he approached the massive walls. He stopped short — he had not expected sentries. With the stealth granted him by *mokaitsh*, he circled the church. There was a sentry at every corner. He would have to return home for a rope. There was no possible way he could enter the church from the front. On the back wall where the church joined the storerooms that enclosed the patio of the priest's living quarters, there was a place he might be able to breach. When he reached his dwelling, he took two hardened, tempered sticks and lashed them together with rawhide to form an X. To this he tied a braided rope. Then, just as he finished, he heard the greeting called up. It was the last person he wished to see and he hid the rope.

"Here you are," said Diego as he reached the roof. "I have been looking for you."

"Be seated."

Aurelio held his face impassive as Diego began to talk of Taos and Popé. He talked on without ever giving indication that he intended to leave. The hours of the night grew late, but Aurelio's worry and growing nervousness did not show.

Dawn could only have been a few hours away when Aurelio was startled to hear Gana cry out. He sprang to his feet.

Diego rose and started for the ladder. "I will finish this conversation later."

"What is it, little Snowbird?" Aurelio asked with concern as he knelt beside her.

She touched his cheek in the darkness. "I am fine. I thought perhaps you needed sleep."

Aurelio kissed her out of relief and gratitude. "You are a good wife," he said. "There is something I must do. I will be back as soon as I can, but if I have not returned by dawn and Diego comes asking for me again, tell him I went to hunt rabbits so we would have meat for when the baby is born."

Gana did not question him.

Aurelio crouched at the parapet of his dwelling for long moments, his eyes probing into the darkness. At length, he descended the ladder noiselessly. When he approached the church, he saw that the sentries were still there. He sought the back wall, making himself a part of every shadow. He threw the sticks attached to the rope over the parapet and pressed himself tightly against the rough wall, not allowing even his chest to move. The sticks made a quiet thud against the wall on the inside. The sentries from either corner approached upon hearing the small noise that was different from the common sounds of night. When they saw each other, they assumed the other had made the sound, for they saw nothing else in the darkness. Aurelio exhaled silently as they walked back to their original positions.

He took his Spanish steel-bladed knife and at waist-height dug it to its hilt into the wall. He hoped it would hold securely, just as he hoped neither sentry would see it there, jutting out. He took a deep breath and with the agility of a mountain lion leaped into the air, one foot coming down onto the handle of his knife as his hands reached upward to grasp the rope as high as possible.

The instant his foot touched the knife handle, he pushed off of it, throwing his body as high as he could, grasping the rope higher still. The sticks held long enough for him to swing his leg over the top of the parapet. He lay still on the roof, listening. When he heard nothing, he pulled up the rope and crossed the roof of the storeroom at a crouch. At the edge, he dropped silently to the ground inside the patio. He found his way carefully to the priest's quarters and entered. He approached the sleeping friar and knelt by his bed. He clapped his hand over Fray Lucas's mouth so that he would make no sound. Instantly the *padre* was awake.

"It is me, Aurelio. Make no sound." He removed his hand. "Father," he said, "there is a plot among the natives. They are going to rise and kill all Spaniards. No one is to be spared — not even women nor children nor priests. This will happen at every pueblo in the province. You must escape before it is too late."

"How do you know this?"

"Diego brought the news when he returned from Taos. The sign to rise up was to be a runner with a knotted cord. Each day one knot was to be untied from the cord. When there were no more, the day had arrived."

He took a breath. "Today the runner reached Áco. Only two knots remain. You must escape tonight. If you get down off the rock and cross the valley during darkness, and push on tomorrow, by the following day you should be out of harm's way. You should be able to reach one of the *haciendas* on the big river. There you may be able to find protection. But you must go now. I will get you past the sentries."

"Sentries?"

"Posted around the church so that you cannot escape."

"How did you get in?"

"I climbed the wall at the back of the patio. I will be able to get you out."

"No," the *padre* said, his voice calm. "I am not going."

"But you must," Aurelio said. "Or you will be killed two days from now."

"That is God's decision, my son," Fray Lucas said. "I do not fear death. Martyrdom is a welcome death. There is no nobler way to die than to die for what one believes in."

"Father, please. Your death can serve no purpose here. Go, while you can."

"No," the priest said, "I will not go. I told you once I would never jeopardize your position here in the village. If I escape, they will know someone has told me of the plot. I will not take the chance that they may discover it was you, my son. I will spend my last days in prayer commending myself to God, and I will beg his mercy for this people and especially for you and your descendants."

"Will you confess me, Father, one last time?"

"Of course, my son," Fray Lucas said. He rose to get his stole and together they knelt on the hard dirt floor as Aurelio spoke words he would never speak again.

The priest went with him across the patio and placed a ladder against the storeroom wall.

"The blessing of God be upon you," Fray Lucas said softly. Aurelio knelt at his feet, and with his thumb the priest made the sign of the cross on the Indian Mokaitsh's forehead.

He did not hear Aurelio reach the ground on the other side. "Do not desert him, Lord," the priest said in silent prayer.

When Aurelio lay down beside Gana, faint fingers of dawn were just becoming visible along East Mountain. That morning, the next to last knot was untied. The merrymaking that had greeted Diego's words in Mauharots did not fill the village streets that day. The White Rock fell strangely silent. People walked to and from their houses merely nodding to those they met. It was as if they feared to jeopardize the morrow with speech that day.

When night fell, Diego came again to Aurelio's dwelling. He seated himself and again began to talk. It appeared he had no intention of leaving. Aurelio kept his face expressionless, although the rudeness of the Apache angered him.

Aurelio had heard it all the night before. He already knew the visions of Po-pé, he knew that Po-pé claimed supernatural powers given him by Po-he-mu, he knew that Po-pé's plan was for all villages to rise up at the same time and fall upon the Spaniards, leaving none with a breath of life anywhere in the land. All roads that led to the *villa* of Santa Fé were to be blocked, cutting off any attempt by Spaniards from outlying areas to reach the capital and safety, just as blocking the roads would cut off the possibility of any aid reaching the *villa* and those who there might have survived the first bloody strike of the uprising. No warrior in the province would rest until every Spaniard had been annihilated.

Then with thorough deliberation they would rid the land of any trace of the hated conquerors. In time there would be nothing left to tell that there had ever existed anything in *Nuevo México* except the native peoples and their way of life. All the strange animals brought into the land by the Spaniards were to be killed — all sheep, horses, donkeys, pigs, chickens, dogs that were not native dogs. Every plant that Iyatiku had not given them was to be destroyed — all peach trees, apple trees, wheat, barley, melons that were not native melons. And most of all — every symbol of the vengeful god the conquerors had brought was to be obliterated, and the people were commanded to wade into rivers and streams and with soap made from yucca root to wash away the water of baptism. They would then live in peace and contentment.

Thus was the vision of Po-pé. It was no wonder that his vision was embraced by almost all. Years of oppression, hunger, and discontent had brought about what had never taken place when the Spaniards came as conquerors into the land — conquering without resistance, without bloodshed, save at Áco. What had now occurred was unity among the native peoples.

Aurelio knew this and understood. It did not take Diego all the hours of the night to tell him. Some slight emotion must have shown on Aurelio's face because Diego's eyes grew darker and his words became more hard.

"Not only will all Spaniards be killed," Diego said, his voice rising, "but anyone — *anyone* — be he native of any village, son or husband, daughter or wife — anyone who would divulge the plan will die a death worse than that of any Spanish dog. Mercy is not a word known by the plan."

Diego paused and peered through slitted eyes at Aurelio for his reaction. Aurelio's face revealed less than any stone there on the White Rock.

Diego continued: "Po-pé has shown that the plan is more important than any life. He held in great esteem and affection the husband of his favorite daughter. But Nicolás Bua, an important man in the pueblo and governor of Ohké, was suspected of treachery to the plan. It was necessary that he die. Nothing could be allowed to jeopardize the plan. Po-pé killed his own beloved son-in-law. None of us will do less."

Aurelio's face revealed nothing. The two men sat in silence looking at each other. Neither dropped his gaze. Then a sudden cry startled them both. Aurelio came to his feet instantly.

Gana's mother stepped quickly out of the dwelling to where the men stood on the roof terrace.

"Tell Hishti," she said to Diego, "that there will be a baby in this house by dawn."

Chapter 41

He started for the room where Gana lay but her mother stopped him. "The baby is coming. When it is here I will call you."

"No," Aurelio said. His words were not harsh but allowed for no disagreement. "I am going to see her."

She was sitting when he entered the room. She smiled, and he knelt beside her.

"Your child wants out," she said, touching his cheek.

"That is good."

At that moment, a fleeting pain crossed her face, but she closed her eyes and chanted a soft high chant.

"Go to the roof for me, husband, and watch for the dawn. I do not want this baby born during darkness—I want it born to light. Tell me when the sun is here."

"Yes, Snowbird," Aurelio said. "I will tell you when the light of day has reached East Mountain."

He kissed her forehead, rose and went out to climb to the highest roof. There he prayed and then sat to await the dawn, his eyes fixed on the east from whence the light would come.

The stars began to lose their brightness and gray took the place of black. The ridge of East Mountain grew out of the darkness, creating a line between the night and the day that came. Feathers of light like tiny pink plumes fringed the backbone of East Mountain. Aurelio rose. The dawn was coming.

He descended the stairsteps from the uppermost roof. A baby's cry rent the air. It seemed to trumpet the dawn.

A wild sound rose from below. People poured off the rooftops and into the streets.

The last knot had been untied.

Aurelio saw them surging toward the church. Po-pé's plan had begun. Begun in blood in the plaza of the *villa* of Santa Fé five years ago, it would end in blood in the plazas of every pueblo, in the patio of every *hacienda* from Taos to Isleta.

"Go in, go in," said Wiika, who had just come out onto the roof terrace. She, too, had heard the people and knew what was to happen as she ran to see if the ladder had been pulled up onto the roof the night before.

"Put the ladder down," Aurelio said. "Do not leave it on the roof." Wiika looked at him, and he saw the fear in her face. "No one will harm us, Sister," he said. His tone was one of assurance. "Let the ladder down. Let no one think we are afraid; let no one think we are not a part of the village in all it does; let no one think we do not join in the plan."

Wiika nodded and let the ladder down as Aurelio stepped into the dwelling.

"You have a son," Gana's mother said. "A fine strong son. He will make a mighty warrior."

Aurelio smiled and approached Gana, who lay on a sheepskin robe, a tiny bundle cradled against her side. He bent and kissed her on the lips. Her eyes were luminous. She lifted away the soft cotton blanket edged with mauve ribbon. A tiny, square face with a shock of coal-black hair looked out at Aurelio. This child would not have the gray eyes of its father.

"He is a beautiful son," Gana whispered. "He shall be strong and wise like his father."

"And he will be beautiful like his mother," Aurelio said.

He picked up the tiny bundle and cradled it in his arms and placed a kiss on his son's forehead.

Gana's mother took the baby. "Sleep now, Daughter," she said. "Your work was difficult through the night."

Aurelio rose and went to a corner of the room where he retrieved something. He carried it out onto the roof terrace and down the ladder into the storeroom below. With his knife he dug out a hole in one of the walls.

One last time he opened the silver box. One by one he took out the contents. There was still left a small piece of faded purple satin ribbon. He looked at the two locks of hair in the dim light. One was black, one flame-colored. He placed them together and closed his hand over them.

"I have a son," he said softly.

He laid the locks of hair aside and picked up an embroidered satin bookmark. His thumb traced the two entwined A's. He touched a silver crucifix, crossed himself, and brought to his lips the tarnished metal symbol. He returned everything to the box and pushed it into the hole in the wall, wedging it securely, and resealed it with mud.

Just before dawn, Fray Lucas de Maldonado rose from his prayers. He dressed carefully, his lips lingering on his stole before he put it around his neck. He intoned the words of the Mass. He consumed all the consecrated host so that it would not be profaned. He lifted the chalice to his lips, then slowly and carefully, wiped it clean. When the solitary Mass was said, he busied himself straightening the sacristy, touching everything lovingly. Then he went back to the altar.

A faint light in the church told him dawn had arrived. He walked down the earthen steps from the altar and toward the massive doors that gave out to the east. He paused in front of the doors and kissed the cross he wore around his neck.

At that moment he heard the voices. He opened the door, and the brilliant light of the sun blinded him. He did not see nor scarcely felt the rock that glanced off his temple. It caused him to stumble to his knees, but he quickly rose and started down the steps toward the surging throng. His prayers never ceased as he was beaten and dragged toward the edge of the rock mesa. He felt blood in his mouth, but he felt no pain. He felt nothing but freedom from his body as he was hurled from the White Rock.

He smiled, for he was falling into God's hands.

The mob yelled and chanted and surged in one body back toward the church. Soon, in a terrific bedlam, in the sanctuary of the church of Juan Ramírez, lay vestments, missals, candles, and censers. The silver paten and chalice, a present of the king of Spain, were thrown on the pile. Holy oil was spilled, and when the fire was touched, everything went up in flames that shot toward the ceiling.

Sometime later, the *latias* of the roof caught fire. The sun was well past midday when a great crashing noise reverberated in the village. The huge *vigas*, carried by hand from North Mountain during Fray Ramírez's time, thundered down like the wrath of God. Turkey vultures circled over the valley floor anxious for the feast that awaited them from the indiscriminate slaughter of sheep and burros. In a land where hunger stalked, Aurelio knew that the destruction of food for whatever reason was a sin. Even Iyatiku would know this.

Toward the end of the day, Aurelio descended the ladder of his dwelling and made his way to the east edge of the mesa. There he saw Fray Lucas, stretched Christ-like on the rocks, a turkey vulture feasting on his open eyes. Aurelio shuddered and closed his own. He turned away and walked back through the streets of Áco to his dwelling. In a village of people ravenous for the blood of Spaniards, no one remarked his presence among them other than to note that the Mountain Lion walked with his head high.

They knew of his son born just that morning; he had a right to walk with his head high. All men walked proud at the birth of their first child.

The dancing lasted late into the night. The revelry was unmatched for the White Rock. People still danced and chanted in the plaza of the village when Aurelio made his way to the eastern edge of the mesa. There were no sentries at the burned-out church that night. Carefully he made his way down the craggy wall to where Fray Lucas lay.

That day when he had looked down to where the friar had fallen, he saw the spot to which he would carry the body. It was not difficult to find at night, but the dead weight of the *padre* made it much more hazardous to cross the rocks. When he reached the spot he had chosen, he wedged the body into the narrow horizontal crevice, and began to fill the crevice with rocks. He pushed them in tightly with all his strength until the crevice was filled. Then he scooped up handfuls of the pink-tan sand eroded by the wind and rain from the rock of Áco itself. Handful after handful he sifted over the rocks and down into the crevice. Fray Lucas would not serve as food for the carrion-eaters.

It was near dawn when Aurelio finally rolled a number of rocks from not far above the new grave down onto it so that they would appear random and not placed there by man. He pulled a large bush out by its roots and swept the ground to remove his tracks. Then he ascended the rock wall and carefully made his way through the village so as not to be seen in the faint early light.

The news of the disappearance of Fray Lucas spread rapidly through the village that morning. Several men descended to the spot where the body had come to rest. They could find no trace of the friar they had hurled from the rock the previous dawn.

A ripple of fear ran through the village, and the wild celebration of their victory ceased. Some suggested that an animal might have dragged the corpse away during the night but admitted there would have been clear evidence of that had it occurred.

The thought crossed many minds that perhaps his god had come and taken him away. Had that not happened to the man who had been killed on the crossed sticks? Had not his body been taken from the grave as the *padre* said? Some regretted their actions of the previous day. What if they had angered his god?

One small girl said she had seen his *capote* spread out as he fell, and it seemed as if he had floated to the earth. Perhaps he had not died as it had appeared.

Talk ceased in the village when Diego made it known that anyone heard to mention the name of the late *padre* ever again would find himself severely punished, or worse yet, might meet the same fate.

Diego spoke in Mauharots that night. He had assumed an air of authority. "The great Po-pé is now the leader of the people. He is supreme over all the land. We will bow down to the great leader whose power comes from Po-he-mu. We will give a tribute in corn each year to him. He has sent a trusted lieutenant to each village to see that his orders are carried out and that no one continues any practice learned from the Spanish dogs. That lieutenant has the power of life and death if he suspects treachery.

"People of the White Rock," he said. "For five years I have lived with our leader. Po-pé has chosen me to be his lieutenant in this village. Starting tomorrow each dwelling will be searched to see if it contains anything of the detested dogs. Anyone found with crossed sticks in his house will be killed as a traitor."

Mauharots was silent when Diego finished speaking. Aurelio's face was a mask of stone as he left the *kiva*.

"Wait, Mountain Lion," Diego said to him, "I have something to discuss with you."

Aurelio paused and turned toward the Apache.

"Let us go out together," Diego said.

Aurelio grunted in response and climbed down the ladder. When they were in the street, Diego said, "Let us walk where none may hear our words."

They walked from the house rows toward the church, whose walls loomed in the darkness.

"Let us go inside," Diego said.

Aurelio followed his lead, not questioning why they entered the gutted building late at night. Stars were now the only roof it had. Diego made his way through the rubble and up the steps to where the altar had once stood.

"Are you Ácoma?" the Apache asked harshly.

"Yes, I was born here on the White Rock."

"Do you believe in the K'atsina?"

"I do," Aurelio answered. His anger, however, did not surface in his voice. He wondered at Diego's purpose.

"Did you once believe in the Castilian god?"

"You know I did."

"Do you still believe?"

Aurelio would not lie. "Yes," he said evenly. He heard a sharp, quiet intake of breath before his interrogator spoke again.

"Do you believe that to lie is a sin that will be punished by your God?"

"Yes."

"Do you lie?"

"No."

"That is your solemn oath as you stand where the altar of your God once stood?"

"I swear upon the altar of God that I do not lie."

Aurelio stood without moving. What was the Apache's purpose? Was he mad—as his piercing black eyes at times seemed to suggest?

"Then you will tell me if it was you who took the friar dog's body from where it lay."

"It was I."

He heard a small animal-like noise come from Diego's throat.

"Where is the body?"

"Where none will find it," Aurelio said. *Mokaitsh* had given him keen eyesight for night-hunting, and he caught the tiny, faint flash of light in the darkness.

"You must die, Spanish dog!" the Apache shrieked, the knife slashing out.

With the swiftness of his namesake, Aurelio moved sideways as he ducked. The Apache flew past him in the darkness and landed at the foot of the steps, but he was agile, and Aurelio heard only the sound of his moccasins and knew he had kept his feet. Aurelio did not move a muscle. He heard the Apache, step by quiet step, stealthily ascending toward him. Still he did not move. Diego sensed his presence and lunged for him.

Again Aurelio stepped to the side, but this time his arms shot out in the darkness, locking around Diego's throat. There was a brittle snap in the darkness, and the knife clattered to the floor. Aurelio felt the unmoving weight in his arms and released his hold. Noiselessly the Apache slid to the floor.

Aurelio reached into the darkness and found the knife. Had there been light and had the Apache's eyes been able to see, he would have witnessed on the Mountain Lion's face a cold, hard smile.

The body was discovered the next day in the church, as two mangy dogs fought over it, the commotion having drawn the curious. There appeared to be no other wound than those the dogs had inflicted on the corpse. No one in the village gave any sign of lamenting the death. No one inquired with whom he had last been seen. Diego's wife's eyes were dry. She felt nothing more than she might have felt at the death of a stranger. No house in Áco was searched that day, nor any day, for relics of the Spaniards' rule.

Aurelio was not asked about the Apache.

On the fourth day, the sun rose brilliantly on a solitary figure standing at the eastern edge of the mesa. The figure lifted its arms and held aloft a small bundle. The figure was bathed in gold, its long hair, flowing red-gold down its shoulders. The form seemed one with the rock on which it stood, made golden by the rising August sun.

"Behold the child, whose name shall be Rohona," the figure said.

The figure lowered the bundle and stood there in the dawn surveying the valley that lay at the foot of the sheer-walled rock.

The Ácoma were free now, free of the strangers who had marched into their land eighty-two years ago to demand submission to their king and to their god. They were free of the strangers who had massacred their village and mutilated their warriors.

"Enjoy your freedom, oh Ácoma," the Mountain Lion said softly to the dawn. "It was bought at a price; it will require a price to hold. But others will come. Others *will* come. But you must endure."

He paused, and the words of the ancient philosopher that he spoke were a benediction spoken to his children and to his children's children.

"Be like the promontory, Ácoma!"

Historical Epilogue

In August 1680, what few Spaniards in and around Santa Fé survived the first bloody strike of the Pueblo Revolt gathered in the meager safety that the governor's palace offered. Armed, mounted Pueblo warriors cut the water supply and laid siege to the adobe-walled compound for nine days before Governor Otermín determined that the only hope of survival was to break out and attempt to flee south to safety.

Fighting only skirmishes, the Pueblo leaders allowed the Spaniards to retreat from the City of the Holy Faith, established seventy years earlier. Popé attempted to secure himself as leader of all the people of the land, but once the hated foreigners were gone, each village zealously returned to its old autonomy.

Governor Otermín made an attempt at reconquest in 1681 but retreated to El Paso, where he and the survivors had established a miserable little colony. It would take a decade before Diego de Vargas reconquered New Mexico for Spain, and the Ácoma were among the last to submit to the returning Spaniards.

Throughout the 1700s, menaced on all sides by Apaches, Navajos, Utes, and a new tribe of fearless, pony-mounted warriors called Comanche, the Spaniards and the Pueblos were forced to cooperate for protection. Then in 1821, Mexico claimed its independence from Spain, but the remote province of *Nuevo México* little felt the change in government. Only short years later, in 1846, however, General Stephen Watts Kearny led American troops over the Santa Fé Trail and claimed the land of *Nuevo México* for the United States, setting in place American government, which profoundly changed the territory Juan de Oñate had conquered for the king of Spain two hundred and fifty years before.

*   *   *

On September 2, 1998, over three centuries after the Pueblo Revolt, a priest arrived early at the pueblo of Ácoma to say Mass. The sky was a brilliant blue, the dawn air cool with only the merest hint of fall, but the day turned hot when the dancers came out of the *kiva*. It was the celebration of the Feast Day of San Esteban.

The dancers' feet moved in an age-old rhythm to chanting, which the spectators from Albuquerque, California, Texas, and France did not understand. Symbols learned from Iyatiku adorned the dancers, as did a turquoise polyester scarf from the K-Mart in Grants.

The dances were Ácoma for the Ácoma; they were not a spectacle performed for the curious, be they anthropologist or tourist. Cameras were banned, as they always are for ceremonies. Between July 10 and 13, the pueblo of Ácoma is closed to all non-Indians. It is the celebration of their most religious ceremony. No white has seen it.

There are intrusions of the old Spanish and the more recent American culture among the Ácoma: the church Juan Ramírez built, although damaged in the Pueblo Revolt, was rebuilt and still stands, its massive walls and beams sources of wonder and beauty today. In the village you will also see Levi jeans, perhaps a Sony Walkman, or a University of New Mexico T-shirt.

What you won't see are the prayer sticks that have been made or the K'atsina masks carefully fed and cared for. But they exist. The jagged sandstone mesa walls exist. Áco still exists, although it is now called Ácoma and sometimes Sky City. It has survived in spite of the Spanish reconquest; it has survived in spite of the subsequent American takeover.

It will survive.

And perhaps someday, if a certain wall in Ácoma is knocked down, there will be found a small, tarnished silver box containing two locks of hair, a faded purple ribbon, and a crucifix.